**Praise for *New York Times* bestselling author Nalini Singh
and the Guild Hunter series**

'Nalini Singh is a major new talent'
#1 *New York Times* bestselling author Christine Feehan

'With the launch of a second paranormal series, Singh provides
incontrovertible evidence that she's an unrivalled storyteller . . . This
book should be at the top of your must-buy list! Tremendous!'
Romantic Times (Top Pick)

'Terrifyingly, passionately awesome . . . you'll love it'
#1 *New York Times* bestselling author Patricia Briggs

'I loved every word, could picture every scene, and cannot recom-
mend this book highly enough. It is amazing in every way!'
New York Times bestselling author Gena Showalter

'Ms Singh's books never fail to draw me in and keep me enthralled
until the very end'   *Romance Junkies*

'*Archangel's Consort* is a great novel that makes me want to read
everything that Nalini Singh has ever written'   *Fresh Fiction*

'A heart-pounding and strongly emotional read'
Publishers Weekly on *Archangel's Blade*

D0308744

Also by Nalini Singh from Gollancz:

Guild Hunter Series

Angels' Blood
Archangel's Kiss
Archangel's Consort
Archangel's Blade
Archangel's Storm
Archangel's Legion
Archangel's Shadows
Archangel's Enigma
Archangel's Viper
Angels' Flight (short story collection)

Psy-Changeling Series

Slave to Sensation
Visions of Heat
Caressed by Ice
Mine to Possess
Hostage to Pleasure
Branded by Fire
Blaze of Memory
Bonds of Justice
Play of Passion
Kiss of Snow
Tangle of Need
Heart of Obsidian
Shield of Winter
Shards of Hope
Allegiance of Honour
Wild Invitation (short story collection)
Wild Embrace (novella collection)

SILVER
SILENCE

A PSY-CHANGELING TRINITY NOVEL

NALINI SINGH

This edition first published in Great Britain in 2018 by Gollancz

First published in Great Britain in 2017 by Gollancz
an imprint of the Orion Publishing Group Ltd
Carmelite House, 50 Victoria Embankment
London EC4Y 0DZ

An Hachette UK Company

1 3 5 7 9 10 8 6 4 2

A CIP catalogue record for this book is
available from the British Library.

ISBN 978 1 473 21759 1

Printed in Great Britain by Clays Ltd, St Ives plc

MIX
Paper from
responsible sources
FSC® C104740
www.fsc.org

www.nalinisingh.com

Age of Trinity

OCTOBER 2082 IS a new beginning.

Psy, human, and changeling, all three races have agreed to work together to unite their divided world.

The Trinity Accord is the fragile foundation of all their hopes and dreams of a future without war, without violence, without shattering loss.

It is a noble ambition.

But the past is not an old coat that can be discarded and forgotten.

It is a scent that clings and clings and clings.

That scent is of blood and betrayal and a chilling, emotionless Silence.

The psychically gifted Psy seek to feel emotion for the first time in over a hundred years.

Changelings with their primal hearts fight their natural instinct to trust only pack, only clan.

Humans look to the future with a grim-eyed determination to no longer be the weakest race.

And others . . . they seek to spread chaos and death and division.

Welcome to the Age of Trinity.

PART 1

PART I

Chapter 1

To be a Mercant is to be a shadow that moves with will, with intelligence, with pitiless precision.

—Ena Mercant (circa 2057)

SILVER MERCANT BELIEVED in control. It was what made her so good at what she did—she was never caught by surprise. She prepared for everything. Unfortunately, it was impossible to prepare for the heavily muscled man standing at her apartment door.

"How did you get in?" she asked in Russian, making sure to stand front and center in the doorway so he wouldn't forget this was her territory.

Bears had a habit of just pushing everything out of their way.

This bear shrugged his broad shoulders where he leaned up against the side of her doorjamb. "I asked nicely," he replied in the same language.

"I live in the most secure building in central Moscow." Silver stared at that square-jawed face with its honey-dark skin. It wasn't a tan. Valentin Nikolaev retained the shade in winter, got darker in summer. "And," she added, "building security is made up of former soldiers who don't understand the word 'nice.'" One of those soldiers was a Mercant. No one talked their way past a Mercant.

Except for this man. This wasn't the first time he'd appeared on her doorstep on the thirty-fourth floor of this building.

"I have a special charm," Valentin responded, his big body blocking out the light and his deep smile settling into familiar grooves in his cheeks, his hair an inky black that was so messy she wondered if he even owned a comb. That hair appeared as if it might have a silken texture, in stark contrast to the harsh angles of his face.

No part of him was tense, his body as lazy limbed as a cat's.

She knew he was trying to appear harmless, but she wasn't an idiot. Despite her offensive and defensive training, the alpha of the StoneWater clan could crush her like a bug, physically speaking. He had too much brawn, too much strength for her to beat him without a weapon. So it was good that Silver's mind was a ruthless weapon.

"Why did you need to see me at seven in the morning?" she asked, because it was clear he wasn't going to tell her how he kept getting past her security.

He extended a hand on which sat a data crystal. "The clan promised EmNet a breakdown of the small incidents we've handled over the past three months."

Those "small incidents" were times when Psy, humans, or non-clan changelings needed assistance in the area controlled by StoneWater—or elsewhere, when members of the bear clan were close enough to help. As the director of the worldwide Emergency Response Network run under the aegis of the Trinity Accord, Silver was the one who coordinated all available resources—and in this part of the world, that included the Stone-Water bears.

Of course, she had no ability to order them to do anything—trying that on a predatory changeling was an exercise in abject failure. But she could ask. So far, the bears had always come through. The data crystal would tell her how many clan members and/or other resources had been required to manage each instance; it would help her fine-tune her requests in the future.

She took the crystal, not bothering to ask why the alpha of the clan had turned up to personally deliver the data.

Valentin liked to do things his way.

"Why does Selenka let you get away with breaching her territory?" The BlackEdge wolves had control over this part of Moscow when it came to changeling access. The city was split evenly between the wolf pack and the bear clan, with the rest of their respective territories heading outward from that central dividing line.

This apartment building fell in the wolf half.

Valentin smiled, night-dark eyes alight in a way she couldn't describe. "StoneWater and BlackEdge are friends now."

If Silver had felt emotion, she may have made a face of sheer disbelief. The two most powerful packs in Russia had a working relationship and no longer clashed in violent confrontations, but they were *not* friends. "I see," she said, refusing to look away from those onyx eyes.

Predatory changelings sometimes took a lack of eye contact as submissive behavior, even when interacting with non-changelings. Bears *definitely* took it as submissive behavior. They weren't exactly subtle about it, either. In fact, bears were the least subtle of the changelings she'd met through her work as Kaleb Krychek's senior aide, and as the head of EmNet.

"What do you see, Starlight?" Valentin asked in his deep rumble of a voice that spoke of the animal that lived under his skin.

Silver refused to react to the name he insisted on calling her. When she'd pointed out he was being discourteous by not using her actual name, he'd told her to call him her *medvezhonok*, her teddy bear, that he wouldn't mind. It was difficult to have a rational conversation with a man who seemed impossible to insult or freeze out.

Bears.

She'd heard Selenka Durev say that through tightly clenched teeth on more than one occasion. While Silver's conditioning under the Silence Protocol remained pristine, her mind clear of all emotion, in the time she'd known Valentin, she'd come to understand the wolf alpha's reaction. "Thank you for the data," she said to him now. "Next time, you might wish to consider an invention we in the civilized world call e-mail."

His laugh was so big it filled the air, filled the entire space of her apartment.

The thought made no sense, yet it appeared like clockwork when Valentin laughed in her vicinity. She'd told herself multiple times that she worked for the most powerful man in the world; Valentin was only a changeling alpha. Unfortunately, it appeared changeling alphas had their own potent brand of charisma. And this bear alpha had a surfeit of it.

"Have you thought about my offer?" he asked, the laughter still in his eyes.

"The answer remains the same," Silver said as a burn spread through her chest. "I do not wish to go have ice cream with you."

"It's really good ice cream." Smile disappearing, Valentin suddenly shifted fully upright from his leaning position against the doorjamb, the size and muscle of him dangerously apparent. "You doing okay?"

"Quite fine," Silver said, even as the burn morphed into a jagged spike. Something was wrong. She had to contact—

Her brain shorted out. She was aware of her body beginning to spasm, her lungs gasping for air as her legs crumpled, but she couldn't get her telepathic "muscles" to work, couldn't contact her family or Kaleb for an emergency teleport.

MOVING far faster than most people expected bear changelings to move, Valentin caught Silver's slender body before she'd done much more than sway on those ice-pick heels she liked to wear. He knew it wasn't the heels that were toppling her; Silver was never in any danger on those heels. The woman walked on them like he walked on his "bigfoot-sized" feet, as described by one of his three older sisters.

"I've got you, Starlight," he said, scooping her up in his arms and walking into her apartment.

He'd been trying to get in for ten long months, ever since he first met Ms. Silver Mercant. But he'd never expected it to be because she was convulsing in his arms. Placing her on the dark gray of the sofa, he turned her onto her side and gripped her jaw to keep her head from jerking too hard. At least she was breathing, though the sound was ragged.

With his other hand, he grabbed his phone, went to call Kaleb Krychek. The viciously powerful telekinetic could get her to help far faster than any ambulance. But Silver's body was spasming too violently for him to both hold the phone and keep her from hurting herself. Swearing under his breath, he dropped the phone and placed his other hand on her hip, holding her in place.

"Not how I wanted to put my hands on you, *moyo solnyshko*." He kept talking so she'd know she wasn't alone, but his blood was chilling with every second that passed. It was going on too long.

Deciding to risk it, he released her hip and, snatching up his phone, managed to make the call. "Silver's apartment," he said to the pitiless son of a bitch who was Silver's boss. "Medical emergency."

He dropped the phone as Silver jerked again. "Hold on, Starlight," he ordered in his most obnoxiously alpha voice, trying to keep her body from wrenching painfully at the same time. If Silver was going to respond to anything, it would be to the idea that he'd dared give her an order. "You're tougher than this."

Her eyes, that glorious silver, met his, the pupils huge . . . right before her body went limp.

Kaleb appeared in the room at the same instant, the Psy male dressed in a flawless black-on-black suit. "What happened?" he asked, his voice as cold as midnight on the steppes.

"Get her to a doctor," Valentin growled, the sound coming from the human male's vocal cords but carrying the bear's rage. "Tell them it was poison."

Kaleb was smart enough not to waste time questioning him. He simply teleported out, taking Silver with him. Teeth gritted at the fact she was out of his sight, Valentin got up and, going into Silver's kitchen, began to pull out anything that could be food. Psy had strange ideas of food—meal bars and nutrient mixes. The only surprise in Silver's cupboard was a block of fine dark chocolate.

Wondering if he'd discovered a secret about the most fascinating woman he'd ever met, a secret he could use to sneak past her defenses— no, he had no shame whatsoever when it came to Silver Mercant—he turned over the block and found a small card still attached to it. The writing was in English. It said: *Thank you for your assistance, Ms. Mercant. I hope you enjoy this small taste of our family business. ~Rico Cavalier*

His bear rumbled inside his chest.

This was the kind of gift a man gave a woman he was interested in— but it looked like this Rico had struck out if the chocolate was sitting in the back of what passed for Silver's pantry.

Good. Otherwise, I'd have had to pound the fool into dust.

The only one courting Starlight was going to be Valentin.

Having collected all possible food items, including some bland-looking "cake" from the cooler that was probably a nutrient-dense protein supplement, he began to go through them. Changelings had the sharpest noses of the three races.

Bears had the sharpest noses among changelings.

Nothing would escape him now that he'd pinpointed the poisonous scent from the millions of others in the air at any one time: the exemplar had come from Silver, her body screaming a warning to his senses as the poison went active.

"Hungry, Alpha Nikolaev?"

He didn't start at Krychek's midnight voice, having scented the cardinal telekinetic's return to the room. Thankfully for his nose, Kaleb didn't have the astringent metallic scent that some Psy did, the ones who were so deep in the emotionless regime they called Silence that Valentin didn't think anything would get them out.

It was as if they'd cut out their hearts and souls.

Silver was pure ice, but she didn't have that metallic scent, either. It gave him hope. As did the faint touch of fire he kept picking up around her, a hidden sunshine that flickered against his skin. Valentin was determined to seduce Silver's hidden wildness out into the light. Who better than an uncivilized bear, after all?

"How is she?" he asked, looking Krychek in the eye.

The telekinetic's gaze was the eerie white stars on black that denoted the strongest among the Psy race, difficult to read even if it hadn't been Kaleb Krychek—a man Valentin respected for his relentless will but mostly for his unexpected capacity for loyalty.

StoneWater did its research on possible business partners. Valentin, a young second to Zoya at the time Krychek first appeared on Stone-Water's radar, was the one who'd dug into the Psy male. And what he'd discovered about Krychek was that if you didn't betray him, he wouldn't betray you.

Valentin could work with a man like that.

Especially since Krychek had had the good sense to employ Silver.

The words the telekinetic spoke were toneless. "The medics are working on stabilizing her."

Valentin's gut clenched.

A deep rumbling building in his chest, he held out a barely used jar of nutrient mix. "This has the same toxic scent as what I scented on her—get it tested. I'm going to finish checking the other items."

Kaleb left at once, no doubt aware that, to treat Silver effectively, the medics needed to know the type of poison she'd ingested. Because while Valentin could tell something was toxic, he couldn't separate out individual poisonous scents—not when he'd never made it a point to learn those gradations.

He saw the half-full glass on the counter, realized he'd interrupted Silver at breakfast. He didn't need to lift the glass to his nose to scent the toxins swirling in the coffee-colored liquid. If he'd been here, he would've smashed that glass out of her hand before a drop touched her lips.

Jaw grinding, he handed the glass to Krychek when the other man returned. The third time Krychek came back, Valentin had found a second contaminated jar of nutrient mix. "It was the third from the front on the right-hand side," he said, knowing the location of the poisoned jars might be important. "The nutrient bars were clean." He'd ruthlessly opened each and every packet, exposing them to the air and to his nose. "Silver's going to be mad I trashed her kitchen."

Kaleb took the jar, examined the label, then teleported out with it.

When he returned, he said, "That was ordinary nutrient mix available at any Psy grocer."

"You thinking product tampering?"

"It's a possibility—those of my race are not universally liked."

That was a vast understatement. Many of the Psy might be attempting to regain their emotions after more than a hundred years of training themselves to feel nothing, but their previous rulers had done massive damage, killed and tortured and created a deep vein of ill will.

Both humans and changelings had long memories.

"The other option is an assassination attempt." Krychek's cardinal eyes took in the mess Valentin had made of the food. "I trust in your sense of smell, but I'll get everything tested regardless."

Valentin felt no insult. This wasn't about pride. It was about Silver's life. "Do it. Now tell me where she is."

Kaleb slipped his hands into the pockets of his pants. "Silver hasn't mentioned a friendship."

"I'm working on it." Had been doing so since the day he'd walked scowling into a meeting and come face-to-face with a woman who made him think of hidden fire and cold, distant, searingly brilliant starlight. And, let's be honest: skin privileges. *Naked* skin privileges. Wild-monkey skin privileges. He couldn't be around Silver and not have his body react. Her own body, it was slender, but with *all* the right curves. And she was *tough*, tough as a female bear out for blood.

Never once had she backed down against his deliberate provocation.

His bear liked that. A lot.

Enough to throw her over his shoulder and carry her off to his lair if only she wouldn't fry his brains for daring. He was tempted to chance it anyway. He had a hard head, could probably take it so long as she wasn't trying to kill him.

That mind of hers . . . He'd never met its like. Silver Mercant forgot nothing, and she had a steely presence that made even rowdy bears sit up and take notice. Woman like that, she'd make one hell of a mate. Too bad she refused to even consider the idea: Silver wasn't budging on the whole emotionless Silence thing.

"My people chose Silence for a reason," she'd said to him three visits earlier. "While parts of that reasoning have proven false enough to topple Silence for many, other parts still apply. I am and always will be Silent. That means I will never be ready to 'run off' and experience 'shenanigans' with you."

No matter. Valentin had a plan.

Because she damn well was going to survive. "Don't even try to stop me from seeing her, Krychek," he said to the cardinal, who still hadn't spilled Silver's location. "I'm bigger and meaner than you."

Krychek raised an eyebrow. "Bigger, yes. Meaner? Let's leave that an open question. However, since she's alive because of you, I think you can be trusted with her whereabouts." He told Valentin the name of the hospital.

It happened to be a short ten-minute run from here. Normally, Valentin would've covered that distance without hesitation—his bear would've barely stretched out by the time he reached the hospital. He could do vehicles, but he didn't really like them. They were all too damn small as far as he was concerned. But this wasn't a normal day. "Can I hitch a ride?"

The other man didn't say anything, but less than a second later, Valentin found himself standing in an antiseptic white corridor, the floor beneath his feet a chilly gray-blue. The chairs on one side were attached to the wall, the seat cushions darkest navy. On the right of the chairs was a door inset with a small square of glass.

Beyond that glass lay an operating theatre where white-garbed doctors and nurses worked with frantic efficiency to stabilize Silver. He couldn't see her, but regardless of the powerful hospital smells in the air, sharp and biting, he could scent the ice-cold starlight and secret fire of her.

"I thought you'd take her to a private clinic." This public hospital was an excellent one, but Silver was critical to the fragile balance of their fractured world—and Krychek could teleport anywhere in the blink of an eye.

"The lead doctor working on her is one of the world's foremost specialists in toxins and poisons and their impact on the Psy body."

"You download that information from the psychic network you're all part of?"

Krychek nodded.

"Useful." Valentin couldn't imagine a life in which his mind was connected to a limitless vastness that included millions of strangers, but as a bear whose clan was his heartbeat, he could understand it. "You didn't leave her here alone." Krychek had been delayed returning to him the first time around. Long enough to bring in someone to watch over Silver.

"No, he didn't." The woman who'd spoken had just walked over from where she'd been getting a glass of water not far down the corridor. Her language of choice was English, and she had a scent that was almost no scent. But to a bear, everyone had a scent, and she hadn't quite managed to erase every thread of hers. The subtle memory of soap, the natural body scent that was uniquely hers, a touch of roses.

He didn't have to ask her identity; this woman was Silver in fifty years. Her hair pure white and her eyes the same as his Starlight's, her facial bones fine, she was clearly a Mercant. And, if the rumors Valentin's third-eldest sister had heard were true, then she was probably *the* Mercant.

He took a chance. "Grandmother Mercant," he said in the same language she'd used, inclining his head slightly in acknowledgment of another alpha.

Silver's grandmother didn't display any surprise at his greeting, so regal, she clearly took it as her due that she'd be recognized—this despite the fact the head of the Mercant family preferred to stay firmly out of the limelight. Yes, the Mercant women were as tough as steel.

More than tough enough to handle bears.

"You have me at a disadvantage," was her polite but in no way warm response.

"Valentin Nikolaev," he said. "Alpha of the StoneWater clan."

"He was with Silver when she collapsed."

Grandmother Mercant's eyes bored into Valentin's on the heels of Krychek's words. "If my granddaughter survives, it'll be because of your quick actions." She shifted her attention to the cardinal who was the third point in their triangle. "Any response from the lab?"

"No," Krychek said, then paused. "I have the report. I'm sending it through."

Beyond the square of glass, Valentin saw a doctor lift up her head. She nodded once toward the window to acknowledge the telepathic message before beginning to issue orders to her staff.

Minutes turned to an hour, more.

Still, they waited.

The Human Patriot

HE DIDN'T CONSIDER himself a bad man. He wasn't in any way like the other self-centered bastards in the Consortium. They wanted to sow division and foster chaos because it would be better for their bottom line. He was disgusted by their greed, had accepted the Consortium's overture only because he intended to use the group to achieve his aims, aims formed of conscience and hope and love for his people.

To him, the Consortium was a tool to help him mount a righteous revolution. Yes, he made ruthless decisions when called for, but that was in business. In life, in politics, he acted on the conviction of his heart, and that heart was telling him the Trinity Accord would lead to the destruction of all that he held dear.

His beloved children, his accomplished and beautiful wife, they'd all be destroyed by this "proto-Federation" agreement being touted as a force for unity. Psy, humans, changelings, people of all three races would be equal, all have a say in the direction of the world.

"Bullshit."

He closed his hand into a tight fist on the aged cherrywood of his desk, the top inlaid with fine gold and semiprecious stones. It was a status symbol, this desk. Worth hundreds of times the yearly income of the common man on the street, it reminded him every day of what he'd achieved through determined intelligence . . . and the genetic luck of the draw.

Without the natural shield that protected his mind, he would long ago have become another casualty of Psy arrogance, another human psychically raped and violated by the emotionless, soulless bastards, his ideas and his freedom stolen.

His eyes went to the photo of his wife on his desk. So *much* light in her eyes. That had been before. She still laughed, she still loved, but she hadn't been the same since that horrific day when she'd come up with an invention a Psy coveted. The monster had stripped her clean before the man who loved her to the core of his being could find a way to protect her.

She no longer created, knowing it could be taken from her at any instant.

But they were supposed to believe the Psy were turning over a new leaf, that they'd suddenly begun to respect the sanctity of the human mind?

Throwing down the pen he'd picked up to sign a contract, he rose to his feet and, stepping out onto the balcony attached to his home study, looked down at the cool paradise of their white-tiled courtyard with its fountain in the center. His children's laughter drifted up from below, their small bodies hidden by the black plum trees that hung heavy with fruit.

"Papa! Papa!" His boy ran out from under the trees, held up a toy truck. "Come play!"

He smiled, his heart so full he could hardly bear it. "In a moment," he called down. "Let Papa finish his work first. We'll play afterward."

Happy with the promise, the boy returned to his play while a little girl jumped into the fountain in laughing delight. Wild, his daughter was, and the apple of his eye. How could it be otherwise when she was so like her mother? And his son, oh, he loved his son, too.

So much.

Enough to fight for a future where they wouldn't be used and discarded. Because if his informant was right, the Psy race desperately needed to harness human minds for some reason the informant hadn't yet been able to unearth. And whenever the Psy needed something from humans, the powerful psychic race just took it.

No more.

If that meant he had to become a monster himself, had to circumvent loyalties and buy betrayal, even order the death of a brilliant woman who—on the surface—appeared to have no bias in sending aid to various humanitarian crises around the world, so be it.

Silver Mercant and EmNet were one of the foundation stones on which Trinity was built. But that foundation stone was set to break, alongside several others.

Soon.

Chapter 2

Betrayal is a rusted sword that wounds long before the first cut is made.

—Lord Deryn Mercant (circa 1502)

THE DOCTOR—AN M-Psy—emerged two hours after Krychek had sent through the telepathic message about the details of the poison; Valentin was pacing the hallway, his bear shoving at the inside of his skin, its fur thick and heavy.

"She'll make a full recovery. No complications foreseen."

Valentin's lungs filled with air again, his chest expanding.

"Did you have to remove any of her organs?" The question came from Grandmother Mercant.

"No." The short, dark-haired doctor took a whisper-thin organizer from a nurse who'd just come through the doors at the other end of the corridor. "We pumped out her stomach, gave her the antidote, but because of the complexity of the poison, we had to monitor her responses and calibrate the antidote drop by drop."

A glance up from the medical file on the organizer. "She was lucky. The nutrients weren't close to digested, and she didn't get the full dose."

Valentin thought again of that half-full glass and of how long it had taken him to climb up to an open window on a lower floor of Silver's

20 NALINI SINGH

building. From there, it had been relatively easy to avoid the security cameras and get to Silver's floor. If he'd been just a minute too late . . . "When can we see her?"

The doctor didn't question his right to be there—apparently, being with the head of the Mercant family and Kaleb Krychek gave him instant credibility, even if he was dressed in ripped jeans and an old white shirt with the sleeves rolled up. That shirt had a drip of blue paint on one shoulder. He'd thought—once—about dressing up for Silver, but he figured if he was going to coax her to the bear side, he should go full bear mode.

No point in false advertising.

He couldn't wait for those cool eyes of hers to give him their usual critical once-over. Last visit, she'd offered to supply him with the name of a good seamstress who could patch up the holes in his jeans. The visit before that, she'd pointed out that most people stopped wearing their T-shirts long before the color faded to a "shade that can be best described as rag gray."

"According to these updated readings," the doctor said, her eyes on the organizer, "she should be conscious in ninety minutes to two hours. We'll be moving her into a recovery room shortly."

The three of them waited in silence while Silver was ensconced in a private room. Valentin watched her grandmother go inside to sit with her, made himself stay outside, though bear and man both wanted to thunder inside. He didn't even look through the partially open blinds on the window beside the door, as he hadn't looked when she was moved from the operating theatre to the recovery room.

Silver *would not* thank him for seeing her when she was so vulnerable.

Except he already had.

He groaned, the bass sound coming from deep within. "She is never going to forgive me for having witnessed her collapse."

Beside him, Krychek glanced at his watch, the cardinal Psy's dark hair gleaming in the overhead light. "Given the current time and the fact Silver keeps to a firm schedule unless she needs to adapt to fit a developing situation, you interrupted her at breakfast, thus saving her life."

"You think she'll see it that way?" Valentin asked on an excited burst of hope.

The other man didn't even pause to consider it. "No. You're out of luck."

Valentin narrowed his eyes, wondering if Krychek was laughing at him.

The cardinal was the coldest man he knew—but unlike Valentin, Kaleb Krychek had a woman who *adored* him. Sahara Kyriakus made no effort to hide her love for her mate. Valentin had seen her kissing Krychek right in the center of Red Square, her joy a bright light. Krychek hadn't so much as cracked a faint smile the entire time—but a man had to have a heart to win that of a woman who wore hers on her sleeve.

So, yes, his bear decided, it was quite possible Kaleb Krychek was laughing at him under that frigid exterior. "Thank you for nothing," he grumbled to the other man, before propping himself up against the nearest wall.

"Do you want a return teleport?"

"No, I'll wait." Just until Starlight was awake. He needed to see her chest rise and fall, hear the frosty control of her voice, feel the laser focus of her intelligence.

"Don't let Silver spot you, or any hope you have of her choosing to forget this incident will go up in smoke."

Now Valentin was *certain* Krychek was laughing at him. "Go count your fleas, you mangy wolf," he said on a deep rumble of sound emanating from his bearish side, the latter words the worst possible insult among StoneWater bears.

Krychek teleported out so fast, Valentin wasn't sure he'd heard. It probably hadn't been the most diplomatic thing to say to a cardinal of such brutal power, but Valentin wasn't the least sorry about it—which was why he tended to leave the Krychek contacts to Anastasia. His eldest sister and second-in-command was much, much better at this type of thing.

Valentin was a "big, deranged grizzly," while Stasya was an "intelligent and thoughtful panda."

That description had come from his second-eldest sister, Nova. Forget that he, Stasya, Nova, and Nika—his third-eldest sister—were all Kamchatka brown bears, and pandas were so "thoughtful" they often took an hour to reply to a question. Apparently it was a metaphor. At least Nova hadn't called him an actual *snearzhnyi chelovek*. An alpha had to have some standards—his included not being called a yeti.

Or a wolf.

His impolitic nature was the reason why it had taken him so long to meet Silver. He'd just never gone to any Moscow meetings. Now, he went to every one where he knew she would be present. Stasya had thrown up her hands when he dug in his feet on the matter—then she'd given him duct tape. To put over his mouth whenever he felt like being his "lumbering beary self." End quote.

Valentin didn't lumber. Not unless he'd downed a few beers.

And none of those thoughts were keeping his mind off the woman in the room beyond the closed door.

When that door opened at long last, he found himself the focus of a steely gaze. "My name," Silver's grandmother said, "is Ena. But you may call me Grandmother."

Valentin was well aware he'd been granted a privilege. When he'd first greeted her that way, it had been because it was the most respectful address that came to mind. This, however, was permission to take a familial intimacy. While he didn't know anything of Ena beyond the fact she was the head of a powerful family, he knew enough of Silver to know this was serious business.

Women like Ena and Silver did not offer such things lightly.

"How's our girl doing, Grandmother?"

Ena Mercant stared at him for long minutes. "You're extremely brash. Nothing like the leopard alpha who's representing so many changeling groups in the Trinity Accord."

"There's a reason Lucas is our public face." It hadn't been a hard decision to trust Lucas Hunter to look after StoneWater's interests in the fledgling accord that sought to unite their divided world.

The other man had more reason than anyone to fight for the tenets of

Trinity. His daughter was both Psy and changeling, the first such child born in a century; and he, like Valentin, had a number of humans in his pack. "Can you imagine me negotiating with the *kretiny* Lucas deals with on a daily basis?" Making a gun of his thumb and forefingers, he pressed it to his temple, set it off with a "bhoof" of sound.

Not responding to that, Ena Mercant sat down in one of the visitor chairs against the wall. Next to her, he stayed upright, alert. "No other windows into Silver's room?"

"No. I'm running a telepathic scan so I'll know the instant anyone teleports in."

So would Valentin, his sense of smell hyper-focused. No one was going to hurt his Starlight. "So, Grandmother, you think it was product tampering?"

Ena's response was indirect. "Silver always has six jars in the cupboard. She starts on the left, pulls the second jar on the left forward once she's finished the first, and so on. It's interesting you found a second tainted jar in the position you did."

Valentin's claws, long, curved, and deadly, threatened to erupt from his skin. "'Interesting' is not the word I'd use." If the poisoner was uncertain of Silver's system, that person would have doctored a jar on each side. Not the first one, so it'd be harder to pin down exactly when the jars had been tampered with, but the second in each row. "She was targeted."

Ena stayed silent for long enough that he managed to talk his bear out of surging to the surface. Now was not the time to rampage in fury. Because "deranged grizzly" tendencies or not, Valentin was also an alpha to the core of his soul; he had the capacity to control his primal urges.

Medical calls came and went over the intercom, and a nurse rushed by in response to an alert, but inside Silver's room, it stayed quiet.

"What do you know of my family?" Ena asked at last.

He noted the possessive. Yes, this woman was an alpha, too. A matriarch like the bear Valentin had succeeded in StoneWater eight months earlier. Zoya was as tough—though far less reserved in her responses. That just made his former alpha a bear and Ena a Psy. It said nothing about either woman's power.

"Not much," he admitted in response to her question about the Mercants. "My sister Janika knows a lot of people"—half of Russia it sometimes felt like—"so we've picked up things here and there, but we've made no effort to dig into Psy politics." They had no Psy in their clan and thus no reason or ability to have a direct line of information. Of course, that would change once he convinced Silver to throw in her lot with him. He'd need the information to make sure she was safe.

As she hadn't been in her own apartment.

Inside him, his bear rose up on its back paws, a massive creature enraged that Silver's home had been violated. Home was safety, was where they raised their cubs and nurtured the bonds of family. Home was warmth and love and play. It was *never* an acceptable target, no matter what the war.

"I don't need anyone to tell me that you personally are a power," he said, his voice dropping into a deeper register as his bear continued to pace inside him. "You wear it like a second skin. It's so obvious even a snow-blind polar bear couldn't miss it. Added to that, Krychek respects you."

While StoneWater and Krychek had had a rocky road to a wary trust that was still a work in progress, Valentin had never doubted the other man's smarts. "He knew you'd be able to protect Silver."

A glance up, Ena's expression impossible to read. "Brash and astute. An unexpected combination."

Valentin shrugged. "Element of surprise." Many people took the bearish approach to life as evidence that bears were dense and unintelligent. Bears made no effort whatsoever to dissuade the idiots.

As Stasya had put it: "Why should we school the stupid out of them when it means we have a huge advantage in almost any negotiation?"

Too bad Selenka's wolves had long ago figured out the truth.

"My family is powerful," Grandmother Mercant said, her eyes on the wall in front of her. "We are the primary shadow players in the Net, the family everyone wants to court to gain intelligence, have our machinery at their back while they climb to power."

Surprised at her candor, Valentin listened in alert silence. One of the things Nika had picked up through her ability to make all kinds of friends—it was as if she'd been adopted from a pony herd or something—was that the Mercants kept their mouths sealed shut when it came to the family.

"Killing Silver would cripple us for at least a decade," Ena added, the reminder of the attempt to end Silver's starlight making Valentin see red all over again, his shoulder muscles bunching tight as he crossed his arms.

Ena continued to speak. "We would withdraw, regroup, become strong again. But we would've lost the person I trust to lead the Mercants into the future."

Her voice never altered, her tone flat, but Valentin knew without a single doubt that Ena Mercant would kill to protect her granddaughter, her love a fierce thing. Ena wouldn't call it love. Neither would Silver. Didn't change the fact that the loyalty tying them together was a bond of the heart any bear would recognize.

"She's also the only one who knows EmNet inside and out," he said, drawing in fine traces of Silver's scent through all the antiseptics and medicines that hung so heavy in the air.

His bear clawed at him, wanting out, wanting to nuzzle her, cuddle her close. Valentin had some trouble getting it under control since he wanted the same thing. "Even if we take her link to Krychek out of the equation," he said, "Silver is a target on multiple fronts. The Consortium"—a greedy, dishonorable group that Lucas Hunter had warned him about—"is anti-peace and EmNet is the flag bearer for Trinity." For the hope of a permanent worldwide peace.

"Yes." Again, Ena said nothing else for so long that he thought the conversation was over. But then she stirred. "Someone got into the most secure apartment building in Moscow. Then they got into her apartment. All without tripping security."

"It's not that hard to get into her building," Valentin told her, furious at the security people. "I climbed in through an open window on the third floor." He couldn't climb for shit in his animal form, his bear too big, but in his human form with his claws out? He hadn't found a wall he couldn't scale.

Not that the alpha of StoneWater made a habit of climbing up apartment buildings. He only did that for his icy Starlight.

"Most people," Ena responded, "including most changelings, don't have the kind of claws sported by bears. You're also heavily muscled and, I'm guessing, extremely strong."

"Teleporters don't need claws or physical strength."

"No, but Silver has worked with a cardinal telekinetic for years. She had scent filters put in, motion sensors. Kaleb tested the precautions to make sure they'd work against someone with his ability. She should've known the instant an intruder entered, but it's clear she registered no such intrusion."

Valentin's bear froze. "You think the poison was added by someone she let in." Easy if the guest was a person Silver trusted, a person she would've left alone in the living area while she went to fetch something from another room or maybe excused herself to take a private call. The kitchen was only steps away.

Ena inclined her head. "If this individual was smart, he or she wouldn't have dosed the jar Silver was using at the time."

"That's what I figured." His bear head-butting him in a stubborn refusal to sit down and behave until it had seen Silver, Valentin thought back to her kitchen cupboards and to the second tainted jar. "How long does a jar last?"

"One month if used nonstop, which Silver doesn't do. Two to three months if interspersed with other sources of nutrients like the bars and protein supplements."

"We need to go through all the visitors she's had in the time since she began using the jar *before* this one." Even though Silver had just opened this jar, they'd have to go back at least four months to be on the safe side.

"No, Valentin," Ena said, interrupting him midthought. "That is not your responsibility."

Valentin's bear roared in outrage.

He clenched his jaw, frustratingly conscious that he had no rights here. Silver wasn't his, hadn't even let him through her front door yet. Today didn't count, and even his bear wouldn't argue that it set a precedent. Starlight had to invite him in for it to count.

"Your job," Ena said, "is to give her safe harbor."

The bear stopped midroar, stunned into silence.

"I'd like nothing better," Valentin said through his surprise, "but Silver won't accept a bodyguard." And he was alpha, his time bound to the clan, a truth Ena had to understand. What she couldn't know was just how badly his clan needed him right now. His short visits to annoy and court Starlight had been the only breaks he'd taken since becoming alpha eight months earlier.

"I know," Ena replied. "I also know she won't go far from her center of work. But she can't continue to live in a place where anyone can walk in and poison her."

Valentin's fur ruffled inside him, his bear's attention caught. "The poison is important." His next question was pure instinct. "Is it a Mercant weapon?" Shadow players would strike with stealth rather than in open aggression.

Ena's response was telling. "I can't offer her any of our safe houses. They're keyed to all Mercants."

Biting back a harsh word in his native tongue, quite certain both Babushka Caroline and Babushka Anzhela would clip him on the ear if they heard he'd uttered that particular word in the presence of an elder, he ran a hand through his hair. "You think one of your own went after Silver."

"Our entire family is built on trust."

"Like a bear clan." Betrayal was a dagger to the heart, and it *hurt*. Valentin knew. He'd felt it stab him to the core, was still bleeding and bruised because of it, his bear dejected by the unexpected blow.

"Why not ask Krychek for a place?" Valentin forced himself to ask; he wanted to haul Silver deep into his territory where no one could hurt her, but these were the same questions she'd ask—better he and Ena have her boxed in before she woke.

The bear inside him snorted at the idea of playing fair when it was Starlight's life at stake.

"Since Silver won't abandon her work by moving to a totally different region, the only possibilities Kaleb can offer her will be in central Moscow. She'd remain accessible to her enemies."

Valentin unfolded his arms, a smile starting to tug at his lips. "Are you asking me to kidnap your granddaughter?"

"Let's call it an enforced move out of the field of danger."

He was fluent in English, thanks to his Canadian polar bear maternal grandmother, but it still took him a second to work out that yes, Ena was in favor of Valentin kidnapping Silver.

Chapter 3

Blind uniformity is a fool's goal.

—Ena Mercant (circa 2072)

ALREADY PLOTTING THE kidnapping, Valentin said, "Silver knows a lot of teleporters." Even the deadly and secretive Arrow Squad, who Nika said were the bogeymen of the Psy, responded to a call from the director of EmNet.

"Given the nature of this incident, she'd ask no one but Kaleb, and Kaleb understands the problem."

Her words confirmed what he'd begun to suspect—Krychek wasn't simply a telekinetic for whom Silver had worked for years prior to taking up the reins of EmNet; the other man had become tightly bonded to the Mercants. "Why trust me?"

"You could've let her die. You didn't. That means you and Kaleb are the two people I can trust without question right now."

"I need to talk to my clan." Valentin was alpha, his word law, but no bear clan would function well with an autocrat at the helm. Clan was about family, about respect, about loyalty.

Pain lanced through his bear's heart as terrible memories rose on the heels of that thought, the wound as fresh today as the day it had been made.

Ena rose to her feet. "I will sit with my granddaughter while you confer with your people."

Valentin pulled out his phone the instant she was inside the recovery room; he'd picked up the sleek black device almost automatically before he entered Silver's kitchen to hunt down the poison. He pressed a familiar code.

"What did you break now?" were Stasya's opening words.

Ignoring the greeting only a big sister would think to offer her alpha, he said, "Security threats if we bring a Psy into Denhome." Like beads on a necklace that tumbled this way and that, Denhome was a mazelike collection of interconnected dwellings dug out of a mountain. It was sprawling and snug and, most of all, safe for the occasionally uncoordinated and always troublemaking balls of fur that were their cubs.

"Which Psy?" Stasya asked with her usual no-nonsense directness.

"Silver Mercant."

"Very funny, Mishka," she said, using his childhood nickname of "little bear"—sisters never forgot anything *and* they told everyone they knew until a man had to remind people his name was actually the very adult-sounding Valentin Mikhailovich Nikolaev.

"I know you have a thing for her, but abducting women is against the law." She said the last very firmly. "Even for bears. Get that into your head."

"No joke." He wished it had been play, that he'd given in to his primal instincts and thrown Silver over his shoulder—she'd have reacted badly, but she wouldn't now be lying unconscious in a hospital bed. "She needs a safe place to lie low, and we're the best available."

"If you're messing with me, I'll put toothpaste in your hair while you sleep," his second-in-command warned. "You know Silver Mercant is a threat as big as an elephant on steroids. She'll have visuals of our den, of our little ones, will pick up our security system, could use it all to mount an attack. It might not be physical, but an economic attack could cripple us as badly. Especially now, with our resources split."

Valentin rubbed a clenched fist over his heart. "I'm dead certain I can make a deal where nothing she learns would ever be used against us." Raw animal instinct told him that Ena Mercant wasn't a woman who gave her word lightly; if he had it, his clan would be safe.

Also, Starlight was his to protect. Yes, she'd argue about his claim, but he liked arguing with Silver. She might be pure frost, but she never shied away from picking up any of the gauntlets he'd cunningly thrown down in an effort to break through her defenses. Though perhaps "cunning" wasn't the right word when he'd been as obvious as Anastasia's elephant on steroids.

"Good," his sister said now, "but the threat isn't as bad as my first-level assessment." Her voice was crisp, direct. "Silver is linked to Krychek, and we know from Nika's many spies and friends that Krychek can teleport to places by locking on to faces. So if he wanted to get into Denhome, he could. But we have an agreement with Krychek—that means if Silver betrays us, she dumps her boss in it."

"I don't think Silver will be betraying us." His cool blonde Starlight was working mercilessly hard to make EmNet a truly cohesive entity; she couldn't afford to alienate one of the two largest changeling groups in Russia. "I'm bringing her in."

"You realize certain bears will probably have a problem with her being here."

"They'll deal, or I'll crack their skulls together until they find their brains." Valentin might not want to handle Trinity negotiations on a day-to-day basis, but he understood the need behind the accord—their world had been divided too long, the fractures running deep and causing wide veins of anger and mistrust.

The defunct Psy Council had done horrific damage in the past, had murdered and stolen and broken, but the monstrous bastards had no claim on the future. Psy, human, or changeling, all three races had to take responsibility for the world they would leave their cubs. Here, in this city, it would begin with a Psy being welcomed into a bear clan.

"I'll prepare a spare cave."

They didn't actually live in caves . . . Okay, they did, but they were very nice caves. He wondered what Silver would think of Denhome. "*Spasibo*, Stasya."

Hanging up, he entered the recovery room after a quiet knock, making a deliberate effort to keep his eyes averted from the bed on which Silver lay so quiet and still. His bear didn't fight him. That primal part of him understood extremely well that getting on the bad side of a female bear's pride was a *very bad idea*—and as far as Valentin was concerned, Silver was a bear under the skin.

Strength and wildness and a relentless—sometimes obstinate—will.

None of that was a negative. Valentin could be obstinate himself. He needed a mate who'd refuse to take any of his shit. She'd also drive him insane, of that he was certain, but bears were lunatics anyway. It'd be fun.

All he had to do was convince Silver of that.

His bear grunted inside him, confident of its charm and ability to court the woman who spoke to both parts of his soul. Valentin decided his animal had the right idea: go in guns blazing and charm at full blast. And he had to be sneaky so she didn't think to put up her defenses until it was too late. Not bear sneaky. *Cat* sneaky.

That began with making sure she ended up in his territory.

"Silver is welcome in Denhome," he said to Ena. "Can she work remotely until the danger is past?" He was already making a list in his head of the tech she'd need. A cat would be sneaky like that, would give the woman he was courting what she needed before she even asked for it.

"I'll talk to her," Ena replied, "make sure she understands that family is not safe for her."

Valentin left soon afterward, aware exactly how much it must've cost this proud, strong alpha to say those words.

SILVER woke to walls that were a crisp white and a ceiling that had a crosshatched pattern that struck her as a design artefact from at least six decades earlier. Her apartment didn't have that type of a ceiling, was smooth. It wasn't white, either, rather a pale gray. Her walls were gray, too. She hadn't chosen the colors. They'd come with the apartment, and

SILVER SILENCE · 33

as the colors didn't distract her or cause any unexpected reactions in her brain, she'd left it.

Her neighbor in the apartment next door, a human executive who was only in Moscow approximately three months of the year spread out over tens of short visits, had already had her place repainted three times in the space of four years. The last time, she'd knocked on Silver's door and asked her favorite of three shades of cream.

Silver had stopped pointing out that she was Psy, didn't spend time on such matters, didn't have favorites. To satisfy the other woman, she'd just pointed to a random shade. Inevitably, it was the one Monique Ling wasn't "loving."

The chaos of thoughts tumbled through Silver's brain in the space of a few heartbeats. Within those heartbeats, her telepathic senses were spreading out, evaluating the threats in the room. She didn't get far. Her head was thick, felt foggy. But that wasn't why. Silver could push through that, could force herself to function even when she was at less than a hundred percent.

She stopped because her psychic senses had brushed up against a mind that had once encompassed her own. She'd been a child at the time, one learning to handle violent telepathic abilities that left her vulnerable to the torrent of noise the world threw at her. "Grandmother." Her voice came out rough, as if her throat were lined with grit.

"Here." Her grandmother, seated in a chair beside Silver's bed, slipped chips of ice between her lips.

Regardless of the questions pounding at her, Silver forced herself to be patient. That was another lesson her grandmother had taught her: to control her psychic abilities, Silver had to learn to leash her impulsive nature.

Ena Mercant didn't believe in flaws or perfection. "We are who we are and we are strong" was her oft-stated motto. It was a motto that had been passed down from one head of the family to the next in an unbroken line.

As a result, the Mercants didn't single out children for traits that would've had them labeled failures in many other families. Instead, all

Mercant children were trained and educated according to their natural inclinations. In some cases, that meant utilizing the natural trait. In others, it meant training the child to be aware of facets that might negatively impact his or her psychic stability.

Today, Silver utilized an old mental exercise to keep her questions from pouring out onto the audible or psychic plane. At the same time, as her brain woke to its usual sharpness, she continued her psychic scan . . . and came up against a mind she couldn't read but that was familiar nonetheless. That hard outer "shell" impervious to psychic intrusion belonged to a changeling.

The presence of a changeling wasn't unusual. From the data she'd already gathered about her situation, she was obviously in a hospital; running into changeling or human minds was to be expected. This mind, however . . .

"What is Valentin doing here?" she asked before she realized what it would betray. She'd recognized her grandmother's mind because they had a telepathic pathway between them that had existed for nearly twenty-nine years, the imprint so familiar the knowledge was ingrained. That didn't apply with Valentin.

Yet despite the fact she couldn't even sense Valentin's surface thoughts, his natural shield too powerful, she knew without a doubt that it was him. If anyone had asked her to explain, she'd have been reduced to saying the mind "tasted" like him.

For a Psy, that was a ridiculous explanation.

It was fortunate her grandmother didn't ask her how she'd so quickly pinpointed his identity. "He's the reason you're breathing right now." No change in Ena's tone, but Silver turned her eyes from the closed door to the room and toward the woman who'd been the defining force in her life. She had highly competent parents who'd shared child-rearing duties when it came to Silver, but it was to Ena that Silver had always looked for guidance.

"Like recognizes like," her mother had once said to her. "She understands you better than I ever will."

It was true. Silver rarely had to explain her thought processes to her grandmother.

"I remember Alpha Nikolaev turning up on my doorstep with a data crystal," she said in response to her grandmother's statement. "Then, nothing." The black spot in her memory brought her up short. "Did I have a seizure?"

"It wasn't as a result of a physical ailment or degeneration," Ena said, answering the most critical question. "You ingested a comparatively fast-acting poison."

Silver took in the information, separated it out into its components, absorbed it. Her mind went back to her morning before Valentin had knocked on the door. Why he didn't use the perfectly functional intercom was not a question she wasted time asking. Bears, she'd learned, often did things that were inexplicable just because they could.

Valentin had turned that into an art form.

"I ate dinner at eight the previous night, went to sleep at ten thirty. I woke sixty minutes prior to Alpha Nikolaev's arrival," she said, working it through. "I spent thirty minutes doing yoga." Another exercise she'd been taught to help her regulate her naturally chaotic mental patterns, the exercise now a part of her.

"Twenty-five minutes to shower and dress for the day." It took so long because she had to put on makeup and fix her hair in precisely the right fashion. Icily Silent or open to emotion, Psy reacted to physical stimuli the same as any other race. Silver's appearance was carefully calibrated to trigger a certain subconscious response.

"I spent the next few minutes going through the messages that had come in during my sleeping hours, at the same time preparing a nutrient drink." She remembered drinking half a glass before the familiar heavy knock on her door. "I placed the still half-full glass on the counter along-side my organizer not long afterward, went to open the door to Alpha Nikolaev."

"Did you know it was him?"

"The only two people who knock on my door that early in the morning are my neighbor and Alpha Nikolaev. As Monique Ling is currently in Hong Kong, that left only him." She didn't say she'd recognized the knock, the psychic sense of him. "I was speaking to him, and that's the point where my mind goes blank."

Staying in her seated position beside the bed, her grandmother filled her in. Some of it Silver had already guessed—including that the poison must've been in her nutrient mix. The rest was new.

"Alpha Nikolaev saw me convulse?" Silver was Silent, had consciously retained her conditioning even as the PsyNet began to fill with emotion around her. As a result, she didn't like or dislike things, wasn't happy or unhappy about any given situation. Valentin seeing her while she was so vulnerable, however, changed the power dynamic between them.

That could not be permitted to stand.

Bears had a tendency to stomp their way over opposition they considered weak. Silver wasn't about to be stomped.

"He contacted Kaleb, got you here." Ena closed her hand over Silver's wrist, the physical contact from her grandmother so rare that it was a severe jolt to her equilibrium. "The bear alpha also found poison in a second unopened jar of nutrient mix."

Silver's lashes lowered. When they rose again, she knew why her grandmother was concerned enough to breach the strict rules by which the Mercant family had functioned and survived the years the Silence Protocol ruled the Psy. Because their genetic line had never been naturally inclined toward emotionlessness.

Mercants had been warriors through time, had roared in battle, had run with "fury in the blood," according to old documents Silver had been given access to six months earlier, when she began to take on some of her grandmother's duties. They'd also birthed fiery poets and playwrights whose prose was lauded to this day. Their line was said to be full of passion. To Silver, passion was a mere intellectual concept, but she understood that it denoted wildness.

As a result, Silence had never been an easy fit for them. But along with passion, Silver's ancestors had repeatedly demonstrated a steely will. That, too, was a trait that ran true in their line, and it had allowed them to not only survive but also thrive under Silence.

As a *family*.

An intense capacity for loyalty was their greatest strength.

"None of my security systems have been set off anytime during the past year," she told her grandmother. "I restocked the cupboard with six new jars of nutrient mix six months ago." They were designed to hold their food value for a number of years. "It took me much longer than usual to finish the first jar because I inadvertently bought several packs of nutrition bars with a short use-by date that I had to eat first."

"Who has been in your apartment in that period?"

Silver held her grandmother's eyes, knowing her words would be an anvil smashing into everything Ena Mercant had fought to build. "Family," she said quietly. "The only people who have been in my apartment over the past six months are members of the family." Usually, that would've meant well under ten people overall—likely her cousin, Ivan, who worked in building security; her brother; and possibly another Mercant or two passing through Moscow who needed to touch base for reasons of family or business, or who'd asked to stay in her spare bedroom while in the city.

However, approximately five months earlier, Silver had hosted a large meeting that focused on Kaleb's acceptance into the Mercant family. Not as an outsider they trusted, but as one of them. He hadn't been at the meeting, the meeting about him. The discussion had been robust, but in the end, they'd come to a unanimous decision.

Silver had always known it would go that way. Ena had already decided, and her grandmother was the one who set the course of the Mercant family. She'd also known Ena would listen carefully to all the pros and cons, on the slim chance that she'd missed weighing an important factor.

"During the meeting," Silver continued, "I kept no track of the family's movements in my apartment." She hadn't thought she needed to be vigilant; these were *Mercants*. Their family maxim was *Cor meum familia est*. My heart is family. The emotional maxim came from a time long before Silence, but they'd left it unchanged because Silence or not, it spoke to what tied their family together, what kept them strong even as others faltered and fell.

Her grandmother's fingers curved over her wrist. "I've already locked down your security and will personally look into every member of the family who has been in your apartment in the past six months. I'll also review all movements in the corridor outside your apartment in the operative window. Whatever it takes, I'll find out who tried to kill my granddaughter."

"Grandmother." Silver sat up, her head having cleared in the interim. "This is my—"

"No, Silver, this is a family problem." Her grandmother's eyes pinned her in place. "You may assist—I will share the data with you, but the most pressing matter is to get you into a secure living space where no one will question why you can't have familial visitors."

Silver considered her options. Because her grandmother was right—if she began turning away those who were Mercants, it would create fine fractures in the structure of the family. That result might even be the poisoner's intent. Silver needed to take herself out of circulation while the traitor was brought to ground.

A single bad seed could not be permitted to poison an entire family.

"I could relocate to the outskirts of Moscow," she suggested. "Family members are far less likely to pass through that region."

"Since there are no secure apartment buildings that far out, you'll have to either hire a full complement of security, or leave yourself open."

That, too, was true. As was another fact: Ena Mercant was too smart not to have used the time Silver had been unconscious to come up with a solution. *Oh.* All at once, she knew why Valentin was outside her room. Ena wouldn't have permitted him that close unless she needed him there.

"StoneWater?" She stared at her normally very sensible and rational grandmother. "Impossible."

Chapter 4

Glasses broken: 132. Chairs broken: 12. Jukeboxes turned upside down because some bear thought it was hilarious: 1.

Bill to follow. (No charge for the spilled alcohol. Your bears were very careful not to do that. That bill's going to Selenka.)

—E-mail to Alpha Nikolaev from Nina Rodchenko, manager of Club Moscow

"WHY?" ENA ASKED. "It's an easy sell—we tell everyone you're spending time with the bears to gain a better insight into how changelings view the world so you can more efficiently run EmNet."

It was a brilliant idea, could well strengthen EmNet's credibility in the eyes of those who believed a Psy shouldn't be at the helm of what was effectively a humanitarian organization. But—"Grandmother, you're unaware of the differences between the various changeling groups."

"Explain."

"Living with leopards might be an option," Silver said. "They're independent and tend to make homes far from one another, while remaining a tightly knit unit. Similar to the predatory bird clans like the eagles. And all akin to our family." She paused to put her thoughts in order. "From everything I know, bears are like wolves but worse."

"In what way?"

"Wolves create large dens where they live in family or couple units, and while they have single-individual residences, each person is still part of a bigger whole. To find true privacy, you'd have to leave the den and go out some distance into the wilderness." Because, apparently, wolves liked to follow packmates and make sure said packmates were okay.

That was what she'd once heard from Selenka when the wolf alpha made a rare visit to Kaleb's Moscow office. Silver couldn't recall what had led to this particular conversation, but the BlackEdge alpha had laughingly told her that though she was alpha, her packmates had come looking for her a few days earlier when she'd taken off for a hard run and not returned for a day.

"Bears," she said to her grandmother, "are worse by a factor of multiples."

Silver had little personal experience with them, aside from Valentin's visits and the odd meeting with StoneWater's second-in-command, Anastasia, but she knew how to listen, and she lived in a region with a strong ursine presence. She'd heard more than enough over the years to build up what she believed was a fairly accurate picture. "They live right on top of one another and have no concept of what it means to be a loner."

"That makes little sense. Natural bears are not community-minded."

"Unfortunately, it appears the human instinct to be social has been supercharged in changeling bear genetics. I'll have an aneurysm with that much togetherness."

Her grandmother didn't reply for some time, her thought processes as opaque as always. "If they're that close," she said at last, "no stranger would ever get to you. According to the research I did while waiting for you to wake, bears also have an incomparable sense of smell, so you'd be in no danger from poisons."

Searching for anything to get her out of this, Silver said, "Do you know how many Moscow bars have a bear surcharge? *All* of them." Silver knew that because she knew her city. "Something always seems to get broken when a group of bears is out to have a good time."

"Yet they aren't banned."

"For some inexplicable reason, people like bears, even if they break things." As with Silver and Valentin, the bar owners kept opening their doors to the rowdiest possible guests.

"Good," Ena said.

"Good?"

"To be so welcome regardless of their propensity for disorderly behavior, they must be generally good-natured. However, their reputation means no one will possibly imagine that you'd want to live with the bears for any reason but political expediency."

Ena held up a hand when Silver would've interrupted. "The poisoner, after all, has no way of predicting exactly when you'll open one of the contaminated jars. So he or she won't assume you're leaving your apartment in response to a security breach."

Silver continued to stare at her grandmother. "You couldn't live in such surroundings."

"No." Ena rose to her feet, her tunic and wide-legged pants a pale shade of green, the ornate ruby pendant she wore on a long silver chain an heirloom passed down from one leader of the family to the next. Depending on the individual wearing it, the pendant sometimes became a watch chain or a brooch. Other times, it was carried in a pocket rather than worn.

Silver had seen it around her grandmother's neck all her life.

"But," Ena added, "you're young enough to adapt. You *must*. The world is changing, and Mercants have survived so many centuries, so many empires, because we adapt without losing the core of who we are."

Silver was having difficulty processing what her grandmother was saying. "Are you telling me to breach Silence?" She knew Ena believed Silence gave them strength when the world around them was falling prey to emotion. But for a single exception, those who could think with crystal-clear pragmatism would always win over the emotionally led.

But that wasn't the deciding factor when it came to Silver—discarding Silence wasn't a choice for her, would never be a choice. Not if she wished to stay sane, stay alive. "You know I can't." There was a reason her sub-designation had been considered extinct pre-Silence.

"Of course I know." Her grandmother's response was a rebuke. "What I'm telling you is that you need to learn to function at peak efficiency in a changed world. Silence has fallen; Psy and changelings and humans are beginning to intermingle, mate, produce offspring. Our family must not be left behind."

Steely gray eyes held Silver's, the power in them a pulse against her skin. "You must understand this new world better than anyone else in the family. You will lead after I'm gone."

Silver did not ever think of her grandmother's mortality; Ena was too strong, too much a force of nature. "You're only eighty-three years of age." Those of her grandmother's generation were forecast to live to a hundred and twenty at least.

"Life is a volatile process, Silver. When you were born, I could've never predicted that, today, we'd be living in a world where the most brutally powerful cardinal in the Net would be openly in love with a woman whose closest friends are emotion-drenched empaths."

Ena's gaze was distant, seeing a past that had once been her present. "Designation E was outlawed then, empaths considered useless. Yet now, it is the Es who hold the PsyNet together. Without them, we'd all eventually fall prey to ravening madness. Even the most gifted foreseers did not see this coming."

Silver had nothing to say to that—her grandmother was right. Change was a juggernaut crashing through the world. It could not be stopped, could not be turned back. Not that Silver would make the latter choice even were it possible. Silence was necessary for her, but for others, it was a cage. Empaths, brutalized by having their natural abilities crushed and belittled, were simply the most obvious casualties.

That wasn't even the worst of it.

It was open knowledge now that the century of Silence had done catastrophic damage to the fabric of the PsyNet. All Psy needed the biofeedback provided by their connection to a psychic network. Cut that link and an excruciating death would follow in a matter of minutes. Silence had poisoned that critical network, fostering pockets of seething darkness formed of all the emotions the Psy refused to feel.

That darkness had turned into a malignant rot that caused the "ravening madness" of which her grandmother had spoken. It was the E-Psy, with their ability to handle even the worst emotions, who had created the Honeycomb, a golden shield against the rot. But even the Es couldn't fix everything. Because what *wasn't* common knowledge was that in constructing a cold world where Psy didn't mate with or love or marry humans, Silver's race had unknowingly removed a vital element from the PsyNet.

The psychic network that was the lifeblood of millions of Psy was in the midst of a slow but catastrophic collapse. Unless Psy could once more win human hearts, bringing their unique energy back into the PsyNet, the destruction of the Psy race was inevitable.

So yes, Silver agreed that the fall of Silence was a good thing.

Still . . . "Bears?" She looked out to where she knew Valentin waited. "There's a distinct chance I will go insane with no help from the PsyNet malignance required."

Her grandmother stood. "You are a Mercant. You can handle a clan of bears."

Of course she could. That wasn't the point. "What did he ask of you in return for safe harbor for me?"

"Nothing but that we will never harm the clan or help anyone else do so. Nor will we ever share anything we learn about StoneWater. I have given my word that the Mercants will honor that request."

Rarely given, Ena's word was as durable as a diamond without flaw. So was Silver's. Mercants might not believe in loyalty to anyone beyond the family unit, but contrary to the popular perception of their family as cold-blooded and mercenary, they also did not betray those who'd assisted them in such ways. Honor still meant something to Silver's blood. "That's all?"

"It appears this particular bear is not cutthroat." Ena paused. "That could be a problem."

Silver knew this was her out; she could convince her grandmother that Valentin was too softhearted to provide any real protection against an external threat—but that would be a lie. Silver did not lie to her grandmother. "StoneWater bears have a reputation for not starting the brawls they're involved in."

The latter was part of why the clubs kept letting them back in. "However, once the fight is on, they will *not* back down. They're also fiercely territorial and overprotective of those they consider under their care. Should I accept StoneWater's offer of safe harbor, Valentin would tear off the head of anyone who threatened me."

"Excellent." Ena turned toward the door. "Get dressed. You'll be weak—an unfortunate side effect that can't be ameliorated by anything except time—but I want you safe before someone not bound by confidentiality realizes what's happening." A pause. "Trust no one, Silver. Especially not any member of our family."

After her grandmother left the room, having first pulled the privacy curtain around Silver's bed, Silver got up with care. Her muscles felt like jelly, her entire body aching, but she could stand as long as she was careful about it. Upright, she reached for the items folded neatly on the bedside table.

They were the clothes she recalled putting on that morning, all except for her panties. Those were still on her body. But since her bra was missing, she thought the medical staff must've had to cut through it to get to her chest. The bruising around her chest area when she opened the hospital gown seemed to bear that out.

Grandmother, why am I bruised on my upper half? she asked telepathically as she took off the gown.

Your heart didn't stop, but the doctors were afraid it might, so they prepped for resuscitation. They say the bruising appeared fifteen minutes after they pumped your stomach. A side effect of the poison.

Silver didn't know of any poison that would do this, but toxins weren't her field of expertise. *I'll need the medical files.*

They're already waiting for you in your secure PsyNet vault.

Thank you. Silver finished buttoning up her white shirt, reached for the cloud gray of her skirt. As she pulled it on over her hips, she consciously regulated her breathing to keep herself from passing out.

If half a glass had put her close to cardiac arrest, then a full glass would've ended her life. Had Valentin not interrupted her breakfast, he would've broken down her door to find a dead woman.

She paused.

Why had she immediately thought that he'd break down the door? As if it were a given.

His sense of smell, no doubt, she told herself. *He'd have scented the first signs of decomposition.* She didn't know if any such scent would be present so soon after death, but why else would she have thought he'd break down her door?

A door that was built to withstand earthquake forces.

Not a determined alpha bear, however.

Silver had a healthy respect for the ursine sense of determination—and also their occasional lack of common sense. Wolves she could negotiate with. Selenka Durev thought like a predator, and so did Silver. They understood each other.

Bears, however . . . Even after all this time, Silver did not understand bears.

At least Kaleb appeared to have the same issue: it had taken him twice as long to come to an understanding with StoneWater as it had with BlackEdge. The bears weren't actually politically aggressive, except in protecting their territory, but neither were they open to sensible negotiations. No, they'd refused to take Kaleb seriously until he'd "have a beer" with them.

Kaleb had instead teleported in with a ten-foot-tall cask of beer and told them he'd be teleporting it into the nearest volcano unless someone sat down and discussed the territorial situation with him. According to her boss, it was only the threat of so much beer going to waste that had caused Zoya Vashchenko, the former alpha of StoneWater, to agree to a meeting.

The negotiations, of course, had taken months.

Because . . . bears.

They might be the most illogical, most wild, and most impossible to understand changelings in the world. And she was about to go live with them. With Valentin. Who called her Starlight and asked her out for ice cream when he wasn't attempting to aggravate her into an emotional reaction.

Grandmother, I think I'd rather start wearing head-to-toe body armor and chemically testing my food.

Think of it as an opportunity, Silver. How many other Psy can say they've lived with bears?

The answer was none. No rebels, no defectors, *no one* had ever infiltrated a bear den after Silence came into being.

That's because most Psy would come out permanently discombobulated, she pointed out to her grandmother. *Did you know the bear idea of courtship is to kidnap their mates off the streets?*

Surely not.

Surely yes. If the kidnapped mate happened to be a bear, it wasn't a major issue—bears expected that type of behavior. For all Silver knew, they encouraged it. But the last time it happened in Moscow, the chosen mate had been a human whose parents had called Enforcement and filed kidnapping charges.

Valentin had turned up to personally explain that their daughter was being courted and in no danger whatsoever. He'd confirmed she was free to come home at any time. The parents had thought him mad. Until their daughter returned, glowing and happily mated to a bear who'd dressed up in a suit and tie for the occasion; he'd also permitted his mate to give him a haircut.

Silver didn't think she'd ever seen a bear so neatly pressed and polished.

"I wanted to make a good impression," he'd said with a sheepish smile when interviewed by a local comm station. "I don't want my in-laws to be mad at me for our entire mating."

He'd had no need for concern. The last time the parents spoke to the media—having gained a local profile after the kidnapping—they'd gushed over how much their daughter's mate adored her, and how the bears were "just the loveliest people you could imagine."

The bear ability to be forgiven for their actions appeared to be a mysterious law of nature. One to which Silver had no intention of falling prey.

If it gets to be too much, send an SOS, her grandmother said, her tone solemn. *I still trust some people without question. I'll get you out.*

Having finished dressing, Silver looked for her shoes before realizing she was in no shape to balance on four-inch heels. *I can survive bears, Grandmother. I'm a Mercant.* Family legend said they had once been the loyal knights of a king. Whether that was true or not, they were a family that had never lost sight of itself, no matter who flexed their muscles in the PsyNet.

A clan of bears wouldn't defeat her.

Neither would their alpha.

Chapter 5

Mate. Family. Clan. That is our heart's heart.
Loyalty. Honor. Courage. StoneWater.

—Words carved into the ceiling of the entrance to Denhome

SILVER WAS A fucking queen, Valentin thought when she opened the door of her hospital room and stepped out. Not a princess, dewy-eyed and soft. A queen, regal, and with a way of looking down her nose at him that said he was a lowly peasant. He felt like one, too, though he wasn't only taller and bigger than her; he was wearing heavy work boots while she was barefoot.

Her feet were narrow and pale, her toenails polished and squared. As polished and precise as she was. A neatly tailored suit jacket lay over the white shirt she'd tucked into her skirt. Notwithstanding the fact she'd almost died mere hours earlier, she now had her hair back in its usual neat coil—and damn but he'd go down on his knees and beg if she'd promise to let it down for him. Then he'd tumble her into his lap and—

Focus, Valentin.

Aside from her bare feet and the paleness of her skin, Silver could've been about to step into a work meeting. Except his Starlight would never go anywhere in clothes that were wrinkled, and these bore inevitable marks from the medics' hasty removal.

"You'll need more clothes," he said, trying to figure out how to get her to agree to his exit strategy. No one else was going to see Silver Mercant with bare feet, that much he knew.

"I'll ask my grandmother to arrange it." She glanced down the hallway, the elegant line of her throat making him want to nuzzle her, draw in the ice and fire of her scent straight from the source. "When did she leave?"

"A couple of minutes ago. Said she had plans to put in motion." Telling his bear to settle down until they had Silver in StoneWater territory, he scratched his jaw, only then realizing he'd forgotten to shave. If— *when*—he courted Silver into a kiss, he'd have to see if his stubble was too rough for her skin. "You have anything but suits in your closet?"

"No, I sleep this way and wake up perfectly pressed."

Grinning at the cool comment that made him want to kiss her until she melted, he put his hands on his hips. "Tell your babushka to pack jeans or other tough pants, T-shirts, sweaters, stuff suitable for a little rough and tumble."

"I don't intend to rough and tumble with anyone." Those extraordinary eyes, so clear and frosty, pinned him to the spot.

A lesser man, or one who had some sense in his head, might've flinched.

Good thing Valentin was big enough to take her, and stupid enough to keep banging his head against a wall of Silver Silence. "No choice in a clan," he said with a shrug. "Bears are handsy." They hugged like it was going out of business and threw each other around for fun. "Adults will respect your personal space, but I can't promise the same for the littlest cubs. Your suits won't survive."

"Noted." Silver tugged her shirt cuffs into perfect alignment. "You need to find me some shoes."

Yes, definitely a queen. "Any particular kind?"

"Low heels that won't clash with this suit."

"I have a better idea." He'd already sweet-talked a wheelchair from a changeling-pony nurse; now he pointed at it. "Sit. We'll hide your legs under the blanket from your bed, and you can wear this hoodie to hide your hair and face."

Picking up the hoodie from the chair where he'd placed it after buying it from the hospital gift shop while Ena was with Silver, he prepared to argue with her over his plan. She never accepted anything at face value. She always had to question it down to the bone.

It was as if she'd been born an obstinate bear and was only faking being Psy.

But today she just said, "A good solution," and sat in the wheelchair.

"We need to get some food into you." He held out a bottle of nutrient drink he'd found in the vending machine at the gift shop; maybe it was the Psy idea of a get-well-soon present.

Not taking it, Silver said, "My stomach and throat are raw."

Valentin didn't give up; he knew how to get under her skin. "Want to be weak instead?"

A dangerously calm look before she held out her hand.

Unscrewing the lid, he gave her the bottle, waited until she was done. After throwing the empty bottle in the nearest recycler, he handed her the hoodie, then ducked inside her room while keeping an eye on her, and tore the blanket off her bed. The sight of her moving slowly as she worked her way into the dark blue of the hoodie, it did all kinds of things to him.

IT was odd to wear something Valentin had bought for her. She'd offer to reimburse him, except she knew he'd take that as an insult. As she'd told her grandmother, bears were intensely protective of their people. The more dominant the bear, the more overwhelming the protective urge.

She wasn't one of Valentin's people, of course, but she'd fallen under his protection the instant she accepted the offer to stay with StoneWater. He'd fight to keep her safe, his big body merciless against any enemy who dared come at her. That body had to burn a significant amount of energy. She wondered what he ate to retain his strength.

That last thought had her freezing in the act of pulling on a garment she would never normally wear.

She was reacting to him.

Again.

Silver did not react emotionally to anyone, her Silence pristine in the subtle Mercant way that worked with each individual mind rather than being a blunt hammer. She hadn't reacted to Valentin the first time he'd come to her apartment or even the second or the third. She'd been impressed by him in an intellectual way, had found crossing words with him an interesting exercise.

So yes, perhaps there *had* been a reaction there—it was unheard of for her to allow anyone to interrupt her, not just at home but also at the office, again and again. But that reaction had been muted, tightly in control. This wasn't. And it hadn't been for at least six and a half months. The math wasn't hard to do: the Honeycomb had come fully into being only weeks before her responses began to change.

That the empathic construct would bleed emotion was no surprise. The once starkly black-and-white landscape of the PsyNet was now overlaid with a fine golden net that was as powerful as it was delicate, and the sparks of color created by the minds of the E-Psy could be found far and wide.

Like all Psy who preferred to stay sane, Silver was linked to the Honeycomb, the connection made via an E-Psy she trusted without reservation. Regardless of that, no empathic sparks should've infiltrated her shields, not when those shields had been modeled on the martial shields of the deadliest men and women in the PsyNet.

And yet, Silver was reacting to Valentin Nikolaev in a way that defied Silence.

WALKING out of the recovery room just as Silver had gotten herself into the hoodie, Valentin waited for her to get into the wheelchair, then he put the blanket over her legs. While she settled the blanket as she wanted it, he reached over to zip up the hoodie and pull forward the hood to shadow her face.

He pretended not to see the look she shot him, the one that said he was crossing boundaries. Being innocently oblivious to silent reprimands was a skill he'd cultivated as a curious bear cub with three older sisters whose stuff he'd liked to nose about in. Not because he wanted it. Just because it was there. "Suits you."

"It swallows me," was the cool response.

"That, too." Mentally plotting how he could swap out the gift-store hoodie for one of his own once they reached Denhome, he began to push the wheelchair manually rather than using the hover capability. Silver was inches from him, and she was about to enter his lair.

As far as the bear priorities in life went, he was pretty much set.

Of course, he thought with an inward snarl that was more mangy wolf than *extremely* civilized bear, the only reason she was coming to Denhome was because someone had tried to poison her.

Grandmother Mercant had been explicit in saying that his job was to protect, hers to unearth the traitor within the family. That was her right as alpha of the Mercants—but he'd make it clear to her that should she need someone to rip off a head or two, Valentin would be delighted to take care of that pesky problem for her.

No one was allowed to hurt one of Valentin's people and get away with it.

"You're rumbling. It sounds like muted thunder."

Valentin's hands tightened on the handles of the wheelchair. "Hazard of being a bear. We aren't good at not showing our mad."

A passing physician gave him a wide berth at that instant. "No one will hurt you again," he told Silver as they exited into the parking lot. "I'll make certain of that." It was an alpha's promise.

Silver's back stiffened. "I'm not yours to protect."

Valentin stopped by the powerful four-wheel-drive vehicle he'd had a clanmate in the city pick up from near Silver's home and drive to the hospital lot. Going around to face Silver, his hands on the arms of the chair, he said, "As long as you're in Denhome, you're one of mine, Starlight."

What he didn't say was that he intended to charm her into making the move permanent. Cats did the suave overconfident thing. Bears knew taking a woman for granted just led to a fall right on your smug face. In this, he'd take the bear approach. Charm first, be smug later.

First, however, he scooped her up and put her in the passenger seat before she could even think about stepping onto the asphalt in her bare feet.

The Human Alpha

BOWEN KNIGHT, SECURITY chief of the Human Alliance and its effective leader, looked at the latest update on his screen with grim focus. Alliance medical investigators and Ashaya Aleine, Psy rebel and brilliant scientist, continued to agree: the chip in his brain, the one that blocked Psy from violating his thoughts, was continuing to degrade.

The rate of decay *had* slowed from initial predictions, but it was going inexorably in one direction. He'd been the first chipped, would be the first to fall if they didn't find a solution. He'd come to terms with that when Ashaya Aleine first made the devastating diagnosis. But now that all of the chipped were past the safe-removal zone—including his sister, Lily—he found his anger spiking into red-hot frustration.

I'm not sorry for the choice I made.

Lily had said that to him when he'd asked her to consider getting her chip out while extraction was still possible. He'd known what her answer would be before he ever asked the question, but he'd had to ask, had to try to protect the woman who'd been his small, big-eyed shadow in childhood.

Switching off the screen, he was about to return to work when there was a knock on his door. As the rest of his team were coming in late after a long night when they'd all pulled punishing hours, he should've been the only one in the building.

He palmed a weapon before saying, "Come in."

He wasn't expecting the man who walked through the door. Raising an eyebrow, he said, "Polite of you not to teleport right into my office."

"Sahara is attempting to teach me manners." Kaleb Krychek slipped into a seat on the opposite side of Bo's desk.

Not about to be fooled by the cardinal's casual attitude, Bo leaned back in his own chair. "Why is a member of the Ruling Coalition in my office?" The Alliance didn't have any kind of relationship with the new rulers of the Psy race. The Coalition's predecessors had been murderous evil, while this new group included an empath and an Arrow, both of whom had saved countless lives, Psy, changeling—and human.

Krychek had done the same.

That was why Bo was listening to him. Because the Ruling Coalition also featured Nikita Duncan and Anthony Kyriakus, who, like Krychek, had been part of the defunct and vicious Psy Council. Word from those who'd know—and who Bo trusted—was that Anthony had always been a rebel in the shadows, while Krychek was the one who'd brought the Council crashing down.

There were rumors he was directly behind the disappearance of at least one Councilor, a cold-blooded sociopath of a woman Bo suspected of having used mind control to turn the former leadership of the Alliance into her puppets.

All of that might've made him more receptive to the Coalition but for one brutal fact: Nikita Duncan may have survived the purging of the Council, may even have given birth to a cardinal empath Bo respected, but that didn't wipe her hands clean of all the blood she'd spilled, a lot of it human.

"Humans and Psy," Krychek said now, "are on an inevitable collision course."

Bo's shoulders knotted. "This have anything to do with the fact your people need human minds for some reason?"

His direct access to PsyNet data was erratic, dependent on a Psy junkie who was a brilliant hacker when he wasn't high. This time around, the other man had managed to get his hands on part of a secure document that talked about the "necessary human element" and "how to achieve integration."

Kaleb betrayed no surprise at his knowledge. "What I'm about to tell you is highly classified. I'm sharing the data because in this, Psy and humans may be able to assist one another."

"I doubt that, but I'm listening."

"The PsyNet was never meant to hold only Psy minds," Krychek said. "Until Silence, humans were part of it through their relationships with Psy."

"How? We're not telepathic."

"Love forms a psychic bond. Changelings call it the mating bond." White stars on black, Krychek's gaze was inscrutable. "A human mind in the PsyNet is connected only to the person with whom they share the mating bond. No one else can even reach that mind, much less hack it."

Bo felt his lips twist, but he held back his cynical comment about how humans outside the PsyNet weren't afforded that courtesy. "You're forgetting an entire race," he said instead. "Didn't the Psy want changelings in their network?"

"Changelings did have a presence, but their numbers were far lower—likely because, in many cases, changelings are able to provide Psy mates with an alternative psychic network we don't fully understand, thus taking Psy out rather than bringing changelings in. Humans, however, were always an integral aspect of the PsyNet. Not peripheral, *essential*."

Bo stared at Krychek, the laugh that erupted from his throat unintentional. "Let me get this straight. The high-and-mighty Psy need humans to maintain your psychic network?"

"Yes." Krychek's expression continued to be impassive. "Coercion negates the effect. The Psy-human bond must be made by choice."

"You're shit out of luck then," Bo said, all laughter gone from his soul. "For humans to trust a Psy is to consign themselves to psychic rape." His tone was hard, his heart even harder.

"Should the Alliance work with the Coalition in encouraging and creating opportunities for human-Psy relationships," Krychek said, "the Coalition will put all of its considerable resources into finding a way for humans to permanently block Psy intrusion."

Bo's hand tightened around the weapon he still held. Of all the things they could've offered . . . "I already have access to the most brilliant scientists on the planet."

"Ashaya and Amara Aleine are undoubtedly that, but they can't think of everything. The Coalition is offering you the entire machinery of the Psy race geared toward one overriding goal."

That machinery was massive, far beyond anything the Alliance could command. "All I'd have to do to get this generous gift is sell out my people, tell them to trust the Psy." Bo shook his head. "The answer is no." He would not betray everything the Alliance stood for on the faith of a nebulous promise from a race that had done so much damage.

"Every human on this planet," he said, rage a cauldron of darkness inside him, "knows at least one person who's had their mind treated like a store or a playhouse by Psy who wanted to steal their ideas or just to defile. We have no reason or desire to help you."

"Strange as it may seem, I agree with you—the Psy have no right to make this request." Krychek rose to his feet as if to leave, paused suddenly.

"My mate," he said, "tells me I need to trust you with a fact we don't often share: Psy need the biofeedback offered by a psychic network. Sever that link and death comes in a matter of minutes. Should the PsyNet fail," he added softly, "it'll mean the near extinction of an entire race."

Bo's hand fisted on his desk, the image a devastating one. Because the Psy weren't only the Coalition and powerful bastards like Krychek. The Psy were also the little girl down the road who waved shyly to him from her nursery window, the M-Psy who saved lives day after day, and the vulnerable openhearted empaths who were helping humans and changelings as well as Psy.

To imagine their lives snuffed out—it was a brutal vision.

As brutal were the other images he had in his brain: of broken humans who'd had their entire lives stripped from them by Psy; of children who'd lost their mothers and fathers to Psy death squads; of men and women who'd committed suicide after losing their lives' work to a Psy thief.

"Do it for nothing in return," Bo said quietly. "Do the research just because it's the right thing to do. Put humans and Psy on equal footing when it comes to psychic privacy. Then, maybe, we can talk."

Chapter 6

I've just been alerted to a serious issue to do with pure telepaths.

—Kaleb Krychek to the rest of the Ruling Coalition (February 2082)

EXHAUSTION BEGAN TO bite at Silver forty-five minutes into the drive to StoneWater territory. Regardless of how hard she tried to fight it, the fatigue seeped into her blood, made her head want to tilt to the side.

"*Moyo solnyshko*, you ever consider saying to hell with it to the Silence?"

Valentin's unexpected question was a welcome dose of cold water. Ignoring that he'd addressed her as his "sunshine," she focused on his question. "I don't see how that is any of your business." No one could ever know that Silver *couldn't* breach Silence; the world had to believe it was a choice.

As far as the Mercants as a group went, the issue of Silence was still under discussion. The overriding consensus was that surrendering to emotion would erode them, make them far too approachable, far too "human" in the wider sense. That didn't mean a Mercant would never break Silence.

One member of her family hadn't ever been truly Silent.

"Of course it isn't my business." Valentin's deep rumble of a voice broke into her thoughts—though she'd never forgotten his presence. Silver wasn't in the habit of forgetting six feet plus several inches of heavily muscled threat next to her.

"But just because it isn't my business," Valentin continued, sounding aggrieved, "doesn't mean I'm not interested."

Bears did appear to have a tendency toward inveterate curiosity. Half the time when they got into trouble, it was because they'd been poking their noses where they didn't belong. A group had even wandered all the way out to Kaleb's isolated home soon after Kaleb bonded with Sahara. When caught and questioned, they'd belligerently said they didn't believe the rumors of Kaleb having a mate, had come to see for themselves.

"Why do bears like knowing things so much?"

A narrow-eyed look. "Probably the same reason you do, Ms. Silver Spy."

Silver doubted it. From all she knew, bears were inquisitive down to the bone. For her, knowledge was power. And she didn't have anywhere near the depth of knowledge she wanted on the bears. That placed her in a quandary.

Valentin put on an act of not being particularly subtle or intelligent, but only half of that was true. He was about as subtle as a baseball bat to the head, but he was ferociously intelligent. All alphas were. Strength alone might be accepted in a changeling soldier, but never in a high-ranking member of a pack or clan.

It was a lesson many Psy still hadn't learned.

So she knew Valentin wouldn't give her any information unless it was an equal trade. "Silence suits me," she said in answer to the question he'd asked. "The calm orderliness it gives to my mind makes me very efficient." Not a lie.

"You remember what it was like before you were Silent?"

As she'd thought—he was clever. He'd picked up the secondary layer of meaning in her response. "My answers aren't free."

A laugh that built in his chest, filled the vehicle. "Ask what you want, Starlichka," he said, "but first you answer my question."

Again, he proved his acute intelligence; he knew Silver would avoid answering the question if she could. It wasn't as if she'd given her word.

"Yes," she said. "Conditioning begins during childhood, but it doesn't 'take' for several years." It had never been difficult for Silver to talk about Silence because she'd never been conditioned with dissonance—a pain loop designed, among other things, to stifle dissemination of information about the Protocol.

"What were you like as a kid? A feral beastie?"

"Feral beastie?" Silver stared at him as she repeated the English words he'd slipped into a conversation otherwise undertaken in Russian.

A shrug. "My great-grandfather was Scottish. He used to call me that. He liked me a lot."

Silver realized that, in bear terms, "feral beastie" was probably an endearment. "My telepathic powers are significant—I'm classified at 9.3 on the Gradient."

"Goes to 10?"

"Nine point nine. Cardinals are off the scale."

"You must be able to speak telepathically across the country."

"Further." Officially, Silver was what was termed a "pure" telepath, her skill to do with communicating over vast distances.

It wasn't so simple, of course, and pure telepaths could be taught to use their abilities in all kinds of ways—including how to use their minds to break those of others. However, thanks to Mercant muscle, the Psy Council hadn't got their hands on Silver. She'd never been groomed to be a torturer.

In truth, though telepathy was her primary ability, Silver wasn't *only* a pure telepath—but as her secondary ability was a useless one that had saddled her with a vulnerability without an advantage to balance it out, she never factored it into her psychic skillset.

"As a cub"—Valentin's bass timbre—"you must've had a chaos of voices coming at you."

"My family protected me while I was an infant, but they eventually had to teach me how to shield myself, and part of doing that meant lowering their shields and allowing me to feel what awaited if I didn't learn to protect myself." The crashing wave of sound had literally put her flat on the floor, the roar of it a horror that threatened to crush her brain.

Valentin's eyes were a primal amber when he glanced at her. "How young were you?"

"It doesn't matter," she said, intrigued at this glimpse of the bear that lived inside him. "It had to be done." She'd had to understand the danger on a visceral level so she'd know why she had to practice so hard with her shields—and with her Silence.

Valentin went as if to reach out, touch her in that tactile changeling way of interacting, wrenched his hand back partway. "I don't understand why you had to lose your emotions to gain psychic control."

"The coming generation of children will test whether emotions can coexist alongside control." Silver would do everything in her power to assist those innocent young minds. "Going backwards isn't an option for me."

"Why?"

Silver took a leaf from Valentin's own book. "Because I say so."

A deep rumbling sound from his chest that sounded very much like the bearish version of a growl. "That wasn't very nice."

Silver wasn't about to get into an argument with a bear, especially over something so nonsensical. Unlike Kaleb, she didn't have a keg of beer and a volcano handy with which to call a cease-fire. "How did you become alpha?"

The grumbling rumble was still in his voice when he answered. "You're asking a very big question."

"So did you." If he was trying to intimidate her with his rumbling, he'd have to try a lot harder. "We had a deal. Answer the question."

"I killed all the other challengers."

She blinked, stared at him. And realized something. "You're lying."

A totally unrepentant grin. "You made me mad."

Another wave of exhaustion slammed into her. Her head spun. But Silver wasn't about to enter an unknown situation asleep and vulnerable. "Keep talking," she ordered.

When Valentin didn't dispute her right to give that order, Silver knew she must look in bad shape indeed.

"I became alpha because that's who I am." A shrug, broad shoulders rippling with a strength that would outmatch any other man in the city, likely in the country. "I always knew I was born to care for a clan. Since I didn't fuck up and turn into an asshole in the interim, the clan accepted me when Zoya decided it was time for her to step down."

Silver caught a hidden undertone in his statement, was certain he wasn't telling her the whole truth. "If she'd evidenced a desire to remain in her position, you'd have challenged her?"

"I respect her too much for that. I'd have left to found my own clan." Shadows fell on the car from the heavy tree canopy above them, old trees with thick trunks lining both sides of the narrow road. "It's hard for two adult alphas who've both come into their power to share the same space."

"That changes once one cedes power?"

A nod.

"It must be difficult," Silver said quietly, "to cede power after a lifetime of leading."

"You're thinking of Ena."

Since he'd clearly already intuited the Mercant line of succession, she saw no harm in answering his question. "The idea of my grandmother handing over the reins is one I struggle to accept."

The heavily forested road turned into a dirt track in front of her.

"I don't think she'd do it for just anyone, but for the granddaughter she's taught herself? I think when the time comes, *moyo solnyshko*, she'll be proud to take a backseat so you can shine."

The emotional interpretation gave her pause. The truth was that while Silver embraced her responsibility to be her grandmother's right hand, she wasn't sure she wanted Ena to cede power anytime soon—her grandmother lived and breathed the Mercant family.

"See those trees?" Valentin raised one big hand to thrust back the messy tumble of his hair. "In a few weeks, they'll be blanketed by snow until, together, they look like a dignified old church."

Silver went to follow his gaze, was distracted by something else highlighted by the beams of sunlight that speared through the canopy. "Are those children from your clan or wild bears?" They were too small to be adult changeling bears. "Is that bear hanging upside down from a tree limb? I didn't know that was anatomically possible."

The rumbling growl beginning again, Valentin brought the vehicle to a halt and stepped out. "Small bears! Here! *Now*." It was a bass drum of sound that wasn't a yell but that carried all the same.

Five bear cubs melted out of the woods to stand around Valentin. Judging from their size and what little she knew of changeling bears in this form, she thought they couldn't be older than seven at the most. At present, they were doing a very bad job of appearing meek while trying to sneak looks inside the vehicle.

One lifted its paw in a wave at Silver.

Valentin put his hands on his hips and said, "Eyes here."

His tone as he gave that order was different from his initial one, and this time, every single bear snapped to attention. Crouching down to their level, Valentin began to speak. She couldn't hear what he said—hadn't known he could speak that quietly—but the child bears all nodded after a short minute before turning and running into the trees.

Valentin was chuckling when he got back into the vehicle. "Arkasha semi-shifted so he could hang upside down. Too damn clever."

"What were they doing out here?"

"Being trouble. They think they're the tiny bear version of gangsters." Laughter in his eyes. "They wait for unsuspecting clanmates to pass underneath and jump on them."

"Wouldn't bigger bears scent the children?"

"The gangsters are just old enough to know how to use the wind shifts to their advantage." He sounded proud rather than angry. "Do young Psy cause their caretakers this much grief?"

"No, not yet. Silence has certain advantages."

Valentin's hands clenched on the steering wheel as he got them underway again. "I was going to say maybe it does—but never having any of the young idiots play tricks? Not watching them grow into their skins in freedom, seeing the idiots become slowly less idiotic until one day they're men and women I'd have at my back any day of the week?"

He shook his head, his hair gleaming blue-black in the sunlight that came in through the sunroof. "I wouldn't give that up for anything." Shifting to hoverdrive when the dirt track came to an abrupt end, he took them into the trees.

Silver watched him maneuver, and she thought of her cousin, Lillya. Currently twelve, she was on the borderland between fully conditioned and just unconditioned enough that she could be nudged either way. Ena hadn't yet made the decision as to which way was better for Lillya. They had approximately three months before her Silence training would've progressed too far to be turned back without causing her psychic and possibly physical distress.

To simply stop as some parents were choosing to do—against advice from the medics and psychologists working for the Ruling Coalition—wasn't an option, either. At that age, a child's needs had to be carefully managed, or that child might be ruined for life when it came to their psychic and psychological health.

"I grew into my skin in Silence," she said aloud several minutes later. "Are you implying that I didn't grow into an individual?"

"*Starlichka.*" A rebuking look. "You know I'd never say that." He brought the vehicle to a stop about fifty meters from what looked like the mouth of a large cave. Several other vehicles were parked nearby, but there were nowhere near enough to account for a full clan.

Not getting out, Valentin turned to brace his hand against the top of her seat. "But are you who you would've been without Silence?"

"I would be mad without Silence," Silver said into the quiet, her words stones thrown into a mirror-still pond. "Imagine being able to hear tens of thousands of voices screaming at you *inside your head*. Now imagine being emotional, and as a result of a surge of shock or anger or grief, losing control of your shields. How many times do you think that could happen before your mind broke?"

"I don't believe it," Valentin said with a scowl. "The Silver Mercant I know wouldn't break, no matter what the provocation—trust me, I've tried."

Silver shook her head. "Prior to Silence," she told him, "a significant minority of pure telepaths chose to end their lives, most in a way that destroyed their brains. The top choice was to put a gun in the mouth and blow off the roof of the head."

That particular fragment of data was buried under thousands of others because pure telepaths weren't considered a problematic designation. Telekinetics, combat telepaths, foreseers, the rare and dangerous X-Psy, they were seen as unstable and in need of extra attention and training. But pure telepaths? Seldom any issues once they learned to manage their shields. At least until they hit about sixty years of age and blew their brains out.

"And now?" Valentin's voice was gritty, his attention so intense that it felt like a furred brush against her senses.

Silver tried to shrug off the irrational thought. "Silence changed the numbers," she said as her eyelids began to grow so heavy it was as if each lash were anchored by a tiny weight. "Pure telepaths have the lowest rate of suicide of any designation in the entire Psy race."

The Silence Protocol had worked for the pure telepaths, a truth that tended to get forgotten. Silver had had to point it out to Kaleb, who usually didn't miss anything. However, because she'd drawn Kaleb's attention to it and he'd alerted his fellow members of the Ruling Council, the educational plans being developed for pure telepaths were different from those being developed for other designations.

And her mind, it was rambling.

She realized that the same instant she realized Valentin was at her side of the vehicle and that her door was open. He was lifting her into his arms a heartbeat later, his big body a furnace. She went to protest that she could walk, but her brain wasn't working right and that was worse than the fact her body wasn't working right.

This was *not* how she'd planned to enter the StoneWater clan's den.

Chapter 7

I want to be alone . . . said no bear ever.

—*The Traveler's Guide to Changelings* (Revised Edition: 1897)

VALENTIN KEPT SILVER'S lax body tucked close to his as he entered Denhome. She'd lost consciousness a second after he took her into his arms, was now a warm but dead weight that had his heart drumming against his rib cage. He'd seen her fire dim in front of him, had felt her light flicker.

Nova, who was waiting for him near the entrance passage that was the narrowest part of Denhome, kicked immediately into healer mode. "She hurt?"

"No, medics said this might happen during the early part of her recovery." Despite the reminder, Valentin couldn't help it. "Check her anyway, all right?" Those other medics weren't his sister and StoneWater's chief healer, who he knew would never lie to him.

"Already in the plan, Mishka." His sister whipped out a small scanner from one of the capacious pockets of her full-skirted yellow dress, ran it over Silver's body as they walked.

Valentin soon exited the passageway to hit the massive space that was the heart of Denhome, despite not being in the center. The Cavern was designed to act as a staging post should a battle ever reach this far into clan lands. Their living quarters could be easily blocked off, noncombatants taken out through hidden back passages while the clan's dominants fought in this space.

Bears could kill almost anything that came at them—all they needed was space to move.

In times of peace, the Cavern was the social heart of his people, so it wasn't surprising when clanmates flowed around Valentin and Nova, curious but not intrusive, the rambunctious little ones kept back by the adults.

Valentin would return to hug the cubs after he'd settled Silver into her room. They needed the contact at that age, now even more than usual, with their strong pack badly wounded, ragged and broken and bleeding.

Valentin's heart flinched as the knowledge that never left him roared to the forefront of his mind. At least the cubs—tiny gangsters included—would be fine until he could come hold them close. He'd spotted Stasya and his third-in-command, Pieter, on the far side of the Cavern. They were more than capable of spreading their arms wide and drenching the little ones in affection.

Being strong in a bear clan didn't only have to do with physical might.

"In here," his bossiest sister said right then. "Stasya and I put her in the room next to yours, since we all know you'd just move her if we didn't." Nova managed to get in an eye roll. "Good thing Nika's away or I'd have had to kick her out."

The room didn't have much more than a bed and private facilities. Nika had packed up and stored her personal items so the space could be used by other clanmates, but it hadn't looked that different even when his sister was living here. Changeling bears, even their least extroverted, didn't like being alone all that much. An introvert bear might choose to quietly read his book, but he'd do it in the Cavern, surrounded by the hum of clan life.

Wondering if Silver would choose to join them or stay in her quarters, Valentin placed her gently on the soft white sheets. Her face was incredibly pale, chill alabaster devoid of the glow that made her such a vivid force. "She's cool to the touch." He went to grab a blanket to put over her.

"Wait, Mishka," Nova said. "I think her temperature may just be inside the healthy range for a Psy." Sitting herself down on the bed, she took another reading, followed it up by manually checking Silver's pulse. "I talked with Tamsyn at DarkRiver after you called me, got a briefing on Psy physiology—said I wanted to be prepared as we were hosting a Psy visitor. I have her on speed dial if I need more detailed information." She tapped her ear, where she wore a high-tech device Valentin couldn't stand.

He kept ripping it out of his ear each time Pavel, one of his senior people and a certified tech geek, talked him into it.

Nova's microphone was a tiny circle attached to the off-the-shoulder collar of her yellow dress. She was also wearing heels. The outfit wasn't sensible in the least, but where fashion was concerned, Nova was never sensible.

"Do I need to contact Krychek and get her back to the hospital?"

"No." Nova rose, her glossy black hair perfectly coiffed and her lipstick a dark pink. "Your Starlight is fine. Just needs to rest so her body can recover from the shock of the poison and the treatment."

Having already lifted a soft blanket in spring green from the foot of the bed, Valentin pulled it over Silver. When Nova frowned and shifted on her heel as if to loosen Silver's clothing, he shook his head. "She won't want to be touched for anything but medical reasons." He wasn't sure she'd forgive him for carrying her from the car, but sometimes, a bear had to do what a bear had to do.

He'd charm her out of her mad.

"Got it." Nova made sure the blanket was comfortable around Silver, then the two of them stepped out of the room. The passageway directly outside was empty, probably thanks to one of Valentin's seconds. Else, the clan would've congregated, asking for updates and offering to help—all the while trying to sneak a peek at Starlight.

The tiny gangsters were probably holding court at this moment, giving equally tiny clanmates the lowdown. Not the adults, however. Valentin had told the misbehaving cubs he wouldn't bust them to their parents if they promised not to leave the safe area on their own again—they usually played their "drop and attack" game far closer to Denhome.

It was their one get-out-of-jail-free card. After that, they'd be facing parental and clan punishment.

"Why," Nova said, "does the frighteningly competent Silver Mercant need safe harbor badly enough to enter a den of disorderly bears? All you told me on the phone was that she'd ingested a complex poison and had been successfully treated."

"Someone tried to kill her." He had to restrain the urge to open his throat and release an enraged bellow. "It had to be a person she trusted, a person she let into her home. They poisoned her food, Nova."

His sister pressed a hand to her heart. "Bastard!" Food was sacred to a bear, the thing by which they connected to one another and to those who would be their friends. "She'll be hungry when she wakes."

"Chert voz'mi." Valentin rubbed his face. "I forgot to pick up the food she likes from one of the Psy shops. I just wanted her safe in Denhome."

Nova patted him on the arm in that way she had of doing, as if she were ten years older than him, instead of a measly three. "Never mind. I'll talk to Tamsyn and find out what real-people food she can eat."

"Nova."

His sister threw up her hands. "I didn't mean anything by it, you know that! I just don't understand people who don't eat for pleasure." Voice befuddled, she looked at him with purest confusion in normally dark brown eyes gone a deep amber. "I checked with Tamsyn—Psy have taste buds same as changelings and humans. Does it make sense to you that they'd ignore the sublime pleasures of food?"

Chuckling despite the worry gnawing his gut, Valentin threw an arm over her shoulders and led her toward the Cavern. His Starlichka was safe now. No one would be able to enter her room without being seen or scented.

Valentin's room was the first beyond the joyous chaos of the Cavern, Silver next to him. Everyone who lived in this part of Denhome had to walk past their rooms. That hallway was normally never empty—and it would be even less likely to be so with his entire clan curious about Silver.

It wasn't every day that a Psy came into Denhome.

In fact, it had been thirty-three years since a Psy walked these stone pathways. Déwei Nguyen had been mated to a StoneWater bear pre-Silence, had watched his people make the emotionless choice from a distance, sad and afraid for what it meant for his race's future. In one fell swoop, he'd effectively lost his parents, his siblings, his nieces and nephews, every Psy family member or friend.

The elder had passed on before Valentin was born, but he'd heard the stories from others in the clan, knew that while Déwei had lived a life many envied, he'd always carried a sadness in his heart for his people. Pavel and Yakov Stepyrev, Déwei Nguyen's identical twin great-grandsons, were two of Valentin's most trusted people.

As for the possibility that Silver's poisoning had been masterminded by the Consortium, while Valentin would never ignore the risk that the detestable group might've gotten their claws into one of his people, he didn't think there was any real likelihood of a traitor in the clan. Stone-Water might be badly fractured, but that was within their own people, would never be exposed to outsiders by either party.

"Did you kidnap Kaleb's aide?" Pavel asked as soon as Valentin entered the Cavern.

"*Bozhe moi!*" Yakov groaned, his eyes the same aqua green as his brother's, his hair an identical mahogany, and his skin the exact same shade of brown caught between light and dark. Despite countless arguments over who was taller, they both stood at five feet eight inches, their bodies compact and strong. The only physical characteristic that differentiated them was their vision. "If you'd decided on her, you should've let us know and—"

"Hey!" Valentin rumbled in his chest to get their attention. "Did Stasya not tell you why Silver is here?"

"Of course I did," his sister said, indignant. "They just don't believe me."

Pieter, the quietest and most introverted of them all, his hair an unusual mix of colors that echoed the hues of a glowing sunset, folded his arms. "Why would a woman who heads EmNet and has Kaleb Krychek for a boss need our help?"

A few of the teenagers skulked closer to the adult talk in the huge living room of Denhome, the natural ceiling of the Cavern at least a hundred feet above. The space glowed with daylight, thanks to a complex system of mirrors that redirected the beams of sunlight that speared into the Cavern via natural cracks in the mountain.

That light caught the teens' nonchalant progress. Valentin glared at them until they hunched their shoulders and, scowling patented teenage scowls, went back to their studies in another part of the Cavern. That part happened to be next to a natural spring-fed pool, where the rain fell when it came in through the same cracks that brought them light. Sand swept out from the gleaming green clarity of the pool, the water shallow enough that even the cubs could play in it without fear.

Lush moss grew on the rocks around the pool, giving that part of the Cavern the feel of being a world within a world. The rest of it was more rocky, though with its own beauty. Veins of sparkling quartz ran through the entire area, while the wall where each of the cubs placed his or her palm print when they turned five was a riot of color.

What would Starlight think of this home he loved with all his heart and soul?

"Silver needs to be cut out of the line of fire for a short period," he told those of his seconds who'd gathered here—three were out of Denhome on long-range patrol missions to ensure no one got ideas about encroaching on StoneWater territory. His bears might like to live on top of one another, but they needed a wide range to wander in.

Zahaan, Taji, and Inara would be back in two weeks. Until then, Valentin kept in touch with them via various comm points the clan had hidden throughout their lands. It was Pavel who'd brief the three after this meeting. "Silver's grandmother knows no one can get to her here, and Silver's agreed with her verdict."

"Silver Mercant listens to her grandparents?" Nova whispered, eyes wide. "She's like us?"

"Yes—and her babushka is as scary as ours, so don't mess with her."

"You talking to yourself, Valya?" Pavel asked slyly, his cheeks creased and his eyes glinting behind the clear lenses of the spectacles he insisted on wearing; the otherwise audacious bear was scared the readily available corrective surgery would damage his already less-than-perfect vision.

Everyone laughed; Valentin's men and women were well aware of his fascination with Kaleb Krychek's dangerous aide. It had been hard to miss after Valentin suddenly began volunteering to act as courier anytime documents needed to be delivered to Silver—or to Kaleb. Because, somehow, it was always far more convenient for him to drop them off with Silver rather than her boss.

"Don't you all have work to do?" he grumbled.

Pavel raised a hand, clearly being an asshole. But Valentin happened to like this asshole. "What?"

"Teleporters."

"Not a problem," he told them. "Silver's grandmother confirmed Silver has some type of shielding that means even the ones who lock on to faces won't be able to find her." It had been part of the final conversation they'd had in the hospital, before Ena left Silver in Valentin's care.

"Huh." Stasya purposely bumped Pieter's shoulder, her height of six feet only an inch less than his.

Subtle, Valentin's sister wasn't. It had become obvious over the past month that she wanted to jump Pieter's bones. Valentin pretended to be oblivious to both the bump and Pieter's responding glance. A man *did not* need to know about his sisters' intimate lives.

Ever.

"Not surprising, really," Stasya added with a self-satisfied smile when Pieter didn't break the physical contact. "She has to have picked up a few tricks working with Krychek all this time."

"You want us to change the security settings?" Pavel asked, his shoulders pulling against the dark brown of his shirt when he thrust his hands into the pockets of his jeans. "I've had the technical elements running at Defcon 5 since we haven't had any major threat warnings."

"Defcon 5?" Yakov—his own outfit a black tee that hugged his biceps, and dark green cargoes—made a face. "Really, Pasha? Have you been playing those American hologames again?"

Pavel made a rude gesture with his hand. "At least I don't lose to ten-year-old ponies from Tajikistan."

Yakov clutched at his chest. "Oh, how you wound me. To think I carried you on my back when we were children."

Used to the twins hassling each other over nothing in particular, Valentin ignored their byplay to focus on the question. "Raise it up a notch," he said. "I want to make dead sure no one can sneak in."

It was an extra and probably unnecessary precaution. Their rugged terrain would, as always, act as their biggest line of defense. Long settled in this region, StoneWater hadn't permitted civilization to advance much farther than a dirt track that they could destroy in a matter of minutes if it came to that.

The only other way to get to Denhome was to teleport in—or to hike in on foot. Good luck with the latter if you weren't trained for uneven terrain set with all kinds of booby traps. Yakov hassled his brother about hologames, but the two of them came up with the best traps when they put their minds together, the hunt a game in itself.

"I'll make that happen now," Yakov said. "We've got more than a few dominants just lazing about in the sun. Time to kick their asses."

"Hey," Nova said, hands on her hips. "They earned that lazing about, and as the clan's healer, I prescribed it."

Yakov was too smart to sass Nova in a disrespectful fashion. Rather, he bowed from the waist. "I will kick their fat beary asses gently, my lady."

"Pasha." Valentin called their technical expert closer as the others began to disperse, Nova stomping beside Yakov to make sure he didn't get too enthusiastic in his ass-kicking. "Anything?"

Chapter 8

THE OTHER MAN pushed up his glasses, his eyes a crystal-clear aqua green. Unfortunately, those pretty eyes had crap night vision. Pavel also couldn't see two feet without his glasses. But his brain was a razor. He also had the same dominance as his brother. Leaving him in a lower position in the clan simply because he had imperfect sight would've been a recipe for trouble.

Now, he shook his head, his shaggy dark brown hair several shades darker than the mid-brown of his skin. That brown came from his and Yakov's paternal grandfather, a bear who was a native of Angola—what the hell a bear clan had been doing in Angola before they moved to a colder clime, Valentin still hadn't figured out. Pavel's dedushka just laughed like a lunatic whenever he brought it up. The aqua-green eyes came from the twins' black bear mother.

Déwei Nguyen's genes appeared long buried, but they were there in the intuition that had marked the twins since birth. If either Pavel or Yakov told Valentin to more heavily guard a section of border, though there was no apparent reason to do so, he listened. The last time that had happened, they'd caught Selenka's wolves trying to sneak in, no doubt to spy on StoneWater.

Déwei Nguyen had been a foreseer.

"Comm traffic shows no suspicious signals that might mean the Consortium has a plant in the clan." Pavel's eyes lit up as he slipped into geek talk. "I've bugged it three ways to Sunday—"

"Pasha." Valentin pinned him to the spot with his gaze.

His second raised his hands. "I'm not breaching anyone's privacy. It's all done by a computer program. Got Brenna from SnowDancer to help me with the code. Man, that woman's *brain*." He sighed. "If only she didn't have the bad taste to be a wolf, and wasn't madly in love with her psycho assassin mate, I'd seriously consider switching teams."

Valentin slapped him on the side of the head. "Focus."

"Right." Pavel shook off the firm hit with bearish insouciance. Any less strength behind it and he'd have taken it as an insult to his honor. "Anyway, it's all automated. Programmed to send up a bright red flag if anyone starts getting cute trying to contact people who mean the clan harm. Nothing so far."

"Good."

"We have had four false negatives that tripped the slippery, sneaky keywords I programmed in," Pavel added. "Juveniles arranging hookups outside of parental view." The other man made a sulky face. "I almost turned them in because no boy ever wanted to hook up with a vision-challenged bear, but I restrained myself."

"I'll cry you a river when I give a shit." Pavel might be vision challenged, but he was never bedmate challenged. Many, many bears and humans found him adorable. Especially when he flashed the dimples he had in both cheeks. Whereas harder-edged Yakov hated the dimples, Pavel had been known to take shameless advantage of his.

Those dimples were nowhere in evidence when Pavel said, "You really think someone in StoneWater could betray us?"

"No, but I'd be stupid not to listen to Lucas's warnings." A good alpha had to take every precaution to protect his clan. "Apparently," he said, "this Consortium group has a way of getting under people's skins."

"You said they're all about money and power." Pavel scratched his head. "I don't get it, Valya. I can't believe they'd disrupt peace just for that."

"That's because you're a bear." The people they loved were everything to them, happiness not found in power or money. The latter two things were only useful because they helped protect the clan, helped keep their cubs and mates safe.

"I don't know what would possibly entice a bear to consider betrayal,"

Valentin added, "but I'd rather catch anything while it's still small." While he could still save a clan member who'd been led astray. "We do have people who don't want me to be alpha." It hurt every cell of his alpha's heart to say that, but it was a fact.

Pavel's face grew grim, the adorable lover replaced by the powerful dominant born with the same lethal drive to protect as Valentin. "None of those people are in Denhome."

Valentin's bear, too, roared that his people were loyal, but the lost part of his clan was a splinter in his soul that reminded him not everyone loved him as bears should love their alpha. "Keep the program running."

"Consider it done." Pavel folded his arms. "I also think the way you're updating the entire clan on this should help protect us. Leaves no shadows for the Consortium to exploit and burrow into."

Valentin nodded. Bears were terrible at keeping secrets . . . except for the very rare outlier, and the secrets the last outlier had kept had been horrific. "Spread the word about Silver, let people know outsiders might mean her harm."

"I know you wouldn't bring a threat into the pack." Pavel's gaze was unusually solemn. "But, I wouldn't be doing my job if I didn't ask if you're sure she's safe."

"About as safe as Nova on a rampage," Valentin said dryly. "But she won't hurt us." Valentin was alpha partly because he could read people, and he knew that in saving Silver's life, he'd earned a certain loyalty from her and her grandmother. Neither woman struck him as the kind who'd forget that act of friendship.

Pavel nodded, taking his alpha at his word. Like all of Valentin's circle of seconds, the other man wouldn't ever hesitate to question him, but he'd also back Valentin when Valentin made a call. "I'm off-shift for the next eight hours. Unless you need me for anything specific, I'm going to go catch some shut-eye in the sun. If Yasha dares kick my ass, I'll tear him a new one."

"Go for it." The other man slept less than any other bear in the clan except for his brother, but it was a natural inclination. Five hours and they were both revved up to go. It had made them little terrors as children. As adults, it made them annoying on occasion, but at least they didn't commit the cardinal sin of being morning people.

After Pavel left to shift into bear form and snooze in the sunshine, Valentin took a look around the Cavern. His tiny targets—gangsters and all—were sitting on a plush rug in the far corner, playing a game under the watchful eyes of two elders. Crossing the massive span of the Cavern to reach the currently sweetly behaved group, he hunkered down. "Can I join in?"

Happy faces lifted up to his, tiny bodies shifted, and small hands patted at his arms as he took his spot on the rug. He listened as they explained the rules of the game; then, as a powerful, fascinating, dangerous telepath slept not far from him, he played with the children of his clan . . .

Not all of them.

Not the ones who'd been ripped from his heart by their parents and guardians.

Aching inside at the loss that was getting closer and closer to becoming a permanent scar, he opened his arms to a cub who wanted to crawl into his lap. The boy's small body, the rapid beat of his heart—it all reminded him of the vulnerable he couldn't protect within his arms, the ones who were out in the cold.

He had time yet. Not much. But some.

The Human Patriot

THE SILVER MERCANT situation concerned him. The plan he'd set in motion when she began to do an increasingly stellar job with EmNet was a good one, but the unpredictability of it chafed. He was a man used to control, and he had none in this. He just had to wait for her to consume the poison.

The outcome of which would now be further delayed unless she had taken her own food with her into the bear clan that was hosting her for a diplomatic stay. It had ostensibly been organized through Trinity and was linked to her position as director of EmNet.

He crumpled the printout of the media release.

How convenient that the Psy were beginning to inveigle their way into powerful changeling packs and clans. Whether they called it true love, or dressed it up as diplomacy, it was all about getting their hooks into the strongest alphas in the world. The second the Psy had enough operatives amongst the changelings, the alphas would no doubt start to die, to be replaced by puppets controlled by Psy telepaths.

It was how the psychic race worked. By going into the bear den as she had, Silver Mercant had proved herself as power hungry as any of her brethren. He'd been right to target her, felt no guilt any longer at the choice. EmNet's "humanitarian" mission was a very clever front designed to give the Psy access to people who wouldn't normally trust them.

"Patience," he counseled himself. "She'll keep." In the meantime, he'd work on fine-tuning the details of his next target.

He wasn't a bad person.

But neither was he a fool about to be railroaded into slavery masquerading as a bright new future. If he had to murder to achieve freedom, so be it.

Chapter 9

Deliver to: Silver Mercant at Krychek Enterprises, Head Office, Moscow
Text to read: Mr. I. M. A. Medvezhonok

—Work order at Astonishing Cakes (September 17, 2082)

SILVER WOKE ALL at once, at full alertness.

It was her usual waking process when she wasn't in a hospital bed recovering from an attempted poisoning. No haziness, no fuzziness, just sleep and then snap, wakefulness. The telepathic scan was automatic, trained into her since childhood. Mercants didn't sleep with one eye open, as was PsyNet myth, but they woke with both eyes open on the psychic plane.

Her scan picked up no Psy minds in the vicinity.

That was such a strange circumstance that Silver opened her eyes to take in her surroundings. Every city had a mélange of minds. Some, her senses glanced off—the changelings, with their adamantine natural shields; others, her mind recognized as like her own; still others, it shied away from—the humans, with shields so paper-thin that if she wasn't careful, she'd unwittingly drill into their brains and drown in their secrets.

Except for a limited number of warped Psy driven by perverse desires or greed, most Psy were like her and automatically "bounced" as soon as they detected a human mind. Having another person's entire psychic presence—thoughts, dreams, nightmares, random pieces of sensory data, echoes of a million conversations—screaming into the brain was not a pleasant experience.

This was not her bedroom.

In fact, it wasn't like any room she'd ever seen. The walls were exposed stone that had been smoothed out only enough for safety. It appeared as if this place had been—literally—hacked out of the stone, then the ones who'd done the hacking had shrugged and said they were done.

Sitting up, she looked around.

The room held no threats as far as she could see, though the front door wasn't deadbolted and there was a door to the side she'd have to check. Other than the bed on which she sat—a bed covered with a soft sheet that was nonetheless not as soft as the blanket half-pooled at her waist—there was an armchair in one corner beside a standing garment rack on which hung a number of clothes.

An aged wooden trunk sat underneath the clothes.

Within easy reach of the bed was a small side table placed against the wall. It held a digital clock, the phone she remembered sliding into the pocket of her suit coat that morning, a sealed bottle of water, and a covered tray.

Leaving that for the moment, she focused on the clock. If it was correct—and a quick check on the PsyNet confirmed that yes, the clock was precisely correct—it was now five a.m. on the day *after* her last memories.

As if the thought had triggered a cascade, the memories rushed back: *Valentin, poison, her grandmother, the hospital, small gangster bears, muscled warmth around her, a bass heartbeat against her ear.*

Silver allowed the deluge to crash over her before slowly separating out the fragments until she understood where she was and why. The next thing was to test her body. Swinging her legs out over the side of the bed, she tried to stand up on the large rug on which the bed sat. A tremor, two, but she managed to stay upright.

Walking to the door beyond which she could sense no minds at all, she opened it to reveal sanitation facilities. Silver wasn't used to being dirty in any sense, and right now, she felt exactly that. The antiseptic scent of the hospital clung to her—but below that was the faint hint of perspiration from when the poison first hit her.

A shower was a priority.

Decision made, she walked back to the door to the room, threw the bolt on this side. It was solid. Made sense in a clan of bears. From what she'd seen in the reports on those Moscow bar incidents, bears broke things without trying.

Only once she felt secure did she examine the clothing. None of it was hers, but it looked as if it would fit. A few pieces appeared crisply new while others were used but clean. In the trunk was underwear meant for someone of her size; it was still in packaging that bore the name of the boutique Silver most often utilized.

Her grandmother must've sent through the new items.

A quiet alert pinged against her mind, telling her she had telepathic messages to which she needed to attend. They were currently corraled in a psychic vault. The vast majority of telepaths couldn't form this type of "waiting area"—only the high-Gradient pure telepaths had the capacity, and even most of them found it too much work. It was, but Silver had always found the work worth the convenience.

She scanned through the translucent bubbles in the vault. Each represented a separate message, kept neatly segregated from its neighbors so as not to risk a garbled crossover. For now, Silver ignored all the messages but two.

The first one was from Ena.

Silver, Alpha Nikolaev organized for a StoneWater bear in Moscow to drive some clothes to you. All are new, purchased by my own hand. It struck me during the shopping expedition that contact poisons may have been placed on your less-used garments as a fail-safe. I will have them tested.

The message ended as Ena's messages always did—with nothing but a crisp silence. Silver knew her grandmother was right to be careful, but contact poisons were unlikely; she had a small, functional set of clothes that she utilized efficiently. Had a piece been compromised, she'd be dead by now.

She opened the second message that had caught her eye.

Silver. Grandmother isn't saying anything, and I can't bring myself to believe the ridiculous "political friendship visit" to the bears touted in the media. Cousin Ivan tells me you've disappeared from your apartment. I can feel you, know you're alive. Are you under duress? Do you need assistance?

Ena had told Silver not to trust anyone, but this bond was one nothing could corrupt. If Arwen ever decided to kill Silver, it would mean their family was broken on a fundamental level. She replied without hesitation to the brother who'd been born at the same time as her but who wasn't her twin.

Their father was the Mercant. He'd signed fertilization and conception contracts with two women. By chance, their pregnancies had occurred within days of each other, one conceiving earlier than expected, one later. Silver and Arwen had been born in the same hospital, only ten minutes between them.

He'd always been an indelible part of her life.

Arwen, she said, reaching out with her mind because her brother wasn't a powerful telepath, his psychic strength lying in another area. To have reached her to leave the message, he must've pushed himself to the point of severe physical pain. *I'm fine. There was an attempt on my life, but it was unsuccessful. Please make sure no one gets to Grandmother.* If an enemy wanted to hurt the Mercants, taking out either Silver or Ena would do it.

Eliminating Arwen would also have a catastrophic effect, but most people didn't realize that yet.

Her brother responded at once, as if he'd been awake and listening for her. *I've spoken to Grandmother in the time since I sent you the message. I'm . . . glad you didn't take her prohibition against trusting anyone to apply to me.*

Silver didn't chide him for believing that she might; Arwen was on his own journey, and it was a difficult one. *Did Grandmother share all the pertinent details?*

Yes. After a certain amount of discussion—whereupon I pointed out that if she didn't tell me what was going on, I'd hack your mind and find you anyway.

Recalling Valentin's words about "rough and tumble," Silver chose a pair of black jeans that weren't new and that Ena was unlikely to have sent. The new pants were all sharply tailored, as per Silver's usual preference, and totally unsuitable for this rugged place. She paired the jeans with a crisp white shirt that had her grandmother's stylistic fingerprint all over it.

To her brother, she said, *You haven't been able to hack my mind since we were four.*

I haven't tried since then. A pause. *I've been going over the security footage. The only non-family visitors you had in the operative window were Monique Ling and Alpha Nikolaev.*

Monique only got as far as my living area and I never left her alone.

And you never let Alpha Nikolaev in at all.

Placing underwear with the clothing on the bed, Silver said what Arwen couldn't. *There is no question then. It was family.*

The incident with the power outage four and a half months ago means there's a gap in the security footage, so there remains a slim chance it was an outsider.

You know as well as I do that the power cut was caused by a freak technical failure, Silver replied. *The poisoner would've had to have the gift of foresight and be waiting all but outside my door to action his or her plan in such a limited time window.*

I know. I just don't want it to be family. Arwen's telepathic voice was as distinctively husky as it was in real life, boosted by his psychic signal to sound as if he stood in the room next to her. *I'm assisting Grandmother to get to the bottom of it.*

Forward me all the data.

Do you want it through your comm account or in a psychic vault?

Ending the conversation after they'd discussed the most secure method of transfer, Silver got in touch with Ena. She had no concern about waking her from sleep—Ena was the one who'd taught her how to set up the telepathic waiting room, would've activated that if she didn't want to be disturbed.

Grandmother, she said, *I'm awake and at full psychic strength. I do feel a certain physical weakness that may take longer to conquer.*

Her grandmother responded immediately. *The doctors said it could take up to three days. The lab has finished analyzing the poison. It's something new, designed to debilitate rather than kill. Had you not received immediate medical attention even after only half a glass, you wouldn't have died. You'd have been left a vegetable.*

I see. That, too, spoke to their enemy's aims. *It wasn't just about taking me out. It was about making me—and by extension, the family—appear weak.*

As Alpha Nikolaev pointed out to me, you are EmNet, Silver. And EmNet is the most visible face of Trinity.

Silver nodded, though no one could see her, the action a subtle breach of Silence that she noted with the periphery of her mind. *Make me weak, make EmNet appear weak, hit it hard while it's not rooted enough to recover quickly from the setback.* It made a ruthless kind of sense. *A dead director could be replaced, but one that was lingering, weak and mindless? The psychological damage would be severe.*

Think about the implications of that, her grandmother said. *Your brother is assisting me.*

Yes, Grandmother.

After ending the conversation, Silver had to sit to get her breath back. Her psychic and physical reserves were very low. She needed fuel.

Shifting priorities, she lifted the lid off the covered tray. No nutrition bars or nutrient drinks, but she recognized the flatbread as one she'd eaten during a long work session in another region. It was created of lentils and was deeply nutritious while not overwhelming to her taste buds.

Alongside sat a bowl of what appeared to be a dip.

She tore the flatbread into small pieces, used it to try the dip. Not a strong taste, but it appeared nutritious. And if Valentin had wanted her permanently incapacitated, all he would've had to do was leave her on the floor of her apartment. The deliberately obdurate bear had also been sending her unexpected and inexplicable gifts of food for months.

Whenever she asked him to stop, he grinned and pretended he had no idea of the identity of her "anonymous admirer with the exceptional taste in food." All the while, they both knew he was responsible for the red velvet cake, the flavored nutrition bars, the individually wrapped nashi pears, the gourmet dinners delivered hot from a restaurant close to her office, and more. The last cake, a dark raspberry, had been accompanied by a card that named her admirer as *Mr. I. M. A. Medvezhonok.*

Mr. I'm a Teddy Bear.

Silver finished everything on the tray, including the two squares of dark chocolate that were bitter rather than sweet. She also drank the full bottle of water. Her body absorbed it all, her psychic abilities burning up far more energy than most people realized. She'd be hungry again in about two hours. Usually it'd take longer than that, but her healing body also needed fuel.

She waited ten minutes to let the food settle before she entered the shower.

Once clean, she dressed and ran a brush through her hair, having found the wood-handled item in a basket of toiletries in the bathroom. There was no dryer, but Silver had no intention of walking out with her hair down. It wasn't about image, but about establishing strength—more important than ever in the middle of a predatory changeling clan known for its brash nature. Especially since she'd been carried in unconscious.

Sweeping up her damp hair, she fashioned it into a knot at her nape. She would let it down to dry once she was back in her room. That done, she opened the cosmetic pack she'd also found on the bathroom counter.

It proved to hold the correct items for her skin tone.

She used mascara and a gloss. Again, it was part of her armor. Silver Mercant was never seen with a hair out of place. She woke up with a face like a "robot that would kill you while looking good doing it."

That particular quote was from a newspaper article written by a human. Hyperbolic, but the description was apt.

Silver did not want to look approachable or "human"—she wanted to be robotic perfection, a woman no one dared to cross. People didn't try to harm robots. So clearly, she needed to work on that, since someone had attempted to do exactly that.

She'd just realized that while she'd found socks, she'd located no footwear, when there was a light knock on her door. It wasn't Valentin. She was fairly certain he didn't believe in the concept of a quiet knock—or wasn't physically capable of it. Valentin Nikolaev did everything with the hugeness of the bear inside him.

The knock came a second time, just as light.

Chapter 10

There is no heart more generous than that of a bear changeling.

—*The Traveler's Guide to Changelings* (Revised Edition: 1897)

CROSSING THE STONE floor barefoot, Silver unlocked the door with her psychic senses at high alert. The person on the other side proved to be a tall, curvy woman with shining black curls styled to perfection and flawless makeup, her dark brown eyes thickly lashed and her lips a pop of rich red that matched the red cherries on her black dress. That black dress had a full skirt and a fitted top with a wide shallow neckline that showed off the smooth honey-dark skin of her toned shoulders.

On the woman's feet were strappy red shoes with two-inch heels.

"Hi! I thought you might be awake." A beaming smile. "I'm Nova, the clan's healer."

"You're also Alpha Nikolaev's sister." It'd be obvious even had she not known anything about Valentin's siblings; the two shared a striking similarity of features, though what was hard and rough edged on Valentin was more an arresting elegance in Nova. No one would ever term her "pretty." She was too uniquely beautiful for that.

"His older—but not eldest—sister," Nova said. "Can I come in?" She stepped inside without waiting for an answer.

Silver could've stopped her, but being rude to one's hosts was not how she'd been raised. "Am I wearing your jeans?"

"*Bozhe moi*, no!" Deep laughter. "Can you see these childbearing hips, as proudly described by my babushka, fitting into those skinny things?" She winked, ebony lashes coming down over one dark eye. "No, those are Moonbeam's. Her parents are a little dippy, but Moon owns that name." Having hauled in two large bags with her, Nova took several small boxes out of the bags while continuing to speak so fast that Silver could have no hope of interrupting.

"But," Nova said, "while Moon has the skinny hips, I have the best taste in shoes in this entire clan and I think we're the same size." A minute pause before Nova gave a pained sigh. "Okay, okay, your babushka did send some shoes, but I will only give them to you so you don't have to lie to your grandmother about receiving them. You have to promise not to wear them."

"Is there a reason for your aversion?"

"The shoes are black and flat and *sensible*." Nova shuddered. "Silver Mercant does not wear sensible shoes, though I bet your shoes are always comfortable."

"Yes, they are." Silver wore spike heels because it was part of the impression she wanted to project, but those heels were custom-made to ensure they never compromised her balance or ability to work.

"I knew you were a woman after my own heart." Nova whipped out a scanner from her pocket, ran it over Silver's chest area, frowned but put the scanner back, and focused on the shoes once again. "I mean, after I saw those photographs of you."

"Photographs?"

"Oh, you know we spy on you and Krychek just like we spy on the wolves and you spy on us and the wolves." Laughter rippled through Nova's words. "Have to know the other predators in the area, right?"

Intriguing that the bears considered her a predator. They weren't wrong, but most people tended to see only Kaleb, disregarding Silver as nothing but an efficient administrator. "You've brought a lot of shoes."

"Ten pairs, and that's not even scratching the surface of my collection. So if you want to borrow all of them, you can."

"Thank you." Silver ran her eyes over the various pairs on display. "While the heels would normally be my choice, it appears I'll have to navigate uneven floors. I'm not practiced at walking in heels on such a surface."

Nova nodded. "Yes, the floors are wobbly all over Denhome. I'm told that big, strong bears don't like anything too civilized." She made a face. "No one listens to my opinion on that, not even Stasya! She told me to start wearing practical shoes."

Hands fisted, Nova pressed them against her hips, her arms akimbo. "Nova Nikolaev does not *do* practical shoes. I fell flat on my ass more than once when I first started practicing with heels at fourteen. Valentin laughed *his* ass off until I dared him to put on a pair and race me. You should've seen the fall he took."

Momentarily diverted by the idea of Valentin wearing heels—even as a boy—Silver had to force herself to return to the matter at hand. "I think I should stick to more stable shoes for the time being."

"Don't even think about the sensible shoes," Nova warned. "Try these little black half boots instead. They're comfortable, cute, and they go with pretty much any outfit."

Since Silver had already decided on those as her first choice should they fit, she sat on the bed and, pulling on a pair of thin ankle socks, slipped on the boots. When she stood to walk on them, she found the fit near enough to her size as not to matter. "These are excellent. Thank you."

Nova waved off her gratitude with a smile. "I have an ankle-boot addiction," she admitted. "Eight pairs at last count, three of them black. Anyway, I think you should have a pair of sneakers as well."

Silver didn't usually wear sneakers, but she wasn't usually in a bear clan, either. "Thank you, I'll try the . . ." She looked between the sparkly blue ones with white glittery moons and stars and the nonsparkly ones with a colorful tropical print.

Nova's laugh was almost as big and warm as Valentin's. "Don't worry,

I'm just teasing you. Here." She pulled out a pair of simple canvas shoes from a bag, the color a solid dark blue. "You should watch for that, you know. We're terrible at making fun of one another. Nothing mean, though." The last was said very seriously, her following question without judgment. "As a Psy, do you understand jokes and teasing?"

"I understand the concept of jokes," Silver said as she changed out of the half boots and into the canvas sneakers. "I don't understand teasing. What's the point?"

"The point is watching Valentin turn red every time I bring up the fact he once wore pink heels and fell on his butt."

"Pink heels?" Silver said before she could censor her words.

"Well, if I was going to make my already nearly six-foot-tall baby brother wear a pair of heels, I wasn't going to choose black, was I?" Nova's eyes danced. "I was also definitely going to get photographic evidence for blackmail purposes in the future."

"Do you still have it? The blackmail material?"

"Why?"

"Because I may have need of it," Silver said, putting the half boots back on after confirming the canvas shoes were a good fit. "Your brother doesn't appear to listen to the word 'no.'"

A rumbling sound from Nova that had Silver coming to full psychic and physical alertness. "You're angry."

Nova's eyes were no longer brown but a pale glowing amber. "My brother has *never* taken any woman without permission."

"I'm not talking about sexual consent. I'm Psy. I don't have sex."

Nova's mouth fell open, amber sliding to dark brown so fast that Silver didn't catch the transition.

Collapsing next to Silver on the bed, the healer whispered, "Never? Ever?"

"Never. Ever."

"It's true then. The Psy reproduce only by scientific methods?"

"That's likely to change post-Silence, but to date, yes."

"Man." Nova blew out a breath, shook her head. *"Man."*

"It's simply another form of exercise." Silver had never had the chance to discuss this topic with someone from the emotional races—it was an aspect of changeling and human interaction that continued to escape her understanding. She'd previously predicted certain behavior, had her predictions fail spectacularly when sex was added into the mix.

"Seelichka, if you think that . . ." Nova patted her on the shoulder.

It took Silver a second to realize Nova had softened her name into an affectionate form. Like Valentin did when he called her "Starlichka"—though "Starlight" wasn't her name, either. Only Valentin ever called her that. She wondered what his friends and family called him. "Valya" would be her guess.

"Can you tell me why I'm wrong?" she asked after realizing she'd been distracted into being silent for too long. "About sex?"

Nova lifted her eyebrows. "I can't really explain sex, except to say the best is with someone who knows you, someone you can laugh with." A soft smile. "We don't say 'sex,' by the way," she added. "We call any touch exchanged between two people who want it 'skin privileges.'"

"I've heard of the concept." Had been working with EmNet long enough to pick up certain nuances of changeling behavior. "You consider it a gift to be permitted physical contact." It was a subtle complexity in the tactile nature of the changeling race.

Nova nodded. "Touch ties a clan together—and so it can never be taken for granted. Though, of course, we don't go around asking permission vocally all the time—like I just touched your shoulder. I wouldn't have done that if you'd pulled even subtly away."

It was Silver's turn to nod. "Communication isn't always vocal." As a telepath, she knew that better than anyone. That changelings were as fluent in body language made perfect sense to her. It also brought home that she was in an environment where she was the outsider. "Would you have the time to show me around Denhome?"

"Sure, but first, if you weren't talking about sexual consent, what did you mean about my brother?" Nova put the fingers of one hand on Silver's neck, having telegraphed her intent by raising a hand in that direction after they both got to their feet.

Silver allowed the healer to take her pulse, breathed in and out when

Nova removed a small sensor from her endless pockets and placed it on Silver's chest after asking her to undo two buttons on her shirt. "I've told Valentin not to come to my door to drop off things, but he does it constantly," she said once Nova had removed the sensor. "I tell him not to send me random items of food in the guise of a secret admirer named Mr. I. M. A. Medvezhonok—"

Nova snorted out laughing. "Sorry, sorry! I can just see Mishka doing that! *O Bozhe!* Mr. I. M. A. Medvezhonok!" Wiping away her tears, Nova smiled. "Look, all that's just dominant bear behavior. You have to push back, and I think you're quite capable of that. My brother would never pull anything like that with a woman who couldn't hold her own. Only an equal."

An equal.

"I'll show you around. As long as you don't overdo it," Nova said as Silver processed the fact that one of the two most powerful changeling alphas in Russia saw her as exactly what she was—a predator as dangerous as himself.

"I won't attempt more than my body can handle," Silver promised Nova when the healer looked to her for an answer. "It'll only cause further delays in my recovery."

Nova clapped a hand to her chest. "A sensible patient. I might die of a cardiac infarction."

"Please don't. You're the first rational bear I've met."

"Oh, I *like* you, Silver Mercant." Sparkling eyes. "Come on then." She reached out as if to hook her arm through Silver's, halted mid-move. "No?"

"No." All Psy were trained to avoid physical contact unless it was impossible; in Silver's case, it also helped keep telepathic interference at bay. Though she couldn't *read* changelings, all sentient beings had a surface layer of thoughts that caused a formless buzz in her head.

Contact with one person, even a small group, wouldn't be painful or detrimental to her psychic reserves, but there *was* a tipping point. Extreme telepathic sensitivity was one of the disadvantages of being a high-Gradient pure telepath. Those of her designation kept that piece of information well under wraps; it was a vulnerability that had, once upon a time, been used to torture pure telepaths.

Just put them in a room with too many people and have those people touch the Psy continuously. At the same time, refuse to give the telepath any food to refuel his or her energy. Sooner or later, the pure telepath would run out of the psychic strength necessary to maintain his or her shields.

It was simpler and safer to avoid all contact.

"Okay." Nova opened the door to Silver's room and the two of them stepped out into the hallway. "From here you turn left to head toward the Cavern. No way to miss it. Turn right and you'll end up in the residential section on this side of Denhome."

Voices drifted down the hallway, followed by three large juveniles. Spotting Nova, they called her name while looking at Silver with wildly inquisitive eyes. Before they could utter the questions they'd parted their mouths to ask, however, Nova gave them a quelling look.

Scrunching up their faces, the trio, every one of whom outweighed Nova by at least fifty pounds, passed in silence.

"That was impressive."

"Healer," was Nova's response. "Unfortunately, the look doesn't work as well on nosy adults. The last time I tried it, Pasha and Yasha picked me up and threw me from one to the other until I threatened to doctor their food with a stomach virus." The other woman gave an exasperated sigh. *"Bears."*

Silver barely heard her, having not expected the massive cavern into which Nova had led her. The ceiling soared high above, the area lit by the haze of early morning to reveal a fresh body of water in the distance, while around her, vines with tiny green flowers wove their way over the rock.

"Does your entire clan live in this complex?" Because it *was* a complex—Denhome might appear rustic, literally a hole in a mountain, but she'd already noted the thread-fine wires high up on the walls interspersed with nearly invisible silver "buttons."

Data connections. Signal boosters.

All on the cutting edge of technology.

"A lot of us do live here," Nova said after a small hesitation. "Bears aren't as much for roaming as a lot of the other predatory changelings, but we do get a few—like my younger sister, Nika—who want to go out." A fond smile. "And with all our business interests, there are smaller groups scattered here and there."

"They don't miss home?" The changeling race's clan-minded nature was both a strength and a weakness.

"We take home with us wherever we go—at least ten other bears tag along." Nova shook her head. "Hard to find privacy sometimes, but honestly, I wouldn't have it any other way."

As if to underscore her comments, multiple voices called out Nova's name.

"Later!" Nova called back. "I'm showing our guest around."

A hundred questions came at them, all to do with Silver.

"Act like bears, not wolves." Nova's stern statement had the entire group laughing big belly laughs. The laughter sent a couple of children rolling around on the rugs scattered across the floor in a riot of well-worn color that somehow wasn't jarring to the senses.

Ignoring the cacophony, Nova led her across the vast expanse and toward what appeared to be an entrance to the Cavern. "Go through this, along the passage, and you'll be outside," the healer told her. "If there's an emergency and you can't reach this entranceway, head for that one or that one." She pointed them out. "Then follow StoneWater bears out through the back way."

"I know you can't detail the escape routes, Nova," Silver said, having picked up the other woman's discomfort. "It's about protecting your vulnerable against an unknown."

Nova's smile returned, the healer's gentleness an almost palpable force. It was the same sensation Silver felt near empaths. As if they had an internal candle that produced a glow strong enough to encompass everyone in their vicinity.

A quite different sensation from Valentin's raw warmth.

"You're unlikely to ever need those back routes," Nova added. "No one would get this close to the heart of the clan without having bombed the hell out of everything around us."

Since even the wolves had apparently never penetrated deep into Stone-Water land, Silver tended to believe her. About to ask another question, she felt a whisper of dizziness. "I believe I better return to my room."

Nova's gaze grew sharp. "Let's go."

It took them longer to return to the room than it had to get this far, with Silver growing progressively weaker. By the time she lay down in bed, she was so exhausted she didn't protest the fact Nova pulled off her boots and covered her with a blanket. *"Spasibo,"* she managed to say.

"Hush now." Nova took several more readings. "I spoke to the physician who treated you—she said the waves of exhaustion will come and go for a day or two, depending on how much rest you get. But after that, you should be as healthy as a bear."

Silver wanted to reply, but her brain had other ideas. She slept.

Chapter 11

Sneaky like a cat.

—Handwritten note pasted to the back of Valentin's door

VALENTIN RETURNED TO the heart of the clan in the late afternoon and immediately caught the barest hint of a familiar scent: frigid ice with a hidden spark of fire. Silver had passed through the Cavern some time earlier. That meant she might be awake.

His bear rose to its feet inside him, its big heart thundering.

"Uncle Mishka!"

Rubbing his hand over the tight black curls of the little boy with skin of darkest brown who'd wrapped himself around Valentin's lower leg, he continued to walk, the changeling barnacle clamped on tight. "It's done," he said to Pieter. "The wolves have agreed to the new perimeter."

The other man's hazel eyes glinted. "Seriously? It took only one meeting?"

"It was difficult for even Selenka to argue against a giant crack in the ground, which meant her sentries would have to grow wings and fly to complete their rounds." Valentin rubbed the barnacle's hair again, the texture soft and bouncy against his palm. "That section was already unstable, and the little jolt we got a month back just pushed it that final bit."

"Flying wolves," Pieter said, his eyes warming with a humor only those close to him ever saw. "Imagine the games Pasha and Yasha would come up with. Target practice with rotten tomatoes, perhaps?"

"Did I hear my name?" A rumpled Pavel, his hair sticking up as if he'd just rolled out of bed after a late shift, bit into a muffin.

"Border with BlackEdge," Valentin explained shortly before glancing at Pieter again. "Selenka wouldn't have been so cooperative if you hadn't come up with the peace offering." Valentin had voluntarily sliced off a comparable section of his territory that backed up against the wolves' land.

The other man—and one of Valentin's two best friends—shrugged. "Not like we used it anyway. Too rocky for us, but the wolves will enjoy it."

"The best thing," Pavel said after swallowing his wolf-large bite of muffin, "would be if we did what DarkRiver and SnowDancer have managed in San Francisco." He thumped a palm against his chest, mimicked a heart pounding hard.

Pieter's lip curled.

So did Valentin's. "Can you see any bear being satisfied with a *wolf*?" He shuddered. "They like to wake up at dawn in *winter* and do insane things like run around in the snow when every sensible changeling who doesn't need to be awake is curled up nice and warm in their bed." It was one of his favorite places to be.

Since the barnacle wasn't showing any signs of breaking off on his own, Valentin reached down and pulled him off in what would've appeared to be an unnecessarily rough action to anyone who wasn't a bear. Bears were tough. Their cubs were tough.

Throwing this cub into the air, he caught the otherwise silent child's laughing body in his arms, then bounced him to Pieter. "Get him back in the Cage." Bear kids were notorious for escaping school—the clan literally had to lock them in and threaten them with outlandish punishments to get them to study.

Valentin's mother had once promised to shave his fur like a poodle's if he didn't stop eating his math homework. Sometimes Valentin wondered how any of them—himself included—were even literate. "And find out how he got out in the first place."

Pieter threw the wriggling escapee over his shoulder and sauntered off, while not-yet-awake Pavel headed to get himself a cup of coffee. Valentin went directly to Silver's room. He pretended not to see all the grinning nosy parkers nonchalantly poking their noses around the corner.

Lifting his hand, he went to knock, then realized she might be resting.

He shouldn't disturb her.

He should leave right now.

Chert voz'mi.

Bear and man both needed to see her.

Just to confirm that she was okay.

Deciding to try a quiet knock and go away if she didn't respond, he lifted his hand, rapped. Damn, that hadn't been so quiet. Yet there was no response. He grabbed hold of his impatience, went to walk away. He wasn't a barbarian. He was a civilized bear.

Crash!!

Valentin slammed into the door, broke the bolt on the other side without trying . . . to find Silver sitting up in bed, her hair down around her shoulders in a cool golden halo, and her hand reaching down for the insulated metal bottle Nova must've given her. It was his sister's favorite way of keeping drinks cold for her patients.

He was inside picking up the bottle, the door pushed firmly shut behind him to discourage his inquisitive clanmates, before he could process the shock of seeing Silver without her armor. "Here," he said.

Accepting the bottle, she unscrewed the lid and took a drink before looking at the door. "Is this how you normally enter guest rooms?" Frost licked the air.

Starlight obviously didn't need her armor to be fully in control. She was doing just fine flaying him alive with nothing but her voice and her eyes.

He grinned and took a seat on the bed.

When she looked *very* pointedly at him, he pretended not to catch her meaning, focusing instead on her face. Not on that glorious hair that wasn't dead straight as he'd always thought but had a slight wave to it that made it appear deliciously soft. He'd stare at that later, when he'd charmed her into not throwing him out of her room. "You're still pale."

"I'm seventy-eight percent Caucasian. Being pale is part of the package."

Sometimes, Valentin swore Silver was jerking his chain. "Paler than usual. And your eyes aren't pure ice," he teased. "There's a little fog drifting in. I woke you, didn't I?" Her face was all soft, her plush lips making him half-crazy.

"Is there a point to this conversation?"

"I just wanted to see if you were doing okay." His hands itched to touch her, but even Valentin wasn't that pushy.

Okay yes, he was when it came to Silver, but he knew how to control himself. "Can I—"

"No." Silver put down the bottle on the bedside table Valentin had built with his own hands.

"You don't know what I was going to ask," he protested.

"You've been staring at my hair when you haven't been staring at my face. You want to touch my hair."

Valentin tried to think like a cat again. Sneaky. After all, Lucas Hunter had a Psy mate. If a leopard could do it, a bear could do it better. "I'll shift and let you pet my fur in return."

Silver froze in place, unblinking.

Bear and man both held their breath . . . and then she shook her head. "No. I have no rational reason to need to touch a bear changeling in his bear form."

Valentin wasn't the most subtle of creatures, but neither was he stupid. He'd caught the hesitation, filed it away. One of these days, he'd talk his Starlight into believing she really *did* need to touch a bear's pelt. And then he'd pet her skin. An even trade . . . even if he was getting pleasure from both. He smiled inside, smug.

See, he could do sneaky as well as any cat.

"What I do need is an organizer and a phone," Silver said, her thoughts clearly not on the same track as his. "I can have the funds for the items transferred into your pack's account."

Valentin didn't take offense at her offer to pay—that was how Psy functioned and Silver liked to follow the rules. "Hold on." Stepping out of her room, he made sure to leave the door nearly closed as a sign to his lingering clanmates that they weren't to go barging in—oh, they'd be cheerfully friendly about it, just ducking their heads in to say hi, but there'd be a hundred of them in under a minute if he gave them the least leeway.

Silver would also end up with enough food for a year.

His bears thought food fixed every hurt. Most of the time, that food came with hugs and loud agreement if you were angry at something. Two weeks earlier, quiet Pieter had said "Hell yeah" while Valentin released his hurt and anger and frustration with what was happening in the clan.

Pieter and Zahaan—currently out on long-range patrol with Taji and Inara—were the only ones he allowed to see him that way; he and Zahaan had been best friends from the cradle, Pieter a natural fit for their small group when he and his family moved to StoneWater while Pieter was a child.

While Valentin trusted Stasya with his life and with the clan, her position as first second never in any jeopardy, she wasn't only the most dominant individual in the clan after him. She was also his eldest sister, their relationship subtly different from that he had with his other seconds.

Her instinct would be to comfort her baby brother while getting angry on his behalf, while Pieter and Zahaan understood that he just needed to let off steam. But Silver wasn't ready for the bearish version of sympathy and comfort, so Valentin scowled at the clanmates who were oh-so-casually hanging around outside her door.

"You all look like you need extra duties."

"Aw, come on, Valya. We just want to welcome her to Denhome."

"You can do that later." He put his hands on his hips and glared.

Dragging their feet, they began to slink away.

More than one shot him a dirty look over their shoulders.

Valentin wasn't surprised by their behavior. To have Kaleb Krychek's famously icy and searingly competent aide in Denhome? His bears were beside themselves with curiosity. There *had* been a few raised eyebrows and three quiet asides to Valentin about how safe it was to have her in the clan's heart, but no one had been angry.

Most understood that this was a time of change, that to stay strong going forward, StoneWater had to form friendships and alliances across the spectrum. Zoya, part of the old guard, had been recalcitrant about breaching the careful isolation that had kept StoneWater safe since the clan was first created. That is, until Valentin pointed out that the wolves were already in the process of coming to an understanding with people like Kaleb Krychek.

Zoya had only moved forward because she couldn't stand that the wolves might end up in a stronger position. But the upshot of her decision to take that first step was that StoneWater was adapting to this changing new world. Not too fast, however. Valentin had turned down good opportunities because StoneWater wasn't ready for too much change. His wounded clan needed time to heal.

So did its alpha.

He blew out a painful breath, shoving aside the thought for this extraordinary moment when the most beautiful, intriguing woman he'd ever met was in his territory. His ungrateful bear grumbled that he should've put her in his bed.

Valentin scowled. "She'd have turned my brains into liquid."

Going to his own room, he found the package he'd asked Pavel to prepare yesterday evening as part of his plan to be sneaky-like-a-cat.

Picking up the sleek computronics carrier along with a toolbox in which he already had the necessary spare lock, he returned to Silver's room. "Here, Starlichka." He put the carrier on her bed. "All the gadgets your heart could desire. I can give you the code if you want to Send using our systems, but I'm guessing you're hooked up to a Psy satellite?"

He was opening his toolbox as he spoke, having set it down by the door. *Be nonchalant,* he told his impatient self. *Don't stare at her to see if she likes the gift. Cats don't stare. Cats just kind of prowl along until they prowl themselves right into their lovers' beds. Be the cat.*

Silver spoke to his back. "My family has a personal communications satellite, but thank you for the offer." A pause. "What are you doing?"

"Fixing your busted deadbolt."

SILVER found herself staring at the wall of Valentin's back as he began to remove the broken lock from the door, his physicality an intrinsic force. "Do you have replacements just lying around?"

A grin shot over his shoulder before he returned to his work. "It *is* a bear pack."

Her eyes lingered on the shift of heavy muscle and tendon in his back and arms under the dark blue of his T-shirt, his words triggering a question she'd been meaning to ask. "Do bears metabolize alcohol faster or better than other changeling groups?"

Valentin's shoulders shook as his laughter filled the air. "Yes. It pisses off the wolves."

That explained the bear liking for alcohol a little more—it wasn't simply the drinking they enjoyed, but the fact they could take it better than the other predators in the area. It put paid to her belief that bears were unsubtle. Bears, it appeared, *could* be subtle. They were just very, very clever about it, hiding the subtle under the blunt edge of an axe.

And Valentin was their alpha.

She stared at the button-collar microphone and paired receiver, the paper-thin organizer, the satellite phone, and the slimline computer that had been in the padded carrying case he'd handed her. Each of the latter three items was of the exact make and model that she preferred. "You've spied on me."

Having removed the broken lock, Valentin put it down beside his toolbox. "I notice everything about you, Starlight." The holes in his jeans exposed part of his lower thigh as he shifted to drill in a piece of the new lock. "If, hypothetically speaking, we did do any spying, it'd be only fair." A very bearish smile. "Can't have you be the only one snooping around."

Silver couldn't refute the latter. She *had* spied on StoneWater. She'd even done a little industrial espionage when her family and the clan had been up for the same contract. StoneWater's espionage had been better; it had taken her three months to work out how they'd done it—by buying a young employee of the company a beer or seven and getting the inside data on the deal.

Bears.

"Did you discover anything interesting during your hypothetical spying?" she said as she began the process of connecting the devices to the Mercant satellite. The first thing that would download after connection was a "clean sweep" virus that would return the devices to factory settings, ensuring she began with a clean slate.

"You have a lot of gray suits." Valentin got up, began to fit in the second part of the new lock. "Light gray, dark gray, blackish gray, gray-gray, gray with fine pinstripes, gray so pale it's nearly white . . ." A shake of his head, his hair all tumbled black strands. "I never knew there were so many types of gray before you."

Satellite connection made, Silver watched the clean-sweep icon come on. "Gray is a very versatile shade."

"I'm no fashion critic, Starlight. My style is 'it's clean, put it on.'"

And yet he had a presence that dwarfed other men's.

"But," he added, "when Nova saw our hypothetical spy file on you, she said you should try sapphire blue and emerald green and deep pink. She says 'winter' shades would suit you, whatever that means."

He put something between his teeth as he carefully positioned part of the lock. "I'd be happy with anything other than gray," he said from around the object. "Makes it hard to see you in the rain."

Silver found herself responding to the sly challenge. "I'll wear a shade of your choice . . ." She waited just long enough for him to turn toward her in open interest. "If you start wearing three-piece suits."

Valentin's scowl was all heavy eyebrows and dark eyes. "I do have a suit, you know. My sisters got it for me for my high school graduation."

"Of course you have only one suit, and it's ten years old." He never turned up to meetings looking as if he'd made an effort. Part tactics, she thought, and part . . . *because bears.*

"How are my bears treating you?" he asked a minute later, his back to her once more.

It was a very broad back. Silver wondered what it would look like if he took off his T-shirt. She'd never been near anyone who was built with that much muscle. "Very well," she said around the problematic thoughts, "but I won't be staying here as long as my grandmother indicated."

Chapter 12

Repeat after me: I will never trust a bear who promises to show me a good time.

—Selenka Durev to BlackEdge juveniles

VALENTIN DIDN'T REPLY at once, his attention on the handheld drill he was using to finish fastening the bolt to her door. Turning afterward, he thrust back his hair with an absent hand, said, "Can't say I'm shocked. Ena's protective of you, but you're not the kind to hide away and let your elder take the risks."

It was an astute breakdown of her nature. "I need to recover to full strength, but that should only take another day or two. After which, I'll return to hunt down the individual who attempted to poison me."

"You think they'll show their hand." Leaning back against the now fully functional door, Valentin shook his head. "Your family is known for being sneaky, yes? Cat sneaky."

"Cat sneaky" was not a term she'd ever heard applied to the Mercants, but it was strangely apt. "Your point?"

"My point is that if I'm right about the sneaky, and your babushka is right about this being an inside job, then the coward responsible will go quiet when he or she realizes the poison failed." His voice dropped into a deeper register. "They'll just wait for another chance, even if it takes weeks or months. Poisoners are patient."

Silver took in that stubbled chin, the messy hair, the corded muscle of his folded arms, and knew none of it was as important as his brain. "You're understanding the subtleties of the attempt on my life very well for a self-confessed rowdy bear who rammed my door open."

"Huh, fancy that." He attempted to look innocent.

"Don't give up your day job for the stage," she advised.

Laughing, all teeth and a charismatic power that hit her with psychic force, he dropped the terrible act. "You going to listen to me, *moyo solnyshko?*"

"Since I've already come to the same conclusion, yes." Silver compartmentalized the reaction she'd just had to Valentin; she'd deal with that later, when he wasn't in front of her inciting further perplexing responses by using endearments that made no sense. She wasn't sunshine. She was ice-cold. "I'll have to action my hunt in a way that doesn't nudge the poisoner into heading underground."

It didn't surprise her that her newly downloaded messages were devoid of any updates from her grandmother.

"Ena going it alone?"

Silver was also no longer surprised by his perceptiveness. "She's used to bearing the weight alone." None of Ena's three children had the drive or the ability to steer the family.

"Zoya was like that," Valentin said. "Even her seconds had to work to gain her trust." His hair fell over his forehead again. "Your grandmother's reverted because you're hurt. She'll settle down once she sees you healthy and strong again."

If Ena didn't, Silver would force the issue.

Valentin nodded at her nest of devices. "Anything urgent?"

"No, it's under control. Lenik has been taking over many of my duties with Kaleb as EmNet demands more of my time." There was no reason to conceal that fact when Anastasia had been dealing with Lenik on various matters of late.

"He's not as good as you."

"He's excellent." She'd trained him herself and knew that he was highly capable; his only issue was a lack of confidence. "You're just not used to him yet."

"Didn't say Lenik wasn't good at his job." Valentin walked forward, engaging her attention despite her order to herself to not be distracted by the bear in her room. "Just said he isn't as good as you." Leaning down, he grabbed her organizer and phone away from her before she could move.

Her computer was next.

"You're going to tell me to rest," Silver predicted, coating her voice with frost. "You should probably know I'm an adult and have been for some time. I do not need to be tucked into bed."

Laughing with an openness that said he wasn't the least chilled by her tone, Valentin put the tech on the bedstand. "Oh, trust me, Starlight—I've noticed you're an adult." He ran his eyes down her face, over her upper half, and to the legs still concealed under the blanket, and made a return journey as slowly. "I've noticed a lot."

Silver tried to ignore the visceral impact of his scrutiny as she ran her own eyes up and down his body. "I've noticed you have more holes in your garments than cloth."

"I like the airflow." Not the least abashed, the bear who'd been provoking her for months affected a put-upon look. "I took your tech because I wanted to invite you for a walk. That's what civilized hosts do."

Silver knew he probably had something up his sleeve, but information was her drug of choice—and she could handle this particular bear. Sliding her legs out of bed, she remained seated on it as she quickly fixed her hair, having placed a hairpin on the bedstand for easy access.

Valentin's mouth fell open, a glowing ring of amber circling his irises.

When he spoke, his voice had dropped several registers, and she had the intense feeling of something big and wild looking at her in utmost fascination. "I always thought you must spend an hour in front of a mirror to get that icy-cool look."

Shaking off her own fascination at the *otherness* of him that oddly wasn't *other* at all, Silver said, "That would be a waste of my time." Which was partly why she'd practiced in the dark until she could do it blindfolded. Power was often about perception. "A moment while I put on my shoes."

She pulled the dark blue canvas sneakers out from just under the bed. "Will I need a coat?"

"Yes, temperature's dropped." Valentin glanced around. "Looks like Nova forgot to lend you one. Hold on." He returned in a minute with a thick sweatshirt. "Here."

Silver stared at the large black item of clothing printed with the logo of a human rock band. "The hoodie wasn't enough?" A hoodie that had disappeared from her room, possibly to be laundered. "You wish to ensure my drowning?"

"Why do I put up with you, Starlichka?" Valentin's growling voice caused the tiny hairs on her arms to stand up straight. "You can get something from Nova later." He lobbed the sweatshirt into her lap. "The light will be gone if we delay."

Silver had the sense she shouldn't be doing this, but she couldn't figure out a logical reason why. Valentin was right; the light would be gone in about an hour, and she needed to make the most of her time here. It'd be wasteful if she didn't use this opportunity to build up her personal database about changeling packs. That information could only help her do her job.

She pulled the sweatshirt over her head, careful not to jar her hair.

It swept over her in a fresh citrus-edged scent that told her it had been recently laundered. However, underneath that was the warm, earthy scent of the man who usually wore the sweatshirt; it felt as if he'd wrapped his big body around her.

Silver went motionless.

But before she could consider what to do about the strange intimacy of being surrounded by him, Valentin was pulling open the door and stepping out. Silver decided she could bear the discomfort, given the advantages of having the alpha of StoneWater as her guide.

She began to roll up the sleeves of the sweatshirt as she walked over to join him.

"Here," he said and took over the task. "Done."

She had to admit he'd been far more efficient with two hands than she had with one. *"Spasibo."*

He smiled.

And it was different.

She couldn't quite understand how or why, but she knew it had something to do with how she'd thanked him without any hint of the edgy challenge that was always present between them, two alphas struggling for control.

Their eyes met. Held.

"Valentin!" A woman of a height near to Silver's, her build athletic and her eyes a stunning greenish gray, jogged down the hallway. "We had an attempted incursion." The woman, who Silver recognized as Anastasia Nikolaev, had a grim expression on her face.

"When?" Valentin's tone was harder than Silver had ever heard it.

"Just now. I got the report from one of the sentries." Anastasia held up a hand, tapped her ear. "Thanks, Yasha."

Dropping her hand, the other woman looked at Silver, then Valentin. "It was a reporter." Her lip curled, her mouth unexpectedly lush in an otherwise angular face. That face was capped by short strands of ink-black hair that suited the handsome lines of her features. *"Parazit.* He was trying to sneak in to get an exclusive of Silver Mercant's torrid affair with the StoneWater alpha."

Silver blinked at the coda. Beside her, Valentin glared at his sibling. "Save the jokes, Stasya. I need the facts."

"Those *are* the facts." Smile wide, the other woman folded her arms across generous breasts. "It was Yasha who caught the journalist. You know how fucking scary he can look—he made the man all but pee his pants. The asshole was from a tabloid."

Silver asked the most pertinent question. "Why would a tabloid reporter think I was having a torrid affair with your alpha?"

Anastasia raised *both* eyebrows. "Sascha Duncan with Lucas Hunter? Or that gorgeous redhead—though her hair's more dark cherry—with the SnowDancer alpha? What made her choose a wolf, I'll never know." A mournful shake of her head.

"Also," the other woman added, "you did disappear into the clan after Valentin was spotted in your vicinity." She returned her attention to her brother. "You got snapped climbing up her apartment building, Mishka."

"I wasn't trying to hide," Valentin said, his expression harsh when Silver would have expected him to laugh and shrug it off. "Any risk the reporter could have gotten through?"

"Our perimeter is solid. Pasha's scanners picked up the reporter, but Yasha acted even before Pasha could feed him the incursion report."

"Good. If need be, we can ramp up security while Silver is in Denhome."

"Got it—I'll keep you updated." Walking backward deeper into Denhome, the other woman smiled at Silver. "In case you *are* in the market for a torrid affair, I know a number of bears far more erudite than this hulking beast next to you."

"According to my understanding of the matter, erudition isn't necessary for a torrid affair."

Valentin laughed, the sound huge and real in a way Silver couldn't explain. "Burned by ice, Stasya."

His sibling didn't seem to take offense. She called out, "Have fun!" from behind them. "Do everything I'd do!"

Evaluating the situation as they reached the Cavern, Silver said, "I didn't believe I'd draw trouble to your pack." The attempt on her life had been a thing of stealth, not orchestrated by an individual who'd expose themselves to the light. She'd never considered that the media would be a concern. "I apologize."

"We can handle it." Valentin pointed a finger at a curly-haired child of approximately three who was about to run headlong toward him. "Not now, Dima. I'm taking our guest for a walk."

The child's face fell for an instant before his dark eyes gleamed and he ran headlong toward Silver instead. Valentin intercepted him with a primal swiftness that would've surprised many.

A bear changeling wouldn't win a race against a cheetah—or a wolf— by any measure, but Valentin would beat Silver in a footrace without trying. A smaller bear might not be able to overtake her, but their physical endurance was legendary. She'd be long down before the bear stopped moving.

Bringing the grinning child to his face, their noses a bare half inch apart, Valentin rumbled in his chest. "What did I say?"

Giving a big sigh, the boy Valentin had called Dima shook his head.

"Exactly." He squeezed the child into a big hug that had Dima smiling again. "Now go join your friends for your own walk, and stop getting into trouble."

After the child ran off to the knot of cubs at the entrance, Silver said, "What was he planning?"

"Dima's suddenly developed the habit of clinging to people's legs like a barnacle." The words held deep affection. "It'll pass, but for now, he's often a one-sided weight when I'm walking around."

"I see." She halted, her eyes on a couple who'd begun kissing in the center of the Cavern the instant the area cleared of children, the male's arms tight around the woman, her fingers digging into his back.

They broke apart an unusually long time later.

"Two minutes, eleven seconds!" called out a woman who'd been watching.

"Beat that!" The couple pumped their fists in the air.

"*Pfft*," a male said. "I can kiss on a single breath for at least three minutes."

"Yeah? How about you show us?"

"Or are you all words and no action?"

The heavily built bear spread his arms. "Which lovely lady wants to volunteer to be the object of my lusty affections?" His gaze landed on Silver. "Ms. Mercant? I could show you— Never mind, I like my head on my neck."

Silver glanced at Valentin. He gave her that terrible innocent look. "You can watch this uncivilized show every night," he told her. "Once the cubs get back from their outing, it'll be much harder to make a clean getaway."

"Let's go." She replied politely to the greetings sent her way, but didn't stop again until they stepped outside Denhome.

The foliage began almost immediately at the entrance, but for two narrow pathways in among the trees and heavy shrubs. There was one larger cleared area that she already knew was used for a limited number of vehicles, though it was empty at present. "Where do the cubs like Dima play?"

"They're free to run amok inside—Cavern's full of natural light and more than big enough. It also has the pond to splash in and rocks to clamber over," Valentin told her. "But we take them out several times a day to let them play in the open air. That play is how we teach them the beauty and the danger of the wild."

He led Silver into the rich green of the trees.

It didn't take extraordinary deductive skills to recognize why the clan maintained such an impenetrable wall of forests across their territory— even from the air, no one would be able to pinpoint the exact location of the place they called Denhome. Looking back, Silver had trouble finding it, even though she knew it was there; the camouflage of trees, shrubs, and moss on the mountain was flawless.

"This way, Starlichka." Valentin shot her an assessing look after pointing out a hidden path through the undergrowth. "Nova'll skin me alive if I overtire you. Then she'll make high heels out of my skinned flesh."

"I'm feeling closer to my normal self after my rest today." It was no lie. "The fact I received immediate medical attention has no doubt contributed a great deal to my recovery. I owe you."

Valentin lifted his hand, the scars on the back catching her attention. Dropping it before his fingers brushed her hair, his gaze strangely gentle, he said, "You would've done the same. We're even—no debts between us."

It wasn't the kind of calculation with which Silver was familiar. In her world, a possible future act didn't hold equal weight to an actual act. But had Valentin collapsed on her doorstep, she *would've* immediately summoned help. Not because it would've been a good political move to have a powerful changeling alpha in her debt—though that advantage would've no doubt occurred to her later—but because the Mercants had more than one guiding law.

The first was: Family. Always.

There was, however, another one that was highly unusual.

"We are the product of an eon of honor," her grandmother had said to her when Silver was a child. "Mercants began as the loyal knights to a great king. Our ancestors were strong and proud and known for their steadfast integrity. That we function in the shadows does not mean we must no longer be true to that lineage."

Silver wasn't sure she believed in the founding legend of the Mercant family, but she had to admit their familial principles were very different from all other powerful Psy families of which she was aware. Because the applicable law in this situation was: Harm no innocents.

Valentin might not consider himself in any way an innocent, but he'd never been an enemy of the Mercants. A business competitor, yes, but that was a different playing field. There was no honor in taking a fight off the field of battle. Another law from their ancestors.

So, yes, Silver would have called for help.

A hidden part of her psyche stirred, struggled against the chains that contained it. *Are you sure family honor is the only reason you would've helped him?*

Chapter 13

SILVER HAD LONG ago learned to deal with that caged aspect of her nature, giving it no freedom but that which allowed it to act as her conscience. The primal, passionate emotions of the girl she'd been had no place in her adult life. She shut it down in instinctive self-preservation.

"Careful." Valentin caught her upper arm when she stumbled over a root, the heat of him burning through the sweatshirt to sear her skin.

She stiffened.

Breaking contact at once, he thrust a hand through his hair. "Sorry," he said, his tone gruff. "I know you don't like contact."

Silver's greatest strength was her mind, so she picked up the subtlety in his statement: He'd said *she* didn't like contact, not that the Psy race didn't like contact. The use of the word "like" was probably inconsequential, simply the way changelings saw the world. "That file you have on me again?"

A smile that didn't warm his eyes, the onyx absent of even a hint of amber. "Maybe."

Silver found herself holding that gaze for motives that had nothing to do with proving her dominance. "I appreciate the assistance. Falling on my face wouldn't have been a comfortable experience."

Amber ringed his irises, his smile a wild thing.

Silver's pulse jerked.

"We're here anyway," Valentin said, "so no more risks."

Following his gaze, Silver saw the spreading branches of a large tree that was a burst of yellow leaves speared to translucency by the late afternoon sunlight. She couldn't spot a single green or brown leaf amongst the shower of pale yellow, but the sloping earth below was carpeted with leaves that had turned brown, orange, and a deeper yellow.

Even more arresting than the natural view was the family of bears busy at play in the large stream at the bottom of the gentle slope on which the tree stood: One large bear with light brown fur and two darker cubs. The adult stood calmly in the water while the cubs splashed and jumped and chased what might've been real or imaginary fish. "Changelings?"

Valentin nodded. "Size and behavior are the clues—though the latter is occasionally negotiable."

Most changeling animals were larger than their wild counterparts. This appeared to hold doubly true for bears. The adult standing watch over the cubs could mow down any predator that came at it. Psy wouldn't stand a chance unless they had the psychic strength to smash a changeling mind or the telekinesis to fight them on a physical level.

"I can't tell if the adult is male or female," she murmured, having never had reason to learn that distinction, as StoneWater bears rarely ever shifted in the city. Even drunk, they seemed to be conscious that if they didn't watch their physical strength, they could very easily kill humans, Psy, and nonpredatory changelings.

"Female." Putting his fingers to his mouth, Valentin let out a sharp whistle.

All three turned toward them, with the romping cubs making excited sounds and jumps, while the adult settled down into the water, the gentle flow parting around her large form as her fur turned water dark. As if now that Valentin had arrived, she could break from her careful watch.

Attention diverted by her move, the cubs tried to climb onto her back. Silver was almost certain she saw the adult bear give a long-suffering sigh. Laughing at the cubs' antics, Valentin jogged down the slight incline and waded into what had to be ice-cold water after kicking off his boots and socks. He splashed the cubs, laughed when they splashed him back.

Running so they could chase him, he turned abruptly and chased them back, to their unhidden joy.

Silver took a seat on the grass. When the female bear looked her way, she inclined her head in a silent greeting. The bear did the same, then they both watched an alpha bear play with two energetic cubs, his hands holding rough care for their small bodies.

By the time Valentin made his way back to her, he was drenched and his eyes weren't human in any way. When he spoke, his already deep voice was so low it felt like thunder against her skin. "Couldn't resist," he said, pushing back his wet hair with one big hand. "If you weren't in recovery and if I wasn't in terror of Nova's wrath, I'd have invited you. The small monsters wanted to play with you."

Silver didn't get to her feet. "Can we stay here a little longer?" It was patent that Valentin had an extremely high tolerance for the cold, but he might want to dry off.

"Sure," he said and, moving away several feet, shook off the wet.

Fine droplets settled on the skin of her cheek, but she didn't flinch at the unintentional tactile contact. She also controlled her urge to reach up and touch the water where it lay against her skin. There was no reason to do that, and Silver was alive because she only did things that were rational.

Settling beside her, Valentin waved at the cubs as their guardian led their tired forms toward a path in the trees that was at the same level as the stream. "Gentler climb," Valentin told her.

"They seem too exhausted to make it to Denhome."

"It's all an act—they're hoping for a ride on their aunt's back." His tone held the same fond affection she'd heard when he spoke of Dima. "It'd take more than a few minutes' play in the water to wipe out those two."

The cubs had played with Valentin for almost a half hour. "They're hyperactive?"

"They're baby bears."

Silver watched as those baby bears turned toward her and rose up on their back paws, as if in challenge. A stern sound from their caretaker, and they dropped down and scrambled to catch up with her. Their bodies disappeared into the trees as dusk began to turn from orange to shadowy gray.

Beside her, Valentin sprawled out, bracing himself on his elbows. His drenched T-shirt clung to the ridged muscles of his abdomen, pulled tight across his pectoral muscles, shaped itself over his shoulders. His jeans weren't much better, outlining the raw muscle of his thighs.

Valentin Nikolaev was a man of violent physical strength even in human form. Yet he clearly had iron control over it; when he'd played with the children, they'd displayed zero fear of their alpha.

To be alpha is to protect.

Words Lucas Hunter had spoken once, according to a media report. It explained much about the dynamics she'd witnessed: Valentin was the most dominant individual in StoneWater by far, but his clanmates understood his strength would only ever be used to protect the clan, never to harm it.

He was like Silver, like Ena.

"You thought about where you're going to live when you escape the bears who've kidnapped you?"

When she raised an eyebrow at him, he grinned. "Fringe netter with his own Internet channel sent out a breaking report last night. Pasha—who obviously needs more work duties—made up a fake account and posted a comment swearing to have seen you being pulled into a black van by six burly bears in bear form."

"You don't seem too concerned." Amber eyes and deep voice, he remained very much a bear in human form.

"Well, according to this 'eyewitness,' the getaway driver was in bear form, too. Must've been tough for him to steer with one paw since he was drinking a beer at the same time."

"Bears," Silver said, making Valentin throw his head back and laugh that huge laugh that wrapped around her.

Hit by the last rays of the setting sun, he was . . . magnificent. It was the only word that applied.

"As for the question of my residence," she said when he stopped laughing and turned to look at her with his cheeks still creased. "I've decided my apartment has some technical issues that require maintenance."

Valentin nodded. "Clever."

"There are a number of secure buildings in the city I can relocate to in the interim."

Valentin made a dubious sound. "Your building was secure, too—and all the negatives your grandmother pointed out still apply."

Unfortunately, Silver agreed with him. "You have an alternative suggestion?"

"There's a changeling complex that might work," he said. "Your relatives won't be comfortable enough to drop by, and it gives you an easy cover story. No need to set up fake long-term repairs in your apartment."

"That I'm further immersing myself in changeling culture to better run EmNet?" Silver guessed. "That means I'll eventually have to live in a human group to ensure no ill feeling across the races."

"Good trade-off for safety. You could reach out to the Alliance to set up a future stay in a mostly human enclave to head off any cries of favoritism . . . even though we bears *are* your favorites."

Silver didn't react to his wink; that would only encourage him, and Valentin Nikolaev didn't need positive reinforcement. "Is it the BlackEdge complex you're suggesting?"

A rumbling sound from deep in his chest, his hands suddenly sprouting lethal claws that dug into the earth as he sat up, palms braced behind him. "Yes. You'd be surrounded mostly by wolves, and that's enough to make anyone deranged, but there's no chance of a stranger getting to you without someone noticing."

"Are there bears in the complex?"

"A few poor souls." Valentin's tone was mournful. "Nowhere else suitable in the city for those strange clanmates who want to work in city-based professions. Like that rebel cousin of mine who's convinced he loves being a prosecutor."

Valentin's "rebel" cousin was actually one of the best young Enforcement prosecutors in the city—and Silver knew full well Valentin had taken him out to celebrate after big victories, the proud older cousin and even prouder alpha. "I've always thought the larger and more predatory changelings must find it difficult in the city." The most dangerous predators lived for wild places.

"That's why the BlackEdge development was so important."

"Don't you mean the BlackEdge-StoneWater development?" At Valentin's sharp look, she said, "I have my own spy files."

A scowl that was all dark eyebrows and bear arrogance. "The wolves and leopards out in California gave us the idea," he said in a grudging tone. "Wolves are mangy and they probably give my clanmates fleas, but we decided a while back that there are certain things it makes sense for us to work on together."

"Ah, this must be the source of your deep and abiding friendship."

Scowling deeper at her reference to his comment the morning he'd come to her apartment, he shuddered. "I don't know how Lucas Hunter does it. Then again, he's a cat. They find the strangest things funny. Maybe he thinks an alliance with wolves is a hysterical joke."

Silver wondered how much of the bear antipathy for the wolves—and vice versa—was real and how much was habitual. "I'd have to check if the complex has any openings." It wasn't built like a Psy or human apartment building—the homes were spread out amidst a large amount of green space; raised pathways that doubled as elevated runs meant every residence, even those sized for single individuals, had a personal exit directly onto a path.

"I already checked. One apartment available on the third floor of a four-story building. Wolves and bears around you. My rebel cousin would be your neighbor."

Silver realized that this was a neat trap into which she'd been gently nudged, but since it happened to be an excellent idea, she had no reason to protest. However, her relocation would be only until they'd unearthed the traitor. She'd permit *no one* to force her out of her home.

The two of them sat in silence for long minutes, the water flowing below and the birds raucous as they finished their business for the day.

Valentin was the one who broke the quiet. "If you want to go for a run after you feel better, Starlight, I can show you a running track through the woods. I know you go running on Moscow streets after dark."

"It's quiet then, the streets comparatively empty."

"Being around so many bears must be driving you crazy."

"No, I'm having no difficulty being in Denhome." Silver had expected to feel suffocated, but she'd forgotten to factor in an important variable: she'd grown up in a tightly integrated extended family unit, had spent her entire childhood sharing quarters with others.

The bear setup didn't stress her on any level.

"My family has a version of Denhome," she found herself telling him. "On a much smaller scale, of course."

"Ena?"

Silver nodded. Her grandmother's home was a place where they were all welcome, and where they gathered multiple times a year.

"Look." Valentin nodded up. "Stars are starting to appear."

Her vision wasn't as acute as his. She couldn't see the stars against the gray of the sky, but she could feel the cooling air, hear the rustling of the trees. "I've never been in this type of environment."

VALENTIN took in her profile, bear and man both deeply contented at being here, beside her. "There's beauty in the night, in wild spaces filled with life." It sang to his soul; he could tolerate the city, but sooner or later, his heart began to keen for the primal forests that were his home.

They kept those forests as natural as possible, but Denhome itself wasn't in any way backward. Having watched and learned while he was Zoya's first second, Valentin had purchased a satellite for his clan as soon as he had the power. It meant their communications weren't reliant on any outside party.

Of course, that satellite was more irritating than a smug wolf when it bounced him calls at moments when he'd rather be left alone. Like right now. Glancing at the screen, he saw Pavel's name. "What is it?" he asked, aware the other man was on sentry duty.

"I have a very pretty dude here claiming to be your Starlight's brother. Silver eyes, black hair, supermodel bones, is giving me a death stare."

Sitting up, his bear at attention, Valentin looked at Silver. "You have a brother?" How had he never unearthed that fact?

A pause, her head angled as if listening. "Arwen is here," she said. "He says he wasn't giving anyone the death stare—that's his normal expression."

"Must run in the family."

Silver's response was a look that was all ice.

Wanting to kiss her so bad it hurt, he told Pavel to guide the other man to a particular section of the territory, one that wasn't too close to Denhome. It was one thing to trust Silver and Ena not to betray them, quite another to trust a brother he'd never seen.

It took them twenty minutes to reach the location.

Pavel leaned against a sleek black vehicle while another male stood nearby. Valentin recognized him at once—he was a regular visitor to Silver's apartment. But the color of their eyes aside, the two had little in common physically speaking.

Arwen Mercant looked to be shorter than his sister, maybe five seven or five eight. That black hair Pavel had already noted, straight and smooth and cut with CEO ruthlessness, not a strand out of place; a skin tone that was more olive than golden; the "supermodel" bones that equaled high cheekbones and a square jawline.

While his eyes were the same shade as Silver's, they were tilted sharply at the corners, giving him a silkily feline appearance.

Right now, he looked about as suited to these primeval forests as a peacock. His suit was dark gray and flawlessly fitted, his tie a stylish black.

"Arwen."

Valentin heard a subtle warmth in Silver's tone that had him listening hard.

"Silver." Walking forward, her brother stopped a foot from Silver.

Silver didn't make contact, either. It wasn't how changelings would greet each other, and it definitely wasn't how bears would greet a sibling who'd been hurt, but Valentin didn't make the mistake of thinking they weren't close.

Back when he'd noticed all those visits by Arwen in the surveillance files Pavel kept on all the major players in the area, he'd been jealous until he'd gotten a close look at the other man's eyes and figured out he was family. Now that he knew their relationship, the visits took on another meaning.

Chapter 14

The E-Psy, or empaths, as they are called in the vernacular, are something of a peculiarity. The powerful among them can heal the most devastating of emotional wounds. Folklore says they can cure insanity. That has never been proven. What has been proven is that they can certainly help people through difficult emotional times, absorbing negative emotion in a way that defies even psychic explanation.

—Introduction to *The Mysterious E Designation: Empathic Gifts & Shadows* by Alice Eldridge (Reprint: 2082)

"WHAT ARE YOU doing here?" Silver asked her brother, keeping the conversation on the audible level so as not to be rude to her hosts.

Right then, however, Valentin moved away to speak to Pavel. The distance was such that neither bear should be able to hear this conversation if she and Arwen maintained a low volume.

"I needed to see you were all right." Her brother let his shields fall; on his face, she saw layer upon layer of deepest emotion.

Arwen's vulnerability was a rare thing in the world in which they lived.

"I'm fine." Of the two of them, Silver had always been the more ruthless and pragmatic. Arwen's Gradient 7.9 empathic abilities sometimes threatened to leave him wide open to the violence and chaos of the world.

She—all of the Mercants—had always known he was precious, had protected him from the cradle, but only now did they understand that he was likely responsible for the deep mental stability of the Mercants over the past twenty-nine years, give or take a few weeks. Arwen made them better.

Better people. Better Psy. Just . . . better.

"Are you sure?" her brother asked. "This environment . . ." Stepping closer, he lowered his voice to a whisper. "Are you aware you're wearing a monstrosity of a sweatshirt and *canvas sneakers*?" A scandalized look down at those sneakers. "I'm half-afraid you've been brainwashed."

"I'm adapting to my circumstances." Seeing below the frivolous comment to the concern that had brought him here, so far out of the city that was his comfort zone, she touched him on the arm. "Thank you for coming to check on me."

He froze for a second, the reaction an instinctive one for siblings who'd grown up under Silence. But he softened far quicker than any other member of the family would've done, lifting his other hand to place it over hers. As she'd learned to give Arwen what he needed to feel emotionally healthy, he'd learned to see through her Silence to the certainty that she'd die to protect him.

Silver didn't know how to love, but she knew how to hold on to her people.

"You look good." Relief colored his tone. "You're recovering?"

"It'll take a little time to get back to full strength, but I suffered no permanent damage."

"You're in a . . . a *jungle* with a clan of bears who don't even believe in proper roads. What if you have a relapse?"

"The StoneWater healer is fully qualified." Silver knew from the research she'd done into the clan that Evanova "Nova" Nikolaev was an M.D. as well as a changeling healer. "I'm in excellent hands."

Arwen sighed. "You're determined to stay here? It's so primitive."

While her brother was a sophisticate through and through.

Gentle and kind and the best Mercant of them all, but a snob when it came to his clothes and the cut of his hair. He'd lay down his life for a stranger in harm's way without thinking twice—but even as he died, he'd probably be judging the clothes and shoes of everyone around him.

Pavel looked over at that instant, winked at Arwen. Who turned right back to Silver. "If you're determined to remain in this den of savages," he said in a tone designed to carry to sensitive changeling ears, "I'll make sure to visit regularly so you don't forget civilization."

Used to him, Silver said, "Come, I'll introduce you." But by the time she reached Valentin, Pavel—whom she knew through her spy files on StoneWater—had melted away into the trees with unexpected stealth. It was a timely reminder never to forget that bears were dangerous predators under the skin. Even bears who wore spectacles and had dimples in both cheeks.

"You're Arwen." Valentin held out a hand in an action that said he'd noted their physical contact.

Arwen shook it. "Alpha Nikolaev," he said formally. "Thank you for offering Silver sanctuary until we get to the bottom of this."

"Progress?"

Arwen shook his head. "I did get access to the report on the poison. It has a unique composition." Slipping out his whisper-thin combined organizer and phone, he brought up the chemical breakdown and turned the screen to face them. "I can run through the components."

"No, I see it." Valentin took the cutting-edge device; his expression turned unforgiving seconds later. "At a guess, I'd say this is designed to badly disturb Psy neurochemistry."

"Valentin has a master's degree in psychology," Silver told her startled brother. Valentin's academic choice had always intrigued her; it seemed so opposed to his forthright nature. "As he was so academically proficient he was strongly urged to do a doctorate, I'm guessing he's aware of certain chemicals as they interact with the brain."

Valentin's expression softened, delight apparent in his eyes at her knowledge of his academic success. "Not something we studied in depth, Starlichka, but I know enough to make sense of this." Handing Arwen's prized piece of tech back to her brother, he said, "It's the combination that's the key, isn't it?"

"Yes, the dosage was precisely calibrated to be devastating to the Psy system." Arwen gave them a précis of the report because he'd already had time to digest it.

"The poisoner," Silver said, "is either a highly skilled chemist or has access to the same."

Valentin's eyes glinted amber. "It's a scent, a place to start." He went to say something else when his phone rang.

The person on the other end had news of a highly unexpected nature.

The Human Alpha

BOWEN KNIGHT TOOK a second look at the header of the e-mail his assistant had forwarded to him. He had an open-door policy to every member of the Alliance, having learned that an out-of-touch leadership could destroy an organization from within. However, with that policy came an avalanche of messages no single human could possibly read. He'd finally agreed with his sister's suggestion that he get an assistant.

Lily had also provided him with the CV of an eminently qualified person.

Not only was Neha trained to the highest level, she was extremely intelligent. Filtering his messages—everything apart from those that came directly to his private address—was just one part of her complex duties. At first, he'd checked the messages she'd filtered out from his inbox; he'd found not a single decision with which he disagreed.

These days, he trusted her judgment.

Which was why he was surprised to see the subject line of the message she'd forwarded, not just to his inbox, but also to his phone, so that it would pop up for his immediate attention.

IGNORE AT YOUR PERIL!!

It seemed like the kind of scam/junky header designed to get people to open questionable mail, but Neha had clearly seen something important in it, so he didn't ignore it.

Scanning it as he stood on his balcony overlooking a canal, he frowned.

Consider this fair warning. If you do not stop your efforts to DESTROY the human race by taking part in this ELIMINATION EFFORT disguised as a PEACE ACCORD, you will pay the price. You are important to the Alliance, have just been led astray. See the ERROR of your ways.

    The first one will be a WARNING. The second will be aimed at you.

There was no signature line, nothing in the generic free-to-get address to show who might've sent it. What was clear was its threatening nature. Bo immediately contacted the tech team that was part of his larger security team and put them on the job of seeing if they could track the sender.

"Also, issue a yellow-level warning to all staff," he ordered. "A crackpot like this might actually turn up and take a shot."

Yellow was appropriate and would be taken seriously. Red was saved for an emergency, orange for when they had details of an actual event that was nearly guaranteed to take place.

After he hung up, he considered the message again. At first glance, it appeared to be written by someone of limited education, but when he looked at it more carefully, he saw that there were no misspellings and, except for the odd capitalization, the grammar and syntax were perfect.

Unfortunately, the writer's pattern of speech wasn't enough to track them down—there were a whole lot of intelligent, unhinged bastards on the planet.

The alert would have to stay at yellow until he had further data.

Closing the message, he was about to slide away his phone when it rang. He answered with a smile. "Phoenix. How's work going?" His closest cousin in age, who also happened to be one of his best friends, had relocated to Mozambique eight months earlier on an engineering contract.

"On schedule, all good to finish in two months," the other man said quickly. "I called you about something else." Before Bo could ask what that was, Phoenix burst out with, "I got mated!"

Mated.

That word had very specific usage.

"A changeling?" Bo grinned. "One of the gazelles you've been admiring from afar?" Phoenix was brilliant and hardworking, but he was also shy to the point that Bo knew he hadn't ever had a girlfriend—despite the efforts of his friends to find him equally gentle women to date. "You actually went up and introduced yourself?" Gazelles tended to be gentle and shy, too, so it'd be a perfect match.

"Not quite." Phoenix sounded like he was grinning so hard his face was about to crack. "Janika came up to me, hauled me into a kiss, and the next thing I know, I'm naked and happy and waking up with the most beautiful woman I've met in my entire life."

Bo blinked. "Not a gazelle then."

"She's a bear."

This time, Bo had to sit down. He did so on the balcony floor. The idea of sweet, blushing Phoenix with one of the toughest predators on the planet . . . "You're sure you're mated and your beautiful bear's not just taking you for a delirious ride?"

"He's mine and he's delightful." Those words were spoken in a throaty female voice that dripped with possession. "You can't have him back."

"I don't want to go anywhere." Phoenix's voice, the timbre unexpectedly solemn. "You're it for me, Jani."

"Ah-hem," Bo said before the two forgot he was on the line. "Congratulations to you both." His happiness for his cousin was no less, despite his shock. "When do we get to celebrate with you?"

"I can't leave the project at such a critical time, but plan for a huge party when I get back. Jani's got a lot of relatives."

Bo felt a scowl coming on. "Your Janika can keep you, but tell her you belong to us, too." Changeling packs and clans had a bad habit of absorbing people; Bo wasn't about to lose touch with a member of his own clan.

"Possessive, aren't you?" The female voice again, her accent distinctive. *Very* distinctive.

Bo sat up straight. "*StoneWater?* You mated a bear from *StoneWater?*" The bear clan controlled an immense chunk of Russia—and its members were notorious for the way they managed to nab business deals right out from under their opponents' noses. Someone in that clan had one hell of a strategic brain.

"Tell my brother I said hi when he calls," Janika said. "I'm now going to ravage my adorable mate."

From the masculine laugh Bo caught before Janika hung up, Phoenix was more than willing to be ravaged. "Jesus. Phoenix with a StoneWater bear." It was like putting a fluffy kitten with a saber-tooth tiger.

He hoped to hell his cousin knew what he was doing.

His phone flashed again. This time, it was a call being redirected from the number the Alliance had on file with Trinity. That it was being routed directly to his phone told him it was important. "Bowen Knight," he answered.

"This is Alpha Valentin Nikolaev."

Bo didn't believe it. "I'm still in shock over my deathly shy cousin mating a StoneWater bear." He banged the back of his head against the railings. "If you tell me Janika is your sister, my head will probably explode."

Laughter filled the line, the sound big and warm and primal. "We are family now, Bowen Knight!"

Chapter 15

Ain't no party like a bear party.
It's the hangover that's the problem.
Worth it. Carpe-the-diem!
Wolves are cool, bears are fools.
Didn't get an invite to the party, huh?

—Graffiti on a Moscow wall, each line written by a different unknown
individual over successive days prior to erasure by the
city works department

TWO HOURS AFTER they'd returned to Denhome, Silver sat in a—comparatively—quiet corner of the Cavern and watched several bears—in bear form—stand up on their back paws to dance. At least two were holding beer bottles in their paws. One had tinsel wrapped around his neck and was, for some unknown reason, wearing sunglasses.

Another was snoring a few feet away from her. Every so often, he'd slap out his paw as if killing dream flies. The cubs who weren't yet asleep kept sneaking up to the sleeping bear on tiptoe and putting flowers and play "jewels" on his fur. By now, he was extremely well bedazzled. Not far from him, a number of clanmates, who hadn't shifted form, were playing a game called bobbing for apples.

No one had so far returned from their shallow dive with an apple, but that didn't stop their stomach-holding laughter. Possibly because the adult barrel was apparently filled not with water but with liquid of a more alcoholic variety. The cubs had a cub-sized barrel that was more traditional.

The tiny gangsters were making up their own games. One was currently standing on her head next to Silver, while another two had stuffed so many cherries into their mouths that they looked like chipmunks. It was a contest from what she could see, with the stems of the cherries neatly lined up beside them.

Two more were in bear-cub form, doing "kung fu"—as told to Silver by the martial artists themselves before they shifted.

"How many seconds?" the head-stander called out.

"Seven," Silver said.

"Nika's mated!" the same child called out. "I like Nika!" Tumbling to the floor, she rubbed at the top of her head before running off toward the food table.

Silver watched the tiny girl duck between much larger bears with fearless dexterity, saw a hand reach down to pluck her up and throw her across the room into another pair of waiting arms. She was lowered to the floor right by the food, a wide grin on her face.

"Boom, boom." A very small cub lurched against Silver's chair, balance not yet his strong point. Someone had shaped and gelled his soft blond hair into a Mohawk, and dressed him in a miniature replica of a biker jacket, complete with fake chains. "Boom, boom!"

"Yes, the music has a strong beat," Silver responded. "It's not as loud as I expected, however."

Big blue eyes looked at her with solemn attention. "Boom, boom!" He then dropped a soggy half-eaten cookie onto her lap.

Plucking the child into his arms, Valentin blew a raspberry on his stomach. The cub giggled. "You should be in bed." Despite the stern words, Valentin cuddled the cub close and began to pat the little boy's back as he leaned up against the wall next to Silver. "Sound's calibrated not to blow out our eardrums."

Silver put the unwanted cookie on a discarded plate nearby. "Of course." Changeling hearing was acute. "I haven't seen you take a drink." It was his sister's mating the clan was celebrating, after all.

A wink. "I'll wait until Nika's home with her engineer. *That'll* be a party."

Silver looked around the wild chaos of the Cavern. The kung fu cubs were now doing kung fu on the legs of adult bears, while the beer-drinking bears were pointing to the whiskey bottle on the bar table, and nodding at one another. Pavel's twin, Yakov, was spinning Anastasia in a dance that kept crashing them both into the other couples. At which point, everyone involved cracked up laughing . . . right before a pie sailed from across the room to nail Yakov on the back of his head.

"Pasha!" With that roar, he took off through the crowd, hell-bent on vengeance.

"If that will be a party," she said, "what is this?"

"Fun, but it'll shut down soon—that whiskey's never going to be opened. People have shifts to prepare for, work to rest up for." He looked down at the child who'd fallen trustingly asleep in his arms. "I'll get this escapee to bed." A glance out of eyes gone amber. "Stay until I get back?"

Silver found herself nodding, though she should've retreated to her room an hour ago, her body yet healing. She watched as Valentin walked toward the residential area, his big body too heavy with muscle to be graceful . . . yet, he was in a way that was all power and strength.

VALENTIN had just returned from putting the cub into his crib—after ridding him of the biker jacket—and was trying to think of a cat-sneaky way to talk Silver into a dance when her eyes suddenly connected with his, urgency in their depths. His phone buzzed three seconds later, a second after he'd navigated his way to her.

The name on the screen was Zarina Saarinen. Head of StoneWater's educational system and mother to Zahaan, Zarina was in the city for a party to celebrate the birthday of her former college roommate, a human female who was now an astronomer.

He answered it as Silver motioned for him to follow her back into the quieter residence section. "Zarina, what's happened?"

"A bomb, I think," she shouted down the line, screams and shouts loud in the background. "I heard the explosion from two streets away, ran over into dust and chaos. Looks like the Dancing Frog bar was the focal point."

A bar?

"Who's on scene?"

"Krychek's here, along with people from neighboring businesses. No emergency crews yet."

"Do what you can." Hanging up, Valentin looked at Silver. "You know?" The telepathic highway was a lightning-fast one.

"Only human victims discovered so far," Silver said, her eyes on her phone, which scrolled with data. "I'm in touch with local authorities to see if they need EmNet assistance."

Anger raced through Valentin's blood. "The fanatics who've been predicting the destruction of the Psy race if Trinity goes ahead?" The threats had been sent to various comm stations, warning of a loss of Psy "superiority" if others were to "interbreed" with them. "Didn't the pieces of shit threaten to attack humans and changelings seen associating with Psy?"

"Word's filtering through that it was a suicide bomber." Silver touched her temple for a second before starting to work her phone again. "No signs of him being Psy at this point. Taking into account the location and the known casualties, as well as the lack of any violent psychic ripples in the Net, there's a high chance it was a non-Psy."

Valentin wanted to say no changeling could do this, but their race wasn't perfect; it was capable of spawning those with hate and violence in their heart. Valentin knew that firsthand. Even if he hadn't, it was changelings who'd stained the earth bloodred during the Territorial Wars three and a half centuries ago. No alpha, no *changeling*, could ever afford to forget that, especially in a time when it would be so easy to blame the Psy for the world's ills.

"I'm heading to the city," he told Silver, raw pain intermingling with the anger. "A StoneWater team will follow." He'd give the order as he was leaving—as he'd said to his Starlight, people had been having a good time, but despite appearances, nobody was drunk. "The cowards behind this will see a coordinated response, see a united city that can't be so easily broken."

"I'll go with you." Silver held up a hand, even as his bear lunged to its feet in rejection of the idea of her going out into the cold night. "Yes, I'm weak, but if I don't show up at an incident in my own city that's claimed mostly—perhaps *only*—human victims, I may as well resign as director of EmNet." With that, she disappeared into her room and when she returned, she'd shed his sweatshirt and changed into a fresh white shirt.

She'd also swapped out her sneakers for ankle boots.

That quickly, she was cool, elegant Silver Mercant again, even in jeans and with not a single gray hue in sight. "People of all races need to believe in me for EmNet to work."

Biting back his protective urge to throw her on her bed, order her to rest, and shut the door—all that would get him was a sore head when Silver turned her telepathic muscles against him—Valentin instead ran to Nova's quarters and borrowed one of his sister's coats. It was darkest gray.

Tracking Silver's scent to the exit from Denhome after he'd spoken to Stasya about sending in a rescue team behind them, he felt his raging protectiveness calm. "No emergency teleport?" He hated the idea of her being out of his sight when she hadn't yet recovered from the attempted poisoning. *Especially* if she'd left without a coat when the temperature had plunged.

"I don't want to split Kaleb's energy." Accepting the coat with a nod of thanks, she added, "I'm used to coordinating resources remotely, so a delayed arrival on-site won't matter." She did exactly that during the drive, using both her phone and her telepathic senses as necessary.

She updated him in the short periods when she was free. "First responders have pulled out three survivors so far, but my sources say the bar was packed for a private celebration. A wedding reception."

Valentin's claws shoved against his skin, the ugly pointlessness of it all infuriating him. "There were probably changelings in there, too."

"No bears identified," Silver said, her tone careful.

Valentin's hands squeezed the steering wheel. "As far as I know, no one was in the city to attend a wedding reception, but I'll alert Pieter to check that all our people are accounted for." The thought of losing even one more person from his clan . . .

The two of them were still ten minutes out from the city when Silver's phone beeped. The person on the other end must've spoken as soon as Silver answered, because she listened in silence.

Valentin couldn't hear anything, Silver utilizing the earpiece that had been part of the tech package he'd given her. A button microphone was attached to the collar of her shirt.

"Yes," she said a short time later. "Moscow does need to show a united face to our enemies, but that can be done by a single high-ranking member of your pack at the scene." A pause. "It would be better if it wasn't you. Alpha Nikolaev will be there very shortly. Kaleb is present already. I don't want all three alphas in the region in one place."

Selenka.

He didn't need to ask Silver to confirm: there were only three true alphas in this region—Valentin, Selenka, and Krychek. And Silver was right. The three of them shouldn't be in the hot zone at the same time. It might prove too tempting a target for anyone who wanted to destabilize the area.

"You should pull in the nonpredatories," he said after she ended her conversation with the BlackEdge alpha.

"Already in progress," Silver replied. "A disproportionately high number of the local mountain-pony herd are in the medical field. The others, I've asked my EmNet assistant to contact."

Valentin knew her assistant was Psy; the stern woman had given him the stink eye many a time when he dropped by to speak to Silver. "You need to have a human and a changeling in your inner circle," he said as he drove hell-for-leather through the traffic in the city proper.

"It's more efficient to work with fellow telepaths."

"Everything you do in EmNet is finely balanced—you made that clear when you came along on this trip." Even though her face was too pale and her strength shaky.

Biting back his bear's bellow of displeasure at how she was mistreating herself, he said, "No one race can be seen to have more influence or power."

"I'll take the suggestion under consideration." Silver's fingers moved on her phone. "The problem with choosing a changeling is that many of you are antagonistic to other changeling species. Predators won't always accept orders from a nonpredatory workmate, while two different predators can get into dominance battles."

Valentin couldn't argue with any of that. "You're the smartest person I know, Starlight." Bar none. "You'll figure it out, but you can't keep it Psy-only at the top."

Noticing the traffic jam up ahead, dust rising up to blur the glittering Moscow skyline and a sea of brake lights coloring the night scarlet, he brought the vehicle to a stop on the side of the street. "Can you walk the distance?" He knew better than to offer to carry her, but he could bull his way through in the all-wheel drive. It'd be messy and noisy and it'd piss off a lot of people, but it was doable.

And he was a bear. It wouldn't be the first time he'd made people swear and wave their fists at him.

"I can walk."

Exiting the vehicle, the two of them moved down the sidewalk; it grew more and more congested the nearer they got to the disaster zone. He made sure he was in the front, so Starlight wouldn't be jostled. Most people shrank back from the force of his dominance—or maybe it was the scowl on his face.

They arrived at the cordon set up by the first responders, were immediately waved in. Controlled chaos lay beyond, with an Enforcement officer attempting to organize the surge of help from various agencies and groups. Sweaty and overwhelmed, he clearly didn't have the training for it.

Valentin saw his shoulders drop in open relief when he spotted Silver. "Ms. Mercant," he said in Russian. "I think this qualifies as an EmNet situation."

Silver caught the ball, ran with it. "Who's already here?" she asked without preamble. "Tell me what resources I have to work with."

The officer, looking much less harassed now that someone else was in charge, listed all available personnel on-site. Valentin forced himself to take a mental step back. He was used to being a caretaker, but if he hovered, he'd do more damage to Silver's reputation than if she collapsed.

It had nothing to do with being the director of the world's biggest humanitarian organization and everything to do with being Silver Mercant. Tough and in control and without weakness. "I'm going to see if I can help scent out survivors," he said when the Enforcement officer paused for breath.

Silver's eyes met his, all frost and sexy intelligence. "Take the southeast quadrant. That sector has no changeling assistance, and the lights currently on-site are limited. Your greater night vision will be welcome."

Realizing she'd received a telepathic update, he nodded, would've left, but she said, "Valentin. Be careful." No change in her tone, but it was the words that mattered. "The debris is unstable."

Despite the circumstances, despite the permanent bruise on his heart, a smile formed inside him. Of all the changelings here, he was undoubtedly the one most able to survive half a building falling on him. But it was him she was warning. "You, too, Starlight."

Bear ready, he headed to his assigned sector—but not before he found the young clanmate he'd scented nearby. "Devi." He squeezed her skinny, dusty body into his arms, held her until her tremors eased. "You hurt?"

A jerky shake of her head. "A few friends and I were about to go into the restaurant across the road when it . . . when it happened." Her voice broke, this member of his clan a bear with a soft heart and gentle hands. "I tried to help, get people out, but Zarina said I should s-stay back."

It had been the right call, given Devi's physical strength and skills. Now Valentin made another one. "Come on." He took her to Silver. "Devi is an athlete," he said when his brilliant Starlichka shot him a silent question. "A runner. Fast, with bear endurance."

Silver didn't question his word. "Wait here," she said to Devi. "I'll be using you to run water to the rescuers in a moment."

"Okay, sure." No longer trembling, Devi reached back to tighten her ponytail. "I can do that."

Valentin was already turning to head to the quadrant Silver had assigned him. He caught sight of Krychek lifting off large pieces of the rubble in the distance, but even the telekinetic was having to go slow, his movements based on information passed to him by a red-haired changeling Valentin recognized as a BlackEdge wolf: an engineer doing double duty, scenting survivors and planning the safest actions Krychek could take.

Krychek was a *power*, but if the cardinal moved the wrong piece, the debris would collapse like a house of cards, crushing any survivors within.

Valentin saw no more of how it went; he'd reached his quadrant to find a mixed group of Psy and human first responders. The medics had been ordered to stand back, but the others were picking up and moving pieces of the broken building with painstaking care.

Spotting Valentin, an older woman called a halt. "Your nose as good as a wolf's?"

Ignoring the tired attempt at a joke, Valentin began to climb the pile of rubble, careful to ensure his weight was in no danger of causing a collapse. Sweat and desperation—the rescuers' own scents—were pungent in the air. But he was a bear alpha. He knew how to filter out unwanted scents— *Chert!*

"Has the gas been turned off?"

Chapter 16

"YEAH! AT THE city's system mains!" The speaker was wearing the gear of Moscow's fire-safety crews, the reflective stripes bright on his jacket. "You smell a leak?"

"There are discrete pockets." Gas wasn't a common fuel any longer, except in older buildings like this one where conversion wasn't worth the cost, but Valentin knew the scent.

"That's probably from right after the initial collapse!" the fireman called back. "It took ten minutes for someone to request the gas be cut off."

Having scented nothing that went against the other man's hypothesis, Valentin continued on—but not before yelling down, "Make sure Silver Mercant has that information!"

He was aware of his every tiny move as he navigated the jagged mountain of debris. If gas was trapped within, a single spark could ignite molten death.

"... *help. Please.*"

Valentin froze. "I hear you." He focused on the area where he'd heard the sign of life, soon scented the air exhaled on a living breath. It was the most precarious part of the rubble. "Is there anyone else with you?"

"Daughter." A gurgle followed that single word. "Just m—..."

The man was dying.

"Will you permit a telepath to scan your minds so a telekinetic can get you out?" he called down, aware even Krychek needed a face to lock on to.

The response came not in the original male voice, but in a shaky female one. "No. Never."

Some things, Valentin thought, were worse than death. "This is Alpha Nikolaev—you have my word that your minds will not be touched," he said, so they wouldn't fear a psychic invasion.

His bears might cause trouble in Moscow, but they were also well-liked because they always stepped in to help if someone was in trouble. Two weeks earlier, Pasha had stopped traffic so an elderly lady could cross the street. The lunatic Moscow drivers had called out a slew of insults as they hooted impatiently, but the lady had kissed Pasha on both cheeks, then taken him home to feed him lunch.

"*Spasibo*, Alpha Nikolaev," the survivor whispered. ". . . trust you."

Shifting his attention to the rescuers waiting below, he said, "Here!" and pointed at the exact spot. "Two alive!"

"Silver's located a couple more structural engineers!" It was the same woman who'd spoken to him when he first arrived. "One will be here in a minute!"

A minute's wait might well prove fatal, but if Valentin began to throw around the wreckage in an effort to clear it off them, he could crush the very people he was attempting to save. "Hold on," he ordered the survivors in his most alpha tone. "We're coming to get you out."

He spent the time till the engineer's arrival searching for more survivors.

The acrid smoke of burned flesh, the metallic sting of blood mingled with alcohol fumes, the warm tones of seared wood, he scented that and more, but no other voices called out to him . . . and he smelled no more living breaths. By the time he climbed back down with careful hands and a heart on which sat a huge metal anvil, the engineer had come up with a plan to get to the trapped survivors.

Valentin listened, began to lift. His muscles burned, but he had no intention of stopping until they'd saved two people trapped in hell.

The Human Patriot

HE WATCHED THE footage streaming in from Moscow with interest. It didn't take him long to spot Silver Mercant. It'd be so convenient to take her out now, but unfortunately, that didn't suit his plans. Nor did it suit the plans of the fools who were helping him achieve his aims while believing him a power-hungry sociopath like them.

Silver had to be removed *quietly* from the equation. He didn't want the world uniting behind her assassination, trying to be better than violence. It was pure luck that his "associates" had the same goal. No one had argued with his idea of a domestic poisoning—the Mercants, after all, would never air their dirty laundry.

Human he might proudly be, but money talked even to Psy, and he had his informants. He knew all about the Mercants and the opaque shield they kept between themselves and the rest of the world. Their cold arrogance could be utilized as effectively against them.

All this, the bombing in Moscow, it was a good distraction from his far more intelligent strategies. Sad that good humans had to die, but that was the way of war. People had to understand what was at stake, the ruin to come if those pushing Trinity were permitted to have their way. He'd kill every human on the planet before he allowed them to be turned into slaves.

Chapter 17

We are, all of us, better than we believe ourselves to be.

—Adrian Kenner: peace negotiator, Territorial Wars (eighteenth century)

SILVER DRANK HALF a bottle of water into which she'd poured a nutrient sachet provided by a member of the emergency medical team. She'd also had Devi run similarly doctored bottles to the rescuers. The girl was thin, but she was bear-tough, and Silver was using her to the edge of her endurance.

Devi didn't complain; she thrived.

Silver, meanwhile, was coordinating every facet of the rescue and security operation—because if this hadn't been a lone radical or unhinged individual, and those behind them wanted to cause secondary casualties, now would be the time to strike. That in mind, she made a call. "This is Silver Mercant," she said into the dot of the microphone mounted on her collar.

"What do you need?" an ice-cold voice responded.

"A security cordon at the site of the Moscow bombing." The locals she'd put on the cordon were doing their best, but there weren't enough of them, and she couldn't request more officers without leaving other parts of the city vulnerable. "Possibility of a secondary strike."

"Understood."

Silver hung up, confident the deadly men and women of the Arrow Squad would respond to her request. Aden Kai, their leader, had made it known to Silver that EmNet could count on Arrow assistance. The only reason they hadn't already appeared was because of the executive memo she'd sent out a month earlier, requesting that signatories to the Trinity Accord not independently respond to an emergency situation that wasn't in their local area and where EmNet had a presence.

All our resources cannot be pooled in one place at one time, she'd written. *Such a concentration makes it very difficult for EmNet to mobilize rescuers to emergencies in other areas. Give us time to assess the situation and send out a call for the help required.*

Now that she'd sent out that call, however, the Arrows appeared in a matter of seconds. *Vasic Zen.* The only known Tk-V in the world, a man who wasn't a teleport-capable telekinetic but a born teleporter, he wasn't worn out by teleporting. For him, it was akin to breathing.

The black-clad men and women he'd brought in spread out on the perimeter, a small but highly effective unit. One Arrow, it was said, was worth twenty trained and experienced soldiers.

Ms. Mercant. A polite telepathic contact, Vasic Zen's mental voice as clear as arctic ice.

She saw him in the distance, a tall form made distinctive in silhouette by his loss of an arm. It had been amputated after a failed biofusion experiment, the details of which were so classified that even Mercants hadn't been able to find out much more. None of that concerned Silver right now. What mattered was that Vasic Zen was the Arrows' second-in-command, with the attendant skills.

Do you have specific instructions for my team?

Do what's necessary, she replied. *You're the security experts.* That the Arrows had broken free of those who'd used them as a death squad didn't change their lethal gifts and skills.

Three minutes later, she received an update. *The cordon is now airtight,* Vasic said. *However, there may be devices planted inside that cordon.*

Silver took in his deadly summation, while on the vocal level, she issued instructions to the traffic controllers to continue to block a particular roadway to general traffic: she needed that roadway for the emergency vehicles moving in and out of the site.

My changeling friends tell me there's a specific scent to the most commonly used family of explosives even before they are detonated, Vasic continued. *Something from that family appears to have been used in the initial attack. You should warn all changelings in the area to be on alert for that scent—if any of them need an exemplar, I've teleported in a sample and am now giving it to your runner.*

Devi returned less than a minute later with a sealed container in the palm of her hand. Silver opened it to see a minute amount of an inert gray-white substance that, to her, had no scent. "Smell this," she said to the girl.

Devi did, twisted her nose. "Ugh. It smells like the explosion but more . . . raw."

"You can differentiate between the two?"

"No problem. It's the difference between a hard green fruit and a ripe one."

"I want you to run this to every single changeling inside the cordon, and tell them to shout an alert if they smell even a hint of it in the area. Understood?"

The girl's nod was immediate. "You think there might be more bombs?"

"We have to assume the worst."

A message popped up on Silver's phone as Devi left on her task. It was an update on the first survivor they'd discovered after Silver's arrival, a man who'd been rushed to the nearest hospital minutes earlier: Dead on arrival. Catastrophic percussive injuries, multiple loss of limbs. DNA identification unsuccessful. Prints unavailable. Image being forwarded.

Silver added that image to the file she'd already opened. Unlike Psy, humans weren't always in a DNA database. That could pose severe difficulties when it came to identifying the injured and dead so their families could be contacted; many of the bodies were being pulled out in shattered pieces. Silver didn't even have faces for several of the confirmed dead.

The bomber had achieved his or her aim of maximum damage.

VALENTIN had to grip his impatience in a tight fist as the engineer called out, step-by-tiny-step, how to safely remove the rubble from above the survivors Valentin had found. Neither the man nor the woman had spoken in the past five minutes. "Next!" he yelled out after passing down a chunk of a wooden beam to the person in the living chain behind him.

"The large piece at fourteen hundred ten hours!" the engineer called out, his eyes on the scanner with which he was mapping the ruin of the bar. "Can you move it?"

Valentin didn't bother answering back. He just reached out and hauled off the piece in a single move. The problem came when he went to pass it to the next person in the chain. It was a changeling—but not a bear. The wolf thought fast. "You and you!" he called to the next two people in the line.

The three of them took hold of the piece with a grunt, started to carry it down. Valentin didn't watch except to make sure they could handle it. If they dropped it, it could crash through the rubble, collapsing it onto the survivors. When he saw that the wolf was managing to take at least half the weight, with the other two supporting effectively, he turned back to the hole he'd created.

"Three seventeen!" the engineer called out.

Valentin shook his head. "It's big enough! Get me some rope!"

That rope was sent up with alacrity. He asked two burly human construction workers who'd moved up the line when the wolf and the other two began to head down, to anchor the rope. "Got it, boss," one of them said, his beard short and orange and his build close enough to Valentin's that he might've been a bear if not for his scent.

Valentin fed the rest of the rope down into the hole, while the two construction workers set their feet apart and gripped the rope tight. "Ready?"

Both men nodded.

Valentin took a grip on the rope and began to lower himself. He could've easily jumped down. He was no feline—they were fucking "bouncy" when they landed—but he was solid. However, when he'd looked into the hole, his bear's night vision penetrating the darkness as if it didn't exist, he'd seen the survivors almost directly below.

He managed to bring himself down to the left of their tangled bodies, the construction workers holding strong even when he swung off to the side. "*Chert voz'mi*," he muttered when he saw the woman's dress.

It was all pretty and flowy and white.

The bride was a broken doll in the wreckage, her father's hand tight on hers as he lay at a right angle to her, his lower body crushed so badly that it was a miracle he'd survived even a minute. Valentin's gut twisted. He knew what he was going to find even before he knelt and checked the gray-haired man's pulse.

Nothing, his skin cold.

"Come, *milochka*," he murmured to the bride, "tell me you made it." He pressed his fingers against her skin. Cool, but not cold. A fluttering heartbeat.

"She's alive!" Sliding out his phone, he snapped a photograph of her amidst the rubble. He sent it directly to the number he'd been forwarded for Vasic Zen.

The bride disappeared a second after he'd sent the photo. An instant later so did her father, though Valentin had tagged the man as deceased. The father had only been in the image because Valentin had wanted to be sure the Arrow had enough visuals to do the remote teleport. The teleporter was only supposed to be asked to retrieve survivors, not the dead.

"You're a good man, Vasic Zen," Valentin murmured before gripping the rope and hauling himself up and out.

"We got a survivor?" one of the construction workers asked with a hopeful smile.

"We got a survivor!" He yelled it loud enough to carry to the engineer and others below. "The bride!"

A huge cheer went up. The construction worker who hadn't spoken wiped away a burst of tears. "Fuck, man," he said in American-accented English before switching to Russian. "There's just been too many dead."

Valentin clapped him on the shoulder. "Let's keep going. We don't know who else is trapped below." Even as he started to do exactly that, he had to battle the urge to check in on Silver.

His Starlight should've been in bed, resting. Instead, she was here, fighting to clean up a mess of violence, fighting to save lives. Because she was Silver Fucking Mercant, and she was as tough as any bear in Stone-Water.

Including its alpha.

The Unknown Architect

THE ARCHITECT OF the Consortium looked at the raw footage feeding out of Moscow. It was being reported as a terrorist strike undertaken by a lone individual, for which no group had taken credit.

The Consortium didn't take credit for its actions, but they also didn't cause violence without significant thought as to the advantages of any such action. They weren't fanatics or ideologues. Their entire reason for being was built on cold, hard thinking that led to political or financial gain.

They weren't anti-Trinity, as often reported. That implied an ideological stance. No, it was the peace fostered by Trinity that was an impediment to their goals. From a purely financial perspective for certain members of the Consortium, there was far more profit in instability and war. For others, like the Architect, peace offered no path to power. War and panic did.

It was all about the cost-benefit ratio.

Whoever had hit the wedding reception in Moscow had undertaken no such rational calculation. If their aim had been to destabilize the city, they'd failed in a spectacular fashion. The media had highlighted Kaleb Krychek in the footage, as well as the problematic-to-the-Consortium Silver Mercant.

A changeling alpha, Valentin Nikolaev of the StoneWater bears, had also been identified by the media, along with wolves from the BlackEdge pack and nonpredatory changelings, including mountain ponies. Human medical staff, engineers, and Enforcement officers were working side by side with their Psy and changeling compatriots.

The rapid, coordinated response was a poster child for Trinity.

As it would be in the city called home by the director of EmNet and by the most powerful telekinetic in the world. Not only that, but the violently powerful StoneWater and BlackEdge changelings also had an open line of communication, offering no room for sowing discord. Moscow was simply not a good target for anyone who wanted to cause maximum damage.

Switching off the feed, the Architect turned their mind to their own business interests. The Consortium had nothing to do with the badly planned Moscow attack and, as such, the bombing needed none of the Architect's attention.

As for Silver Mercant . . . perhaps it was time to get an update on that operation. A shame to eliminate someone of her abilities, but she'd chosen her fate when she accepted the directorship of EmNet.

If the Architect had believed she could be turned, an approach would've been made. However, while the Architect had rethought the invitation to Ena Mercant after deciding the woman was *too* intelligent and might prove a threat to the Architect's role as the puppet master of this operation, the reason for not approaching her granddaughter was far different: Silver Mercant appeared to be taking the "equal treatment of all parties" aspect of her job seriously.

Unfortunate.

Chapter 18

Trust to a Mercant is a complicated thing. It usually requires years of acquaintance, several background checks, and a probationary period.

—Ena Mercant (circa 2074)

DAWN WAS A bare two hours distant when Silver made the call no one in her position ever wanted to make: The rescue effort was now a recovery operation. No survivors had been discovered over the past two hours, and the rescuers all agreed on a lack of signs of life: Psy with their telepathic scans, changelings with their peerless sense of smell and acute hearing, and humans with a high-tech imaging scanner that had been brought to the site by a local geology professor.

"No heat signatures," the black-haired woman with dark brown skin and softly uptilted eyes had said to Silver, lines of exhaustion bracketing her mouth as she stood with her back to the wreckage of the bar.

Valentin, his body and hair covered with dust and his mouth set in a grimmer line than she'd ever seen it, had just shaken his head. He'd found the final survivor, a young man he'd carried out of the rubble in his own arms after the teleporters had been called away to take three severely wounded survivors directly to the trauma ward. The doctors had asked them to stay and lift the wounded using telekinesis so that the victims' crushed bodies could be examined without causing those bodies any further harm.

No one had found anything since then.

Bathed in the hard white glow of the powerful lights Silver had organized early into the rescue effort, the ruins of the bar appeared a spotlit tomb.

While Valentin and the others began to do what they could to help retrieve the bodies, Silver sat and collated the numbers. She already knew them, of course. "Seventy-five-percent fatality rate," she said to the head of the on-site medical team, the man who'd triaged the victims. "Another ten percent are so badly injured that their chances of survival are low to negligible."

The doctor, his face stark, sat on the tailgate of an ambulance and stared out at the destruction. "I guess we got lucky there wasn't a secondary explosive."

"Yes." The changelings had reported no signs of any suspicious scents, and the Arrows had done a sweep for covert devices and unearthed nothing. "You should stand down your team."

The doctor glanced toward the exhausted group. They sat in silence in the cordoned-off part of the dusty street, their heads hanging. "It's hard, being a healer and not being able to do anything." With those quiet words, the human male left to pick up the pieces of his devastated team.

Silver, her own legs shaky from fatigue, nonetheless made time to personally speak to all the other team leaders, bar one. Valentin, she saved for last. As the most senior changeling, he'd taken charge of the other changeling responders—no one had disagreed with his leadership, partisan lines laid aside in this time of emergency.

She found him with Kaleb.

He greeted her with a scowl. "You planning to face-plant?" he asked in a low rumbling tone, his eyes suddenly ringed with amber.

"I wasn't planning to, no," Silver said coolly, though her entire body was warning her it had reached critical. "The recovery teams are en route, will be here in three minutes." She'd put them on standby an hour earlier.

"I've cut all the rescuers loose—the retrieval teams have the right equipment to safely clear the debris and recover the bodies and body parts still trapped in the blast zone."

Valentin's expression didn't ice over at her cold recitation as changeling and human eyes so often did when she spoke. They thought that because she could be so calm, the loss of life meant nothing to her. Silver had never bothered to tell people that just because she didn't feel didn't mean that blood and death skated past her without impact.

So *much* potential had been lost this night, the vast majority of those inside the bar, people just starting out in their adult lives. That most of them had been human didn't change anything . . . or perhaps that made it even more of a tragedy. Statistically, humans tended to be at the forefront of cutting-edge technological and artistic advances—though under Silence, the Psy Council had often stolen their tech work.

The human ability to think outside the box was why the business arm of Mercant Corp. employed a significant number in its science and tech enterprises. Hiring good people and paying them well—and also protecting their minds with their own telepathic shields—was far more efficient than forcibly stealing ideas.

"Silver," Kaleb said, his tone as impossible to read as always. "Valentin is right. You'll set back your recovery by days if you keep pushing yourself."

"I'm well aware of that."

"You're finished here then?" Valentin angled his body slightly toward her, as if to break a fall he saw coming.

"Almost. I need to complete the handover to the recovery commander when he arrives. The Arrows have agreed to provide security during the recovery process, in conjunction with a team of BlackEdge soldiers Alpha Durev is sending in."

Valentin's face held the harsh echo of sadness, his alpha heart feeling too much, but his lips kicked up a fraction. "So we two *idioti* should shut the hell up and stop telling you what to do?"

"I knew the dust hadn't fogged up your brain." Silver walked away to the sight of his eyes burning a wild changeling amber.

. . .

VALENTIN opened the passenger door to his vehicle, having driven it closer now that the area was horrifically quiet, somber with resignation and the shadow of death. Silver got in, would've slipped if he hadn't caught her arm, given her a boost. She didn't say anything until after he'd gotten into the driver's seat and begun to back the vehicle in preparation for a turn.

"*Spasibo.*"

Valentin wanted to grumble at her for letting herself get to this state, but Starlight had made her point earlier—Valentin wasn't about to lose her by being a rampaging bear, all wild emotion and no sense. Even if he wanted to yell at her, then cuddle her close, hold her safe.

Gritting his teeth, he found some human words. "What do you need once we're home? I'll tag Nova, have her on standby."

"I just need to rest. No medications, no other treatments."

"You eat at the site?"

"No, but I'm not sure I have the strength to chew right now."

Bear half-mad by now, Valentin made a call, asked Chaos to prepare a nutritious soup. "No need to chew," he said to Silver afterward.

He was expecting a smart comeback, but she stayed silent. Her profile was a clean line, her lips soft, her skin pale, and her eyes heavy. The vulnerability of her—the trust it exhibited that she'd chosen to come home with him when she could've asked for a teleport anywhere—it caught his bear's heart in a grip both soft and steely.

That grip was formed of pure starlight.

He got them to Denhome as fast as safely possible. Chaos hadn't let him down, despite the early morning hour, and had hot bowls of soup waiting. Silver barely got half a bowl into herself before she fell asleep, her head pillowed on her arms. Resisting the temptation to sneak a petting stroke of her hair was *hard*.

Better nature finally winning out over his bear's grumbling protests, he scooped her up into his arms to carry her to her room. First, however, he had to scowl at Yakov, who'd tried to beat him to the punch.

The other man shrugged. "I just wanted to touch her hair."

"Go pet Pasha's hair." Valentin snuggled Silver's sleeping body closer. "She's mine."

"She know that?"

"I'm working on it." Glaring away any other bears who might be tempted to come close, he got her into her room without further interruptions.

She was dusty from the site, no doubt sweaty, too, but he wasn't about to strip her. He told Nova not to, either, after his sister responded to his request to check on Silver and make certain that rest was indeed all she needed.

"I'm taking off her boots at least." Nova put those boots by the side of the bed, while Valentin pulled a blanket over Silver's body.

"Rest well, Starlight." His own body ached, but he was an alpha bear, could've gone on for another day if necessary. If he had his way, he'd spend that time watching over Silver. Ah, who was he kidding? Give him free rein, and he'd curl himself around her like a living blanket. He'd listen to the beat of her heart, feel the soft heat of her breath, the delicate strength of her bones.

"Come on, little brother." Nova wrapped an arm around his waist. "You need to finish your own meal, then you can grab some sleep and dream of your Starlichka."

Throwing an arm around her shoulders, he tugged her close, this sister of his who'd become the one he went to with his childhood hurts once his mother, Galina, stopped seeing him, stopped seeing all of them. At only a year older than Valentin, Nika had been as young and bewildered, while Stasya had been their fire, so angry for their shattered family that she'd picked a hundred furious battles with clanmates who couldn't see through her rage to her pain.

It was Nova who'd held them together with her healer's warmth, Nova who'd refused to embrace anything but love, Nova who'd made him his favorite snacks and told him she was proud of him when he did well at school. Their maternal grandparents had taken the adult role when it became clear Galina was barely hanging on, but it was Nova all three of them had turned to in their darkest moments.

Valentin often thought healers had the strongest hearts of any change-ling. "I love you, Novochka."

A startled smile. "I know, Mishka." She patted his chest, her hand that of a healer, nails clipped short and devoid of the ornamentation she so loved on every other part of herself. "Your love is like a force of nature—even as a cub, once you decided a person was yours, you didn't let go." Smile fading, she said, "Tell me how it was at the site."

"Horrible," he said honestly. "So much death, so much loss. The only good thing about it was Silver." He forced himself not to look back at her room, more than a little afraid his bear would waltz right in and make itself at home. "You should've seen her at work. She's like a contained storm." Handling a hundred things at once with no sign of strain or stress. "People trust her to be competent because there's no way a woman that powerful and that in control would ever be otherwise."

"Your crush is getting worse." Nova patted his back, but when she looked up, her eyes were solemn. "I like Silver, but she's incredibly Psy, Mishka. No cracks that I can see."

Valentin knew what she was trying to say. "She's in Denhome now." In bear territory. "Anything's possible."

"Just take care of yourself, okay?" Nova leaned her head against him, her glossy dark curls tumbling around her head. "You're carrying too much on that heart of yours already." She pressed her free hand over his heart. "The weight shouldn't all be yours."

Closing his hand over hers, he shook his head. "I'm alpha, Nova." Meant to carry that weight. Meant to bleed to fix what was broken.

And meant to love a woman as strong as a fiery star.

SILVER woke to the feel of data at the edge of her senses, messages and information having built up against her mind while she slept. She held back the flood as she took stock of her body and mind. After she deter-mined that though her body ached, she was otherwise healthy, she checked the time and realized she'd been asleep for almost twenty-two hours.

No wonder she was thirsty and hungry.

Pushing up into a seated position, she saw two notes on the bedside table. Both were propped up against a jug of water in which swam slices of fresh orange. Silver poured herself a glass, drank it down, then read the neatly folded notecard: *Someone in Denhome is always up, so there's always food available. Don't worry about asking for it, no matter when you wake. Just ask to be directed to the kitchen.—Nova*

The other note was a piece of paper torn from a notebook: *Hope you had a good sleep, Starlight. Now go eat so much you want to burst.—Mr. I. M. A. Medvezhonok.*

What kind of an alpha signed his message *Mr. I Am a Teddy Bear?* Only Valentin. Carefully placing the note under her phone, she pushed back her hair. Her hands came away coated with dust.

No one, she knew, had touched her after Valentin put her to bed. He wouldn't have allowed anyone else to handle her. He was incredibly possessive, and she was well aware he was trying to brand her as his in ways he probably thought were subtle; he wouldn't succeed, but she appreciated that he always protected her.

It *was* slightly disconcerting to realize she hadn't awakened, even when he'd picked her up and brought her here. Then again, her trust in him was hardly inexplicable, she thought as she rose to her feet. Valentin Nikolaev had saved her life. More than that, she'd come to know that the rough-edged alpha of StoneWater was a man of blunt honor and unimpeachable integrity.

She was safe with him.

The thought sank deep inside her, an echo that reverberated through her bones. Telling herself the unexpected sensation was nothing but a sensory blip, she began to strip off her filthy clothing. She also needed to strip the sheets on the bed, but that could wait.

Getting out of the hot shower after a long twenty minutes that helped ease the lingering aches in her body, she prepared to leave her room. This time, she decided to leave her hair down.

Fresh underwear, a pair of dark brown corduroy pants, and a thin gray sweater was her choice of outfit. On her feet went socks and the half boots that were no longer covered in dust but shined to a mirrored gloss.

She paused with the left boot in her hand, staring at the gleaming leather.

She understood enough of the changelings' communal nature to guess that whoever had done it had done so for no reason but to be helpful. They wouldn't expect anything from her except a *spasibo* if she happened upon their name. Cooperation and a sharing of resources was the foundation of the changeling way of life.

Psy families were meant to work the same way. The Mercants did. But not even in her own family would anyone have cleaned her boots. They'd have checked her health status, made certain she had any and all medical help she needed, but this small touch of care wouldn't be on even Arwen's radar.

It was simply the way they'd been raised.

Pulling on the boot, Silver had to accept the realization that even her tightly knit family had lost something in Silence. But what had been lost could be regained. All it would take was a change in how Mercants raised their young. Making a mental note to speak to her grandmother about that, she got up to locate the kitchen. She would strip the bed after she'd eaten and caught up on the messages crowding her brain.

As for the ones stacked up on her e-mail, she began to download them onto her phone to see if there was anything urgent. While that was in progress, she scanned the telepathic messages.

Kaleb's psychic imprint caught her eye.

Silver, he'd telepathed, *Selenka's team informs me that cleanup at the site will be complete in thirty-six hours. Autopsies are in progress, and Enforcement forensic teams are working double shifts to process as much material as they can. They have recovered parts of the individual believed to be the bomber—a human local to the area. DNA verified.*

The date and time stamp showed the telepathic message had been routed to her about two hours earlier. He hadn't sent her any further updates. Neither had her grandmother or Arwen.

Deciding to follow up after she was fed and at full strength, Silver glanced at her phone as she exited the room. Valentin's name jumped out. The message was untitled.

He'd never before e-mailed her. She tapped his message open:

You're right! This e-mail invention is amazing. You can even send photos!

He'd included a photo of two bear cubs in bear form, tidily eating ice cream from cones held carefully between their paws. Below the image were the words:

It's *really* good ice cream.

Closing—but not deleting—the message that continued their long-running ice cream conversation, she realized she'd reached the Cavern.

The den was quiet this early in the morning, and she hadn't run into anyone else. But now she found herself on the receiving end of a brilliant smile from Devi, the young woman fresh-faced and with her hair in a ponytail. She was dressed in black running shorts and a blue athletic tee with white stripes on the sides, her feet bare.

"You must be hungry," Devi said. "Come on, I'll show you to the kitchen. Did you have a good rest?"

"Yes, thank you."

"Here you go." Devi pointed out a wide internal entrance. "Sorry to show and take off, but I'm meeting a friend for a run." A pause, her smile fading. "Thank you for letting me help at the site. I needed to help."

"You were an asset." The young woman hadn't stopped until Silver did. "I hope you rested as well."

"Oh, sure, but I'm a bear. We're tough." She left with a smile and a wave.

Silver watched her go before walking into the huge communal kitchen to which Devi had led her. It was nearly empty, holding just a few people preparing what appeared to be items for breakfast. The youngest looked to be about six years old. Wearing pajamas of pale blue fleece, his hair sticking up in light brown tufts, he was sitting on a counter carefully peeling mandarin oranges and putting them into a bowl.

"Ms. Mercant."

Turning at the sound of that deep male voice, Silver found herself facing a tall, square-jawed male with skin of ebony. If Valentin was all rough edges and crags, this man could've walked out of a modeling catalog or from the files of those families who aimed for not only psychic power in their bloodline, but also physical beauty.

"Please take a seat here, and I'll bring you something to eat." Unlike all the other bears she'd met to date, he didn't smile at her.

Chapter 19

Food is to a bear what a hug is to a human.

—Author unknown

"THANK YOU." SILVER took a seat on one of the stools at the counter nearest the door. Bowls of fruit, snack bars, and a clear jar of cookies sat on one end.

The model-beautiful man brought her a tall glass filled with a familiar liquid. "I was able to source a jar of nutrient drink for you."

Having not expected that courtesy after his cool greeting, Silver said, "Thank you. I appreciate it." Nutrient drinks were the fastest way to beat psychic fatigue.

"Not a problem." Still no smile, his face all smooth skin and flawless symmetry, his shaved head only serving to bring the perfect lines of his face into sharper focus. "I'll bring you a plate of solid food, too."

From his curt manner, Silver came to the conclusion that this changeling was unhappy about her presence in Denhome. Then he brought her the plate of food; it held high-energy items, all of which she knew were naturally light on flavor.

As if correctly reading her response, though she'd made no betraying movements or sounds, the man—who she guessed to be the cook—said, "I did a little research. Recipes are creeping online now, with Psy starting to step out of their comfort zone."

"You took extra time out of your day. I appreciate that."

The faintest thawing of his features, his light brown eyes wrinkling at the corners. "You're welcome."

After he moved back to supervise the other workers in the kitchen—who were shooting Silver curious looks but, oddly for bears, keeping their distance—Silver watched him without appearing to watch him.

He was calm and competent and clearly respected. Pair those traits with his symmetrical good looks and, if anyone should've provoked a reaction in Silver, it was this man. Yet she couldn't stop herself from keeping an eye—and ear—open for Valentin's booming laugh, his overwhelming, uncivilized presence.

"Hey, if you have a thing for Chaos, you'd better tell Mishka now."

Silver glanced at Nova as the healer took a seat beside her at the counter. The other woman was wearing a scoop-necked and wide-skirted dress in leaf green with small white flowers dotted randomly over the fabric. It had three-quarter-length sleeves that exposed the tattoo on her forearm, which Silver had already noted. Two letters, one big, one small, circled by a pattern of hearts and stars. Neither initial was Nova's.

"What," she said, focusing on the most pertinent matter, "is a 'thing'?"

"Aw, come on, Seelichka." Nova reached up to fix the jaunty ponytail she'd tied with a white ribbon. "You know exactly what I mean, so don't pull that 'I am a Psy robot' stuff with me."

Silver returned to her meal, considered her answer in between keeping an eye on her steady stream of phone and telepathic messages. "I'm Silent, Nova. I choose to be Silent."

"You sure?"

"Quite sure."

"Hmm . . . Then why were you checking out Chaos?"

"I wanted to see if he wasn't smiling at me because he doesn't like Psy, or if he simply doesn't smile at anyone."

"Weirdly, that makes sense." Nova sighed and, propping her elbows on the counter, cupped her chin in her hands and turned huge dark eyes in the direction of the cook. "That hunk of a man *does* smile, but he doles it out like it's a rare spice, and he's only got a limited supply."

Chaos, who'd been walking toward them, shot Nova a scowling look. "Eat this." He thrust a plate across the counter with that terse command in English. "And stop telling lies about me."

Blowing him a kiss, Nova beamed at the small, perfectly decorated cake Chaos had given her before answering in the same language he'd used. "Chocolate cake for breakfast? I love you, honey bunny."

Scowl deepening, the changeling male reached over and, gripping Nova's pointed chin, kissed the healer on her lushly painted lips. When he drew back, she lifted the cloth napkin he'd brought over and wiped the hot pink color off his lips. "Good morning to you, too, *moy dorogoi Alik*," Nova said, alerting Silver that Chaos had a given name quite different from how he was usually addressed. "Now go be your sexy, tall, gorgeous, and silent self."

Chaos gave what Silver read as an exasperated sigh before he moved back toward his work crew—who did a very bad job of hiding their grins. "You all want a second kitchen shift?" he growled and got a wave of shaking heads, grins still wide. "Then back to your jobs."

"He's your mate?" Silver asked under the cover of industrious activity.

"Yes." Nova's smile was gleeful. "All mine since we were eighteen." Forking up a bite of cake, she made a humming sound in the back of her throat that had Chaos watching her with intense interest from the other side of the kitchen. Nova blew him another kiss. "My love always says he won me by winning my stomach."

"Did he?"

Nova gave a throaty laugh. "I knew that grouchy polar bear was mine the day I first saw him in Babushka Caroline's birth clan, when she took all us grandchildren along for a visit when I was sixteen." A dreamy smile. "But I had to play a little hard to get, didn't I? Give him a chance to court me."

Another bite of the cake. "Boy, does that man know how to court a woman."

"Do you have children?"

"The Barnacle is ours." Her eyes shimmered with maternal love. "Stasya looked after him last night, so he'll still be cuddled up in bear form with her—he likes sleeping over at his aunt's because, like aunts the world over, she spoils him silly," Nova said before raising her voice. "Talking of small bears, I see *someone* is still sneaking out of bed before dawn."

The little brown-haired boy giggled.

Smile wide, Nova nudged her plate toward Silver. "You want to go wild and try some?"

Shaking her head, Silver replied to an urgent message on her phone. "I apologize," she said to Nova afterward. "I'm receiving EmNet updates."

"Sure, I get it." Nova's expression turned serious. "I did a shift at the hospital while you were asleep—I'm officially on staff in case of emergencies where a bear is taken in, but I figured they could use all possible backup with so many badly wounded."

Silver met the other woman's eyes. "I haven't had a chance to read the report on the survivors."

"Thirteen made it past the first few hours." Nova put down her fork. "Eleven look like they might recover fully, but it's contingent on no infections or complications. The other two are hovering in that twilight that could go either way."

Chaos moved across the kitchen with a mug of coffee. After placing it in front of Nova, he ran his hand over her hair. Though the couple exchanged no words, Nova's sadness no longer seemed as heavy a black cloud when her mate returned to his work.

"I don't understand people who carry out these crimes," she said. "I mean, what does it achieve?"

"Logic isn't what drives them." Silver had seen evidence of that truth over and over again. "The Pure Psy fanatics who attacked the SnowDancer pack in the Sierra Nevada mountains were convinced theirs was a righteous war that would make the world turn in the direction they wanted."

They'd believed the Psy race was stronger and more powerful under Silence, that any alternate existence was untenable. "It never occurs to them that others may not agree with their goals." Silver needed Silence, but that was *her* choice. No one had the right to dictate it.

Nova's lips parted before she looked over her shoulder without warning. Silver didn't need to turn to see what had caught the other woman's attention. The tiny hairs on the back of her neck had just reacted as if electrified, her heart slamming against her rib cage. Not in primal warning. In an awareness she'd been attempting to stamp out since the day Valentin Mikhailovich Nikolaev first entered her life.

"You look terrible, Mishka." Nova got up, slipping a scanner out of the—now expected—large pockets of her calf-length dress. "Sit, let me take your readings."

"I'm fine, just tired." Valentin grabbed the stool beside Silver's, sitting with his back to the counter, elbows braced on the granite and his big body humming with energy.

His scent washed over her, clean sweat and more, a layer that was distinctly earthy. Distinctly, roughly Valentin. Ignoring the telepathic and electronic messages pinging at her, none of them urgent, she took in the lines of strain on his face, the bruised shadows under his eyes. "You haven't been to sleep."

"I got four hours. We had a senior sentry go down with a broken leg, and another because of idiocy." Pure aggravation in every word. "I covered for them rather than put someone less experienced on the perimeter."

Silver knew she was a big part of the reason he'd made that decision. She'd changed the balance of his clan, needed to leave before she caused any damage. About to suggest she move out today—her physical state not at a hundred percent but far better than it had been yesterday—she was interrupted by the sound of running feet.

Pavel all but fell into the kitchen. "Did you see this?" he cried before the distinctive aqua green of his eyes landed on Silver.

He snapped his left hand behind his back with bear swiftness, the dark brown of his hair falling over his forehead. "Um, never mind."

"Spill it before I beat it out of you, Pasha." Valentin's voice was a growly rumble.

"Remember, you asked for it." Pavel placed the organizer between Valentin and Silver before retreating out of reach. "Don't shoot the messenger."

Valentin swiveled in his stool so he faced the counter and the organizer that lay on it. His shoulder brushed her shoulder, but Silver's attention was on the headline that took up the entire screen but for the square reserved for a full-color photograph: THE MOST SURPRISING PSY-CHANGELING ROMANCE YET!

A telepathic contact touched her mind at the same instant that the meaning of the headline actually penetrated. The contact was from one of the few people who had direct access to her, the telepathic pathway between them nearly twenty-nine years in the making. *Silver? Should I take these reports of your romance with the StoneWater alpha seriously?*

Of course not, Arwen.

Her brother withdrew, needing nothing other than her word. Silver, however, was still staring at the article. "Where is the romance in this image? We're both dusty and sweaty and standing at the incident command center speaking with Kaleb."

Nova leaned between them to look at the article. "Body language," she said in a definitive tone. "Turned toward each other, standing closer than Psy usually stand to other people, way closer than either one of you is standing to Krychek." She tapped her lower lip. "Also, Mishka's body is angled as if to protect you from anything that might come."

"Give us a minute." Valentin's tone was alpha in the truest sense.

Stepping away, Nova went around to cuddle the boy who was peeling mandarin oranges, while Pavel returned the way he'd come.

"You can't take this too seriously," Valentin said with unusual quietness. "Making up stories out of thin air is what tabloids do."

"It's not only in the tabloids." Silver had already scanned the PsyNet, found multiple other reports along the same lines—albeit less hyperbolic in tone. "Bring up the *Moscow Daily*."

Valentin hissed out a breath at first sight of the newspaper's home screen.

"*Bl*—" Glancing over at the little boy with Nova, he cut off the rough word she was sure he'd been about to utter. "I thought this was an actual news site."

"The EmNet director's connection to a powerful changeling alpha *is* considered news." The *Moscow Daily* article was nowhere near as melodramatic or as long as that in the tabloid, but it was more danger-ous. "They did their research—it states that you've been spotted leaving my apartment building multiple times." Valentin had enough bear arro-gance to have walked boldly past security on his way out, taunting them with the knowledge that he'd once again skirted their systems.

Valentin's body rumbled beside her, the bear in him apparent in the primal timbre of his voice when he spoke. "It says the information came from a woman named Monique."

"My neighbor—it's unlikely to have been malicious on her part. She talks about everything to everyone." Silver didn't quite understand how Monique Ling held such a high-powered position in the fashion world, but perhaps fashion people all talked without pause. "We were once trapped together in a malfunctioning elevator for ten minutes. At the end of it, I was aware of her entire life history."

VALENTIN couldn't read Silver, but he guessed she was coldly angry under her precise exterior. His Starlight did not like being at the forefront of the public's consciousness. She preferred to be in the background, tugging strings, gathering information, ensuring things moved in the direction she wanted.

Valentin wasn't exactly a happy bear, either. He knew the best way to lose their private battle was to, in any way, corner Silver. Like a wild falcon, she'd fight to the death to get free.

That was the whole reason why he'd launched plan "sneaky like a cat."

"Starlichka," he said gently, trying to fix this. "The interest will fade—the pictures aren't exciting enough." Though Nova had been eerily accurate about the body language—when the tabloid photo was taken, he'd been fighting the urge to wrap Silver's exhausted body in his arms and haul her off to his lair.

His Starlight was brilliant and she was tough, but she was still flesh and blood.

Silver's response to his rough attempt at reassurance wasn't what he expected. "From the comment thread on this article, it appears humans and changelings are responding well to the possibility of such an improbable romance."

"Unexpected." Valentin's bear scowled inside him. "Not improbable."

"With Silence having fallen," Silver said, rather than replying to his grumble, "I believe a percentage of Psy will also find it intriguing—there's certainly significant chatter in the PsyNet for what should be nothing but a fringe topic." She ate a bite of the food on her plate. "It could end up being a positive."

Valentin's bear roared to the surface at this hint that she might be open to being his, the animal's thick fur attempting to erupt out of his skin. "What if I asked you to have a real romance?" he said, abandoning sneakiness for a directness that fit far better.

Her response was quiet, potent. "I'm not like Sascha Duncan or Faith NightStar, or even Vasic Zen."

"No," he said, unable to look away from that crystalline gaze that made the bear inside him rise to the surface, his vision shifting to that of his animal. "You're Silver Fucking Mercant, a woman who makes her own rules."

"That woman chooses Silence." No hint of an expression on her face, her eyes searing, unreadable starlight. "I have access to all the data on the pros and cons of breaking Silence, and I've downloaded all available information about what it is to be in a relationship. I've also had a close view of a highly stable relationship."

Kaleb Krychek and his mate. "None of this changes your mind?"

"No." She continued to hold his gaze.

Not many people could do that, changeling or not. Yet Silver had never flinched, her dominance his equal. Thunder in his heart, man and bear both in her thrall.

"The one thing that is often forgotten in the discussion about Silence," she continued in that same quiet tone, "is that terrible as it was for the many, for a small minority, it worked exactly as intended. I am one of that minority."

Chapter 20

To be Silent is to be without emotion. This emotionless state allows for a statistically significant increase in psychic control while having the opposite effect on any tendency or inclination to be violent.

The Silent will be an intelligent, controlled people who do not waste their energies on battles or wars or interpersonal aggression. They will be perfection.

—Arif Adelaja's first speech to the Psy Council on the matter of the Silence training proposed by the Mercury group (late twentieth century)

VALENTIN KNEW SILVER expected her statement to be the final word on the subject, but, while he was conscious he could never make Silver Mercant do anything she didn't want to do, he also knew she'd never been up against an alpha bear who was fascinated by her on every possible level.

"You sure you have all the information?" Catching an apple Chaos threw over, he bit into it with a crisp crunch.

Silver's eyes went to his mouth, flicked away as fast. "I'm very good at research."

Valentin's cock wanted to react, react *hard*.

Chewing and swallowing the bite he'd taken as he fought his hunger for this smart woman who smelled more delicious than his favorite honey, he pulled out his pocketknife and began to cut a slice from the part of the apple he hadn't bitten into. All the while attempting not to fall into erotic daydreams of licking honey off his Starlight's skin.

He'd die and go to beary heaven should that ever come true.

"I don't doubt your skills," he said. "But you're not the kind of woman who lets other people make her decisions for her."

"You're being extremely subtle for a bear."

Valentin smiled inside because he was certain he could almost hear aggravation in her tone. Right now, he'd take any emotion. And aggravation was a good one. Mates to bears often got aggravated.

He held out the slice of apple.

When she accepted it, he had to stop himself from beating at his chest like a gorilla. Or a bear who'd succeeded in feeding his mate. Watching as she took a testing bite, her lips derailing his honey fantasy for another one that was all rough heat, Valentin had to scramble to find his brain cells again. "All I'm saying is, how can you possibly have all the data if you've never let go of your Silence to see what happens?"

"I wasn't born Silent."

"I get that." Though he still couldn't understand how anyone could train emotion out of a child. Children were huge, wild creatures full of promise and hope and dirt and mischief. How could anyone crush them into a box?

From what he'd heard, it had been an act of desperation, even an act of love, but it remained difficult for him to comprehend. At the same time, it gave him a painful insight into how bad the situation must've been for the choice to be made.

But Silver wasn't a child.

"No child has control over their urges," he pointed out. "Human, Psy, changeling, doesn't matter the race—cubs need rules and boundaries for a reason."

Silver finished her slice of apple, accepted another from him. This time, his bear stayed quiet, finally getting with the "sneaky like a cat" program. Today an apple, tomorrow ice cream, the next day licking honey from her body, it was all about strategy . . . and stubborn bearish hope.

"Agreed," the woman who fascinated him said after a long pause.

Valentin wasn't about to back off now. "After a child grows up, they begin to make their own decisions. I often do things my mother wouldn't have permitted while I was a cub. I use sharp knives, I go out alone in the dark, I drink too much." Of course, the rare times when he did the latter, his grandmothers still threatened to box his ears.

His mother was alive but . . . gone, lost to them in a way Valentin couldn't stand to think about too hard. The wounds on Galina Evanova's soul were too grievous to allow her to fully exist in this world. He and his sisters did their best to reach her, but their mother preferred to roam StoneWater territory in her bear form. The last time he'd spotted her, she'd been asleep under the dappled shade of a poplar.

She'd looked so peaceful that he'd left without disturbing her.

"Valentin."

Realizing he'd gone silent, Valentin dug up a grin. "I think you're an adult, Starlight, and adults make choices a child never could."

Silver's eyes looked at him with a perceptiveness that threatened to strip him bare. "And I think you, Alpha Nikolaev, are far better at keeping secrets than anyone knows."

Valentin stopped playing. He locked his gaze with hers, let the bear rise to color his voice, his eyes. "To understand my secrets, you have to understand emotion."

The air shimmered with the words he didn't say, the challenge he'd laid down. Silver didn't look away. And his blood—it grew so hot it scalded.

AN hour later, Silver walked back alone to the stream where she'd seen the cubs playing in the water. She knew Valentin had an ulterior motive for his oh-so-rational argument. He'd made no attempt to hide his desire for her.

He was also an alpha bear. Challenge was part of his psyche.

Yet none of that negated his point: she *hadn't* ever attempted to live without Silence as an adult in full control of her abilities. Was it possible she could safely use the "sharp knife" of emotion?

Silver.

Arwen, she said, her eyes on the water that sparkled under the morning sunlight, *what did you find?*

Nothing, but I've finally convinced Grandmother I'm definitely not the one who tried to kill you.

I'm sure Grandmother never believed otherwise; she was simply being cautious.

Ena had once told Silver that the family had been changing in subtle but terrible ways before Arwen's birth. "Without your brother," Ena had said, "and given the powerful influence of the Psy Council and their mandates, we could well have crossed the line from ruthless to cruel. He is our conscience and our soul."

Whoever did this, her brother said now, *they wanted clean hands. Distance.*

You know that only further implicates the family. Mercants were experts at sleight of hand.

Arwen didn't reply with agreement—none was needed at the self-evident fact. *I'm assisting Grandmother in every way possible, but so far, there is not even a hint of a smoking gun.*

No unusual financial or other transactions?

I dug deep. Nothing.

It's possible there are no external factors to find. It could've been a purely internal job. A power play.

On current data, that probability is medium to high. But why would anyone in the family want to harm you if they hadn't somehow been turned by outsiders? Anger and frustration vied for supremacy in his voice. *No one else has your skill and financial expertise—lose you and the family fortunes would dive.*

Silver's skin grew suddenly sensitive, her head turning without her conscious volition. *I'll speak to you later, Arwen.*

It was no surprise to see Valentin heading toward her, his big body at ease in this primal landscape. Because he was as wild, civilization a thin skin that he could shrug off without hesitation. Thrusting a hand through his hair, he came to a standstill in front of her.

"Do you own a comb?" she asked, her eyes on the incongruously silken strands.

Valentin shook his head, sending the strands flying. "There," he said afterward, "it's neat now." He sounded absolutely serious.

Silver lifted her hand. He went motionless. Her fingers were a centimeter from pushing back the tumbled strands when data blasted her mind, picked up by the monitoring alerts she had in place.

Explosives. Unknown casualties. Multiple strikes.

In front of her, Valentin's gaze turned grim. "What's happened?"

"Attacks in Shanghai, in Berlin, and in Melbourne. Identical characteristics to the Moscow attack. Majority human casualties forecast, with limited but not zero Psy and changeling casualties."

Heart thumping in an uncontrollable physical response to the deluge of information, Silver nonetheless already had her phone in hand. "I have to activate EmNet, get in touch with the people on the ground."

"What do you need?" Valentin asked as they moved quickly back to Denhome.

"A larger computer would be useful. At least two screens. A comm I can take over for the duration."

"Follow me."

Silver began to make calls at the same time, alerting the nominated EmNet contacts in the affected areas that she was aware of what had happened and was about to initiate the emergency network. "Send me local data, as much as you can," she told them. "It'll help me mobilize the right resources."

Once inside Denhome, Valentin led her down several corridors to a medium-sized room set up with cutting-edge tech. "We use this for comm conferences. It should have everything you need."

Settling in and hooking up the system to EmNet's servers, Silver discovered the StoneWater system was higher spec than her EmNet office. She was able to handle the triple emergencies with comparative ease, technologically speaking. The only issue was that she and her assistant were only two people. This needed at least five.

Creating an EmNet team would go to the top of her list after this was over.

When hot nutrient drinks appeared at her desk through the hours that followed, she drank them. In a distant part of herself, she realized that this, too, was different. No one fed her when she was caught at home during a situation. She worked alone and in silence.

Though no bears interrupted her today, she was aware of Pavel and Nova looking in on her. The bear male had silently added another screen to her system after seeing the amount of data she was handling, while Nova had left a high-energy nutrient bar on her desk.

"You want my help?" Pavel asked at one point. "I'm not on shift for another four hours."

About to say no out of habit, Silver abruptly realized that would be foolish. "Yes," she said. "That screen over there—can you collate the emergency data coming in and give me a précis every half hour?"

"Summarize?" Pavel pulled up a chair, his eyes already on the screen. "I don't like to brag," he bragged smugly, "but I was the king of last-minute summaries for school essays."

She'd been concerned the gregarious bear would keep on speaking, but that was all he said, his focus on the work. She should've remembered that while bears could be rowdy, StoneWater wouldn't have become a power if they weren't also capable of intense concentration on things that needed to be done.

He turned out to be as good at winnowing the data down into manageable bites as he'd boasted. "Are you in the market for a permanent position?" she asked after the first hour.

"Yasha would cry if I left him." Pavel kept his eyes on the screen in front of him, even as he spoke. "But maybe if you throw in your scrumptious brother as my bonus."

"Arwen should be coming to see me again soon," Silver replied. "If you're half the bear you claim to be, you'll get his call code from him."

"Oooooh, that was a burn as cold as Siberia!" Pavel thumped his fist onto his chest, shooting her a dimpled grin over his shoulder at the same time. "I can melt a Mercant, just you wait. I'm a bear."

With that, they returned to their work and to the dark reality of an emergency that could have no happy ending.

Valentin didn't reappear after showing her to the tech room. It wasn't a surprise. She hoped he was catching some sleep but knew it was unlikely; as the alpha of a large and powerful pack, he had multiple calls on his time and attention. Which made it even more extraordinary that he'd come to see her at her apartment so many times.

Regardless of all that, part of her listened for him.

VALENTIN'S heart was a pulsing ache when he returned from the part of StoneWater territory the dissenters called home. No matter how many days passed, the pain remained as hurtful as the day he'd first felt it . . . the day a quarter of his bears had rejected him to walk out into the cold. But despite the freshness of his hurt, time *had* passed. He'd soon have to make a final decision.

His bear hung its head, its big body no shield against this wound.

"Mishka!"

Halting at the sound of that childish cry, he immediately tracked a fresh trail of scents to find three unsupervised cubs, ages six, six, and seven. All tiny gangsters. He scowled and folded his arms. "What is Arkasha doing?" he asked, nodding at the furry butt hanging out of a hole in a stone formation.

It was hard to keep a straight face as those little legs kicked and the butt wriggled.

"He's stuck!" Sveta cried. "We were going to explore the cave, but the hole's too small."

Biting the inside of his cheek to choke off his laughter, Valentin raised an eyebrow at the other miscreant. "Why is Arkasha so shiny and slick?" His fur looked like it had been slicked down with hair conditioner, but that wasn't what Valentin's nose was telling him.

Fitzpatrick Haydon William, tiny owner of a very long name, took his hand from behind his back to reveal a familiar wrapper. "We thought if we rubbed him with butter, he'd slide in," he admitted.

"Did you ask Chaos for that butter?"

Two shaking heads, while the butt went still, Arkasha in full listening mode.

"Hmm, we'll talk about that later." Valentin hunkered down by Arkasha's small body. Patting his furry back to make sure the boy wouldn't get scared, he considered their options. Despite his antics in hanging upside down on the tree the other day, Arkasha was too young to have fully mastered semi-shifting, or Valentin would have asked him to shift parts of his body to his smaller human form.

Which left only one option.

"I'm going to crack the stone," he told the boy. "Close your eyes and duck down your head. Kick your left paw when you're ready."

The kick came nearly at once.

Slamming the side of his fist against a section of stone that appeared the weakest, Valentin created a crack, then carefully wrenched off a piece. It left that edge ragged, and he had to act quickly to clamp his hand on Arkasha's side to protect him as the child wriggled free.

Plopping down on his back, the cub lifted his paws to his face . . . and sneezed.

Valentin couldn't hold in his laughter any longer. Cracking up, he sat down with his back against the hole and opened his arms. Arkasha crawled into them at once, Sveta and Fitz slamming their bodies against Valentin's the next second. He held all three, calming the butter-covered cub and his friends from their fright.

And his heart, it hurt a fraction less.

When he returned to the den with the gangsters—after first blocking up the newly enlarged hole with stones they wouldn't be able to move— he marched them to the kitchen to confess their butter thievery. Chaos, hands on hips, gave them his patented glare. "No dessert tonight for any of you."

"But it's gonna be *medovik*!" Arkasha said, his body clad in Valentin's checked shirt. The cub had destroyed his own clothes when he'd shifted from boy to bear, and hadn't wanted to be a "naked criminal." The sleeves Valentin had folded, but the tails dragged on the floor, giving him a woebegone look.

"Yeah!" his friends said. "We love *medovik*!"

Valentin loved the layered honey cake, too.

Remaining unmoved, Chaos said, "That's why it's a punishment." The clan's chief cook rubbed his jaw. "Or you can wash dishes all day."

Sveta gulped. "All day?" A big-eyed whisper.

"Yes. Or no cake."

All three cubs looked at one another, with Sveta the one who spoke. "We'll wash the dishes."

They swarmed Chaos, wrapping their arms around his legs. "We're sorry for taking your butter, Mr. Chaos."

Chaos's lips twitched above their heads at the attempt at formal address, his hands going down to rub the top of their heads. Valentin knew the imps would likely be asleep in a corner within ten minutes of starting their dishwashing sentence, and that Chaos would care for them with utmost gentleness. But every time they woke, he'd make them wash an unbreakable dish or two—in their cub minds, that would equal an entire day of hard labor.

It'd be the talk of the tiny gangster circle for months.

Right then, Arkasha tripped over the tails of Valentin's shirt and fell over onto his butt. "Ouch."

"Come on." Valentin hauled the cub up onto his back. "Let's go get you some proper clothes before you do your day in the salt mines."

"What's a salt mine?" Arkasha asked, while Chaos put the two other felons to work at the sink. They had a bench to stand on—this wasn't the first time StoneWater had had to deal with miniature-sized gangsters.

Valentin explained the concept of salt mines to his felon, got him dressed, then—after a stop to grab a fresh shirt for himself—dropped Arkasha off to serve his sentence. His heart lighter, he was about to find Silver, aggravate her just so she'd play with him in that icy Psy way, when Pieter found him.

This time, the problem wasn't a laughing matter.

Chapter 21

To be alpha is to have a heart big enough to love every single member of
your pack or clan. That is the one constant of all the strongest alphas I've
ever met. They are men and women with an astonishing capacity to love and
to forgive.

—Adrian Kenner: peace negotiator, Territorial Wars (eighteenth century)

VALENTIN DIDN'T NEED Pieter to lead him to the group of sullen
teenagers; he could've followed their scents across the territory. He did,
however, need his friend in other ways. "They're reacting to the fracture
in the clan," he said to his third-in-command as they stalked through the
forest.

Pieter had ordered all seven teenagers to stay where he'd left them,
and he was dominant enough that they'd have obeyed. Now, the other
man nodded, the sunset colors of his hair glowing in the late afternoon
light. "Yes. It's messing with their heads."

The other man blew out a breath. "Mina apparently attacked Olive
when words were exchanged about Mina's aunt's family being traitors.
Friends of both jumped into the fray."

"Fuck." Valentin had tried to keep the problems to the adults, but
while the cubs just asked after their missing friends, sad they couldn't

play with them, the teens were old enough to understand this separation was shaping up to be permanent. "This isn't right, Petya."

"You know what I think." His friend's voice was hard. "They made their choice. You've been too patient."

Valentin rubbed a fist over his heart. "I can't let them go without trying everything. They're part of me." So many tiny threads, alpha to clanmate. "Cutting them loose will bloody us all."

"The dissenters did that when they made unfounded accusations." Pieter had never had any sympathy for the clanmates who'd turned against Valentin. Perhaps because Pieter's entire family had joined StoneWater when Pieter was a child of eight, after they'd left their previous clan because the asshole alpha had wanted Pieter's much older sister, and she'd said no.

The alpha had made Pieter's sister's life so untenable that the family had made the decision to move. That alpha had soon been toppled by a far better bear, but Pieter's family had never returned to their old clan. They were violently loyal to StoneWater, which had taken them in with open arms. Pieter, in turn, was violently loyal to Valentin.

"Your heart's too big, Valya," his childhood friend said. "*No one* has the right to stomp on it just because you have a capacity to forgive that shames the rest of us."

Valentin squeezed his friend's shoulder, his heart full of love for this man who was his brother in every way that mattered. "The time is coming. Until then, I need you to help me watch over them."

Pieter said nothing on that point. It was understood that he'd always be there for Valentin and vice versa. "What about the girls?"

"They're wounded, too." This wasn't ordinary teenage rebellion and angst. "Let me see them before I decide what needs to be done." The instant he did, he realized battle fury was riding them yet. Changeling bears didn't often fight among themselves, but when they did, they were bloody-minded about it.

Three girls sat on one side of the forest clearing, four on the other. They glared daggers at one another. All their eyes were different shades of amber, their claws out and raking furrows in the earth. "Eyes here," Valentin said in a tone that rumbled with his bear's presence.

Seven heads snapped toward him, the girls getting to their feet and coming to attention. Not a word escaped their lips, though he could all but see the hot air building up in their brains, ready for an explosion. "Follow me," he said without warning. "Petya."

"I have the rear."

Valentin took them on a run so grueling that by the time they returned to the clearing, every single girl collapsed into a limp heap. The anger was gone, extinguished by the burn of their lungs and the whimpers of their muscles. Someone moaned. Valentin ignored it, well aware of what these girls could take—they were dominants, every single one. Even more, they were all extremely physically fit.

Hunkering down in front of them afterward, he said, "We're clan. We're strong *only* when we're clan. When we're one."

Mina looked at him with tears swimming in her eyes. "But they left us," she whispered. "My own aunt and her family. They *left* us."

Her erstwhile opponent, Olive, put her arm around Mina's shoulders. "I'm sorry," she said, her throat working as she swallowed. "I didn't mean what I said. I'm just mad because your aunt took Temür with her."

Temür was a teenage boy with whom Olive had been flirting up a storm before his family made the decision to move. As Valentin watched, Mina sniffed and patted Olive's knee. "I'm mad at them, too, but they're my family. I have to defend them."

"I know."

Valentin ran his hand over Mina's hair, then Olive's. "I'm working on the situation." They had a right to know what was going on. "There's still time." Not much, but it wasn't all over.

He wasn't about to give up on his divided clan.

And he was never going to give up on his Starlight.

His babushka Anzhela had once said to him that his middle name might as well be "obstinate." He'd taken it as a compliment.

WHEN he finally saw Silver again near dinnertime, he had to bite back a rumbling growl. Purplish bruises under her eyes, lines of strain, it all spoke of exhaustion. She simply hadn't given her body and mind enough downtime after the poisoning.

At least she appeared to be heading to her room.

"Have you eaten?" he demanded, unable to help himself. "Here." He gave her a chocolate bar from his pocket before she could respond. "Think of it as fuel."

"I did eat." She didn't return the chocolate bar despite her statement.

His bear settled. "Rumor is a group called HAPMA is taking responsibility for all four attacks."

Silver blinked, her fingers tight around the chocolate bar. "What?"

"Inside, sit down." He pushed open her bedroom door. "Do you block off all other data while you're handling EmNet?"

She entered, took a seat on the bed without argument. *Chert voz'mi*, his Starlichka had to be exhausted to the bone if she was following his orders. Placing the chocolate bar on the bedside table, she began to take off the little ankle boots she seemed to love. Valentin had asked Nova where she'd bought them, had placed an order for Silver so she'd have her own pair.

"It's the only way to handle the deluge," she told him. "I have to focus on facts and figures, on numbers of responders, on medical triage." One boot off, she worked on the other. "I do need a team, and I need it quickly."

He bent down to pull off the second boot for her, barely restraining the urge to take her slender foot in his hands, work the tension out of it. "Nova's mad at you for going so hard when you haven't recovered from the poisoning." He was mad, too, but mostly, he needed to take care of her.

Since she was letting him, he could forget the mad.

"I wish I could argue with her." She rubbed at her shoulders.

Valentin's hunting instincts came to full wakefulness, but he didn't roar like a barbarian bear with no manners. *Sneaky,* he reminded himself, *be sneaky and wily.* "Want a massage?" Rising, he attempted to look like the harmless teddy bear he'd told her to call him. "I've got strong hands, and I promise to be a gentleman unless you ask me to tear off your clothes and kiss every delectable inch of you."

Govno! Why had he added that last? That was *not* harmless-teddy-bear behavior. Neither was it the least sneaky!

Silver's mouth opened on what he glumly figured would be a firm rejection. "All right."

It took him a frozen second to realize Starlight had given him permission to put his big clumsy hands on her. Bear and man both wanted to throw back their head and howl like a deranged wolf. This made up for his entire hellish day.

"Over my clothing." Silver was giving him a look that said she didn't entirely trust his vow to be a gentleman.

Valentin smiled his most innocent smile, the one that made even hard-ass Babushka Anzhela kiss him on both cheeks and call him her "pretty little Mishka." His paternal grandmother clearly had vision problems, but Valentin wasn't stupid enough to point that out to her.

Silver's eyes narrowed. "No skin contact."

"You make the rules." He kicked off his own boots in preparation to get on the bed behind her. "You must ache a hell of a lot if you're allowing an uncivilized bear so close." It was a tease to hide the thud of his heart, the raw need of his body.

Valentin was well and truly hooked on his Starlight.

SILVER watched Valentin walk toward, then behind her, a large predator who took up all the air in the room, felt the bed dip as he got on. The heat of him buffeted her back in a thick wave that threatened to melt the ice in her veins, ice she'd looked at today and found wanting.

In the short gaps between EmNet decisions, she'd thought about a single personal decision, come to a conclusion.

"I've decided you're correct," she told him as the warm, heavy weight of his hands landed on her stiff shoulders, their size and strength unmistakable. It caused a hitch in her breath. She had to consciously think to finish her statement. "I can only judge the efficacy of Silence if I test it now that I'm an adult."

Valentin's motionlessness reminded her once again that, playful or not, he was a bear alpha, could be deadly. "Just like that?" His voice was so deep it vibrated in her bones.

"There's no point in hesitating when a decision must be made."

Valentin began to knead at her with his hands. "Silver Fucking Mercant." The words were the opposite of an insult, his tone drenched in primal admiration. "You're an alpha under your pretty, soft skin . . . which I am *not* going to touch tonight."

Silver heard the want in the naked roughness of his voice, but her attention was on his touch. It was strong but controlled, the "uncivilized bear" clearly tempering his strength; it mattered little—the heavy burn of him sank into her flesh, soreness kneaded out as he unerringly read her body language to zero in on the worst spots.

She could barely resist the temptation to close her eyes and just drift.

Because Valentin Nikolaev was safe, would never harm her.

"HAPMA, tell me about it?" She was too mentally tired to trawl the PsyNet.

"You need to sleep, *moyo solnyshko*, not think about this." Again, Valentin's rumbling voice reverberated through her entire body, a now-familiar sensation that felt oddly intimate.

"But," he added, "since I know my Starlichka will go looking if I don't tell her, I'll give you the lowdown. HAPMA seems to have sprung up fully formed out of thin air."

"Nothing this coordinated was thrown together in a few days." The timing had been too precise, the strikes too coordinated. "The Consortium may have a hand in it, but even if it doesn't, HAPMA can't be a wholly new entity."

"I agree with you, Starlichka." The bear who was trying to seduce her brought his fingers perilously close to her neck, but didn't cross the line between clothed and unclothed skin. "Some twisted *mu*— er, *gad* has been planning this for a while."

"Valentin, I know every curse word in your vocabulary. Including *mudak*." She pronounced the extremely impolite word exactly as she'd heard dockworkers say it while she was supervising the unloading of a shipment during one of her training placements.

"I was being a gentleman bear," Valentin chided her.

"My apologies," Silver said in a solemn tone that had him rumbling at her and muttering about "some telepaths being smart alecks."

"HAPMA," Silver murmured several minutes later, her body leaning back into Valentin's without her conscious volition. Once she was in the position, the massive width of his chest a warm wall, she couldn't make herself move forward again. "*H* and *P* in the same acronym," she said after a yawn that caught her unawares. "Humans against Psy?"

"Humans Against Psy Manipulation," Valentin told her. "That's how the letters to the media were signed—e-mailed via public Internet access points, using throwaway accounts." He dug deep; Silver's bones felt as if they were liquefying. "Bo told me the Alliance was sent the same e-mails."

Silver struggled to think past the lethargy invading her body and mind. "You appear on highly friendly terms with the security chief of the Human Alliance." She had a good working relationship with Lily Knight, the Alliance's EmNet liaison, but Bowen Knight was a man who tended to keep his own counsel.

"We're family now," Valentin said. "Bo understands what that means to a bear." A gentler touch. "It means the same thing to a Mercant."

Silver could find no reason to argue with him. "HAPMA's targets make no sense," she said after forcing her eyelids open. "The victims were mostly human."

Valentin dug into a particular spot. Endorphins flooded her bloodstream.

He was so warm. How could he be so warm and still want to wear clothes?

"Letters said HAPMA was sad to cause harm to their own people"—Valentin's chest vibrated against her as he spoke—"but that if Trinity succeeds, humans will be eradicated or enslaved. HAPMA is just giving everyone a sneak preview of how humans will be treated as disposable under this new totalitarian regime."

"Fanatic logic."

"No logic involved, Starlight. The Alliance put out a statement disavowing all knowledge of, or support for, HAPMA."

"Anything else I need to know? Moscow?"

"Is safe. Kaleb, Selenka, and I had a security meeting before dinner." The three alphas.

Suddenly, despite the heaviness in her limbs and the fog in her brain, she understood something that had escaped her till now. "Though you and Selenka take responsibility for changeling access, neither of you consider the city part of your territories, do you?"

"We keep an eye on it, but it's Krychek's territory. Not much use to bears or wolves, so we let him have it."

Silver wondered what her lethal boss would think of that interpretation of things. "What did you three decide?"

"To let loose all our various spies with only one aim: find the HAPMA terrorist cell in Moscow if one exists."

Silver had no doubts that they'd succeed.

"They hit Moscow first for a reason—I think it was meant to show up EmNet in the city where its director is based." Anger rolled through the deep timbre of his voice.

Silver found herself patting his thigh. "They failed." The muscle bunched under her touch.

Breath no longer even, Valentin moved his hands to her upper arms. "Okay?"

At her nod, he leaned close to her ear and whispered, "Imagine, Starlichka, how much better this would feel if you were naked."

Silver knew he was teasing her, the bear in him unable to maintain the good behavior. But she'd learned a few things after watching how the bears interacted with one another. "I've always been interested in sex, in why it causes such inexplicable and often irrational behavior."

Chapter 22

Regular sexual contact with another individual causes the formation of psycho-chemical bonds that are disruptive to Silence. It is recommended that all such intimate contact be eliminated from Psy life.

—*Practical Application of the Silence Protocol*, a study by
Catherine Adelaja for the Psy Council (1976)

VALENTIN WENT STOCK-STILL behind Silver. "What?" It came out a strangled sound, his bear sitting dazed on its ass, like little Arkasha this afternoon.

"It seems important to humans and changelings. I want to understand it." Reaching back, she touched a part of her shoulder. "You missed this spot."

First she hit him with a virtual roundhouse punch, and now she was giving him orders exactly like the queen she was. Silver Mercant was Valentin's kind of woman. "You want to try sex?" he said, his bear's heart pounding like a drum and his eager cock in serious danger of prematurely spilling its seed, like a teenage boy faced with his first naked woman. "I volunteer as a willing sacrifice."

"Humans don't launch these types of attacks," she said, instead of responding to his generous offer to be her sex crash-test dummy.

Groaning inwardly, Valentin shifted his brain from his engorged cock to his head. "You're right." As a race, humans generally got on with the business of life while Psy and changelings engaged in a centuries-long power struggle. The revitalized Human Alliance *was* making waves, but they didn't do it with indiscriminate violence.

"So why now?" Silver murmured, her lashes shadowing her cheeks. *"Oh."*

Valentin was smug at having petted her into boneless laziness, but he knew that last utterance hadn't been of pleasure. "What aren't you saying, Starlight?"

"The information is classified. I was briefed only because I'm the director of EmNet."

Valentin wanted to rampage bad-temperedly around the room. Not because he didn't understand loyalty. But because he wanted Silver's. "You think your classified information is behind the surge of violence?"

"It would explain HAPMA's rhetoric." Silver knew the empaths had determined the PsyNet needed human connections if it weren't to collapse, but no one had worked out how to foster those emotional bonds, not after over a century of ill treatment of humans by Psy in power.

The vast majority of humans hated the Psy.

If HAPMA had gained access to the report on the need for human energy in the PsyNet, they could believe the Psy were planning to force the issue. The irony of it was that the bonds *couldn't* be forced. The Es were adamant the connections had to be organic.

"Secrets cause rot," Valentin murmured, a profound darkness in his tone that didn't fit the warmth of his nature. "They give fear room to grow."

Silver didn't take her hand from his thigh. "If this information were to go public, it could cause catastrophic panic." How could the Ruling Coalition or the Empathic Collective tell millions of people that the psychic network they needed to survive had a fatal disease without offering them hope of a cure?

Silver had been briefed so she could come up with a game plan for EmNet's response, if and when a leak did occur and the forecast panic led to riots or other chaotic incidents.

"Or," Valentin said, "you make this classified problem public and all those clever minds working on it might figure out a solution."

Silver gave up trying to open her eyes and turned a fraction to lean deeper into Valentin. "That decision isn't mine."

Apparently not the least discomforted by the physical liberties she was taking, Valentin said, "Then let's talk about the decision you *have* made. In case you've forgotten, it's the one to do with sex." Heat in his voice, his fingers working muscles that had turned to honey. "How about we start with kisses and ice cream?"

Silver mumbled her response. "Kisses aren't on the menu. Neither's ice cream."

"I thought you wanted to experience sex."

"Intercourse, yes."

"I think you have the wrong idea about intimate skin privileges, Starlight." His breath brushed her ear, his husky words a near-tactile caress. "We could do the physical act, but that'd teach you nothing about why sex can cause people to do insane things."

Silver made herself open her eyes, though she didn't shift from her position curled into Valentin—despite the fact that she couldn't recall pulling her legs up onto the bed, or moving her hand from his thigh to place it over the steady beat of his changeling heart. "Explain."

"Sex and emotion," he murmured. "That's the explosive combination. People kill for love, die for love. But even if it doesn't get that far, affection is a prerequisite to intimate skin privileges in my book. Kisses have to be on the menu, along with a million other small acts that build bonds no one can break."

Silver ignored the latter part of his statement; it was too dangerous. "I don't understand affection."

"Let me show you." A deep rumble. "Take a chance, Silver. If you're going to test your adult control, do it for real. Nothing halfway."

Silver was so drowsy, her muscles so relaxed, she was certain she was already breaching Silence. However, she couldn't bring herself to move away. The strength of Valentin's hands, the heat of him pulsing against her, it was . . . good. "You want to convince me to live with emotion."

"Never exactly hid that." His jaw brushed her temple, his stubble abrasive but not in any way painful. What was disquieting was her need to feel it again. Even then, Silver didn't withdraw.

She'd made her decision, would not be held hostage to childhood memories and the horror of her mind being crushed by a building roar of noise. She needed to learn who Silver Mercant was without Silence. For this experiment, she would assume nothing. Not even that her life depended on purest Silence, a truth she'd been taught as a child and never before questioned.

Her grandmother would've never lied to her about that, would've *never* hobbled her, but given all the recent revelations about the flaws in Silence and the Psy Council's manipulation of their people, she had to assume that Ena herself might not have had all pertinent information. Most important, she'd stop fighting an undeniable truth: that the only reason she'd permitted Valentin to touch her was that he caused her to react in ways no one else ever had.

Rough, tough Valentin Nikolaev had gotten under her defenses from day one.

"You have to know one thing before we do this." She deliberately moved her hand to the bare skin of his forearm.

Valentin shuddered. "An uncivilized bear might take that as permission to break the rules about not touching you skin to skin, but since I'm a gentleman bear, I'm going to ask." Deep and rough, his voice scraped over her skin like he was rubbing his stubbled jaw against the most sensitive parts of her. "Skin contact okay now?"

"Yes, but that's not what you need to know." His skin was hot under hers, the dark hairs on his arms giving it a texture that wasn't smooth but wasn't rough, either. He had hair on his chest, too—she could feel the springiness of it under her cheek through his shirt.

"There's a high chance I'll return to Silence." Her grandmother might not have had all the information, but one truth no one could change: pre-Silence, Silver's sub-designation had been considered extinct.

No Tp-A had ever survived to adolescence, much less adulthood.

"I'll take that risk." Valentin's right hand curved around her throat.

"But I should warn you, too, Starlight," he whispered against her ear. "I'm playing for keeps."

Her pulse sped up, her skin flushing as blood surged to the surface in a primal response to the gauntlet Valentin had thrown down. Her first instinct was to stifle the physical response under a wave of arctic ice . . . but she was Silver Fucking Mercant and she'd made a decision, would see it through.

Valentin wrapped his hand more firmly around her throat.

It should've felt like a threat. It felt like something else altogether, the sensation one she didn't have the experience to process. Ignorance was not a concept with which Silver had an acquaintance. "Explain what's happening."

"*We're* happening." Valentin stroked her throat with a gentleness that did nothing to hide the blatant possessiveness of the contact. "But you're exhausted and now that I've made you boneless"—unconcealed smugness—"I'm going to allow you to sleep. The Church should give me a sainthood."

Silver yawned, her eyes gritty. Yet she didn't want to stop.

Want was a forbidden concept under Silence. Under the Protocol that stripped Psy of emotion, things were framed in terms of necessity and checks and balances. But that prohibition no longer applied, and Silver was discovering the craving power of want. Such as the need to feel Valentin's not-rough, not-smooth skin against every inch of her.

His hand went motionless on her throat without warning. "Will it hurt you? To break out of the Silence?"

"No. I have control over the structural scaffolding of my Silence." Ena had made dead certain no Mercant child had pain controls built into his or her mind. Silver would not be crippled by an excruciating backlash should she breach the Protocol.

Valentin began to stroke her throat again. "Good." A rumbling sound in his throat. "If you get changed and slip into bed, *moyo solnyshko*, I'll massage you some more."

Silver realized he was negotiating with her, decided the compromise was acceptable. "I need a minute."

Valentin brushed his fingers over her skin once more before getting off the bed. The loss of his earthy scent; his heat; his big, solid presence, it was disorienting enough to cut through her drowsiness.

"I'll leave the door slightly ajar," Valentin said, his eyes ringed by amber and his voice still holding that rough depth that said she was speaking to both parts of him. "If you say my name, I'll hear it."

Silver watched him until he left the room, then got up to ready herself for bed. All the while, she considered the disorientation she'd felt when he broke contact, the sudden . . . howl of emptiness. Emotion was dangerous. It created need and need created vulnerability. The smart thing would be to step back, return to the cold insulation of Silence.

Be yourself.

Words her grandmother had spoken to her when Silver was a child of ten, the two of them standing at a Mercant property in the country, the landscape flowing out endlessly in front of them. The wind had tugged at Silver's white smock, unfurled a strand of hair from Ena's chignon.

"In a world of those who follow the rules without deviation," Ena had added, "those who innovate even in the shadows, will rule. Never be a carbon copy."

Having changed into white pajama pants printed with the outlines of trees and a simple black tank, Silver brushed out her hair before getting into bed.

"Valentin."

He entered so quickly she knew he'd been waiting impatiently for her. Shutting the door behind him, he ran his hand over the light panel to pitch the room into total blackness. She could feel him walking toward her regardless, the size and sheer power of him disrupting the air patterns.

"Lie on your front."

In the dark, his voice reached even deeper inside her. Skin aching in a way that wasn't pain, she turned over onto her front and swept her hair to the side out of habit.

The bed dipped.

Her pulse accelerated.

"I'm definitely going to play with your pretty hair now." A hot breath against the back of her neck, a tug on her skull, as if he'd gently fisted his hand in the unbound strands. His body was a wall of primal power over her. "So soft. I want to hold it in my hands while I kiss you wet and deep."

Silver's breath lost its rhythm.

Then Valentin put one big hand on her upper arm. An electrical surge arced through her body, smashing out of every single nerve ending she possessed. Her eyes snapped open, her heartbeat so jagged it was in her throat. "Stop."

Valentin broke contact at once. "You're hurting." It was an angry charge, the sound all bear. "I am *not* going to do anything that'll cause you pain."

Silver felt the bed begin to move, as if he were getting off. "Don't go."

A rough, grumbling sound, but his weight came over her again, his elbows braced against the mattress on either side of her head. "I want to bite you right now." It didn't sound like a playful sexual threat.

Fingers curling into the sheets, Silver said, "We rushed it." Her fault. "No more skin contact tonight. I have to build my tolerance."

Valentin didn't touch her even through her clothing; she could feel the waves of fury coming off him at the thought he'd caused her pain.

"Have I ever lied to you?" She should've known the first time she told him the truth when she didn't have to, that Valentin Nikolaev was dangerous to her.

He grumbled against her again. "Why do you sound so pissy when I'm the one who's got a right to be mad?" Teeth closing on her shoulder, over the delicate cloth of her tank top, but despite his threat, he didn't bite.

The pressure was enough. It made her toes curl, the physiological response inexplicable. "Valyusha," she said softly, having the sense of calming a wild creature she'd startled. "I'm not hurt. I was just being Silver Fucking Mercant, trying to do it all right now."

Releasing her shoulder, Valentin came down more heavily over her, his erection a rigid brand against her lower back.

Chapter 23

Male bears are excellent and generous lovers, albeit demanding. Be enthusiastic. Be demanding in return. And whatever you do, never ever look bored. Your gorgeous bear lover could have a surprisingly fragile ego.

—From the December 2079 issue of *Wild Woman* magazine: "Skin Privileges, Style & Primal Sophistication"

STARLIGHT HAD FALLEN asleep.

After calling him Valyusha, which made him feel petted and adored.

Valentin had been determined to stay mad regardless, had wanted to grumble some more at her. But half a minute after he'd settled his body onto hers, and while he was still building up his growling words, she'd gone liquid with sleep under him.

Good thing he had an ego "the size of an elephant"—as per Nika—or he might've taken Silver's descent into sleep as a mortal insult. As it was, he wanted to cuddle her close and kiss the life out of her. All was forgiven. Because Silver Fucking Mercant had fallen asleep under his heavy, powerful bear body.

If that didn't betray deepest trust, he'd eat his own foot.

Tempting as it was to curl himself around her and play with her hair, stroke her body, he got up and, after pulling a blanket over her, made himself leave. If she'd reacted that badly to his hand on her flesh, she wasn't ready to handle being tucked possessively into his body.

Valentin scowled at the memory of how she'd gone so stiff and still. "No more rushing," he said, bear and man in agreement. "We're going to be as patient as those stupid pandas."

After he left Silver's room, his plan was to head to his own room, but a loud noise had him changing direction. Pavel and Yakov were on the floor of the Cavern, apparently in the throes of attempting to murder each other.

He hauled them apart with no care for their bodies. The two were damn hard to break. "Quiet," he said in a tone that brooked no disobedience. "Silver is sleeping."

They gave him identical disgruntled looks. "Why do we have to be quiet?" Yakov demanded while his brother tried to fix the bent left arm of his spectacles.

He shook them. *Hard.* "Because Silver is sleeping. Make any more noise and I'll pound you both flat."

Spectacles on, Pavel straightened his half-torn shirt like it was a tuxedo. "How come you like her more than us?"

Valentin was well used to that gleam in the other man's eye.

He pointed a finger first at Pavel then at Yakov. "I'm going to bed. Make sure the clan doesn't fall down around us."

Leaving StoneWater in their care because despite their current behavior, the twins were powerful and loyal to the pack—and as thick as thieves when not attempting to kill each other—he went to his room and stripped for bed. The erection he'd barely got under control after getting out of Silver's bed returned in full force the instant he was alone.

Her skin had been so silken under his touch, her body so lithe. She smelled like darkest honey. Lush and complicated and with a hidden bite. He wanted to lick her up. Use his tongue on her until her thighs clenched on his head and she pulled his hair so hard it hurt.

No control, no distance. Just his Starlight wild for him.

Groaning but quite willing to torture himself further, he lay down in bed . . . and his mood shattered, his eyes locked on the ring he kept on his bedside table. It was a deliberate reminder to be vigilant, to never forget the blood that ran in his veins—and the terrible price it had extracted.

StoneWater had been *the* strongest pack in the country in his grandfather Kirill's generation. His father's father was now a deeply wounded man who couldn't bear to live in Denhome, the reason Valentin saw his beloved babushka Anzhela only rarely. But in his prime, Kirill had been one of the strongest bears in a proud clan.

Back then, StoneWater had controlled such a vast swath of land that, in changeling terms, Russia had been all but theirs. BlackEdge had taken over a quarter of that territory in the time of the alpha before Zoya, the wolves becoming increasingly powerful while StoneWater crumbled.

Looking back, it was no surprise they'd lost what they had. StoneWater had been under bad management, with a resulting loss of bears to other clans leaving them shorthanded—because in the changeling world, you only kept what you could hold. A brutal law that kept the peace.

Predatory changelings were hesitant to attack any clan or pack that could protect what was their own. Conversely, clans didn't overreach, conscious they'd get no support from fellow changelings for their arrogance. Which was why StoneWater had pulled back when the wolves started growing stronger than they'd been in previous generations. They'd let part of their territory go rather than lose hundreds of lives in a pointless territorial battle.

It all made sense . . . except it hadn't had to be that way.

Valentin had been ten when his father made the decision not to fight the wolves. It should've caused Mikhail Nikolaev incredible anguish that StoneWater was weakening under his leadership, but Valentin's father—Valentin's *alpha*—had already begun to change from the man who'd taught Valentin how to track, how to semi-shift, how to do a hundred other things.

The loss of land, however, that wasn't the deepest wound, wasn't the one that bled and bled without pause.

Zoya had tried to stanch the flow, failed.

Valentin had come to power on the driving need to fix the worst hurt, heal his clan, but his ascension had instead led to the loss of a quarter of his people. *That* loss, he couldn't ever forget, no matter what else he was doing. StoneWater's festering wound had split families, friendships, lives.

It kept him awake every single night.

Not the land gone before he was alpha. Not the territory now held by wolves.

It was the people. *His* people.

Out there in the darkness all alone. Alphaless because they'd rather live broken and lost than accept Valentin and the tainted blood that ran in his veins.

Something brushed his mind, a strange awareness.

He frowned. He knew what it felt like to have Psy knock on his brain. Some idiot was always trying to be the one to break changeling shields, but this didn't feel like that. It felt . . . gentler, a caress rather than an attack. Sitting up, he tried to follow the sensation, but it was gone, a gossamer thread whipped away by the jerk of movement.

Had Silver reached out to him in her sleep?

His fisted hand opened, his bruised heart starting to beat again. "Good night, Starlight."

The Ruling Coalition
of the Psy

"WE HAVE A leak—it has to do with the information about the necessity for human minds in the PsyNet." Nikita Duncan's voice was frigid as she made that pronouncement.

Kaleb leaned back in the chair in his home study, his body in Moscow while a significant part of his mind attended the Ruling Coalition meeting in a secure psychic vault. Of course, he was never totally unaware, even while on the Net—no one would ever get close enough to harm his body while his mind was otherwise occupied.

"It's confirmed?" Anthony Kyriakus asked, the other man's mind surrounded by impenetrable shields. As the leader of a family that had many of the world's best foreseers, he was both extremely intelligent and extremely strong.

"Yes." Nothing in Nikita's psychic voice betrayed that she and Anthony had a relationship outside of the Ruling Coalition. Exactly *what* that relationship was, no one was quite certain.

Nikita was a former Psy Councilor, ruthless and focused on her bottom line. Anthony had only joined the Council toward the end—and he'd proven to be a rebel who'd fought for a new world order. The only thing Nikita had in common with Anthony appeared to be their blood loyalty to family.

Both would kill to protect their own.

"Here." Nikita uploaded data into the closed vault of the Coalition chamber. They'd built the chamber together, the decision not to use the previous Council chambers unanimous. No one knew what codes or back doors were buried within, what nasty surprises might lurk behind the slick walls.

Nikita's document flashed up against the black of this vault, silvery streams of data that their minds interpreted into the correct forms for understanding.

Kaleb shifted forward physically. "Where did you get this?" They were looking at an internal HAPMA document that was short and to the point.

The Psy want to enslave us to save their HIVENET. They need a pound of HUMAN FLESH for every pound of Psy. We all know what they'll do to get that. Brothers and sisters, we will not be SUBJUGATED! We will RISE! We will FIGHT!

Freedom, independence, humanity! HAPMA!

"The group appears to be small, the members fiercely loyal to one another," Nikita said. "I've been unable to track any real information about them. I received this from an informer in the Alliance—it was sent to Bowen Knight an hour after the second round of attacks. My informer was in the right place at the right time, was able to make a copy."

Once again, Nikita proved why she'd survived so many decades. Kaleb hadn't been able to break anyone in Knight's inner circle, but Nikita had obviously found a spy on the periphery. Likely someone as innocuous as a sub-assistant to an assistant.

"Could it be a double bluff?" Anthony asked Kaleb. "Knight feeding the information you gave him to this group, then having it be redirected to him to give him plausible deniability?"

"No," Kaleb said. "Bowen Knight understands this information could cause widespread panic in the Psy. He might distrust our race, but he's not capable of inciting a genocide."

"I agree." Ivy Jane Zen's voice, the president of the Empathic Collective speaking for the first time. "I've met Bo. He's a hard man, but he's not evil or vindictive."

It was Aden Kai, leader of the Arrows, who spoke next. "How certain are you that the note is genuine?"

"No way to confirm." Nikita's psychic tone remained as cold as the emptiness of space. "HAPMA is too new, but it doesn't matter who sent it, or even if my informant is a double agent who made this up to fool me."

"No," Anthony said quietly, "because the fact that humans are necessary to the Net is true."

"HAPMA could cause catastrophic terror in those of our race by blasting this information to the media," Aden said. "Why are they using it only to inflame their own people?"

"Hivenet," Kaleb murmured. "If they really believe that, they must believe all Psy already know and are working together to enslave humans." To this group, the Psy weren't individuals but a single hateful mass.

"Secrets are poisonous." Ivy's psychic voice was gentle but firm. "I still say we need to share the truth."

Aden Kai remained silent. The Arrows always watched first. And they backed any calls made by the empaths. Not because the deadly men and women of the squad didn't have their own opinions, but because they believed the empaths were the Psy race's conscience—and Arrows had a lot of darkness in their past.

"I would agree with you, Ivy," Anthony said in his calm, tempered tone, "but Sophia Russo and Max Shannon remain the only Psy-human bond in the PsyNet. *No* such bonds have formed since the fall of Silence. We'd be giving our people terror without even a flicker of hope to balance it out."

Kaleb didn't think in those terms, but he understood them because his mate did. His heart was hers, every broken, twisted part of it. Sahara also believed true love would win in the end, conquer hate and anger and fear. He called her a dreamer. She just smiled and told him she'd be proven right.

I loved you right into my arms, didn't I?

How could he argue with that when he'd been a scarred, dangerous monster she'd coaxed to her with nothing but laughter and tenderness and love?

"We have no reason to rush a decision," Nikita said. "These HAPMA fools are killing their own people. Only a small percentage of the victims have been Psy. Our populace isn't screaming for answers."

Cold-blooded and practical, that was Nikita. She was also right, except for one thing. "Sooner or later—I'd guess sooner—the tide will turn." Kaleb had seen too much darkness to believe otherwise. "If they manage to convince enough humans of the truth of their claims, Psy will become the targets." Kaleb didn't care about his race as a whole, but Sahara did. She'd asked him to save them.

Kaleb didn't break his promises to her.

"Kaleb is correct." Aden's voice was gleaming obsidian, as black as the martial shields around his mind. "This will only have one outcome, and that outcome is bloodshed on a massive scale as ordinary humans turn against the Psy."

Nikita shrugged off Aden's warning. "Most Psy can defeat humans."

"No," Anthony responded, "they can't. Not if humans take shots from a distance or use grenade launchers to blow up Psy houses or any of a million ways in which they can kill without ever getting within psychic distance."

"*No.*" Ivy Jane's voice shimmered with empathic power, the wave of it hitting them all. "No more blood, no more war. We are not the Council and we will *never* be the Council. We have to find a way to save our people *and* the humans." Her mind blazed with empathic sparks. "We give Bowen what he wants. We build a way for humans to shield their minds."

Kaleb had known it was Ivy who'd make that call. He'd also known Nikita would object to it. "We hand that over, and we lose all negotiating power."

"This isn't about negotiating," Ivy countered. "It's about honor and integrity and goodness." Potent emotion in every one of her words. "Today, here, this is our chance to be different, to not be Ming LeBon and Shoshanna Scott and Tatiana Rika-Smythe and Marshall Hyde and all the Councilors who drove our people into hell."

She didn't add Nikita's name to that list, but the implication was there.

This was Nikita's chance for redemption, too. Kaleb didn't need it. He'd never walked the Council's path, despite being on it, Sahara's the voice that held him back from evil no matter how twisted his soul.

"A vote," Anthony said. "Those in favor of Ivy's motion?"

Ivy. Aden. Kaleb. Anthony . . . and Nikita.

Chapter 24

Hope is the greatest gift and the greatest evil.

We hoped for so many eons that we could contain the firestorm of our minds, that we could use our psychic abilities without going mad, without shattering into violence, and so we continued on despite the heartache of losing our children and watching our children's children get ever more fractured.

Hope saved us and hope might yet kill us.

—Extract from *The Dying Light* by Harissa Mercant (1947)

THIS TIME WHEN Silver walked into the Cavern after her morning shower, she hit the breakfast rush. Seeing her, Dima the Barnacle ran over but didn't clamp onto her leg. Huge brown eyes, shaded by the thickest lashes she'd ever seen on a child, fearlessly held her own.

"You wan' bweakfast?" he asked in accented but readily understandable English.

"Yes, thank you."

He slipped his hand into hers, his flesh soft. "I show you."

Having readied herself for physical contact after noting how the cubs always touched the people in their vicinity, Silver permitted Dima to lead her to one of the large tables—with bench seats—that had been set up nearest the freshwater-fed pond in the corner of the Cavern.

Sunlight beamed down on the table from high above. That light, as well as the closeness of the moss-covered rocks and the scent of the tiny white flowers on the vines that crawled over the walls, made it feel as if they were eating outside.

Dima scrambled onto the bench seat alongside her. "I eat breakfast, too," he said, switching to Russian with the ease of a child who'd grown up speaking two languages.

"Where did you learn English?" she asked him.

"Great-gamma Caroline," he said in English. "Uncle Mishka says I'm smart." An angelic smile before he returned to his half-eaten bowl of what appeared to be oats with dried fruits. Dipping his spoon into the oats, he lifted it up, put the spoon into his mouth.

A drop of oats fell onto his blue jeans.

Not thinking about it, Silver picked up the cloth napkin beside his bowl and wiped off the food before it could set. Dima kept eating while she dampened another corner of the napkin with a drop of water from the jug on the table, and further wiped the spot clean.

"*Spasibo.*" The Barnacle finished his oats with enviable speed, put down his spoon, then stood on the bench seat. He'd pressed his lips to her cheek and was scrambling off the bench, chortling, before she realized his intent.

"You gotta watch bears." Anastasia Nikolaev slid into the empty place beside Silver, her long legs clad in black jeans over which she wore knee-high black boots. Finishing off the outfit was a thin round-necked sweater in cherry red, which showed off her impressive breasts. "They have a way of getting their paws on you. Even if they're tiny paws."

"I think I'll survive." Silver could still feel the soft, slightly wet kiss against her cheek, the contact lingering.

"You eat this, right?" Anastasia passed over a basket of bread that had been making the rounds of the table. There was a dangerous grace to even that small action; Anastasia Nikolaev moved like the dominant protector she was.

"Yes." Choosing two plain wheat slices, she passed the basket to the person across from her, a teenager who was inhaling his food as if it were about to become a scarce commodity.

"Hi, Silver. Chaos said this is for you." The juvenile who'd put a small jar next to her was gone in the direction of the kitchen before Silver could respond.

"Kitchen duty," Anastasia said, spreading peanut butter onto her slice. "All the kids do it as soon as they're old enough." A nod at the jar. "What'd Chaos get you?"

Opening it, Silver saw a familiar substance. "Nutrient spread." She picked up a knife and began to spread the nutrients onto a slice; she needed the burst of concentrated energy. "Does Chaos look after all guests this way?"

"He looks after all of us." Anastasia's attention was diverted at that moment by an older packmate who'd taken a seat on her right. White-haired, face wrinkled with life, the female had a soft voice Silver couldn't hear from this distance.

Silver took the opportunity to look for Valentin, saw no sign of him. She did, however, pick up an odd emotional resonance in the Cavern that had her instincts prickling.

"Good morning, Silver." Nova slipped into the seat the starving teen-ager had vacated. "You going into the city today?"

"No." She had to see this through, had to find out who she was with-out Silence . . . and with Valentin.

Nova waggled both eyebrows. "That decision have anything to do with you having a certain alpha in your bedroom last night, hmm?"

"Privacy seems to be an unknown concept in the clan."

Eyes dancing, Nova poured a mug of coffee from the carafe on the table. "We can mind our own business—once a day. Maybe twice if we're very strong willed."

"Novochka should know." Anastasia took the mug of coffee her sister passed over, while Nova poured another for herself. "She's got her nose in every pie in the den. Sniff, sniff, oooh, then sniff, sniff again."

"Healer's business." Nova's expression was the definition of prim. "How's the leg, Jane?"

The white-haired woman beside Anastasia released a deep sigh. "I'm getting old; that's how things are."

"Oh?" Anastasia looked askance at the elder. "Way I heard it, you were climbing a tree with your mate when you injured yourself."

Nova threw back her head and laughed a laugh nearly as big and warm as Valentin's. "*Busted!* I knew it had to be something interesting when you refused to tell me how you'd ended up with an eversion sprain."

The elder, her cheeks pink, said, "I have no idea what Stasya is talking about. I turned my ankle during a perfectly ladylike walk."

"Talking of walks," Nova said after the laughter died down, "anyone want to wander down with me to look in on the wild bears on the other side of the lake?"

"I'll come," a woman down the table said, her accent lyrical. "I need to waddle a little more while this cub grows fat enough to pop out." She rubbed her rounded belly.

"We'll go slow," Nova promised.

"That's my current fastest speed." The pregnant woman stretched as Silver identified her accent as Irish. "I love my cub, but I can't wait to run again. *Really* run."

Silver had seen the brown-haired woman move around the Cavern and could categorically say she was far more mobile than Silver would've expected of someone in her advanced stage of pregnancy. Especially since she wasn't changeling but human.

"I'll join you if that's all right," Silver said. "I didn't leave Denhome for most of yesterday, should get some fresh air."

"You're not too busy dealing with the fallout from yesterday's violence?" Anastasia asked, her crisp tone far different from Nova's warmth. Anastasia, Silver thought, always had her eye on the clan's overall security, as was her job as Valentin's first second.

"I do need an hour and a half to clear up a few matters." The emergency part of the response was over, thus ending EmNet's involvement. It was now all in local hands. "If you don't mind waiting," she said to Nova, "I can come then."

"Sure, that works. Moira, that okay with you?"

"Yes, I need to wrap up a present for my pen pal so Leonid can drop it off in the post." She waved at Silver before she left. "See you soon."

It only took Silver another minute to finish her own meal. In that minute, she finally realized what had been disturbing her about the atmosphere in the Cavern. The boisterous moments at the table aside, it was quiet. The Cavern was never quiet, much less with this many bears gearing up for the day.

"Something's wrong," Silver said to Nova as the healer rose to leave the table. "Is that why Valentin isn't here?"

Nova's expression became tight. "Not yet, Seelichka. You're not one of us yet."

With that and a touch of her hand to Silver's arm, she walked away. Silver glanced at Anastasia, got a hard shake of her head. "I like you, Silver, but I don't have a big crush on you like my baby brother, and I'm not gentle like Nova. You want my trust? You earn it."

Silver held the greenish gray of the other woman's gaze. "You're very much like me, Anastasia."

Lifting two fingers to her temple, Anastasia saluted. "I figured that out a long time ago." A faint smile. "What I said still stands."

"Understood—but is there anything I can do to assist Valentin in dealing with whatever problem he's handling?"

The other woman's smile faded into what seemed to be a deep-rooted anger. "This, only my alpha can solve—even though he shouldn't have to."

Soon afterward, her mind pulling at the reins in a futile effort to search for Valentin, Silver made her way to StoneWater's tech room. Taking a seat at the system she'd commandeered, she used it to handle matters that didn't require impregnable security. For those, she used the organizer she'd picked up from her room on the way.

When the hairs rose on the back of her neck, her skin prickling, she wasn't in the least shocked. Part of her had known he'd find her. "You weren't at breakfast."

Valentin leaned down to brace his arms on the back of her chair, his scent and the unapologetic size of him taking over the space. Rubbing his jaw against her hair, the stubble catching on the strands, he said, "Miss me, sleepyhead?"

Silver sent an e-mail, began to read another. "Why should I miss you?

There are any number of virile males in the den who I'm sure would be happy to volunteer for my experiment."

A rumbling sound behind her, thunder rolling across a storm-dark sky. Claws pricked her throat as he closed his hand around it. "That," he said, speaking against her ear, "was mean."

"It was truthful." Silver found herself leaning her head back against him, her words breathy and her breasts feeling full in a way that seemed to demand Valentin's big hands massaging the aching flesh.

The rumble came again. "Take it back." Teeth nipped at her ear.

She jerked, having not expected the act—having never even thought about it in her entire life. Her nipples tightened against the deep cerise of her vee-necked sweater. "Don't you believe other men would volunteer for my sex experiment?"

"*Silver.*" His voice wasn't human any longer.

Lifting her hand, as her thighs clenched in a response she couldn't explain, she reached back to weave it into the heavy strands of his hair. "It appears I only wish to run this experiment with a certain gentleman bear."

Another rub of his cheek against her hair, his hand sliding up and down her throat. "I can smell you, Starlichka. You want me." The words were a pleased rumble. "When can I lick you?"

Chest rising and falling in rapid breaths, Silver said, "Now."

He growled at her, as if he were a lion and not a bear. "No, I can't. You know what happened last time when we rushed it." Despite the harsh words, he didn't break contact. "Distract me from imagining you naked, all soft and open for me, your pussy glistening with your honey."

Silver lost the train of her thoughts. All she could see were Valentin's wide shoulders between her thighs, the dark strands of his hair brushing her skin in a thousand caresses as he licked her up. "You're putting sexual images into my head."

An unrepentant chuckle. "Good. I woke up with a cock so hard it hurt." He began to play with her hair with his free hand. "What have you been doing this morning?"

Silver told him, then asked, "Did you have early duties in your territory?" She was careful to keep her voice neutral; if he wished to speak to her about what had muted an entire clan of bears, he would . . . but it mattered that he didn't trust her.

"An alpha always has duties."

Silver was no expert at emotion, but she knew she wasn't mistaken about the sadness she heard in his voice. "Valyusha?"

"I just need to pet you this morning. Let me?"

When Silver leaned back a little further into him, he kept on stroking her throat, the skin there far more sensitive than she'd ever realized.

"What's this?" he rumbled a while later, indicating her computer setup.

"EmNet work." Though she hadn't answered any messages since he circled her throat and began to talk to her using words she'd always considered coarse, but that had taken on a whole new meaning when spoken in Valentin's deep tones. "You're a distraction."

A satisfied chuckle that was pure bear. "Good." He rose after another gentle stroke that rubbed his callused palm against her skin. "Now stop making me crazy and do your work. We'll continue our experiment tonight." A pause, a rough kiss pressed to her temple. "Thank you, Starlight."

She turned to watch him leave, this big, brash bear who had so much more to him than most people would ever know. It was a near-compulsion to go to him, ask him to tell her what was wrong so she could help fix it, though she had no claim on his secrets.

Silver wanted that claim.

A pounding in her ears, her heartbeat a drum.

It took her a long time to calm her mental pathways enough to finish her work. Valentin was far more than a distraction. He threatened her very stability, made her consider a life she'd always believed was for other people, impossible for her.

A telepathic ping. *Silver.*

What is it, Arwen?

I hesitate to mention this, but there's been a change in your emotional equilibrium.

Of course, Arwen would notice. *Is that a problem?*

It's not bleeding out. I know simply because of our connection.

Because Arwen was the sole E in the Mercant family. He was the one who anchored Silver to the Honeycomb, keeping her sane and mentally healthy in a badly damaged psychic network none of them could leave. *Will you report this to Grandmother?* Silver would do that herself when the time came, but right now, she needed to walk her own path.

Of course not. Empathic ethics forbid such disclosures. It was a rebuke. *Even if they didn't, I'd never betray you.* A pause. *Are you sure? The risk—*

Is significant, I know. She was always listening for a breach, for her brain to begin to rebel. *But I need to know if Silence is the only path. I need to know if I have a choice.*

Arwen's simple response held an undertone of intense hope. *If anything does threaten to bleed out into the PsyNet, I'll contain it until you regain control. Good luck, Silver.*

Luck. If only that were the final decider and not the mutant piece of genetic code that had marked her from childhood.

Silver's hand curled on the desk.

She found herself reaching for her phone, inputting Valentin's code. But she didn't press Send. He was having a hard day; she didn't need details to understand that for a man like Valentin to be so sad, the pain had to be devastating. He'd thanked her for giving him a moment of peace.

She wouldn't ruin that.

Putting down her phone, she got back to work. She was seventy minutes into it and all but done when Yakov poked his head into the room. "Sorry to interrupt, Starlight—"

He winked at her icy look. "I mean, Silver," he said, with no sign of repentance in his tone, "but my brother says the 'supermodel cutie pie,' end quote, is here. I can guide you to the meeting spot."

Chapter 25

Every decision has a consequence. Nothing can change that law of nature.

—Anonymous

SILVER FINISHED THE last bit of work, shut everything down. Curious as to why her brother hadn't telepathed her to say he was in StoneWater territory, she looked to Yakov after she rose to her feet. "When did Arwen arrive?"

"Ten minutes ago, I think." He shrugged, his shoulders taut with muscle. "I swear my lunatic twin hasn't thrown him over his shoulder and run off pounding his chest."

Not certain she believed him, Silver nonetheless didn't reach out for Arwen. While he might be gentle, her brother could also take care of himself. So she was in no way surprised to reach the small forest clearing to find Arwen leaning against the front of his car, arms folded, while Pavel stood several feet away, his hands on his hips.

The bear scowled at Silver, light glancing off the clear lenses of his spectacles. "Why didn't you warn me he had claws?"

"You're a big bear." Silver walked to meet her brother. "May we have some privacy?"

Yakov hooked his arm around his twin's neck and all but hauled him away. "We'll be out of earshot but not far, just in case you're thinking of a hostile invasion!"

Waiting until the twins were indeed far enough away that they couldn't hear her and Arwen's conversation, she touched her fingers gently to her brother's clean-shaven jaw. Though she dropped her hand almost at once, Arwen swallowed at the contact. "How did you get here so quickly?"

"I haven't left Moscow since you were hurt. I . . . I thought you might need me."

Silver looked at this man who was the reason she'd never become cruel or without conscience. "I did," she said, admitting to need for the first time in her life. "Thank you for coming."

A shaky smile. "You want to sit with me awhile? I have a meeting with Grandmother that I have to drive back for soon."

Perching next to him against the front of the car, she didn't ask about the investigation. That could wait. "Pavel?"

Color touched Arwen's cheekbones. "Bears are the most irrational creatures I've ever met."

"Agreed."

"But there is something about them." His eyes flicked to where Yakov was ruffling his brother's hair while Pavel tried to kick him. "He found my call code. I don't know how. He sends me ridiculous messages."

"Do you reply?"

"He'd think he'd won if I didn't."

"I think they do that on purpose." Silver was starting to wonder if bears could be far more sneaky than she'd ever known. "Appeal to our competitive instincts."

Arwen crossed his legs at the ankles, his shoes shiny boots she recognized as being from an exclusive designer label. "He's very good at it."

"What will you do?"

"I'm a Mercant. I can out-strategize a bear." A searching look out of eyes the exact same shade as her own. "And you, Silver? What will you do?"

"Not turn back. Not until I know."

The Human Alpha

The peacemaker must have the strongest heart and the toughest will in the room.

> —Words spoken by the alpha of the FireDawn Leopards, Daniel Emory;
> to Adrian Kenner, Peace Negotiator; on the day the Peace Accord
> was signed, ending the Territorial Wars. As noted in the
> official record of the historical signing. (Eighteenth century)

BO LOOKED AT the data on HAPMA that he and his people had collected. The news was bad. These fanatics knew the Psy needed humans to save their race, but they had a pathologically skewed idea of how to stop any manipulation that might be involved in achieving that aim.

"The message got through?" he asked Lily over their internal comm system.

"I got a read receipt. Old-fashioned, but it's a confirmation."

Bo glanced at his e-mail. He'd been given an e-mail address to contact HAPMA in the last message they'd sent him. He'd used that e-mail to tell them what Krychek had told him: that humans had to *choose* to be with Psy. He knew why the Ruling Coalition was holding on to that information, understood it was to stop panic, but HAPMA already knew—and Bo couldn't worry about hypothetical Psy panic.

Not when humans were dying.

He'd made it clear in his e-mail that he'd had the information direct from the highest sources and that he'd confirmed it by reaching out to a contact he trusted. That contact was Lucas Hunter. The leopard alpha's mate wasn't just Psy; her mother was on the Ruling Coalition. Bo wouldn't believe a word out of Nikita Duncan's mouth, but Sascha Duncan was a cardinal empath.

Even after over a century of hate and division, humans remembered empaths, remembered their hearts and how hard they'd fought for a better world. More recently, empaths were working to give peace to as many mentally hurt humans as Psy. Bo trusted Sascha in a way he'd never trust Krychek and his ilk.

She'd told him that *she'd* confirmed the details via multiple sources, including having had the information directly from Ivy Jane Zen.

Another empath.

The sources couldn't be more trustworthy. He'd made that clear in his message to HAPMA, not noting specific names but stating that his data had been verified by empaths who were independent thinkers. Sascha wouldn't lie for the Ruling Coalition, and while Ivy Jane Zen was on that Coalition, she had no reason to pander to anyone. Not when her mate was part of a powerful and deadly group that could take on even Krychek.

Bo had asked the fanatics to stop the violence, stop the killing.

Ping.

He opened their reply, swore.

Picking up the paperweight on his desk, he threw it at the opposing wall. It left a dent, falling to the floor with a dull thud.

Breath harsh, Bo's eyes went to the note again:

Your mind has clearly been MANIPULATED. That's not your fault. We will FREE you of their hold, but you must STEP DOWN as Security Chief for the good of the human race.

We are here now to FIGHT for our PEOPLE.

Chapter 26

Even the most open heart has its secrets.

—Adina Mercant, poet (b.1832, d.1901)

SILVER WAS LATE by two minutes to her meeting with Moira and Nova, but found only Moira at the main entrance to Denhome.

"Sorry I'm late." Nova's breathless voice breaking into their conversation, her feet clad in sparkly pink trainers, her body in the same creamy yellow dress she'd worn to breakfast. "Little Zhenya started throwing up. I was worried it was a stomach virus, but it turned out she'd eaten a mushroom she'd found outside in the minute her father was dealing with her brother.

"But"—Nova took a deep breath, released it—"she's fine, sleeping cuddled up in her daddy's arms, and Lizabeta is well able to handle any small matters that arise, so we can go for our walk."

Silver didn't speak much on the first part of that walk, the two Stone-Water women carrying on the conversation. She didn't feel sidelined—she wasn't a huge talker by nature, and she had a deep interest in the still-unfamiliar flora around Denhome.

The women caught on to her interest, began telling her the names of plants and the seasons in which they grew the strongest. Before long, they'd passed the small lake Nova had mentioned and were nearing the den of wild bears.

"They won't react badly to me?" Silver asked. "They may have never scented a Psy before."

Nova laughed. "It's too late, Seelichka—you smell of us now. Mostly of Mishka, but a little of my Barnacle, hints of others who you've been around."

Silver realized she was at a sensory disadvantage in ways she hadn't truly comprehended before now. "There are no secrets when it comes to relationships within a clan?"

"Not really." Nova's glance was penetrating. "That bother you?"

Silver took time to think about it. "Only because I don't have the same advantage."

"Oh, that." Nova waved it off. "The information gets around so fast, you'd think we were the telepaths. Trust me, you'll never miss out on the freshest gossip."

Moira's laugh was cut off with a harsh suddenness. Moss-green eyes wide, she clutched her belly. *"Nova."*

Nova went from smiling clanmate to highly competent healer in a heartbeat. "Silver, watch for the wild bears. They won't harm us, but they may get too curious. If that happens, growl and look big."

Silver had never growled in her life. "I'll make sure they don't get close." She took in Moira's position—the other woman had gone to the ground on her hands and knees, her face stark white.

"Do you want me to contact the clan, request help?" She had her satellite-linked phone in her pocket; had she left it behind, she'd have telepathed Arwen, had him make the call for her.

"Yes. Ask for Lizabeta," Nova said, her attention on Moira. "She'll know what to bring." Nova rattled off the comm code.

Silver did as asked, then kept watch on the bears who'd exited the den and were lingering nearby, until she heard Moira cry out. Going to the other woman's side without turning her back to the wild bears, she knelt down and put her hand on Moira's back, careful to watch for any sign the contact was unwelcome.

SILVER SILENCE

Moira didn't throw off her hand. Instead, she put one hand on Silver's thigh, bore down hard. "It's too early!" The words were a scream.

"Bear babies are tough," Nova said, her voice perfectly calm. "You just listen to your body and push when you feel the urge."

Silver stroked Moira's back through the contractions. When the laboring woman begged for distraction, Silver began to tell her of the current hot topics in the PsyNet news cycle.

"That is the most boring thing ever," Moira complained. "Don't Psy gossip?"

"Right now, the current hot topic is Silver Mercant's torrid affair with a bear. Most people believe I've either a, lost my mind; b, decided to attempt mind control on a notoriously uncontrollable race; or c, lost my mind."

Moira snorted with laughter that turned into a moan. "Nova?"

"You're doing fine, *milaya moya*. Better than fine. Just one more push."

Silver brushed Moira's sweat-damp hair out of her eyes. "Have you decided on a name for your child?"

"What?" Moira lifted a dazed face up to Silver, the moss green unfocused. "No, we're still thinking." Her breathing grew even more jagged. "Wanted to see him first. Name him so it suits. Like you with your eyes."

Silver didn't correct the other woman; yes, her name matched her eyes, but the name itself was a familial one born of the tendency for that eye color in their genetic line. "All newborns look like they've been squashed, so you'll have to wait some time."

Moira laughed, her eyes lighting up. "Silver, I think we're going to be friends."

Then there were no more words. The largest wild bear rumbled out of the trees in a beeline toward them, Silver did her best imitation of an alpha growl, and Moira screamed right before a child's thinner cry split the air. Collapsing against Silver, the other woman tore at the top of her dress so it split open, then held out her arms for the squalling child Nova held with firm tenderness.

The adult bear—who'd frozen at Silver's growl—took a few more steps forward, this time with cubs at her heels. Silver didn't need to scare them away this time. Two other bear changelings had just emerged from the woods. One of them was Valentin. He was sweaty, his hair wild from the run, and his grin at seeing his tiny new clanmate a dazzling thing.

Another man, almost as sweaty but with a far more bloodless face, collapsed onto his knees next to Moira. "Damn it, *a chuisle mo chroí*." A hard kiss as he spoke the latter words in a language Silver guessed might be Moira's native tongue. "You had to do it your way."

Laughing, Moira placed the baby into his arms. "Kiss our cub, handsome. Then we have to let Nova do her thing. He's come too early."

When Nova did reclaim the child within seconds, Valentin went to stand behind her, his thickly muscled arms cradling his sister's softer ones. As if he were giving her his strength in an unknown changeling way. In Nova's hold, the small baby gained a noticeably healthier glow before the healer tucked him back against his mother's chest.

"He looks like me." With that proud statement, which made Moira laugh, Moira's husky mate lifted mother and child both into his arms to put them on a stretcher two other clanmates had brought out in the interim.

Valentin, meanwhile, was leaning companionably against the large wild bear, the smaller bears padding along beside Moira's stretcher until their mother called them back with a low sound.

"Come on, Starlight." Valentin held out an arm after he'd petted both cubs. "I have to spend more time with my new clanmate, especially with him coming so early."

Silver rose to her feet at last, realized her legs were shaky.

"Whoa." Valentin tucked her close to the heated brawn of his body, his size comforting in a way she couldn't explain.

"Do you know what he said? *A chuisle mo chroí*?"

"A pulse of my heart, I think." Cuddling her in a possessive hold, Valentin added, "Leo drove us crazy repeating the Gaelic over and over when he was trying to learn it so he could shout it up to Moira's balcony on the second floor of a college hostel." A pause. "I *climbed* up a building for you," he said pointedly. "That's better than shouting love words from the street."

"Bears." The word came out shaky. "I've dealt with terrorist attacks without blinking," she said in an effort to find her equilibrium. "Why is this affecting me so intensely?"

"You saw a life come into the world. Even an alpha's heart beats harder, faster at that instant." He looked affectionately at the wild bears who'd decided to shadow them. "They're excited, too. Tonight's party will be *zaebis*, Starlichka. We'll blow off the roof."

"A party? With a premature infant in the clan?"

"He's a bear. He'll like it."

IT turned out that the infirmary section of Denhome was well insulated against noise—a fact Silver learned from Pavel after Valentin left to help settle the infant in the infirmary.

"Little guy will be fine," Pavel reassured her. "When Yasha and I were born, they put us in baskets in the center of the Cavern and put up a disco ball so bright it permanently damaged my eyes." His grin turned into an "Ouch!" when a tall woman with aqua-green eyes identical to his, her hair a silken fall of red, slapped the back of his head.

"Pavel Mayakovskevich Stepyrev," she said, eyes flinty, "are you accusing your parents of mistreatment?"

"Aw, Mama, no." Pavel wrapped his arms around his mother. "I was just—"

"Being a bear," Silver inserted.

The other woman's lips twitched. "You want the truth? My mate and I had to carry this menace and his twin strapped to our chests for weeks. They'd howl like banshees anytime we dared put them down."

Pavel, still holding her, kissed his mother on the cheek. "I love you as much today as I did then, Mama."

His mother gave an exasperated shake of her head. "My charming troublemaker." Pulling him down by the ears, she kissed him on both cheeks. "Go find Yasha and tell him I expect you both at the family quarters for dinner tomorrow."

Nodding a friendly good-bye at Silver, the older woman continued on her way. Pavel rubbed the back of his neck, looking more like a sheepish toddler than a grown dominant. "Your parents still treat you like you're five?"

"No." Silver didn't have that type of relationship with her mother and father. "My grandmother, on the other hand, occasionally forgets I can look after myself." As now, with the investigation into who had tried to kill her.

"What about your brother?"

"You hurt him and I'll turn your brain to soup without blinking."

Rocking back on his heels, Pavel scowled. "I'm the one who needs protecting—he totally fooled me with his sweet pretty-faced exterior."

"You seem to have survived."

"I'm a bear. I can handle claws made of ice." With that, Pavel jerked his head toward where a group of people were bringing out boxes. "Want to help with the party setup?"

Silver nodded, though she felt as if she'd lost a layer of protection out there with Moira, a layer of shielding she hadn't even been aware existed.

She was put to work untangling the strings of lights the clan intended to put up as decorations. She'd just finished when Valentin walked back into the Cavern. He was stopped by several of his clanmates, all clamoring for information about the newest member of the clan.

Grinning, he put two fingers to his mouth, let out that piercing whistle. "The cub is fine," he said in the ensuing hush. "Healthy and cuddled up to his mother. He's going to need a little extra care for a while, so Nova will be less available for nonemergency matters. Visitors will be permitted from tomorrow in small groups. Lizabeta will put up a list outside the infirmary where you can sign up."

"What's his name?" Pieter asked in a quiet voice that nonetheless carried.

"That's up to Moira and Leo to announce," Valentin said, then clapped his hands. "Back to work now. And I don't mean party prep if you're assigned to other duties."

Silver was still looking in Valentin's direction when the knot of people around him dispersed, so she saw the small dark-haired woman who went to him. Unlike everyone else, her face wasn't suffused with joy. This emotion was bleaker. Going into Valentin's arms, she just held on tight as he held her in return, his own joy fading away like water rolling off a slope to leave only craggy rock.

Silver looked away from the silent tableau to give Valentin and the dark-haired woman some privacy. Others were doing the same—and she saw pain mirrored on more than one face. Even Pavel, the always laughing joker, had a brutal tension to his jawline as he worked with single-minded focus.

And Silver still didn't have the right to know what would take the laughter out of a clan of bears who never seemed to stop smiling.

That irrefutable fact settled in her gut like a rock.

In an effort to distract herself, she decided to get an update on the investigation into her poisoning. *Arwen.*

Her brother took a few minutes to reply. *I was in a meeting with three of our cousins,* he told her. *All were present when the poison was planted.*

Do you believe it was one of them?

All three are ambitious, particularly Hunter.

He's very loyal to the family.

He was against Kaleb's inclusion.

Yes. Hunter Mercant had argued that they could trust only blood, that Kaleb Krychek was too ruthless a predator to allow into their midst. *He wasn't the only one who didn't agree with that decision. Even you remain uncertain of Kaleb.*

Yet I backed you when you made the call—I trust you to know him far better than any of us. Hunter didn't back you. He voted against Krychek.

That doesn't equal disloyalty. Hunter had always had a strong personality. *Our aunt Ada was also against the measure, and none of us would ever question her loyalty to the clan or to Grandmother.* Because to harm Silver was to harm the line of succession Ena Mercant had personally put in place.

Agreed. But we have to ask these questions, Silver. No matter how much it may hurt.

Arwen only ever betrayed his emotional nature with those he knew would never use that nature against him. Even now, with Silence having fallen and the empaths a power in the PsyNet, he kept his own counsel much of the time.

Today, Silver found herself asking something she hadn't to this point. *Have you made friends with other Es, Arwen? People who understand how your mind works and who can help you decompress?* She was a vault with Arwen's secrets, would protect him to the death, but she'd always been tied to Silence.

Her brother didn't answer for a long time.

Chapter 27

I'M SLOWLY BEGINNING *to do so,* he said at last. *I've formed a growing friendship with an empath named Jaya who works out of the Maldives, as well as a Russian empath named Ruslan. But they both know me only as Arwen, an E of no particular lineage.*

I understand. Sometimes it was difficult to gauge if a person wanted a Mercant for the Mercant's skills or personality, or if it was about gaining access to the Mercant network. The latter was how it had begun with her and Kaleb, but their relationship had undergone a fundamental change years ago.

I'll tell them the truth, Arwen said. *But not yet, not until our friendship is secure, and the fact I'm a Mercant won't change it either way.*

The good thing is that Jaya is completely apolitical—she probably won't have any reaction to my last name except to ask if my family treats me well. A sense of a smile in Arwen's voice, something he rarely betrayed on the psychic plane. *Her family is like ours, very close-knit.*

According to Jaya, they're also half-crazy, but in a good way. Arwen sounded confused about the latter—he clearly needed further exposure to StoneWater bears. *Her mate is an Arrow who I've been avoiding because he'd undoubtedly dig up my family connections. He is very protective of her.*

Arrows and empaths, it was becoming a familiar pairing, the most dangerous predators in the Net protecting the most vulnerable Psy of all. Or perhaps, Silver suddenly thought, it was the other way around: Es using their ability to love to pull the Arrows out of the blood-drenched shadows in which they'd lived for so long.

What about Ruslan? she asked, making a mental note to check up on both Es to be sure they were no threat to Arwen. *Is he apolitical, too?*

Ruslan cares mostly for very old things. He's an archaeologist. I can see him asking for access to our archives to track down an old artefact, but he won't reach for power through me.

Good.

"Who're you talking to?" Valentin's deep rumble of a voice, his hand touching her nape in a blatantly public caress before he took a heavy rope of lights and passed it up to a bear on a tall ladder.

"My brother." Silver's fingers curled into her palm, the urge to touch Valentin coming up against decades of Silence. "How did you know?"

"I have secret psychic powers." A wink, no hint of sadness.

Silver gave in, touched her hand to the beat of his changeling heart. "Are you all right, Alpha Nikolaev?"

Amber eyes locked with her own, his body motionless, the power of him a leashed force. "Why do you ask, Ms. Mercant?"

"I see your hurt," she said, forcing herself to be blunt. "I sense the pain in your clanmates."

The amber didn't dim. "Maybe I'll tell you one day." Valentin tugged on a strand of her hair that had come loose when a light caught on it. "But you'd have to be mine for me to share clan secrets."

Silver's heart kicked. She had a sudden vision of a life where she walked into Denhome every day . . . and slept every night in the protective warmth of Valentin's arms.

You must survive first.

The cold reminder came from the part of her that had grown up conscious of the ticking time bomb in her head. It was currently encased in the remnants of Silent ice, but what would happen when the ice melted?

"A mating bond," she said. "It's a formidable psychic connection." A number of Psy, most famously Sascha Duncan and Faith NightStar, had survived dropping out of the PsyNet when they mated with changelings. *Something* had to be giving their brains the necessary neural feedback.

Else they'd have died within minutes of disconnection.

"It's a bond of the soul." Valentin's voice. "It's a leap of faith."

Silver broke the eye contact, her hands busy on the lights she'd already untangled. Some leaps of faith, she thought, shouldn't be made—not when it put the other party at risk.

This world needed Valentin Nikolaev's big heart and wild spirit.

She couldn't tell him the darkest truth yet, focused on another. "That bond cuts Psy from the PsyNet."

Valentin's frown was in his tone when he said, "You sure?"

"Without a doubt. Mating with a changeling—an alpha or one of his closest people at least—pulls the Psy into what must be a changeling neural network of some kind." Shutting down all access to the psychic highways of the PsyNet.

"I have too many responsibilities in the Net to abandon it," she added before deciding she no longer wished to talk about the harsh realities that lay between them. "I've had minor tactile contact with other members of your clan today without any repercussions. We can continue our physical experiment tonight, this time skin to skin."

Valentin groaned. "Now I have a hard-on," he accused with a scowl.

Feeling the faint edges of an emotion that might have been self-satisfaction, Silver answered the question he hadn't asked but that blazed in his eyes. "Yes, I'm certain it won't hurt me. The minor touches have primed my body for more intimate skin privileges. I may even chance being naked while you—"

"You're deliberately messing with me now, Starlight," Valentin interrupted bad-temperedly. "I'll get my revenge. Just you wait."

Toes curling inside her shoes, Silver said, "Tell me of your new clanmate."

Valentin accepted the change of topic. "He knows he's clan, knows his alpha accepts him: bear cubs need that knowledge to feel secure, feel happy."

Glancing up at the change in his tone, all aggravation and sexual heat lost, Silver glimpsed the shadows that danced across his face, knew once again that StoneWater's secrets were painful ones for its alpha to carry. "It's about family."

Valentin had no need to reply, his response manifest in the way he interacted with each member of his clan and in how his clanmates responded to him.

Valentin was the heart of StoneWater.

Her phone alarm buzzed at that instant, alerting her that she had to return to her work.

Silver turned off the alarm, saw the raft of messages waiting for her. Yet she didn't want to go, the depth of her reaction a silent indicator of how far her Silence had crumbled in a dangerously short time. "I'm the director of EmNet," she reminded herself. "Lives hang in the balance."

Valentin's hand shot out, tugged her against him. She landed with both her palms on his chest, a gasp of air rushing out of her lungs. The kiss he pressed to her lips had shouts going up all around them . . . and her mind threatening to short-circuit.

But she was Silver Fucking Mercant. She could handle a kiss.

Even if it threatened to melt her bones.

Illogical. Irrational.

And yet . . .

He was pure brawn and heat against her, his lips firm, the stubble on his jaw abrasive, the tongue he licked across the seam of her lips bluntly aggressive. Silver should've been put off by that bluntness, but when had she ever been put off by Valentin? Her breasts ached, her blood pumped, and when he scraped his teeth over her lower lip as he released her from the kiss, she felt her eyes flick open, and only then realized she'd closed them to savor the sensations.

Grinning, Valentin ran one hand down her back, lower, squeezed.

The possessive action incited another round of whistles from his clanmates. Pushing off his chest, Silver raised an eyebrow. "Careful, Alpha Valentin. Don't forget who you're tangling with."

"I know you like me, Starlight. Just admit it." He clasped her hips with the rough care of his hands, raised his voice. "She likes me, right?"

"I dunno . . ."

"Looks like she wants to fry your brains . . ."

"But that's normal for a woman with a bear . . ."

"So . . ."

Ignoring the dubious comments, Valentin pointed at Silver. "All your dances are mine tonight, *moyo solnyshko.*"

"We'll see," Silver said, because the man who'd kissed her was an alpha bear who had to be kept on his toes.

IT took her far longer to finish her work than she'd anticipated. Lenik called her in a panic—a Silent panic, of course—because Kaleb had asked him to handle a business matter with which Lenik had zero experience. Neither had Silver when she first started as Kaleb's aide, but she'd been able to lean on the experience of her grandmother, who'd talked her through the complicated steps.

Lenik, by contrast, came from a family that was by no means united. He was alone in a way Silver couldn't comprehend. "There's no need for stress," she said in a calm tone. "Here's how you do it." Connecting with him telepathically using her greater psychic reach, she walked him through the process.

Later, when he came to her and asked her to double-check his work, she did so.

You're far more competent than you give yourself credit for, Lenik, she said, impressed by how quickly he'd absorbed the new information. *Be confident in your work.*

I never expected to be at the forefront, he admitted. *I'm fine when you deal with Kaleb, but dealing with him on my own . . .*

Silver was starting to realize that might be an issue they couldn't solve. Lenik was highly intelligent. He spoke seven languages, had a memory that was near-eidetic, and mathematical skills that surpassed hers, but what he didn't have was the self-assurance necessary to deal with a man of Kaleb's power and demands.

Would you be willing to work under another? It wasn't a question she'd expected to ask, since Lenik was otherwise so well suited to the position of senior aide.

His answer was immediate. *Yes, but I don't know if Kaleb will accept anyone else in the position.*

I'll speak to him. She'd already decided that she couldn't keep her position as Kaleb's senior aide while running EmNet. Both positions suited her, but EmNet was the one that stretched her more now—it was so new and unformed that she was literally laying the foundations as she went, building it from the ground up.

Making a mental note to speak to Kaleb about the senior aide position, she ended the conversation with Lenik, then began to scan the applications that had come through for positions on her team. Though she'd been exhausted last night, she'd placed the ad before she logged off. The recent series of events had brought home to her that she couldn't continue to run EmNet with only an assistant.

In an effort to be transparent and open to all voices—because Valentin was right about EmNet needing to be seen as impartial—Silver hadn't asked for recommendations from the various powerful groups. Rather, she'd placed the job advertisement through major news organizations around the world.

The ad requested that people with various specialist skills apply for a position on the EmNet team, those skills including: administration, coordination of resources, experience managing food supplies and water networks, engineering, and other knowledge that related to disaster relief.

The caliber of the people who'd already sent in applications was extremely high, and they came from across the racial spectrum. One in particular stood out—a human engineer who'd led a military search-and-rescue unit for over a decade, but who could no longer do the work because of a debilitating spinal injury that had left him without the use of the right side of his body.

She'd have to dig deeper into his work history before she decided, but for now, she put him at the top of the list of candidates. Someone with that depth of experience could run entire operations from a remote base.

Silver.

Kaleb's voice was midnight in her mind, immediately recognizable. *Sir.*

I've just received a call from your building manager. She needed to contact you and said she'd lost your personal number.

Silver felt her brow furrow in a physical response to the information.

Thank you. I'll follow up with her. How did she get through directly to you? It was Lenik's job to be a wall through which inconsequential items did not cross.

Sahara is helping Lenik deal with incoming matters, and she thought it might be something important. A short pause. *It appears I need at least three people to replace one Silver Mercant.*

Silver took the opening. *You need to get another aide. Lenik is very good at what he does, but he doesn't want to be at the forefront.*

You mean he thinks I'm the bogeyman. Kaleb's tone was as difficult to read as always. *I have someone in mind*, he added. *I'll have you interview her if you're agreeable, see if she's competent enough to take over.*

Of course, sir. She should've known he'd be two steps ahead. Kaleb Krychek hadn't become the youngest Councilor ever by standing back and letting events overtake him. *When would you like the interview to take place?*

It can wait until your safety is assured. Lenik is doing far better than I expected, and Sahara doesn't mind juggling her duties with the empaths with assisting at the office.

She likes being with you, Silver said, and it was the most intimate thing she'd ever said to her boss. *I apologize, sir*, she said as soon as she realized what she'd done. *I overstepped my bounds.*

I think, Silver, you've earned the right to say what you want to me. And call me Kaleb. You're no longer my senior aide. You're now the director of EmNet, the world's biggest humanitarian organization.

After Silver ended the conversation with Kaleb, she leaned back in her chair and considered the changes in her life over the past months, culminating in her attempt to discover if she could exist beyond Silence. Even now, her mind strained, *listening*. Nothing. No breaches. Her shields were intact even as her Silence fractured.

But this was only the start. A touch. A kiss. Affection.

What would happen when Valentin ran those big hands over her naked body?

Chapter 28

Bears have big bodies and big hearts. No one can ever argue otherwise. But there is a school of thought that says these big, blunt, gorgeous, and often aggravating creatures are the most sensitive changelings of us all. It's hard to hurt a bear . . . but if and when you succeed, their pain is enormous.

—From the March 2078 issue of *Wild Woman* magazine: "Skin Privileges, Style & Primal Sophistication"

VALENTIN RETURNED TO the infirmary an hour after his previous visit. Once again, he found his tiny clanmate sleeping tucked up against his mother's chest, his father's hand on his back. Neither party objected when Valentin picked up the child and—having stripped off his T-shirt as he came in—placed the child against his own bare skin. The baby opened his fist against Valentin's skin, and the fragile new thread inside him, the tug that told him this was one of his clan, grew infinitesimally stronger.

The baby's pulse was so fast, his skin so soft, his bones so fragile. Valentin held him with utmost care, his alpha's heart pounding in joy and fear both. Joy because this was a new member of his clan, a new clanmate to love. Fear because the cub was so very small, so vulnerable. His bear rose to the surface, a powerful beast. Nothing and no one would harm this child so long as Valentin drew breath.

What of the others?

The children who weren't in Denhome, the ones who were far from their alpha's protective arms.

He set his jaw, knew what he had to do. It was the same thing he'd been doing since the terrible day that had shattered StoneWater and left a permanent bruise on Valentin's heart. He'd swung by for a reconnoitering visit early this morning but hadn't made contact.

That was about to change.

Pressing his lips to his newest clanmate's forehead, he murmured to the cub that he was home, that he was safe, that his alpha would permit nothing to happen to him. The boy was in a deep sleep when Valentin handed him back to his parents. "I'll be out of the den for a while," he told them, stroking his hand over Moira's hair, his other hand on Leonid's shoulder.

"If he becomes unsettled, Stasya, Petya, Pasha, or Yasha should be able to soothe him." Bear newborns needed significant contact with their alpha during the first days of life—but if the alpha wasn't available, a strong pack dominant could take his place for a short period.

Moira's eyes grew wet when they met his. "Bring them home, Valya." It was a heartbroken whisper. "I don't like it this way. It's not right."

Her mate's voice was more serrated, less forgiving. "They made their choice. They chose to blame Valya for something that has *never* been his fault."

Squeezing the other man's shoulder, Valentin said, "The adults made the choice. Not the cubs."

Leonid shuddered, blew out a breath. *"Chert."* He took his mate's hand. "Go hug them for all of us."

Valentin left the infirmary only to feel an immediate tug toward the tech chamber, which was slowly becoming Silver's personal domain. Nobody—not even their resident tech expert, Pavel—was worried about the takeover. StoneWater bears were good at a lot of things but most didn't particularly like computer work; they figured if Silver liked it, they could ask her to do things they were supposed to be doing.

Valentin didn't resist the temptation to go to her.

She had on a headset, was having a rapid-fire conversation that seemed to be about the movement of food across borders. A flood, he figured out. There'd been a flood somewhere and people urgently needed clean water. They'd get it because it was Silver Mercant doing the work. He shouldn't interrupt her, but he couldn't leave without letting her know, didn't want her to think she wasn't important to him.

She looked over her shoulder at that moment, a silent question in the crystalline clarity of her eyes. After walking across the rough stone of the floor, he ran the knuckles of one hand over her cheek, then picked up her unlocked organizer and typed in a note.

Heading out for a few hours. Be back in time for the party. Don't dance with anyone else.

Silver responded to whomever she was speaking with, even as her eyes scanned the note. Her fingers flew over the touchscreen.

I've never danced with anyone. I'll wait for you.

His heart, it threatened to burst in his chest.

Dropping a kiss to the curve of her neck with a possessiveness that would claw him bloody if she didn't become his soon, he left her to her work—and went out to confront the heavy cloud of pain that lingered over every single member of his clan, no matter how happy they appeared on the surface.

His bear's fur brushed against the inside of his skin.

No one stopped him when he strode through the Cavern; the cubs who might've rushed him were turned in other directions by parents who accurately read the sense of purpose in Valentin's stride. The crisp chill of the air outside was a welcome kiss, but it did nothing to ease the scalding pain deep inside him.

Valentin had grown up knowing he would one day hold his clan safe.

He'd never expected the horror that had divided them.

Pounding over the earth with the solid, relentless stride of a changeling whose animal was a bear, strong and built to endure, he passed endless groves of trees, the dark green and brown whipping past him in a blur that would become a blanket of white with the oncoming winter. He scented clanmates at times, made sure to avoid them.

Valentin didn't like speaking to anyone when he was on this particular task.

Their pain gouged his own to bleeding.

Erupting out of the trees about fifty feet from the cave system where the members of his clan who'd forsaken him made their home, he caught his breath, shoved back his hair. The sentries spotted him, but they could no more stop him than they could a hurricane—and it hadn't gotten that bad yet. These bears, they weren't disloyal.

They were just lost . . . and heartbroken.

"Fariad, Ilya," he said in greeting. "Any threats I need to be aware of?" He and his strongest dominants made sure to cover this area during their patrols, but the local sentries had responsibility for those who lived inside the cave system.

Both men shook their heads, deep grooves on either side of their mouths. One parted his lips, closed it without making a sound.

Valentin answered the question the blond male couldn't bring himself to ask. "Oksana won't wait forever," he said bluntly. "She's a strong, beautiful woman. If you're not there to be her lover and partner in life, she'll move on." A harsh thing to say, but true; Ilya and Oksana could've been something special—but by leaving her in favor of this group, Ilya had made a choice she might never forgive.

The other man flinched.

His fellow sentry squared his shoulders. "If she truly loved him, she'd wait."

"*Govno*, Fariad." The other man had to know he was talking shit. "No bear female wants to know she comes low on her man's list of priorities."

Both men paled this time. Because Fariad, too, had a woman he adored, but whom he'd left behind. Irina was even prouder than Oksana.

Valentin hardened his heart against the instinctive urge to reassure clanmates in distress. "Are the cubs inside?"

A jerky nod from Ilya.

Leaving them, Valentin entered the cave system and—ignoring the adults who looked at him with wan, drawn faces, or with a deep confused anger that blamed him for this division yet expected him to fix it—went straight to the center. It was nothing like the heart of Denhome, a small dark room in contrast to the sprawling light of the Cavern.

No water, no moss, no vines, a bare glimmer of natural sunlight.

"Mishka!" The shout went up from two tiny mouths, was immediately echoed by a chorus of others. All five cubs who lived here tumbled into him. Laughing, he allowed the small pack to take him to the floor, not chiding them when some shifted in their excitement and clawed him a little. These were his cubs, his babies to love.

"What're you eating out here?" he said, pretending to be flattened by their weight. "You're all getting so big."

They butted against him in pride. Being big was a compliment from and to a bear. He continued to hug them, continued to praise them, until at last, they exhausted themselves into happily limp balls against him. Staying seated on the floor, he looked at the others who'd come to linger in the general area. The teenagers and older children, caught between their primal need for their alpha's approval and their love and loyalty toward their parents.

Valentin wasn't about to make them choose: They were children. This war was not theirs. Rather, he smiled to show them their alpha's love for them was as powerful as ever, his bear in his eyes and his voice as he spoke. "You kissed a girl yet, Marik?"

The teenager went red as, around him, his friends clapped and stamped their feet. But the smile that dawned on his face was real and a far better thing than the stricken look he'd worn before Valentin's teasing comment. "Bears don't kiss and tell," the boy replied. "My alpha taught me that."

Valentin laughed deep in his chest, causing the cubs to chortle and the teens to look a touch less ragged.

Slowly, one by one, the older kids and teens ended up seated around him, telling him their news. Of studies and play and the myriad small pieces of everyday life. Most asked about their friends in Denhome. He shared the news he had, including that of Nika's mating, but kept the biggest piece till last.

"You have a new clanmate," he announced. "Moira gave birth to her and Leo's cub this morning."

Gasps—and not just from the children. The adults who'd whispered quietly into the space were also straining to hear. Valentin caught their shining eyes, their hunger, and the alpha in him couldn't deny them this knowledge of clan. He spoke to the children, but his words were for all of them. "He was more impatient than even you," he said, tickling a bear cub who was trying to crawl up his chest.

The little girl broke out into bearish giggles, her friends jumping in on the fun by tickling her with their little hands and paws—which Valentin made sure weren't clawed. "He wasn't supposed to come for at least three more weeks. It was a good thing Nova was with Moira, as was another friend." He didn't name Silver, because he couldn't trust these clanmates with that precious piece of his heart.

It was a vicious blow to an alpha to even think that about members of his clan, but he had to start getting hard-eyed about this. The time for a final decision was nearly here. But not today, not on a day of celebration.

"Nova's the best!" a tiny boy cried. "I like her *shoes*!"

Grinning, Valentin grabbed the cub into his arms to smother his face in kisses. The boy squealed with laughter and clambered up to sit on Valentin's shoulders afterward. "Nova's looking after the cub right now—but don't worry, he's tough."

"He's a bear!" the children said in concert.

"Exactly." Valentin nodded proudly. "He'll grow strong enough for play soon."

The solid little boy on his shoulders pulled his hair. "Can we see him?"

He felt the shift in the emotions that swirled around the adults and teens in the room. Instead of facing a question that could shatter the joy, he tumbled the cub over his head and into his lap. "What do you think you're doing assaulting your alpha?" he grumbled. "Big bears have been known to eat small bears who aggravate them."

He faked growling as he brought the cub's arm to his mouth as if to take a bite.

Laughing too hard to speak, the boy just said, "Mishka!"

His infectious laughter distracted the little ones and the older ones weren't about to poke that particular bear, so Valentin left the question unanswered. Not long afterward, a teenager asked another question, his tone wistful. "Are you having a big party to celebrate?"

"With dancing?" the girl next to him said.

Valentin nodded. "Of course. It's a new life in the clan, a new voice in Denhome." A Denhome that was far too empty right now.

Normally, he'd have said, "All are welcome," but today, he swallowed those words, despite the hurt that caused inside him. "You should have a party, too."

The cubs took up the cry, and he knew it'd be an easy wish for the adults to approve. What they'd have a difficult time with was that they hadn't been invited to join in the celebration at Denhome. As he rose after interacting with the kids for fifteen more minutes, he saw shock in more than one pair of adult eyes.

There was anger, too. Clenched fists and red bursts on cheekbones.

Valentin held each and every gaze, showed them he was about to make the call he should've made months ago. The only thing that had held him back was his abiding love for his clan. But even an alpha bear's heart couldn't take blow after blow without breaking. "Celebrate," he said in a quiet tone. "The rest can wait."

HE returned to the den *needing* touch, needing comfort. He didn't want it from any of his clan. He wanted it from a telepath who'd barely begun to accept her capacity to feel. But he'd go to her anyway. Not to the tech room, but to her own. He could scent the ice and fire of her in that direction, a thread that whispered his name.

Yet, though he wanted to arrow straight to her, he was alpha. His needs didn't come first. He cuddled the little ones who ran over to him, spoke to clanmates who asked hesitantly about family or friends in the lost group. He discussed ongoing business matters with two of his seconds, congratulated the team that had so beautifully decorated the Cavern, went to the infirmary to see his newborn clanmate again, and dropped by the kitchen to say hi to the cooks working hard to put together a celebratory feast.

By the time he got to Silver, need was a wild creature gnawing on his bones.

He forced himself to knock.

Silver pulled open the door almost at once. She was still wearing the headset, had an organizer in hand. But the instant she saw him, she said, "I'll call you back," and took off the headset. Putting that and the organizer on the bed behind her, she held out a hand. "What's wrong?"

He couldn't speak.

Taking her hand, he stepped inside and kicked the door shut. Then he wrapped his arms around her and crushed her close, his body vibrating with the force of the emotions tearing him apart. Inside him, his bear roared in anguish.

Chapter 29

This child of my child, Silver, she is brilliant firelight, incandescent in her intelligence and inner strength. To watch her become Silent . . . it is the only way, and yet I cannot help but wonder if we will lose part of her under the weight of the conditioning.

—Personal diary entry, Ena Mercant (November 14, 2059)

VALENTIN EXPECTED SILVER to protest at how he'd engulfed her.

But Silver Mercant, he should've remembered, was made of sterner stuff.

She put her arms around him and, after a brief pause, began to stroke his back. He knew at that instant that he was the absolute focus of her attention. She wasn't telepathing, wasn't doing anything but concentrating on him. He knew that in his gut, as he knew each and every member of his clan—even the ones who'd walked away.

When Silver finally spoke, it was many minutes later. "I've never known you to be lost for words, Valyusha. I should take advantage of this momentous circumstance to tell you all the ways in which you've annoyed me since we first met."

Light began to dawn inside him, his bear suffused with joy. His Starlight was *playing* with him. Really playing.

"First," she said, "bringing over documents in hard copy but never in triplicate as requested. Then asking me to copy them for you right then because you wanted to be sure we didn't mess with the contract."

His lips curved. He remembered how she'd icily do the task personally rather than passing it on to her assistant. Then she'd hand him his copy, usually with a pithy comment about how his satisfaction was her utmost priority. He'd almost kissed her a hundred times during those exchanges.

"We won't mention how you continually breached my security, forcing my cousin to run a full security update five times in the space of a single month."

As well he should, Valentin thought with a scowl that came straight from his bear. His first few entries had been ridiculously easy.

"Also the *zefir* you somehow managed to leave on my desk while I wasn't looking. The sweets would've been wasted if I hadn't been aware of a family on the lower floor of my building who would appreciate them."

"You didn't eat even one?" he grumbled at her, the sound a roll of thunder.

"I was Silent," was the prim response.

Bear and man both froze. "Was?"

"Partially." A pause. "The process is gradual regardless of the individual concerned, but I have to be more careful than perhaps even an Arrow."

He rubbed his jaw gently against her temple, cuddling her impossibly closer, no longer for himself but because he needed to look after her. "The suicide numbers you told me about?"

"Yes," Silver said. "And no. I have a mutation in my genome."

Valentin squeezed his eyes shut against a storm of emotion. For a Psy of his Starlight's standing and power to admit a vulnerability, it was a trust so deep that he knew he had to reciprocate or he'd break something fragile that had barely formed. "My clan is hurt in a way no clan should ever be hurt. We're broken in two."

Silver shifted back enough that she could look into his face. "To the outside world, StoneWater remains a powerful clan no one wants as an enemy."

She was trying to comfort him. Cool and in-control Silver Mercant felt his pain and wanted to ease it. Valentin had never had a chance resisting her. Now . . . now, he could easily become her slave.

Needing to caress her, he ran his hand over her hair, then, ah hell, he unraveled her neat twist so he could fist all those silky blonde strands in his hand. "Oops."

"You've been wanting to do that since day one."

Valentin gave her his patented innocent expression.

Silver didn't speak, just took a sudden, jagged step back. He held on, not understanding she was trying to sever their physical connection—not until her eyes lost all color, turning a fathomless black. He broke contact on the chilling realization that she was overloading. "Tell me what to do."

Silver lifted her head, her eyes obsidian and her breathing erratic. "Don't go."

Valentin's heart pulsed, held inside her slender hand. "You couldn't make me leave if you had a forklift and a pack of feral wolves to drive it." He looked deep into her obsidian eyes, saw his Starlight staring back at him. "You look like a magical warrior princess with those eyes. All wild and deadly."

"I attempt to look deadly every day."

"Yes, *moyo solnyshko*, but usually, it's lethal ice princess."

SILVER heard Valentin's words, but she couldn't concentrate on them; data cascaded through her brain, threatening to short-circuit her ability to think. Something had fractured. Not her PsyNet shields, or Arwen would've been there, protecting her against exposure to the millions of minds in the psychic network.

Internal shields.

She tracked the breach, saw immediately what had triggered the cascade: *Too much sensation.*

She'd seen the raw anguish in the rigid tension of Valentin's body, had reacted instinctively to give him what he needed. Knowing he'd come to her when he needed an anchor, this big alpha bear, it had fundamentally altered the balance of emotion inside her.

It wasn't just the physical contact that had pushed her over—it was the torrent of feeling that had smashed through her defenses. She felt a compulsion to reach out to him, even knowing it would undo all the work she'd just done to get her mind in order. "Emotion makes me stupid." Silver's intelligence had always been her biggest weapon.

Valentin folded his arms, his eyebrows drawing together over his eyes. "We're all a little stupid when it comes to the people who matter."

"I'm not."

"Would you stand in the way of a bullet aimed at your grandmother?"

"She's my alpha. Of course I would."

"She's older, while you're young, ready to take over. You should let her die."

Silver stared at the hard angles of his face, a face that wasn't beautiful by any typical measure and yet that was *her* standard of masculine beauty. Harsh and rough and unashamedly male. "Stop making sense. Go back to being unbearable."

His eyes went amber, his arms uncrossed, and then he began to laugh, the sound filling the room, filling her. When he looked like he wanted to grab her and tumble her to the bed in that wild bear way, she didn't tell him not to do it. That he didn't caused her awakening emotions to twist into a knot—this powerful alpha was fighting his instincts for her . . . as she was fighting hers for him.

"I'll be beary good," he promised, his face lit from within.

She had the sense of playing with a wild thing. "Now you're just beyond bearing."

He laughed so hard he fell onto his back on the floor like one of the cubs. It took her only a small movement to lie on the floor beside him. Bracing herself on her forearms, she said, "This is a ridiculous conversation."

"But fun." He tugged on a strand of her hair, seemed to get fascinated with the cool gold fall, bunching it in his hands, running it through his fingers, taking a lock to rub it against his cheek.

Silver's heart felt too big inside her.

Careful of her newly rebuilt shields but unwilling to turn back at the first hurdle, she put one hand on the massive width of Valentin's chest. "If I was yours," she said, "how would you treat me?"

"Like a fucking queen." A slight pull on her hair, Valentin tugging her closer with his fisted grip. "I'd also probably drive you a little insane," he said with a shrug. "Bears can be a bit hardheaded—that's not just rumor. But I think your head can be just as hard, so we'll be fine. I'd also touch you. A lot."

The scowl returned, as did the grumbling rumble in his chest. "But only if it wouldn't hurt you. So long as it didn't, I'd probably throw you on a bed, or against a wall every single spare second and tease you, kiss you, pet you until you hauled me down and demanded naked skin privileges."

That primal mental image spoke to the long-dormant wildness in her, the girl who'd once run through a country lane screaming because Silence was a cage and she wanted to be free. That country lane was on a Mercant estate where their children were trained—and where Silver had accepted the cage as a necessity.

The rules, however, had changed. "I want to kiss you again." Wanted to feel his stubble against her cheek, taste the blatant masculinity of him with her tongue.

A harsh exhale. "Come here then." He placed his hand on her lower back, nudging her up and onto him. She didn't resist, soon found herself on a warm wall of muscle, his scent overlaid with a hint of sweat that only made his scent deeper, earthier.

"Is my weight bearable?"

His cheek-creasing smile made her stomach flip, the sensation startling. "Starlichka, you can use me as a mattress anytime and for as long as you please." He moved his hand to her lower curves, squeezed with a blunt appreciation that had her fingers digging into his pectoral muscles.

"You, Ms. Mercant, are the sexiest woman I've ever laid eyes on." This time when his chest vibrated, it was against the hard points of her nipples. "I've been wanting to peel you out of your suits since the first day I saw you."

Shifting higher up his body as a hot pulse coalesced between her legs,

Silver traced the shape of his lips with a fingertip. He groaned, tried to bite her finger. "Stop teasing me." The next bite was on her throat.

She felt it through her entire body.

Putting one hand on his shoulder, she pushed down. It was like trying to budge a brick wall. A warm, muscled wall determined to stay exactly where he was. "I'm doing the kissing." She made her tone icy.

Of course it had little effect on the bear below her. He squeezed her buttocks again, cupping the cheeks with smug possessiveness. "Do it then."

"My way."

Thunderclouds darkened his expression. "You're not a kissing expert."

"I'm a fast learner." She shut him up by pressing her lips to his.

He groaned and licked his tongue over her lips.

She broke contact. *"Valentin."*

Dropping his head to the floor, he patted the flesh he'd been fondling. "Sorry. Gentleman bear. Promise."

This time when she pressed her lips to his, he let her lead. The contact was intensely intimate, the feel of his jaw under her palm rough, while his lips were firm but mobile. Taking her lead from him, she licked her tongue over the seam of his lips. Shuddering below her, Valentin moved his free hand to gently cup the back of her head. His conscious tenderness made things deep inside her tug, melt.

As if he were caressing her heart.

Valentin parted his lips. It was an invitation. It was also a dare.

Silver took it. And he brushed his tongue against hers.

Shivering, she broke contact, feeling drunk on him.

His pupils were dilated, his skin flushed, his hands still on her. "I think, *moyo solnyshko,*" he said solemnly, "we should kiss a lot so you can become an expert."

Silver brushed her cheek against the stubble of his jaw just to experience the sensation, drank in his groan. "I begin to understand why my race fought so hard against Silence when it was first introduced."

Valentin squeezed the back of her neck. "Give me your mouth again."

Silver knew it was a bad idea to escalate things so quickly, but she was discovering she had few defenses against this alpha bear. Bracing her palms on either side of his head, she kissed him with unleashed possessiveness of her own. "Will you carry my scent now?"

His smile was slow and very, very satisfied. "You're trying to brand me."

Locking eyes with his, she fisted a hand in his hair. "Answer the question."

He fondled her some more. "I already carry your brand, Starlight." A nuzzle against her before a sudden scowl marred his features. "Some *durak* is coming this way."

Silver didn't have a chance to respond before there was a knock on her door.

VALENTIN had to yell at Yakov to go bother someone else before the other man would stop his irritating knocking. Yakov yelled back, "Here I was, doing you a favor! Pasha would've barged in, and Stasya would've had a camera to capture you in flagrante."

"Do you want me to beat you dead?"

Yakov laughed. "I smell a frustrated bear."

"*Yakov.*"

Laughing without remorse, his second finally left, but not before calling out, "If you don't come join the party, Stasya will be your next visitor!"

By that time, Silver, her lips kiss-swollen because he was a barbarian gentleman bear, had pushed off him to ready herself for the party. On the floor still, Valentin tried to think of frigid showers and mangy wolves. His erection laughed at him. So he made himself think of how Silver's eyes had gone black, of how she'd so abruptly broken contact.

Ice trickled down his spine, took care of his eager cock.

Silver wasn't his yet. Silence might yet succeed in stealing away his mate. His bear's heart had known who she was to him for a long time. It was the man who'd shied away, scared of falling so hard and deep for a woman who might never look at him the same way.

But, *chert*, who had he been kidding? He'd been hers from day one.

Today he watched her put on her makeup; she'd already fixed the hair he'd had such fun messing up, and she'd changed into a thin green sweater with winter sparkles that Nova had given her. He knew she'd say nothing about his own T-shirt and ripped jeans—Silver saw him exactly as he was—but he was sweaty from the run to and back from seeing the cubs in the dissenting group.

"Wait for me," he said before going to his own room.

Jumping into the shower, he washed off the sweat. That done, his wet hair rubbed dry and left to do what it would, he changed into less-ripped jeans and a clean shirt in a dark gray that he hadn't worn before. Folding up the long sleeves, he walked over to knock on Silver's door.

She opened it, looked him up and down. "I'm not sure I recognize you."

Wanting to kiss her perfectly glossed lips, he spread out his arms. "How do I look in your favorite color?"

"Inexplicably respectable, though I see you still haven't found your comb."

Chuckling because he could tell Starlight liked his hair just fine, he held out his hand.

She gave him a cool look . . . but she took his hand, his ice queen who burned with a passionate fire.

Silver Mercant, he knew, would fight to the death, break all the rules, ignore every boundary, for those who were her own.

Valentin wanted to be one of those people.

His bear's heart stubborn with the determination to win her, he led her to the Cavern and into the warmth and joy and chaos of a party thrown by StoneWater bears. This time, it would be a big one, as the following day was a weekend. His heart swelled. "No one throws a better party." Silver's touch, the happiness in this room, it took the edge off the gnawing pain that was his sundered clan.

"For some reason, I don't see you as an impartial judge."

Valentin grinned before holding up a hand for silence. For a clan of rowdy bears, they shushed each other very quickly. Especially after an elder or three whacked the backs of certain heads.

"Today we celebrate the birth of a new clanmate!" He held up his hand again to quiet the second round of roars, this time accompanied by foot stomping. "Before we start the party, however, I think we should know the guest of honor's name."

Before the noise could start up again, he hollered, "Settle down! This is a newborn bear we're talking about, not one of you ruffians!"

Laughter, followed by more shushing, elbows being dug into the sides of the overloud. "Keep it at this volume until our littlest clanmate is back in the infirmary," he ordered. "Or I swear I'll crack some skulls."

Leaving Silver with a pat on the butt that had her raising a pointed eyebrow and clanmates smirk-smiling as they tried to pat the butts of their own lovers, he turned to go bring Moira, Leo, and their cub into the Cavern.

And Silver's hand patted his ass in full view of his clan.

Chapter 30

THE NOISE THIS time around was of a level that threatened to blow off the Cavern roof. Ridiculously pleased, Valentin looked over his shoulder and met those eyes of glorious silver that hid so much. "Can't keep your hands off me? I knew it."

Her gaze lit with an inward fire in answer.

Feeling happier than he had in forever, a damn puppy dancing on his heart, he said, "You calm them down before I get back here with the cub."

He knew she'd get the job done. Clan of bears versus Silver Mercant? No contest.

He was proved right five minutes later when he returned with Moira and Leonid, Moira cradling their newborn in her arms. The baby was awake in that drowsy infant way. He'd focused on Valentin's face long enough to know his alpha was there and happy with him, but was now blinking sleepily against his mama's skin, Moira holding the baby to her chest, her shirt buttons open to permit it.

No one would've cared if she'd turned up buck naked; changelings were far more comfortable with nudity than either humans or Psy. But Moira needed to stay warm, as did her baby, so she was wearing loose fleece pants and one of her much bigger mate's checked shirts. The sleeves were rolled halfway up her forearms, the tails hanging loosely, her hair in a careless knot.

She glowed, a woman who shone with love.

"Oooh." The subdued sound of awe and delight whispered toward them from an otherwise silent horde of waiting bears, deathly excited tiny gangsters included.

Silver stood a little to the side, but when Valentin held out his hand, she didn't hesitate to join him. His Starlight had made up her mind, and she'd decided on him. Valentin wasn't giving her back. He wanted to stomp his feet and roar his defiance to the heavens. Only his alpha awareness of the baby stopped him.

"You have the floor," he said to the new parents.

Moira, in turn, smiled up at her mate. "You tell them, honey."

Cuddling his mate and baby to his side, Leonid said, "Our cub's premature arrival caught us a touch unprepared with a name—but then we saw his sweet face and saw the mischief well-hidden, and we had it." He kissed his mate on the temple. "StoneWater, meet Danil 'Danusha' Popov."

Wide grins split every face in the Cavern except for Silver's—she was looking at the baby with intent care. When Moira passed the infant to Valentin, and he went down on one knee so all the curious small bears could come greet their new clanmate, he was aware of her staying close, as curious as the cubs.

When more little bodies wriggled closer, however, she moved out of the way to give them room. A few small plump fingers dared touch the baby's cheek. The newborn's happiness at meeting his tiny clanmates pounded inside Valentin, the knowledge of an alpha nothing he could explain.

He just knew the newborn was happy to be here, in amongst his clan. But he also knew when the littlest one of them all began to tire. "You can see him later," he promised the cubs. "He needs to rest now."

"Good night, baby," whispered several voices in unison.

Valentin rose and returned the newest member of StoneWater to his parents before escorting the couple back to the infirmary. Afterward, he found Nova. "Come play with us," he said, because healers had a way of giving and giving without pause. "I think those three will be happy alone for an hour or two."

Nova's eyes searched his face. "How are they?"

Valentin knew she wasn't talking about the young family. Smile fading, he said, "Not tonight, Nova."

Tonight was a celebration.

Tonight, Silver had patted his ass.

The memory cut through his renewed anguish to put a grin on his face.

Nova immediately narrowed her eyes. "What have I missed?"

"You'll have to ask Chaos." Blowing her a kiss when she glared, he backed out of her office. "See you later, Evanator."

She threatened to throw medical supplies at his head. It only made his grin deepen as he returned to the Cavern and to Silver—who was currently seated in the middle of a semicircle of astonished cubs, ages three to seven. The noise level in the rest of the Cavern—the party in full swing—kept him from picking up their conversation until he was less than two feet away.

". . . really not allowed to smile?" Nurlan asked in an awed whisper.

"No," Silver said. "Under Silence, no one is allowed to smile or laugh or cry."

"But what if you hurted yourself?" another small voice asked.

"It doesn't matter," Silver said. "You are expected to control your reaction and to not cry or otherwise betray your emotions."

A small hand patted Silver's knee. "Did you cry inside?"

Silver's eyes locked on the speaker's face. "You're very clever. What's your name?"

"Svetlana Valeria Kuznetsov," was the carefully spoken answer. "Mostly, I'm Sveta. My mama and papa and Mishka call me Svetulia a lot."

"Yes, Sveta, when I was small, I cried inside because it hurt to hide my emotions," Silver said with a razor-sharp honesty that made her more like a bear than she knew. "But after a while, I learned not to cry inside, either."

"That sounds sad." Dima's expression was mournful.

"It was all I knew," Silver said. "As being a changeling bear is all you know."

Thoughtful frowns on a number of faces. "Do you like being noisy now?" Sveta asked after a long pause.

"Noisy?"

"'Cause you were Silent before?"

"Oh, I see." Silver took time to consider the question. "Emotion—being noisy—is new to me. But . . . yes, I think I like being noisy. The world is a much more eclectically beautiful place with emotion in it, despite the clear disadvantage of losing the power of pure rationality."

"You talk funny," Arkasha volunteered. "I like you though."

"Thank you. I like you, too."

"And me?" asked more than one voice.

"All of you," Silver said. "You've been very welcoming to me."

A rainbow of smiles, pure innocent joy.

"Now," Silver said, rising to her feet, "I think you should go join the party."

Valentin came forward before the cubs could swarm her with hugs. Gathering them up in his arms with a growling rumble that made them squeal, he squeezed and kissed and played until they ran off to go raid the dessert table. No one would be too strict today, though it was likely they'd be given actual food at some point to make sure they didn't turn into sugar monsters.

"You're good with the little beasts," he said to Silver, putting his hand on her hip just because he could.

"Children are children. But Sveta is perceptive—this isn't the first time I've heard her ask an incisive question for a child of her age. Have you had her tested for empathy?"

Valentin scratched his jaw. "A psychic power?"

"Psy did intermarry and intermate with other races pre-Silence. The genes are swimming around in the wider gene pool."

"I've always known she was sensitive, that I had to take extra care with her"—even with her tiny gangster buddies, Sveta was always the caretaker—"but I figured that meant she's a baby healer. Nova thinks so, too."

"Interesting." Silver fixed the collar of his shirt. "Empathy might be present in all changeling healers. There are so many things the races don't know about one another because Silence split us in three."

Valentin turned so she could more easily fuss over him. So everyone could *see* her fussing over him. No, he wasn't subtle. He was a bear. "I don't know if it was all Silence," he said as she smoothed out a wrinkle. "Changelings do a good job of staying in our caves." Their close-knit pack and clan structures gave them their strength, but also made it difficult for outsiders to break through.

Music boomed into life, a heavy bass beat.

Unable to wait to hold Silver in his arms, Valentin hauled her into a dance. He made sure to keep her back to a wall, so that people wouldn't bump into her, the bulk of his body her living shield. His reward was to have her snuggled deliciously close, until his bear rolled in her scent like a cub.

"You move like you were born to move against me, Starlight," he murmured against her ear. "We're going to be so fucking good together naked."

SILVER ran her hand up Valentin's shirt, flicked open one button, two. Her fingers curled into the crisp mat of hair below. She wondered what it would be like to rub her naked breasts against the crispness.

"Silver." Dark eyebrows gathering over eyes of onyx, his expression stern. "Stop that or I'll forget to be a gentleman bear and start devouring you."

The rumbling sound vibrated against her fingertips, made her breasts ache. "Okay."

"Okay?" Eyes going amber, he glared at her. "You have terrible timing." He pulled back, grabbed her head with both hands, looked into her eyes. "I'm alpha, Starlichka. I can't leave the party yet."

"We can come back." A sense of urgency pounded at her. A nameless panic that said she had to take this opportunity before it slipped forever out of her grasp. Because a knowing had begun to buzz at the back of her brain, a buzz she didn't want to hear.

Expression altering to a perceptiveness that reminded Silver that this wild, affectionate bear was also a highly intelligent opponent on the business field, Valentin searched her gaze. "What's wrong?"

"I'm eager to experience intimate skin privileges."

"You're lying to me, Starlight," he said, making no effort to hide his hurt that she'd do that.

And Silver learned that his hurt was a blow to her own heart. "It's a lie of omission," she whispered, their bodies and minds locked in an intimate world surrounded by the thunder of a bear celebration. "I'll tell you the rest after." When it wouldn't taint the memory, when it wouldn't shatter the moment into jagged splinters.

"I'll hold you to that."

"I would expect nothing less." Sliding her arms around the warm bulk of him, she placed her cheek against his shoulder, her height suiting his.

He enveloped her in the warmth of his embrace, one hand sliding up her back and the other down to her lower curves again. Yet this time, it wasn't sexual. It was possessive and protective in that rough Valentin way, a way to which she was becoming used.

"You going to overload?" he asked as the bass beat of his heart became her anchor. "Don't you dare lie to me about that, *moyo solnyshko*. If you make me harm you, I'll never forgive you."

Silver threw up another desperate layer of shielding. "I have it under control." No lie. Not yet.

Sinking into this instant when she was free of a cage that had saved her and imprisoned her, she cleared her mind of all other thoughts, her attention only on the wild, beautiful man who called her his sunshine and who saw starlight in her eyes.

The steady beat of his huge heart.

The raw warmth of a body that would protect her against every threat.

The earth and green of his scent, so familiar to her now that she searched for it when it was missing.

The clan's joyous celebration was background music, shouts and footsteps all part of the larger whole.

Then came the tug of small fingers on her leg.

Startled, she looked down to see the Barnacle; he was dressed in dark blue jeans and a black shirt that was—as yet—unstained with food. "May I have this dance?" he asked with such perfect politeness and enunciation, she knew he was repeating the exact words someone had taught him.

Though Silver wanted to drown in Valentin, to build a lifetime of memories in a moment, not wounding a child's heart took priority. She'd have made the same decision in Silence, though then, she'd have justified it by saying the child was more vulnerable and needed attention.

"I'm afraid," she said to the bear who'd hold her forever if she asked, "I have a better offer."

Valentin scowled down at the tiny interloper. "You trying to steal my girl, Dima?"

Throwing out his arms, the three-year-old did an excellent imitation of a bearish bellow. Laughing in an open pride that had Dima strutting, Valentin released Silver. "I'll be back to reclaim what's mine, Starlight."

The promise rang with the power of an alpha.

A second later, he was tugged into a dance by a clanmate holding a glass of champagne, and Dima was gripping Silver's hands as they "danced." And Silver heard whispers from the trees far beyond the thumping noise of the Cavern.

Not yet, she told her brain. *Give me a little more time. Just a little more.* Enough to build memories that would have to last her through the coming decades of Silence.

Chapter 31

Dear Aunt Rita,
   I'm about to share intimate skin privileges with a highly dominant bear for the first time. Any advice?
   ~ Excited Non-bear

Dear Excited Non-bear,
   Cancel all your engagements for the forthcoming week and hold on for the ride.
   ~ Aunt Rita

—From the February 2080 issue of *Wild Woman* magazine:
"Skin Privileges, Style & Primal Sophistication"

IT WAS MIDNIGHT by the time Valentin could get away, and by then, his gentleman tendencies had worn so thin, he'd have been terrified of scaring his mate—if that mate weren't Silver Mercant, who was as tough as steel and who said a firm yes when he asked her if she was ready for a night of wild debauchery.

Then she patted his ass again.

Cock threatening to snap in two if he didn't feel her possessive fingers on his skin soon, he took her not to his room but to hers. So she'd be comfortable. So she'd permit him to do even more naughty, sexy things to her.

He had plans to devour her from head to toe then go back for seconds.

Shutting and locking the door behind him, he rid himself of his boots and socks, began to unbutton his shirt. Silver's eyes followed his every movement, and then she was there, parting the sides of his shirt and pushing it off his shoulders. It fell to the floor in a soft murmur of sound he barely heard over the pounding of his heart.

"I love the way you feel." Silver ran her nails through his chest hair, the light scratch like a red rag to a bull. Grabbing her up into his arms, he strode to the bed, threw her down on the mattress. He didn't say she could tell him to stop at any time—if Silver Mercant wanted him to stop, she'd make it head-ringingly clear.

"I want these off," he said, and pulled off her boots, throwing them over his shoulder.

Eyes on him, Silver sat up and lowered her hands to the bottom of that thin sweater with sparkles in it. It was gone a second later and he could see her bra. It was plain black, no frills, and it set him afire. Crashing onto the bed, he took her down—careful to make sure his weight and strength didn't hurt her.

He was a bear, not a goddamn savage.

"You have amazing tits," he said, his filters all off and one hand on a creamy globe cupped by the black of her bra.

She arched under his hand. He squeezed harder. She shuddered, her eyes going black. But since she didn't tell him to stop, he figured that, this time around, the obsidian was a good sign. Gripping her jaw with his free hand, he pressed his mouth to hers, his kiss all tongue and demand. Silver gave back as good as she got, wrapping her arms and legs around him and lashing her tongue against his.

Groaning, he ground his erection into the vee between her thighs. "I'm going to fuck you so hard, Starlight."

Silver's response was to bite down on his lower lip.

Her filters, too, were clearly off.

Chest rumbling in pleasure that his mate was as mad for him as he was for her, he lifted up, breaking her hold so he could rip off her jeans. He did literally rip them off, the fabric shredding under his claws and harsh pulls. Her panties were black, too. He left them for the moment because he liked how the black framed her otherwise creamy flesh.

Throwing the shreds of the jeans aside, he ran his hands up her thighs. Eyes dark and mysterious, Silver spoke. "Take off your pants." It was a demand. He liked it.

Playing with her, he braced himself on his arms above her and bent down as if doing a push-up. "Make me," he dared against her lips.

Silver scissored her legs, surprising him onto his back.

"Where did you learn that?" he asked, happy to be bested because it meant her hands were now at the waistband of his jeans. *O Bozhe!* Silver's fingers were brushing his engorged cock as she worked.

Making no attempt to hide his desire, he just watched her.

"Simply because I'm not a physical person doesn't mean I don't know how to defend myself should the need arise," she said, the cool words at odds with the flush on her skin, the scent of her arousal thick in the air.

"Oh, I think you're a very physical person, Starlight." Without Silence, Silver Mercant was a bear under the skin.

As she proved when she tugged off his pants to reveal the black boxer briefs he wore underneath. He let her get the pants off and drop them over the side of the bed before he retook control, flipping her onto her back and nuzzling a wet kiss to her neck. Her response was nails digging into his back. "You like my tongue, *moyo solnyshko*?" he asked with a stroke of his hand down her body. "Let me show you what else I can do with it."

Taking off her bra with more care than he'd shown her pants—he liked that bra, liked how she looked in it—he threw it aside and filled his hands with the bounty of her breasts. Her nipples were a deep pink, and they made his mouth water. Not one to resist temptation when that temptation was Silver—*his* Silver—he lowered his head and feasted. Her cry was sharp, her hands gripping his hair tight and her body twisting under his.

Sucking not just her nipple but part of her breast into his mouth, he drew up with his teeth scraping her flesh, then flicked his tongue over the tiny hurt. When he repeated the caress on her other breast, his hand squeezing and petting the breast he'd already wet with his mouth, Silver said, "I want to bite you." The words were breathless.

"Good." He returned to his pleasurable task. "You taste even better than I imagined. I want to eat you up."

Silver's nails scored his back.

Making a deep, rumbling sound in his chest, he bit lightly at her nipple in mock punishment. She jerked . . . and pulled hard at his hair. He laughed against her. Yes, his Starlight knew very well how to deal with her bear mate.

Kissing his way down the center of her body, he licked a line along the waistband of her panties. It took him a second to remove that impediment. Two rapid claw swipes and he was done.

"I don't have that many clothes," Silver reminded him as he drew one of her thighs over his shoulder.

"Stop wearing panties. Problem solved." Before she could respond to his very sensible suggestion, he gave in to the compulsion to taste the erotic musk of her and, pulling her other leg over his shoulder, buried his face in her pussy.

Her jerk all but arched her off the bed this time.

But she didn't tell him to stop.

Thank God.

Valentin licked and sucked and petted and drank her in. She was liquid need and delicate softness and so intoxicating, his head spun. By the time he attempted to slide a finger into her sheath, she was wet enough that he had zero trouble. Except for one fact. "*Chert voz'mi.* You're too tight." He looked up with a scowl, saw her looking down.

Licking her lips, her breath coming in gasps, she said, "I didn't plan on having sexual intercourse with an overendowed bear or I would've stretched myself out."

He growl-laughed, delighted with her. "Yes, I *am* overendowed. Glad you noticed." His bear swaggered, full of himself. "Now let's make sure you can take me over and over and over again." Dipping his head, he proceeded to do his best to drive his mate deliriously insane. So insane that maybe she'd lower the shields that kept them from mating.

He was wide open to her in every possible way.

Her thighs quivered, her pussy clenching on his tongue and the thick intrusion of his fingers, and her scream of pleasure loud enough to please his primal heart. But he was just getting started. Rising back over her deliciously limp body, he kissed every inch he passed, rubbing his stubble against her to mark her all over. He fondled her breasts because he could, kissed her already swollen mouth hot and deep.

"I can taste myself on your lips."

The huskiness of her voice was a band around his cock that squeezed mercilessly. "You taste like the best kind of honey," he said before making his way back down.

This time around, he was all about the main course.

He used his teeth on the delicate folds of her pussy, pushed in his fingers with a little more force, spread them inside her to prepare her for the intrusion of his cock.

She came again in a screaming rush, two of his fingers inside her, the pads pressing on a spot he'd made it his business to learn as a young man who *was* big enough that even bear females gave him a jaundiced eye. It had all been for this, to make sure he could pleasure his slender mate with her tight internal muscles and her eyes gone midnight and her pussy that was so, so wet for him.

Getting up onto his knees after a last possessive lick, he managed to tug off his briefs, then lifted up her legs, her knees hanging over his arms, and said, "Ready?" The eager head of his cock nudged the scorching heat of her.

Fuck, he was going to lose it.

Silver raised her arms above her head, her breasts taunting him . . . and smiled. "Do it."

Valentin's mind short-circuited. The only thing that kept him from just rutting into her like a caveman was the knowledge that this was her first time. Shoving her thighs wide, he pushed in, slow but relentless. The instant he saw pain whisper across her features, he froze. "No?"

"I said," she growled, "*do* it!"

Rumbling back at her, he did, pushing in hard and deep. Her gasp was lost in his loud groan of pleasured pain. "Your pussy is like a vise around my cock."

She squeezed her muscles even tighter.

"Mean, mean Starlichka." Dropping her legs, he shifted so that he was braced over her.

She wrapped her legs around him. "I read an article in a magazine I found in the Cavern that said men like it when women do that during sexual skin privileges."

"This man does, except when he's about to blow his nut on a single stroke." Kissing her, he drew back an inch, maybe two, then thrust back in. And the mean, mean woman in bed with him squeezed him tight again.

Valentin was only a bear. He lost it, pulling out and shoving back in in two hard, fast strokes before his spine locked and he exploded inside her in a gush of wet heat.

SILVER had made a conscious decision to deliberately breach the final walls of Silence and face the consequences. She'd known going in what those consequences were likely to be—especially after the earlier overload. Yet despite her foreknowledge, it still felt as if her mind had exploded outward, bloody shards digging into her.

It didn't matter.

Not when she could feel Valentin's heart pounding against her, his body a heavy weight. She could barely breathe and still it made no difference to her. Because she understood now, understood that it wasn't the sex that complicated things.

This, what she'd done with her bear, it had had nothing to do with a simple physical interaction.

"*Solnyshko moyo.*" A kiss to the dampness of her neck as he roughly spoke words whose meaning had deepened to raw intimacy with a simple change in order.

Sun of my heart. Sunshine of my life.

The passionate, romantic words from her brawny, blunt bear hammered her straight to the soul, made her search for words to give him in return. She wasn't like Valentin, didn't always know how to show her love. "Valyusha," she said, then got stuck, the power of what she felt for him choking her throat.

But he lifted his head and smiled. "Say that again. I like it."

"Valyusha," she said, her next words coming from deep in her psyche, words that crashed through all reason and sense. "*My* Valyusha."

Eyes wild amber in unhidden delight, Valentin rolled off her, breaking their intimate connection. The aloneness was sudden, startling, but fleeting. He was drawing her up against his chest almost before she'd felt it. She shifted until she was on top of him, could look down into his face. His eyes were heavy-lidded, his skin flushed, his lips curved. "You pack a punch, Starlight."

"And consider," she said, "I'm only at the beginner level." Her lack of experience was an ache between her thighs, an intriguing ripple of pleasure and pain that made her feel used—in a way that felt *right*. Because she'd used Valentin, too, but none of it had been done to cause pain or to take more than was freely given. An even exchange where neither one of them was keeping score.

Valentin had focused nearly exclusively on *her* pleasure.

"I plan to learn to drive you to the breaking point as you did me." She'd have to advance at light speed, time spilling from her cupped hands like water.

"Starlight, you do that by existing." Valentin slid his hand down her back, lower. "You have one fine ass. Have I ever told you that?"

"You may tell me that at any time," she said, just to see his eyes fill with laughter, even as her own heart ached. She'd never known the organ could do that through the sheer weight of emotion. It hurt.

Valentin's laughter faded before her greedy gaze. "Talk to me. What's got you sad?"

Sad.

Such a simple word. Such a powerful word.

The ache in her heart grew deeper, harder, darker. "I don't trust easily."

"I figured that out after the eleventh time you gave me that blank do-I-know-you face when I turned up to say hi."

Her lips wanted to curve. Why should she have that physical reaction to a feeling of amusement? Not that it changed anything. She couldn't cup her hands tight enough to hold the rapidly passing seconds. "But," she whispered, "I've learned something about you in the time since we first met."

"What?" A rumble of sound against her, his hand still on her buttocks and his heavily muscled body a wall of searing heat full of a primal power that would never be turned against her.

She met the intense dark of his eyes. She could read those eyes now, read them so clearly that she wondered why she'd ever thought them impenetrable. What she saw, it made her own eyes burn in another inex-plicable emotional response. "I've learned that my Valyusha does not lie to me. Sometimes, he won't tell me things, and other times, he'll tell me only a little, but he won't lie."

A scowl. "Do I look like a *durak*? Of course I'm not going to lie to my mate."

She didn't dispute his claim; she felt it, too, the sense she was the lock to his key. Or perhaps it was a case of two keys mutually unlocking each other's souls. "Do you know how extraordinary that makes you in my world?" He was a gift beyond comprehension. "I trust my family, but I trust only Grandmother and Arwen never to lie to me."

Lines carved into his forehead. "But your family is about loyalty."

"We are shadows in the Net. Lies are a part of our lexicon."

Valentin's scowl grew deeper. "You don't lie to me, Starlichka." It was an order. "Not even by omission. Not anymore."

"Never," she promised, touching her fingertips to his jaw. "I vow this."

Silver gave her word as rarely as her grandmother did, and for the same reason—once she gave it, she wouldn't break it. As long as her memory remained, as long as her mind worked, she would keep her word . . . even if she could no longer understand why she'd given it. "I will not lie to you, Valentin. Not so long as I live."

Valentin made that deep rumble in his chest that had her hand vibrating where she'd placed it against his skin. "Tell me what you aren't saying," he demanded. "I will fight all your monsters beside you, *solnyshko moyo*. You just have to point them out."

Beside her, not for her. Yes, this alpha bear understood her as no one else had ever done. And she was about to break that huge heart of his—because this monster, not even her bear could fight.

"People talk about Psy gifts, Psy powers." For over a century, the rulers of the Psy race had made sure that when others thought of the Psy, they thought of power. "Even after the outbreaks when Psy became mindless killers, most people just believe we got hit with a mental virus. Bad luck, but not enough to diminish the aura of Psy power."

How could it be otherwise when Kaleb was a living symbol of that power, when the Arrows were heroes using their violent abilities to help rather than harm, when the M-Psy continued to diagnose countless illnesses and the Es opened their hearts to all who needed them?

"What's the other side?" Valentin fisted his hand in her hair, a big predator who'd die for her. "That's what you're trying to tell me, isn't it, Starlichka? That it isn't only about gifts and powers."

"Yes." Silver wondered if he knew she'd not only die for him; she'd kill for him. Mercants had few boundaries when they loved. But that fierce woman, the one who felt the passion of her ancestors, would soon be erased from this earth. "What no one ever talks about are the curses in amongst the gifts."

Chapter 32

Even so young, it's clear that Silver has the intelligence, spirit, and strength to lead this family after I am gone, but she can't do that if she's dead. I have to find a way to keep her alive.

—Personal diary entry by Ena Mercant (March 7, 2057)

VALENTIN RAN HIS hand over her hair, his attention a dominant wave.

There was no more time to delay, no more time to hope for a miraculous reversal of her personal curse. "Do you know what Nova is doing right now? She's talking to Chaos about how Dima took off his pants and ran around half-naked this morning just because it was fun. Every so often, he'd stop and do a 'butt dance.' Nova couldn't catch him because she was laughing too hard."

"Boy's got a point," Valentin rumbled. "It is fun to run around pantless—though I'd go the whole hog and take off the shirt, too."

Despite Valentin's light words, his lips weren't curved, his amber eyes aglow . . . and suddenly acute in their perception. "How can you possibly hear them?" he asked, muscles bunching beneath her. "I have far better hearing than any Psy should have, and I can't hear a word of their conversation."

"That's because it's taking place out in the forest where the two of them are going for a moonlit walk while their cub sleeps, watched over by his doting grandparents." She paused. "Your parents?"

He shook his head, a shadow passing across his face. "My father is dead. My mother prefers the wild." Short words that said so much and not enough. "Must be Chaos's parents—they just arrived this morning for a visit after spending time with his sister in the Rockies. She mated with a grizzly. Bad-tempered creatures, grizzlies."

Silver had so many questions, but tonight, she was the one telling secrets. "I can also hear one of your sentries sending in a report to Pavel."

"The miscreant is heading the watch tonight." Valentin kissed her slow and deep, as if savoring her, before flipping them so she was below the powerful bulk of his body. "Super hearing doesn't sound like a curse. It's considered a strength for changelings."

"I'd consider it a strength, too, if I could control it." She pressed both hands to her ears. "This is what I did as a child when my grandmother lowered the secondary shields she'd had around me. I had my telepathic shields already, didn't understand why she was pushing me to create military-grade shields so strong they were titanium." Silver had always had a strong will.

"Grandmother didn't want to do it," Silver said, because it was important Valentin know that, "but she had no choice. I had to know my greatest weakness so I could protect myself." She thought back to the child she'd been. "I screamed and screamed and screamed until I lost my voice."

Valentin's expression grew ominously dark. "Ena—"

"Hurt far more than I did, though she'd never admit it." Silver knew, was the one who'd woken cradled in her grandmother's lap, being rocked like a far younger child. "She had no choice. I had to understand the danger. Because, you see, unlike those with normal hearing, those of Designation Tp-A can't block out sound by plugging the ears."

Valentin's face was all craggy lines now, his voice so rough it was barely human. "*A* for audio?"

"Yes." She brushed back his uncontrollable hair. "The sound I 'hear' comes in via a psychic pathway. No one really knows how it translates into sound—audio telepaths are so rare that research on the sub-designation is nonexistent." What was the point when it had long been considered a death sentence?

"You're saying the noise will overwhelm you if you allow your shields to fall?"

"That's what happens to *any* pure telepath who lowers her shields." A roar of crushing noise. "The telepathic noise of the world is chaos—depending on a telepath's strength and the number of unshielded people in the vicinity, it could mean being overwhelmed by tens or hundreds or thousands of minds. Millions of random thoughts, no rhyme or reason to it."

Valentin kissed her again, his chest rumbling with the bear's agitation and his voice increasingly primal. "Like being in an extremely scent-rich environment for a bear changeling," he said. "Lock one of us in a per-fumery, and we'd be in physical pain within a very short time."

"Exactly." Silver petted his shoulders, the muscles hard as rock with tension. "Too much input through channels that are *meant* to process that information—as a result it can be controlled through various methods. You could squeeze your nose closed; I could slam down telepathic shields."

Valentin nodded.

"It's also a matter of degrees." Silver had had a lifetime to think of this. "If I want to use my telepathy without being overwhelmed, I can. I simply have to adjust the strength of my shields."

"That doesn't work with audio telepathy." Not a question, because her alpha bear was too smart not to have worked out where she was going.

"It's either all or nothing." Silver pushed back his hair again for the simple pleasure of touching him. "I can block it, or I can have it open. That means when my audio channel is fully open, all I hear is *noise*. I could be alone in the middle of a national forest with not a single mind in the vicinity, and it wouldn't matter." Silver had done exactly that so she'd be certain of her hypothesis.

"In such a situation, I hear the rustle of the trees, the fall of the water, the crackle of the earth settling, magnified a thousand times over for every tree in the forest, every drop of water, every foot of earth." Nature turned into a brutal hammer. "If I didn't have my shields, it'd take a minute at most to crush my mind; cause of death would likely be an aneurysm or just pure shock."

Valentin's hand tightened in her hair. "Why are you hearing Nova and Chaos if you block the audio channel?"

No more time. No more hope.

"The shield is crumbling." Like a brick wall with parts eaten away. "Right now, my audio telepathy is at a point where I can use it. Though it's irregular, like a radio channel broken up by static, I can hear actual conversations, separate one voice from the other, one strand of sound from its neighbor." It was a painful glimpse of what her ability could've been if it weren't so impossible to control.

"It's astonishing," she said. "I'm so deeply aware of the world. The whisper of the wind through the trees, the way the leaves rustle, the scrabble of small creatures in the forest, the laughter of one of your clanmates as he runs from a chasing friend . . . Is that what it's like to be changeling?"

"The world is music around us," her bear told her.

Heat burned Silver's eyes until a droplet rolled down the side of her face. Valentin leaned down and licked it up. "Don't you cry, Silver Mercant." It was a rumbling order. "Don't you *cry.*"

"I didn't know I could." She kissed his jaw, his cheek, her heart breaking for this man who would move mountains for her. "It's beautiful what you said, about the world being music around you." Nuzzling against him, drinking in the tactile contact as if she could take it with her into the darkness, she drew in his scent.

Valentin nuzzled back; the affectionate contact made more tears roll from her eyes. He kissed them away, growling once again at her to "stop it" and yet his touch was tender, his kisses so gentle they hurt. "Why?" he asked at last.

Silver needed no further words to know what he was asking. "It's emotion." She clamped her palm over his mouth when he would've spoken.

Scowling, Valentin licked her palm.

She wanted to smile, couldn't. "Because of the lack of research," she told him, "I don't know how or why, but audio telepathy has always been linked to emotion. Pre-Silence, audio telepaths were considered extinct. We simply didn't survive childhood."

"Not even the weaker ones," Valentin asked after she dropped her hand, "the ones who would hear less?"

It was a good question, a smart question. "As far as I've been able to determine, audio telepathy only appears as a secondary ability and only in high-Gradient telepaths." Which meant powerful telepathic channels. "The oldest surviving pre-Silence audio telepath who was identified as such was three years old. Chances are very high that others died before ever being identified as Tp-As."

"Then you go Silent," Valentin said, the words hard. "If it will keep you safe, keep you alive, you stop feeling and you *go back* to Silence."

Silver's throat was crushed glass. "I can't."

"Don't you argue with me on this." He gripped her jaw. "You *go back*." An alpha's command, wild storms in his eyes. "I'd rather have a frosty Silver alive and well than a feeling, loving Silver dead in a box. You shut it down. Be who you were before you decided to lower your shields."

She loved him so.

Silver had never truly understood love before this instant when she knew it, like a bowstring snapping tight inside her soul. With that one potent glimpse, she saw the other strands of love in her heart. For Arwen. For her grandmother. Even for her parents. All shining bright. All unbreakable.

"You go back to being ice-cold, Starlight." Valentin's words were unyielding, but the pain in his big body, it was a dark turbulence. "You go back."

She cupped his face in her hands, his bristly jaw a familiar sensation against her palms. "I'm not being stubborn, Mishka." She used the family nickname as a gentle tease, but there was no joy in her. "I've realized over the past hour that I *can't*." The knowledge seeping into her in a slow wave until it was unavoidable.

"Why?" A harsh demand. "You were fine before."

"Before?" She laughed, the sound fractured but holding a humor he'd taught her to feel. "Before, I was opening my door to an alpha bear and having conversations with him when I should've called security." Instead, part of her had waited for that heavy knock. "A truly Silent individual wouldn't have interacted with you as I did, wouldn't have thought about you when you didn't show up for a few weeks."

"I was trying to play hard to get," Valentin said, turning his head to bite at her fingers, as bad-tempered as the grizzlies he'd maligned. "You're telling me your Silence was breaking down before you made the conscious decision to try a life without Silence?"

She nodded. "The Honeycomb changed everything." The empaths had created the network to keep the PsyNet alive, keep Psy from going insane. But— "It's a product of naked emotion."

"Can you cut yourself loose?"

"Yes." Silver had already considered how it could be done. "I'd risk madness, but that could be managed by short bursts of contact with the Honeycomb—only I think it's too late." The fractures in that brick wall could no longer be repaired.

She had tried already in an effort to disprove her dark theory, only to have all her attempts fail. "Taking into account all I know of audio telepathy," she told this bear who was a gift she'd never expected, "the disintegration of my audio shields appears to be a genetic inevitability."

"Your research could be wrong."

Silver had never wanted to be wrong so much in her life. "Even before Silence fell, my shields were starting to crack under the weight of the avalanche of sound my mind is built to hear."

To *hear*, not to *survive*.

"I just didn't see the cracks until the sound levels reached a critical point." There was no other explanation for the depth of the damage to her shields—it hadn't happened over weeks or even months. "The Honeycomb accelerated the effect, but only by a matter of weeks. My shields were always going to fail."

Valentin pushed off her, got off the bed. He strode around the room, proud in his nakedness. When he slammed his hands against the wall, it was with a cascade of curses that turned the air blue.

His fury was an untamed, beautiful thing. Like him.

Eyes wild, his hair whipping around his face, he strode to her, hauled her up onto her knees on the bed.

CLASPING Silver's head in his hands, the moonlight of her hair tumbling over his big rough hands, Valentin roared at her. She didn't flinch, not Silver Fucking Mercant. His mate. His tough, proud mate.

Who would die if they didn't figure out a way to shut off the increasing scream in her head.

"There *must* be a way."

Silver closed her hands over his wrists. "I've thought of everything."

Valentin wasn't used to thinking about the brain in such ways, but he wasn't stupid. He could learn new things. And maybe an outsider could see options Silver couldn't. She was brilliant, but she'd been raised in a certain way, taught certain things. "If you don't feel, if your brain literally *can't* feel, could you rebuild your shielding?"

Silver's eyes grew darker in thought. "If I *actually* didn't feel, there would be no need for the shielding. Audio telepathy is tightly linked to emotion, remember? That's why it continued to exist in Silence—we always had the capacity for emotion, even if we trained ourselves not to respond to it."

Valentin squeezed his eyes shut, his bear trying to make sense of a wholly unfamiliar world. *Think, Valentin.* He snapped open his eyes. "Is it possible to physically stop your brain from processing emotion?" He hated that he was talking about maiming her, but damn it, if it would keep her alive, he'd consider anything.

"If that were possible," Silver said with no hint of anger, her tone gentle in a way he'd never heard from her, "the Psy Council would've done it long ago."

The Psy Council.

A chip to force Silence on the biological level.

Valentin's heart thundered.

"The scientist who mated with a leopard in Lucas Hunter's pack." A woman with startling blue-gray eyes against skin of deepest brown, her hair a wild mass of near-black curls. "She did that public broadcast." An act of rebellion that had further pushed Silence closer to collapse. "She talked about the Council wanting to use a chip to make people Silent."

Silver sat up straighter on her knees, the sadness fading from her face to be replaced by acute concentration. "Ashaya Aleine?" Her tone was better now, more his smart, strong Starlichka.

"Yes, her. Have you ever talked to her about your audio telepathy?"

"No, but my grandmother was able to get access to data about the chip. It wasn't designed to fix an error in the brain—it was designed to suffocate normal emotion and create a hive mind."

Valentin could see her struggling to find a way to explain.

"It's . . . like a sphere designed to perfectly encompass a flower. A construction of exquisitely precise detail," she said at last. "But if the flower is shaped differently, if it has longer petals or is misshapen, the sphere will no longer be able to enclose it without damage. It might cut petals in half or crush a critical part."

"Tell me you didn't just call yourself misshapen." Fury had him glaring at her.

Silver raised an eyebrow, every inch the queen. "I am perfectly shaped, Alpha Nikolaev."

Grinning, he kissed the life out of her, tumbling her back into the bed so he was braced over her. "That's my Starlight."

Frost in her expression, but she touched him with possessive hands, pushing his hair back from his face in a way that made his bear smug. "I have no problem with who I am," she said. "I am made up of all parts of me, and they are all critical to Silver Fucking Mercant."

His bear adored her. The man loved her beyond bearing.

"I was simply attempting to explain why a chip designed for ninety-nine percent of minds may not function on the one percent who don't fit the mold of what is considered normal."

Valentin got what she was saying, but he also understood another critical factor. "Mercants are all about secrets, right?"

"That's a fair enough estimation." Her tone was slightly suspicious.

It made his grin widen—bear mates often got that tone in their voices. "So I know, *moyo solnyshko*, that you've never considered asking Dr. Aleine if she could modify her original chip to work on your brain." He saw from her face that he'd hit the bull's-eye. "Doing that would've exposed a Mercant vulnerability, and Mercants don't expose anything if they can help it."

"Again, for a bear alpha who disavows an interest in politics, you have an acute grasp of it."

He bit at her jaw. "Stop being mean."

She laughed. Starlight actually laughed. It was short and cut off almost at once, her hand at her mouth. But he'd heard, and it was the most beautiful sound in the universe. "Do that again," he whispered.

Eyes wide, she said, "Did I laugh?"

"You're a goddess when you laugh." Hell, she was stunning no matter what, but when she laughed he felt as if he could conquer the world.

Eyes still wide, she ran wondering fingers over her own lips. The lingering warmth in her face made her glow. "You're right. I've never really considered reaching out to Dr. Aleine or her twin."

"Her twin?"

"Identical in every way except that Amara is a psychopath. They've always done their most brilliant work together." The glow faded. "Rebels blew up the original lab. Ashaya destroyed her own files. All information on the chip is gone."

"Do you think it's gone from her brain?"

Chapter 33

Not long ago, an attack on my lab put the development of the implant back to square one. But it can be rebuilt. I'm not the only scientist with the capacity to do the work.

—Excerpted from transcript of Ashaya Aleine's broadcast (June 2080)

VALENTIN'S QUESTION CIRCLED in Silver's brain.

Ashaya and Amara had two of the *most* brilliant minds in the world. They would've forgotten nothing, even if they'd chosen not to pursue their research—or more correctly, Ashaya had made the choice and Amara had decided to accept her twin's decision.

"If I do this," she said to Valentin, "if I ask them and they can create a chip that deletes my emotions, I'll no longer be the Silver you know. I won't even be the Silver you knew before I decided to consciously drop my shields."

She had to make him understand the consequences. "My emotions were already beginning to make themselves felt on a subconscious level when I first met you. Otherwise, I would've never sparred with you as I did."

"Regret that?"

"Not for a second." She *liked* the person she was with emotion, liked the woman who loved her brother so very deeply and who knew her grandmother as far more than the matriarch of their family.

And this man, this wild changeling . . . "You make me more myself than I've ever been."

"You make me better," was his deep, rumbling response.

"Valyusha." He made her better, too. So much better. "I can't lose this."

Valentin's jaw set again. "If it'll keep you alive, we take the hit." Making no attempt to hide the anguish tearing at that huge heart of his, he said, "You're Arwen's beloved sister and Ena's hope and the linchpin of EmNet. Most of all, you're my Starlight. You *have* to survive."

"Will you?" She understood now what it would cost him to have her be cold toward him. Cut off from her emotions, she wouldn't feel the pain. He'd feel every terrible second.

"So long as you live and breathe," he said, his eyes a deep, glowing amber, "I can bear anything."

She didn't respond with another play on words this time, couldn't. "I'll ask," she said. "On one condition."

"Always negotiating," he grumbled. "What's your condition?"

"Tell me about the mating bond." She felt a wrenching pull toward him, had done so for far longer than she could admit to herself. She'd fought it because, in some distant part of her, she'd understood the inevitable—and the whole world knew changelings didn't do well after the death of a mate. Many didn't survive.

Valentin nuzzled her, surrounding her in muscled warmth. "Will you come for a walk with me?"

"Always." While she was herself, she'd walk anywhere with Valentin Mikhailovich Nikolaev.

Tonight, he led her out of the den—after swamping her in his sweatshirt and pulling out her hair from where it had gotten caught against her back. Hand clamped around hers, he tugged her through the Cavern. They had to step past more than a few drunk bears sprawled on the floor in their animal forms. One raised his head groggily, swiped at Silver's leg.

His fur was decorated in pink little-girl barrettes and ribbon.

Silver allowed herself to be caught, found his grip was gentle. "Go back to sleep," she said in a stern tone.

The bear yawned and went right back to sleep, his hand going limp as his snores filled the air. She retrieved her foot and carried on with Valentin. Who was grinning. "See? Not a single problem handling a bunch of rowdy bears."

"Of course not. I'm Silver Fucking Mercant."

His laughter infused the night with wildness as they stepped out of Denhome, the arm he threw around her shoulders warm and heavy. "You're also my Starlight."

She felt that clenching in her heart again, so deep and tight. "I know, Mr. Medvezhonok."

He rubbed his chin against the side of her head. "I'll be your teddy bear. I'll even put on the suit if you like . . . Oh, wait. I have a built-in suit. Want to see?"

"Yes." Breath lost, she turned to him. "I want to see."

"Really?"

"Why do you sound surprised? I've wanted to see your animal form since the day we first met." Since the day he crashed into her life, big and brash and aggravating.

"You never let on," he accused in a grumpy tone.

"I like to keep you on your bigfoot-sized toes."

"You've been talking to my sisters." He laughed again, so warm and generous and impossible to offend, unless you insulted someone he loved. For that insult, he'd pound you into the earth. But never her. Because she was his Starlight.

"Well?"

"Patience." He kept his stride short to accommodate her own, and they strolled through the trees to the edge of the wide stream where she'd seen the bear cubs playing. The grass was soft under her feet when she took off her shoes, the air crisp and cold. Beside her, Valentin stripped, scattering his clothes on the grass.

Rolling her eyes, she bent down and folded them, before putting them in a neat pile—while he showed off, his muscles taut and his eyes primal. "You're beautiful," she said truthfully.

His smug, happy smile was her reward.

The air filled with light a heartbeat later, so many particles of it, and where Valentin the man had stood, now stood an incredibly large bear. The biggest she'd seen in StoneWater by far. His fur was a deep, lush brown, his eyes that glowing amber she'd seen on the man. And the head he butted gently against her stomach heavy enough to tumble her to the ground.

The fall didn't hurt in the least, the grass soft.

But the bear jerked back as if he'd accidentally stepped on a kitten.

Laughing again, the uncontrollable sound coming from deep inside her, she scrambled up onto her knees and grabbed Valentin's ears, holding his face to hers, those amber eyes so clear and deep and not in any way human. His fur was softer than it appeared, his breath warm, and the way he looked at her intimately familiar, despite the wildness of him. This was her Valyusha, just in a different form.

"You're *definitely* bigfoot sized," she teased.

He lifted a paw, showing it off. She put her palm against it. It dwarfed her many times over. She didn't know why she said it—the thought was barely formed before the words tumbled out. "You're big enough that I could ride you."

His eyes grew impossibly brighter. He nudged at her with his head again, this time very, very gently. She didn't have to be an expert in body language to know he was telling her to climb on board.

Silver Mercant did not do ridiculous things like ride a changeling bear. A big changeling bear with sharp hooked claws. Which was the reason she couldn't quite understand why, a minute later, she was attempting to climb onto said bear's back.

She slipped once. Twice. And the bear laughed, its body shaking.

Glaring at him, she pointed to the grass. "Get down so I can climb up."

Body still shaking, Valentin sprawled down on the ground as if he were fast asleep. He even made a snoring noise. Feeling her lips curve, she grabbed handfuls of his fur and managed to get onto his back. He was warm, and when she leaned down and threw her arms impulsively around his neck, he made a sound that she knew meant pleasure, though how she knew, she couldn't say.

Then he was rising beneath her, a huge living rock. But when he began to move, he was no rock, his movements far smoother than she'd expected. And far faster. She bared her teeth against the wind and held on for the ride. As Valentin said, she was Silver Fucking Mercant. She had this.

VALENTIN had always been open to the idea of a mate who was Psy or human rather than changeling. All he'd wanted was a mate to adore and fight with and play with. The one thing he had worried about was that his bear would feel left out of a relationship with a non-changeling. Today, as Silver laughed while he ran through the forest with her on his back, he knew that had been a foolish worry. The bear was ecstatic—and more than a little bigheaded at both her delight and her fearlessness.

So it ran and it showed her secret places in the land around Denhome and it kept her safe, easing its speed anytime Silver needed to adjust her grip. But for a woman who'd never before been on the back of a large beast, she was a star. By the time they'd done this a few more times, she'd probably be trying to put reins on him.

Valentin laughed before he remembered there wouldn't be more times if Silver succeeded in erasing her emotions.

Raw pain scored his insides, but the bear was in agreement with the man: as long as Silver lived, he could take the pain, take the loss that would haunt him always. He had this big body for a reason. It could take a lot of punishment. As long as she breathed, he'd survive. He'd watch over her from afar, and he'd survive because his mate was alive.

Shoving away the agony of the future because this night was a memory he'd treasure forever, he ran until they were on an outcrop that gave them a startling view of the stars, the Milky Way a scattering of diamonds in the sky. He went down so Silver could slide off his back, then he shifted.

Exquisite pleasure and wrenching pain, that was the shift and it was over in a moment. Naked to the skin, his blood hot from the run, he lay on the grass, head braced on folded arms, and nudged his head again. Silver scrambled onto his back to lie with her chin propped on his shoulder, her arms wrapped loosely around his neck.

Her weight was nothing and it was everything.

He drank her in, the scent of her, the softness of her, the steel of her. Never again, he knew, would he meet anyone like his extraordinary Starlight. "Mating is once and forever, *solnyshko moyo*," he told her, because he could deny her nothing. "Once a changeling mates, that changeling will never again mate with anyone else, never want to mate with anyone else. Many don't survive the passing of their mate."

Silver pressed her lips to his shoulder. "I hear so much pain in your voice, Valyusha, so many memories."

Throat thick, he swallowed. "My mother survived the breaking of her bond with my father, but she's never been the same. She no longer shifts out of her bear form." He blinked away tears that made him feel a cub as small as Dima. "I haven't spoken to her in over fifteen years."

Galina Evanova had held on for nearly two years after her mate's death, but the instant Stasya turned eighteen, it was as if she'd given herself permission to break—though Nova had been only seventeen, Nika fifteen, and Valentin fourteen. "Even if I go to her as a bear, she looks right through me."

Silver's response was fierce. "That is unacceptable. Loss of a mate or not, she is a parent. That responsibility is forever."

Valentin found himself chuckling through his pain. "I think my mother, when she was herself, would've liked you—she was one of my father's seconds before they mated." Two strong women, they would've probably struck sparks off each other that Valentin would've winced at and pretended not to see.

A man didn't get between his mate and his mother when they had a difference of opinion. He pretended to be a dumb bear who saw nothing, heard nothing, had no opinions on the matter whatsoever—anything else was just asking for trouble. Unless of course, his mother crossed an invisible line, in which case, said bear had better become not-dumb very fast.

Pissed-off mothers could be coaxed and calmed after a cooling-off period. Pissed-off mates would rain down fire and brimstone and, in Silver's case, storms of ice frigid enough to turn his balls blue.

How he wished that was a tightrope on which he had to balance.

"Hmm, perhaps," Silver said, her tone icily doubtful. "From what you've said, the mating bond is a deep psychic connection."

He shrugged, Silver's breasts momentarily pushing down into him as he lifted up. "It just is."

"If we don't complete the mating, will you be able to find someone else?"

He wanted to lie to her, but bears were terrible liars to start with—and Valentin did not lie to Silver. "I've heard rumors that mates can repudiate each other," he said, a hitch in his voice, "but I'm never going to repudiate you. Who would ever measure up to Silver Fucking Mercant?"

Another kiss, the small touch from his glorious ice queen melting him. He was pure mush, would do anything she asked if only she'd reward him with little kisses and petting strokes.

"Are you sure, Valyusha?"

"It's you or no one." Nothing would change that. "But don't you dare allow that to influence your decision when it comes to contacting the Aleines. If I have to protect my Starlichka by letting her go, that's what I'll do." His chest hurt with the force of his need to protect her. "Don't steal that from me."

"How could I?" A brush of warm air against him. "No one will ever measure up to Valentin Mikhailovich Nikolaev, either."

His chest puffed up, his bear strutting. "So we're stuck with each other." Until she wasn't the Silver he'd fallen for any longer, until she didn't understand what it was to love, what it was to find a mate.

"Since we are and since you won't ever find another mate," Silver said, "can we mate?"

Valentin froze, his mind hazed.

He had to physically shake his head to snap out of his shock. "No."

"Why not?"

Trembling inside, Valentin tried to think, to explain. "The mating bond is a *powerful* force. You can't block it, and breaking it with anything other than death is next to impossible." He knew of only one case of the latter. *Ever.* No other rumors, no other whispers. Nothing. Just that one horrible case.

"Talk to me." A firm order that said she'd heard his renewed pain and was through with giving him room to hide.

He had an alpha's strength, could've kept his most shameful secret, but Silver was his mate, bond or not. "My father's name was Mikhail," he began, his bear's heart a black bruise all over again.

"He was alpha of StoneWater from the time he was thirty-two. A good alpha, one who was respected and loved, even though he could be stricter than usual for a bear. He was always Mikhail to clanmates. Only my mother ever called him by any other name. '*Moy dorogoi Misha,*' she'd say and pull him into a kiss."

"Was he strict with you, too?"

Valentin tried to smile, failed. "He had to be. I was worse than Dima and the tiny gangsters combined. Petya and Zasha—Zahaan—were my accomplices. Petya when his family joined the clan when he was eight, Zasha from the cradle."

"I've met him," Silver said when he paused to breathe past the ugliness of the memories to come. "He used to drop off papers occasionally before you took over the task."

Valentin scowled. "I wasn't about to let him try to seduce you with that pretty face of his." Zahaan looked like he'd walked off a movie set, complete with perfectly styled hair and a meticulously groomed goatee.

When his friends ribbed him about looking like a sly, sneaky cat instead of an honest bear, Zahaan just smiled and said he had to leave for a date. The man hadn't spent a night alone since before he was technically legal. He was also a dominant who'd die for StoneWater, and a friend Valentin knew would walk through fire for him.

"I prefer bears who don't own combs," Silver said with another little kiss that made warmth uncurl inside him, fighting the heavy dark.

"As small bears, Z and I got up to as much trouble as we possibly could between daybreak and falling asleep out of exhaustion." He could remember his father's strong arms lifting him up from wherever he'd crashed, to put him to bed. "My father—he was always just Papa to me—would discipline us in his role as alpha . . . but it was never cruel. It was exactly what we needed."

Silver ran her fingers through his hair. "What went wrong?"

Valentin drew in a rough breath, faced the horror. "He changed in his forty-seventh year—it was like he released a part of himself he'd shut away. Some people say maybe he suffered a traumatic brain injury that changed his personality, but there's no proof of that." No matter how much Valentin and his sisters wished for it to be true.

"All we know is that he began to withdraw from everyone, including my mother, Galina." Valentin could still see the numb confusion in his mother's eyes as her mate—the same man who'd kidnapped her so he could court her with sparkly jewelry and handmade food, the same mate who'd tumbled her into his lap and kissed her every single day—began to treat her with disinterest.

"She thought she'd made him angry, really angry in a way a bear never gets with his mate." Valentin might blow up at Silver, but he'd still cuddle her close, and if she so much as stubbed her toe, he'd be there to yell at her for hurting herself.

Never would he go cold toward her as his father had done his mother.

"So even though she was a dominant at nearly the same level as him," he told Silver, "she apologized, asked what she'd done." His mother had been worried she'd hurt her mate in some terrible way. "He just . . . didn't really react." Being ignored by her beloved Misha had devastated his mother.

"Despite the upsetting behavior, we didn't know how deep the change ran until it was too late. Until he became such a monster that, one day, the mating bond broke without warning." The stark words were as much a shock today as then. "My mother . . . it was like she broke from the heart outward that day. I saw her go down, saw her convulse, then I saw her lie there with dead eyes."

Silver stroked his side, petted gently. "But she lives."

"Through sheer, grim determination. She might be broken, but she wants no one to forget that my father tried to fight his psychopathic tendencies for forty-seven years and that he succeeded well enough to win a mate whose honor and integrity no one can question." Valentin would kill anyone who tried. "The day the bond broke was the night before he committed his first murder."

Chapter 34

"NOTHING YOU SAY will ever change who you are to me, Valyusha," Silver said in an uncompromising tone when he went silent. "One of my ancestors was an infamous poet who said that Mercants are miserly autocrats when it comes to our hearts—we give it only once in our lifetimes. And once given, we expect it to be held forever."

Valentin shuddered, not knowing until then how much he'd needed those words. But Silver wasn't finished. "Adina Mercant went to jail for stabbing her lover when she mistakenly thought he was trying to leave her." A pause. "He brought her roses in prison and married her afterward."

Warmth spread inside him. "Are you sure you're not bears?" he said, before forcing himself to continue. "The elders in the clan say the mating bond must've broken because my father became a totally different person, a person my mother's bear sensed and couldn't accept."

Valentin shook his head. "I don't think that. My mother loves him to this day—she'd have hunted him down for his crimes if need be, but she wouldn't have repudiated him. I think he triggered the repudiation when he lost the part of himself that made him capable of love and loyalty."

Silver rubbed her cheek against his when he turned his face to the side, the soft strands of her hair drifting over his skin. "Did your mother suffer psychological damage?" she asked. "Did she worry that the reason she and your father had mated successfully was because she, too, had a seed of darkness inside her?"

Had another person asked that question, it would've been an accusation, an insult. Not so with Silver. With her, these were just questions.

"Yes," he said. "That's why she spends so much time in the wild." So much time in her bear's skin.

"She's searching for an answer to the question of how she could've mated with a man who became a serial killer—and how she can love his ghost still. The ghost of the man who was her lover, who created four children with her, children he raised with love and honor until he was forty-seven."

Silver tapped a finger on his shoulder. "It's highly unusual for a psychopath to so successfully maintain bonds and relationships. Especially given the tightly knit nature of your clan—there were no earlier indications?"

"Afterward, everyone thought back. *We* thought back, but there was *nothing*. He didn't torture animals, he didn't set fires, he didn't do anything strange or troubling. He was a wonderful alpha, an incredible mate and father, a good friend."

"You're sure there was no head injury?"

Valentin clenched his hands into fists. "I want to believe that. My mother wants to believe that. Most of StoneWater wants to believe that. The *only* piece of evidence that supports that theory is the fact my father was on long-range patrol for two weeks before it all went wrong. When he came home, he had black and blue bruises on his face, said he'd fallen into a ravine during his patrol."

"There is," Silver said, "another possibility."

Valentin knew what she was going to say. "Psy manipulation? The clan thought of that at the time, but there were no signs of incursion into the territory, and Psy can't manipulate changeling minds that way."

"Kaleb gave me access to highly restricted files when I took over EmNet," Silver said, her tone quiet. "Including to files he dug up himself."

Valentin just waited, his heart thundering.

"At the time of your father, a fringe group of scientists was running experiments on changelings. In almost all cases where they were successful, it took significant time and effort and a large number of Psy. And the change was never long-term. The changelings either self-destructed or went 'active' without warning."

His throat was dry now. "Who? Do you know?"

"The subjects had no names, but I remember seeing Bear Subject M in Moscow."

The thunder in his heart turned to a raw hope. "What was the purpose to breaking the changelings?"

"To use them as sleeper agents to harm the pack or clan. The experiment was shut down after all of the subjects failed to act as programmed."

Harsh laughter escaped his throat. "Oh, no, they didn't fail. My father's chosen victims were Psy, but he nearly succeeded in murdering Stone-Water, too. My clan is split in two. The ones who've left Denhome believe I'll go the same way as my father, my blood tainted."

"They're fools." The words were icy.

"You sure about that, Starlight?"

"Don't make me hurt you, Valyusha."

Bringing her hand to his mouth, he pressed a kiss to her palm.

"Clearly," Silver said in a tone that made it plain he wasn't yet forgiven, "they don't feel the same way toward your sisters, or you'd have torn off their heads by now."

He was glad she understood that; *no one* hurt the people Valentin loved. "It's because I'm male. Changelings hardly ever spawn serial killers, but the rare times it happens, it's always a male. Stasya likes to torment herself by doing research on the topic, and she's found no mention of a female serial killer. Murderers, yes, but not serials."

"And you're alpha, hold the same power as he did."

"Yes, they're afraid I'll finish what my father began and poison Stone-Water from the top." He kissed her palm again. "You really think that was my papa? Bear Subject M?"

"It's possible. The timing is right. I can dig further."

"Will it put you in danger?"

"No, it wasn't an official Council project. Even if they did secretly support the experiments, the Council is gone, and the Arrows are no longer bound to protect their secrets."

"Ming LeBon is still alive," he said, referring to the brutal Councilor who'd made more than one changeling enemy. "So are Nikita Duncan,

Shoshanna Scott, and Anthony Kyriakus." No one knew what had happened to Tatiana Rika-Smythe—the Councilor had disappeared off the face of the earth.

"I'll be sure I don't make any waves that could attract dangerous attention."

"No risks, Starlight."

"Mercants are used to getting information. Trust me."

"Do you think you ever have to say that?" he grumbled at her, his bear scowling inside him.

"Are you sure you're not a grizzly?"

"Grr."

They were quiet for a long time after that, Silver's fierce, unconditional love healing broken things inside him.

"Even if the Psy broke my father," he said at last, "there must've been a seed in him to turn him into a murderer."

"No," Silver said. "That's partly why the program was shelved—because the results were so unpredictable. Messing with a changeling brain takes too much effort, and the results are nonlinear. If they did this, they broke a fundamental part of him."

Valentin had been so angry with his father for so long. Today, for the first time, he hurt for the man who may have been murdered, too. "If I accept that possibility, Starlichka," he said, his tone raw, "I also have to accept that maybe he *was* born that way."

Accepting only the good and ignoring the bad achieved nothing. "I have to consider whether he was just really, really good at fighting his psychopathic instincts, good enough that he convinced himself he didn't have them, burying them to the point where he was able to mate, have children, take up the position as alpha."

Silver didn't try to argue that he was wrong. "We Psy are our minds to a large extent, so we understand the mind better than any other race— it is an extraordinary organ and it has an ability to compartmentalize that can stun. Your father *may* have so totally compartmentalized away his psychopathic tendencies that even he may not have been aware of them."

"Until the dam broke."

"Yes." A kiss on his neck. "It's also possible his bear balanced out his psychopathic propensities in some way for most of his life. Psy have often studied changeling mental health patterns, and most haven't been for nefarious reasons—it's *because* changelings have so few serial killers. My race wanted to see if they could duplicate that result."

"'Few' isn't 'none,' Silver."

"Let me do my research before you condemn him. Let me give you this closure."

He released a harsh exhale. "No unnecessary risks. Promise me."

"I promise."

The next time she spoke, her words had nothing to do with psychopaths or serial killers. "Consider this, Valyusha: if the mating bond is so powerful, it might survive the excision of my emotions."

"If it did, it would eliminate the whole aim of the operation," Valentin pointed out, instead of bellowing his claim then and there as his bear rampaged to do. "The mating bond is a thing of primal emotion, no logic, no control."

"We're talking a physical operation to block my emotions, not a psychic shield. The mating bond would either break—and the pain would be violent for you—"

"I'd take any pain for you," Valentin snarled.

"I know." A hard bite on his shoulder that told him to stop growling at her. "But if it *doesn't* break, it could provide a nucleus from which my emotions can regrow."

"No." It was a rumbling refusal. "I won't risk the operation not working." That operation was theoretical right now, but for Silver's audio telepathy to be blocked and *stay* that way, she had to stop feeling. How could she do that if he were inside her, loving her with bearish ferocity? "You can't leave the PsyNet, either, and you said it yourself— mating with a dominant changeling seems to pull Psy permanently from the Net."

"It'll be harder to do what I need to do from outside the PsyNet," Silver said, "but I'll adapt. There *must* be a way for non-PsyNet-linked mates to have access to the data in the Net."

"No." Valentin had to fight every one of his instincts to say that, but this was about Silver's life. "It's not worth the risk."

"It's not your choice, Valyusha." The soft words were his only warning.

Silver dropped all her shields.

Man and bear both *knew*, felt the roaring openness of the connection deep inside him. Before he could fight the draw, before he could control his heart's joy to protect her, the mating bond smashed into them, a slender hand reaching out and clasping his heart, as his hand cradled her own heart.

It was the most wonderful moment of his life.

It was the most horrific moment of his life.

He might just have killed her.

"Damn you." It came out a harsh whisper.

Silver's response was to hug him tight from the back, her breath hot against his ear. "I feel you deep inside me." Her voice was as unrepentant as a bear's. "So big and dangerous and mine. Always *mine*."

Her ice and fire burned inside him like a steel candle, a flame his bear curled its big body protectively around. His mate was everything he'd ever dared dream. He scowled nonetheless, refusing to cuddle her back for at least a minute.

He lasted ten seconds before taking her hand and pressing a kiss on her palm. "Are you still in the PsyNet?"

"Yes." Stunned surprise, followed by a pause. "It's strange—I can see a bond to you, I know you're at the other end, but it disappears into the fabric of the PsyNet like it's entering a part of the psychic plane I can't access."

The terrible, disobedient Mercant who owned him body and soul kissed his neck. "People say the psychic plane is alive, that the neosentience that guards it makes more decisions than we know. Maybe it decided I needed to stay in the PsyNet."

Valentin had nothing to add to that, but he did have certain things to say to his mate. Flipping over onto his back with a speed that meant he caught her before she tumbled off, he glared at her. "Do you know what you've done?"

A cool-eyed glance. "Yes, Valyusha. I've loved you."

And damn his heart, it melted all over again. "You may have killed yourself."

"No." A single—and very alpha—word. "The chances of my survival are infinitesimal. I weighed all the factors and decided I'd rather know what it is to belong to you than reject that gift because it might gain me a little more time."

He gripped her arms, shook her. Gently. Very gently. "Stubborn, willful, infuriating—"

"Stop calling yourself names."

"Argh!" Driven to distraction, he hauled her down to his mouth and kissed her wet and deep and angry.

She took it, gave back as good as she got. His mate was Silver Fucking Mercant.

The Human Patriot

HE LOOKED AT the data HAPMA had sent him, saw the e-mail exchange with Bowen Knight, and felt his gut clench. Damn it. Bowen had always been a good man; he'd done more to raise humanity's profile and increase their strength than anyone.

He sent HAPMA a quick reply: Do not harm him. He can still be saved.

He didn't believe Bowen had been psychically compromised. The other man had an experimental chip in his brain that blocked psychic interference. No, Bowen was simply being led astray by Psy he thought he could trust. Yes, the empaths were probably trustworthy—they were the only Psy the Patriot had any time for—but the empaths were getting their information from others.

Their leader, Ivy Jane Zen, apparently sat on the Psy Ruling Coalition, but who was her lover but Vasic Zen—a member of a death squad that was attempting to rebrand itself as heroic. Loyal as empaths were known to be, she'd probably accept anything he told her as gospel and pass that on to her fellow empaths.

Bowen should've known that the empaths' information had to be treated as compromised.

HAPMA responded to his message: He must be made to see reason.

Yes, the Patriot wrote back. Bowen is too important to lose, but there are others around him who are disposable. That was how the Psy thought of humans, after all. I will make him see that the future holds only pain if he trusts the Psy.

How?

The Patriot wasn't beholden to HAPMA, but he answered because they were dogs on a leash who had to be kept fed so they could be controlled. There must be no hint of HAPMA involvement. We're going to pin this on the Psy. It'd take some planning, but he was good at that. Do not waste this opportunity by being impatient. I'll handle it personally. When I'm done, Bowen Knight will hate the Psy to his dying day.

The Patriot's eye fell on the image of Lily Knight that he had on the pinboard he used to map out his plans, her uptilted eyes a huge dove gray in a fine-boned face framed by a blunt black bob. Picking up a red marker, he used it to X out her image. "Sorry, Lily, but your death will ignite his fire, make him realize that he can trust only those of his own race."

Chapter 35

Doubt thou the stars are fire;
Doubt that the sun doth move;
Doubt truth to be a liar;
But never doubt I love.

—From *Hamlet* by the human artist William Shakespeare
(seventeenth century)

SILVER SLEPT DEEPLY that night, peaceful in a way she'd never been. She'd made her choices and she would stand by them. Neither her grandmother nor Arwen had contacted her. Though she'd shielded the bond with Valentin the instant it formed, they would've known nonetheless. Even if her grandmother *had* somehow missed the change in Silver, Arwen wouldn't have.

Yet he hadn't contacted her.

She smiled. Of course he hadn't. He was an empath and he was her brother. He understood that this time was precious. Arwen rarely went against Grandmother, but he had a spine as steely as Silver's when required; he'd no doubt made Ena agree to keep her distance, too.

She'd talk to them both, but not now.

This morning was for lying skin to skin with Valentin while the clan woke around them. She could hear many voices, could still make out the individual conversations, but the pressure, it was building. It was just as well that Valentin had made her get in touch with Ashaya Aleine the previous night, both of them aware Aleine would be awake—it had been early afternoon in San Francisco by the time they returned to Den-home.

The scientist had been shocked to learn of Silver's secret, had promised to keep it. "I *can* re-create the implant for single-brain use," she'd said, a shadow of horror in the blue-gray of her gaze as she revealed her own secret, one that could make her a target for the likes of Ming LeBon.

"I can't forget the details," the scientist had added, "no matter how hard I try." Folding her arms over the deep green of her long-sleeved top, she'd said, "Before anything, I need thorough scans of your brain—and I have to be there to supervise those scans, to ensure we get the necessary information."

It was then that Silver had made a decision that held nothing of logic. "Not tonight, Ashaya. I need tonight."

Expression softening with the knowledge of a woman who understood exactly the loss Silver was facing, Ashaya hadn't argued. "In the morning your time is soon enough. I'll spend the time till then resurrecting the specifics of the chip with Amara."

A pregnant pause had followed. "I also need the scans to make sure you're telling the truth. The only reason I've taken your words on faith to this point is because you're mated to an alpha my own mate and my alpha both trust. I need to know I'm not creating something that could be used to do harm."

"I understand. The implant is a piece of tech many would kill to possess." Especially the modification that permitted certain chipped individuals to control the minds of others who were similarly implanted.

"If you've seen the classified files, you know there's also a serious degradation issue." Ashaya had rubbed her forehead. "So while I can re-create the chip, I won't be putting it in your brain—that'd be a death sentence. We'll use the chip as a starting point to create a solution tailored to your needs."

"Is a solution possible?"

"We never begin a project assuming we'll fail."

It was akin to Silver's own philosophy. "My audio input is increasing hourly."

"Amara and I will make this our priority." Shadows under her eyes. "I'm currently banging my head against a brick wall in another time-critical project, going around in circles. This may help me think in different patterns that could save more lives than just your own."

"The human implant to block psychic intrusion?" At Ashaya's raised eyebrow, Silver had shrugged. "I'm a Mercant." Information was their business. "I know you can't discuss the project, but you have my full support. If humans can block Psy intrusion, the world becomes an even playing field, and Trinity might actually succeed."

On this morning, however, a morning that might be the last one she had when her mind wasn't in danger of a catastrophic breach, Silver pushed all thoughts of politics and treaties out of her head and snuggled closer to her bear. He grumbled at her. "I'm mad at you for the bond."

"Can I have naked skin privileges anyway?" Turning in his possessive hold, she drew her leg up the hair-roughened skin of his.

His erection was stone hard against her thigh, but he scowled at her, dark and beloved. "You're not taking this seriously."

"I've decided to adopt the bear approach to life." She kissed him.

He kept scowling but he still kissed her back, he still touched her with rough tenderness, he still loved her until she was limp and drenched in sweat. Silver knew Valentin would always love her—even when she forgot the meaning of love.

Her heart broke.

THE next twelve hours were a blur of scans and tests.

Aware of how much Valentin carried on his shoulders, Silver had convinced him that she could handle this phase on her own. "I'll call you when I need you," she'd said in a tone with which even a bear couldn't argue. "Treat me like a simpering fragile flower at your own risk."

He'd given a short bearish roar before pressing his nose to hers, his eyes narrowed. "You," he'd said, "are an impossible woman."

"Exactly what you need."

After dealing with her bad-tempered mate, she'd told Kaleb what was happening, and he'd provided both the medical facility and the teleport for Ashaya and Amara Aleine and their guard, a white-blond male with lethal blue eyes who Silver recognized as Dorian Christensen.

A leopard sentinel and Ashaya's mate.

With Silver's permission, Ashaya had also looped in Samuel Rain, a brilliant scientist who worked in experimental biofusion. As for the telepathic scan to verify the truth of Silver's request, Ashaya did that herself—the scientist was only 1.1 on the Gradient when it came to telepathy, but as Silver was cooperating, she didn't need anything but basic telepathy to do the scan. For it, Silver had to drop her external shields, but she could only keep them down for three seconds before the telepathic noise of the world threatened to crush her.

Ashaya staggered physically back at the same time that Silver slammed down her shields. Christensen caught his mate, his eyes no longer human but a dangerous green that spoke of the large cat that lived under his skin. "Shaya?"

"I'm fine," the scientist said, though her breathing was erratic, the pulse in her neck rapid. "My ears are ringing. The sound . . . it's dual layered."

Shocked or not, Silver realized, Ashaya Aleine was a scientist first and foremost, one who was already analyzing the data she'd gathered.

"The first," Ashaya added, "is the telepathic noise all Tps hear when their shields are down—and it's violent because Silver is a pure telepath of incredible strength—but below that is actual *sound*."

Amara spoke, her affect curiously flat. "Can't we simply remove her capacity to hear? It would be a far more efficient exercise than neurosurgery."

Silver went still. "Will it work?"

"No," Ashaya said after a thoughtful minute. "You're not hearing through your auditory canal or any other part of your ear. The input is definitely coming in via a psychic pathway." She looked at Amara.

Purest quiet reigned for thirty seconds, the two sharing data.

"My twin is correct," Amara said afterward in the same flat tone.

And so it went.

All the while, she felt Valentin inside her, a huge presence full of an intrinsic wildness wrapped around her like a living shield.

HAVING received a message from Silver that she was on her way home after "having her brain mapped to the last neuron," Valentin had intended to wait for her at the border to StoneWater lands. He'd planned to see if he could pull off a modified tiny-gangster trick just to make her laugh.

All his plans changed when he felt a painful yank inside him just as night began to fall. That sensation was of a healer reaching out desperately for their alpha's strength. Not Nova. A younger healer who was nonetheless bonded to his alpha.

Valentin didn't delay even long enough to send his Starlight a message. He headed straight for the healer in distress. Silver would understand. She was an alpha, too.

"Sergey," he said, stepping out of the trees in front of the cave system that held those of his clan who'd left him. "Who's hurt?"

The tall man of his father's generation, a man who had been first second to Mikhail, folded his arms. "You have no right to be here." White lines bracketing his mouth, he stood his ground, though he was having difficulty meeting Valentin's gaze.

While Sergey's human half had rejected Valentin, the animal knew he was alpha, knew that Sergey shouldn't be trying to oppose him. But Valentin wasn't here to win by force. If it had been about that, he could've subjugated this group eight months ago, when he'd taken over from Zoya and they'd broken away.

"I don't have time for a pissing contest." Valentin was too angry to watch his words—if what he suspected was true, Sergey had let down not just a clanmate but a healer at that. "Someone is badly wounded, and you have only a trainee healer." That trainee, Artem, had come with the splinter group because Sergey was his father—and because a healer needed to come with them. "Why haven't you called Nova?"

"Artem is helping him," Sergey insisted. "There's no need to further stretch Nova. She's already been to see us twice in the past week."

That statement might've softened Valentin if not for one thing. "Your son is killing himself for you." Claws shoved at his fingertips, his bear enraged. "Nova warned me that Artem is already worn down to the bone. I knew you were a stubborn *durak* but I didn't think you'd be stubborn enough to put your own child's life at risk. *Now, who the fuck is hurt?*"

Sergey went white under the roaring force of Valentin's dominance. "It's Jovan." His shoulders slumped. "He got into a fight with Laine and they both shifted. It went to hell in a heartbeat. Laine is scratched up but otherwise fine—he got Jovan in the gut with his claws."

Valentin saw the pain on the other man's face, saw the stress. But he also saw the guilt: the teens were becoming aggressive in the absence of an alpha to calm their bears, and Sergey knew it. They would discuss that later. Right now, Valentin had other priorities. "Take me to them."

Sergey didn't argue again, just turned and led Valentin into the cave system. Pinched faces and stark eyes met his when he walked in. A few jerked toward him, held themselves back at the last minute.

Valentin's bear raged, wounded and angry, but Valentin couldn't force this. These clanmates had to come to him, had to choose to trust him. He made eye contact with every bear he passed, and he smiled at the cubs—who *did* run to him, crying "Mishka! Mishka!"

Easily lifting two children into his arms as he went down on one knee so the others could gather around, he kissed them all on the cheek, squeezed them hard one by one, murmured reassurance that they were still clan, still his. He could only stay a minute or two, but that time was necessary.

These cubs were also becoming stressed in a way that made him beyond furious.

Leaving them chattering happily, he stepped into the small cave that was acting as this group's infirmary. He saw Artem at once; the young male was on his knees beside a comfortable mattress on which an unconscious Jovan had been laid. There was a bed in the room, but the injured boy had been placed on the mattress—which lay directly on the floor—because Sergey and the others obviously knew Artem was too weak to stand for long.

Tamping down his fury with conscious effort of will, Valentin strode to the trainee. "I'm here now, Tyoma." He put one hand on Artem's shoulder as he spoke the affectionate nickname, the other on Jovan's uninjured shoulder. "Take what you need."

A sob from Artem, tears rolling down his bloodless face. But he was a healer to the bone, swallowed his pain to work on the wounded boy. The primal energy of the clan ran from Valentin to Artem and from Artem to Jovan, changed by healer alchemy to be what the body needed to mend itself. Valentin barely felt the draw, the entire strength of the clan behind him . . . even that of the broken shards.

Because he hadn't lied to the cubs who played down the corridor: These bears were still his even if they didn't want to be, their animals reaching out to be part of StoneWater. If there had been a total break, he wouldn't be able to do this, wouldn't be able to help Artem heal his clanmate.

His phone vibrated in his pocket about ten minutes later. Ignoring it, he continued to hold contact with both Jovan and Artem. The healer finally stopped working on Jovan a half hour after that, his trembling body collapsing into Valentin.

Wrapping the young male in his arms, Valentin pressed his lips to the boy's hair.

Over the worn-out healer's head, he checked on Jovan. His stomach wounds were closed, and he was breathing far easier. "Rest now." He held Artem against him until the healer's body grew lax, his breathing even.

Scooping up Artem's far-too-light form in his arms once the healer was asleep, he laid his clanmate down on the unused bed. He was aware of Sergey and his mate hovering in the doorway, but neither interrupted as he pulled the blanket over their son and made sure he was comfortable. Returning to Jovan's side, he brushed the hair off the boy's face, spoke to him, because an alpha's voice was especially important when a clanmate was wounded.

Getting to his feet only after he was sure both the wounded boy and healer were in a deep natural sleep, he headed to the doorway. "I need to get back to the clan."

Sergey swallowed at his curt tone, stepped back, his mate Enja doing the same. The space behind them was filled with a large number of the adults who'd left. But it was shy Enja who spoke, her voice tremulous. "Are Jovan and my son . . . ?"

"They'll both be fine," Valentin reassured her.

When he spoke to the man who'd precipitated the breaking of Stone-Water, however, it was in a much harsher tone; as of today, the time for private talks was over. "Don't allow Artem to get to that state again." His bear was in his eyes, in the claws that erupted from his skin. "He's your son, but he is also a gift to the clan. Look after him, or I'll send someone here who'll make sure of it."

The older man looked as if he'd been struck.

Valentin didn't take any pleasure from the reaction—but it was one thing to be stupid and angry and full of hate toward Valentin, quite another to let a young trainee healer get to Artem's current state. "I'll be back tomorrow to check on him." Jovan would be fine, but Artem would keep giving and giving until he snapped.

Not trusting himself to speak any further, he began to stride out.

A young woman sobbed and stumbled into his arms. He crushed her to him, ran his hand over her hair. A gentle submissive, she was here out of loyalty to her mate, rather than because she'd wanted to leave. Valentin felt only love for her, well aware the competing needs inside her had to be tearing her apart.

However, when he spoke, it was to all of them. "Small bears, you have ten seconds to leave the area and go to the nursery."

Only after that order had been followed, the little ones out of earshot, did he continue. "Denhome is open to you anytime you decide to come back." Then he made the most painful decision of his life as alpha—because what tonight had shown him was that this situation wasn't just deeply hurtful to him and his clan; it was dangerous.

It was time.

"But," he said, "I can't have you camped here anymore. You need to acknowledge an alpha so your young will thrive rather than turning on one another." Bears were predators, big and powerful.

They could do a hell of a lot of damage to each other.

"You also need an alpha so your healer is safe." Several of the adults dropped their heads in shame. "Most dangerous is that you can't hold this territory, which means I have to assign extra clan resources to secure the border. The instant I withdraw the patrols, the wolves will see it as a weak point to claw more territory for themselves."

Selenka was holding to their negotiated truce, but wolves were predators just like bears. Sooner or later, one of her border sentries would figure out that this wasn't simply a satellite part of the clan, but a broken shard of it. At that point, he'd have to rely on BlackEdge's better nature—and despite what bears liked to mutter, the wolves *could* be civilized. It would, however, last only so long.

Wolves were wolves as bears were bears, and changelings could only claim what they could hold. That law existed for a reason.

"You have a month to get off this land or to find yourself an alpha who will help you defend it against the wolves and against StoneWater." Because the instant they brought in another alpha, they became an unknown force in his territory.

Total silence around him.

It was an older woman who finally broke the shocked silence. "Valya, you wouldn't . . ."

He knew her. She'd been a friend of his mother's. He'd played in her cave as a child. "I have a clan to protect," he said, still holding the yet-trembling clanmate who'd come to him. "You can choose to be part of that clan, or you can choose to leave. There is no middle ground." He'd given them eight months longer than anyone else would've done. "One month."

Releasing his clanmate, who was now sobbing in huge gulps, Valentin walked out. His heart *hurt*, but it had to be done. He wouldn't endanger those who chose to be clan for the sake of those who couldn't—wouldn't—forgive the past.

Chapter 36

I will guide this clan. I will cherish my clanmates.
I will dispense justice. I will offer love.
And I will hold StoneWater's secrets as my own.
I take this oath on my honor.

—Part of the oath spoken by Zoya Vashchenko,
Interim Alpha of StoneWater

SILVER WAS OVERWHELMED by a sense of peace when she walked into Denhome. It was noisy here, her head full of countless voices, but it was *home* in a sense her apartment had never been. That had been a place to sleep and to keep her things.

This was a place where the Barnacle barreled straight for her and clamped himself around her leg, a cheeky grin on his face. "Siva!"

She touched her hand to the tight curls of his hair, the texture soft against her palm. "I'm wearing heels, Dima. If I try to take a step with you attached to me, I'll fall flat on my face."

His smile full of mischief, Nova and Chaos's son tightened his embrace for a moment before releasing her and running off to attack another victim. Stepping forward—and only then realizing she'd handled herself on the uneven surface just fine—she found herself accepting more than one teasing congratulations on her mating with Valentin.

After going to her room—their room now—to put away her bag, she returned to the Cavern and to her clanmates. It wasn't difficult to converse with bears; they weren't quick to take offense, and found her direct nature perfectly normal. Possibly because they thought questions such as, *Did Valya tie you up to get you to agree to the mating?* were also normal.

Valentin's arrival was a brush of fur against her senses, her psychic awareness of him a bone-deep pulse. But despite her need to gorge on him, to store away a thousand memories, she didn't rush toward him. She turned, waited. In seconds, he was swamped by children as he always was when he returned to the den after time away.

His eyes met hers over their heads, their chatter music in the air.

She spoke to him with her own eyes, let him know she was content to wait. He was hers, but he was also StoneWater's, an alpha to the core. "Until I met him," she said to Nova, to whom she'd been speaking, "I didn't know one person could love so many people, truly *love* them."

Nova slipped her arm through Silver's. "That's what defines a really great alpha—yes, it takes intelligence and skill and strength, but most of all, it takes a heart huge enough to hold an entire clan. Mishka has always had that. From the day he was born, he made our family better."

Silver closed her hand over Nova's where it lay on her forearm, having caught the bleakness in those final words. "No family is perfect."

"He told you?" A pause too short for Silver to speak. "Of course he did. He's your mate."

Nova leaned her head against Silver's arm. "Our father was a wonderful papa until he began to change. Mishka had it the worst in many ways—he got that wonderful father for the shortest time, and he felt the loss most keenly. He and Papa used to stick together, two men outnumbered by four women." Memories in her voice of a time of innocent happiness. "Mishka was our father's shadow and our pet. Now he's bigger than all of us, with far too much weight on his shoulders."

"He would choose nothing else," Silver said, certain of that beyond any doubt. "He was born with those big shoulders and big feet for a reason."

Nova gave an open-throated laugh. "I like you more each time we meet, Seelichka. And I already liked you a whole lot."

Silver felt the weight of the future smash onto her like a boulder designed to crush. How could she tell Nova and the rest of her friends in the clan that she might soon be incapable of reciprocating their friendship? That, or she'd be dead.

Valentin's heart would break in either case.

"It looks like I'd better grab my son and make sure he eats his dinner rather than his friend's arm as he's threatening to do."

"Shouldn't they be asleep by now?"

"Bears, Seelichka. Small bears, but bears." With that very descriptive answer, Nova went off to grab not only Dima but also his two friends. She held one wriggling body under her arm, gripped another child firmly by the hand, and made the third child hold that one's hand.

The third child looked to be considering escape but one stern look from Nova and he fell in line.

"She's good at cub corralling." Valentin's arms wrapped around her from behind, unrepentantly possessive.

It felt like coming home all over again. Emotion threatened to overwhelm her, a pain in her chest that spread to every corner of her being.

"*Solnyshko moyo.*" A nuzzle against her temple. "Don't be sad."

The simple, rough request threatened to shatter her. "Our bond," she whispered to him, "it's like earth and green and starlight entwined."

She'd never know what Valentin would've said in reply, because loud sobbing interrupted the ordinary conversation in the Cavern. Valentin was moving to intercept the woman who'd run out of one of the many passageways that honeycombed Denhome before Silver realized he'd taken a step.

Slamming against Valentin's massive chest, the woman wailed, "Why didn't you bring her home?" It was a scream. "I want my baby home! How could you tell her to go? She called me! She said you told them to go!"

Valentin's voice was quiet, but Silver heard it with crystal clarity, her audio shields having lost further cohesion during the day. "She's an adult." He held the sobbing woman in a gentle embrace. "She made the choice."

"No!" The distraught female pounded at Valentin's chest with fisted hands. "You're alpha! You *make* her come back!"

Wrapping her totally in his arms, Valentin murmured to her—and again, Silver heard every word. "She'd only leave again." His voice was ragged, his huge heart wounded but still beating because it needed to beat for his clan. "I can't permit her choice or those of the others with her to jeopardize the clan."

The woman screamed again.

Silver's head pulsed.

She slammed up her most powerful shields, the ones she didn't usually use because those shields muffled her senses in a thick fog.

The stab of pain faded at once—but so did her crystalline awareness of her surroundings. She could see and hear everything around her at a normal level, but she felt disconnected from it all. As if she'd cut off part of herself.

Lowering the shield, she braced herself for the pain, but it was more manageable after the short respite . . . and because the mating bond was taking some of the impact. Valentin's big heart was taking some of the impact. Silver tried to stop it—her mate didn't need any more pain—but found it impossible.

The mating bond was as stubborn as the bear to whom it connected her.

In front of her, the woman Valentin had been holding was now sobbing in the arms of a white-haired man with lines carved into his face that spoke of deepest anguish. Valentin looked little better.

It was instinct to go to him, slip her hand into his.

Around them, the Cavern walls dripped with sorrow.

Thankfully, the cubs had all been moved swiftly away the instant the woman ran in.

"The decision has been made," Valentin said, his voice carrying to every corner of the huge space. "It's the only choice that could be made." His words were final.

His eyes locked with hers for an instant, a question in them. Silver answered through their bond—*Yes*, she'd stay. She was his mate, was clan, would stand with him no matter what.

When clanmates came to her, she opened her arms and held them close.

LATE that night, seated on the edge of the bed with Valentin beside her, she fought the infamous Mercant temper as he told her about the ugliness of the day he'd become alpha. What should've been a day of celebration had been marred by a jagged break in the heart of the clan.

"Sergey said I was a good man, a man he respected, but that I came from bad blood," Valentin said, a grittiness to his voice. "Blood that couldn't be trusted. Sergey was my father's best friend and his first second—he became Zoya's first second when she took over."

Silver asked a question so he could pause, his anguish such a huge thing, she worried it would crush him. All the time, her own fury bubbled inside her, a creation of cutting ice. "I don't understand how StoneWater had an alpha available, especially someone of Zoya's age."

"She was the retired alpha of a small clan to which StoneWater has blood ties," Valentin told her. "She stepped in to shepherd StoneWater after we lost my father 'in a terrible accident'—that's what we told everyone, what the rest of the world believes."

He exhaled in a harsh gust. "Only the clan knows that my father was executed by his seconds—he was so strong it took all of them working together to contain him. Even Zoya was only told the truth once she became alpha and had pledged to keep our secrets. Her term was to run just until a new alpha came of age."

"Sergey had to know it would be you." Valentin's dominance was a force of nature.

"I think he hoped he was wrong, that I'd only be a second to another bear." He stared ahead, his shoulders rigid. "In the darkest depths of night, I wonder if Sergey is right, if I'll turn one day, become like my father."

"That's not a possibility." Silver had never known anyone more honest, more centered, more earthy and true. "I feel you inside me, Valentin Mikhailovich Nikolaev, and I'm trained to know the mind. There is no darkness in you." Bad-tempered and arrogant and aggravating he might be, but beyond all that, he was purest light.

Hands fisted between his knees, Valentin's tone was bleak when he replied. "I look like him. I sound like him. Half of me comes from him. And we can't be certain his degeneration wasn't organic."

"The other half comes from your mother." When he still looked defeated, a look that simply did not belong on his face, she allowed her anger to color her tone. "What would you do if you felt such a vicious darkness begin to wake in you? If you felt murderous compulsions?"

"I'd end me," Valentin said without hesitation. "I'd protect my clan by taking the threat out of the equation."

"There's your answer." It was the same answer she'd have given had their positions been reversed.

Amber eyes glowing in the muted light of the room. "Why do you see so clearly?"

"We all see clearly when we haven't lived the pain—and what I see is that I need to kill Sergey."

Looking distinctly alarmed for a man who was twice her size, Valentin scooped her up into his lap. "Was the stabby poet a direct ancestor?"

"Traced back in an unbroken line," Silver confirmed. "Tell me what this Sergey looks like."

"I don't think so, Starlichka, not when you're looking so bloodthirsty."

"He hurt you." No one was permitted to do that. "Now tell me where he lives."

"*Bozhe*, but I love you." Valentin kissed her.

Still coldly furious on his behalf, she kissed him, drank in his laughter. And all the time, the noise continued to grow in her head.

THE next day, Silver managed not to track down and kill Sergey. She also worked a full day despite the pounding in her temples, and she returned to Denhome at a reasonable hour. Given the high caliber of applicants and the fact she might soon be out of commission, she'd sped up the hiring process of the EmNet team. She'd spent the day interviewing and had sent through the first three names for Trinity approval before she left the office.

The approval came through as she reached Denhome. She'd expected as much: She'd chosen one human, one changeling, and one Psy. All, as it turned out, the best people for the job. That they covered the racial spectrum had simply made it difficult for anyone to object. She'd need more than three people, of course, but these three were experienced enough to cover her absence during her healing . . . or if the operation didn't succeed.

She made the calls to the applicants from the car, then told them she was going to run them through a mock disaster scenario. That took an hour, and by the end of it, she was certain beyond any doubt that they'd be able to fill in with the help of her assistant. Everyone would be told that she'd been diagnosed with the beginnings of a cancerous tumor. That wasn't a death sentence if treated at once—no one would be concerned if she was unreachable for a few days after the op, and only available remotely for several weeks afterward.

Valentin, who she knew had gone out to see the young healer in Sergey's group, found her at the table where she was eating dinner with clanmates who'd also driven back in from jobs in the city or who'd just finished their shifts in work within the clan.

Putting one hand on Pavel, who was seated next to her, Valentin shoved the other man aside without the least semblance of politeness. Pavel made sure to grab his bowl of dessert as he moved—giving his alpha a grunt of welcome at the same time.

Valentin sat down, his thigh and shoulder pressing against Silver. In the middle of passing a platter to a clanmate across the table, Silver didn't immediately respond.

"Hey, pay attention to me." Valentin closed his hand over the back of her neck.

"Subtle, Valya," the dominant across from them said with a roll of her green eyes. "Bears really know how to court a woman."

As Valentin grumbled at the older woman, Silver said, "I prefer blunt-ness. Subtle emotion is more difficult for me to read."

The other woman's laughter was full throated. "In that case, you chose your man well. If he ever does subtle, the world might end."

Silver thought of the shadows of memory she'd glimpsed in Valentin's eyes, of the determined cheer that hid the deep sadness at the heart of StoneWater. Bears, she thought, could be far more subtle than the repu-tation they liked to foster.

Waiting until the others had returned to their conversations, she put her hand on Valentin's thigh under the table. Heavy muscle clenched under her hand, Valentin's gaze limned with amber. "You feel exhausted," she murmured, sensing him through the mating bond.

He closed his hand over hers, rubbing the pad of his thumb over her skin. "Our bears are trying to deal with the fact we're about to lose a chunk of our clan. I have to be there for them." No hesitation in his tone at taking on so much emotional weight. "How was work?"

"I have the beginnings of a team." She told him about the three she'd hired, including the partially paralyzed human male who'd previously held the military rank of sergeant. "I've appointed him as my deputy. You were right—my mock scenario showed we'll have no difficulty commu-nicating in an emergency. All of us simply need to wear earpieces so we have direct access to one another."

"I'm always right," her brash bear said with familiar arrogance, but his next words were a rough whisper against her ear, potent with emotion. "And you?"

"Holding on." She hadn't heard back from Ashaya Aleine, but then she hadn't expected to—she was asking the scientist to come up with a quick solution to a highly complex problem.

Placing his hand on the back of her neck again, Valentin tugged her closer. "Have you spoken to your grandmother?"

"No. But I will—when we have a course of action." She leaned into him, knowing that, to the bears around her, such affection was nothing unusual. To her, it meant far more—something Valentin alone would ever truly understand.

"Ena is tough."

"Even the tough can break."

A sudden commotion at that instant had Silver jerking around to look behind her. Valentin was up and running toward the sentry, even as the woman pounded into the center of the Cavern. Whatever words were spoken, Silver didn't hear, her audio telepathy drowning her in a sudden, painful crescendo of noise that couldn't augur anything good. It passed quickly, but the sentry had finished speaking by then.

Valentin's reaction, however, told her all she needed to know: a shudder tore through him, his eyes closing for a long second before he opened them again and said something to the sentry that sent the woman racing back out.

Chapter 37

VALENTIN'S EYES SEARCHED for her, met hers. Their bond flared deep inside her. And somehow, she knew what he was about to say, though he wasn't a telepath and she would never breach his shields. At that instant, the psychic form of an alpha bear filled her to the brim, her skin feeling as if it were coated with luxuriant fur, her hands powerful beyond compare.

Hands on his hips and eyes amber, Valentin shifted his gaze to speak to a clan that had gone unusually silent. "Our clanmates are coming back home. Make sure their rooms are prepped."

A moment of utter motionlessness before everyone exploded into action.

When Dima clambered up to sit next to Silver, quickly followed by three other cubs of a similar age, she decided to assist by keeping them amused and out of the way. Even as she drew the cubs into a logic game, however, she kept an eye on the entrance to the Cavern. It wasn't the entrance to Denhome, but it *was* the heart of this sprawling place, and it was where Valentin stood waiting.

He shot her a speaking look minutes later, holding out his hand.

"Stay here," she said to the cubs in a tone she knew they'd obey.

She was standing by Valentin's side when the air changed. Everyone went quiet, the frenetic activity coming to an abrupt standstill. Suddenly looking down at her, Valentin said, "Don't kill Sergey."

Silver narrowed her eyes. "I'll decide once I hear what he has to say."

The man who appeared in the large entranceway was tall and thin with granite-colored hair and deep grooves carved into his face.

Pain scored that face as he took in the solemn expressions of those who waited. His body was heavy when he stepped inside. Others came in behind him, including two people carried on stretchers. Nova walked next to the stretchers. She was barefoot, her commands crisp and clear as she ordered that the two be taken to the infirmary.

Cubs tumbled into the Cavern after the adults, went immediately to Valentin. He laughed and cuddled each one before giving them permission to join their excited friends at the table and around the Cavern. Dima and the others had stayed in place—though they were bouncing up and down and waving.

Under their chatter was a taut silence.

The adult newcomers, their faces gaunt with strain, lingered near the entrance as if unsure of their welcome. More than one gaze went to Silver.

"Small bears," Valentin said into the mass of unspoken words, "you're out of here. Thirty seconds."

The cubs slid off their seats and ran, the bigger ones holding on to the hands of their younger friends, the cubs who lived in this den reminding their returned friends which way they had to go.

The area was clear of children well within the mandated thirty seconds; two of the adults who Silver knew were in charge of the nursery went with them. The teenagers remained, clearly having permission to stay when the "small bears" order was given.

"There will be no punishment," Valentin said at last, his eyes locked with those of the tall man with granite-colored hair who had to be Sergey. "We've all been punished enough."

Tears on many faces, stark-white shock on others.

"But"—Valentin's tone was brutal—"I *will not* accept disloyalty. Punishment for any such action from this point on will be immediate and harsh."

He looked around, his eyes hard and his voice a boom of sound. "StoneWater as a clan will stay strong, stay a safe place for those who call it home. If that means I have to banish or kill threats to the clan, I will."

Silver was watching the returnees closely, saw the flinches at his use of the word "kill." They had no idea her Valyusha wasn't the real threat. Silver would annihilate anyone who dared hurt him again.

"If you can't live with my 'tainted blood'"—shamed looks from many of the returned—"leave now and you'll live. After this, there will be no second chances."

No one moved.

"Then"—smile open and genuine, he wrapped an arm around the shoulders of a middle-aged male who'd been inching closer to him during the entire speech—"welcome home."

The man turned in to Valentin, hugging him tight before breaking away so someone else could do the same. Only Sergey kept his distance, his expression openly torn.

When he did approach—while Valentin was speaking to two others—it was to come to Silver. "You're Psy."

His harsh words were bullets shot into stone. The Cavern turned deadly quiet.

"She is my mate." Valentin responded before Silver could, his tone as harsh. "If you have anything to say about that, Sergey, say it to your alpha."

The older male looked away, his jaw working.

Others, meanwhile, were staring at Silver, waiting. And she knew this moment was critical, would determine who she was as Valentin's mate. Much as she wanted to turn Sergey's brain into neural soup, that was not what her bear wanted. So she'd give this man and the others a chance to redeem themselves. "Welcome home," she said. "Your clan has missed you."

More than one shaky smile, the pinched look fading from their faces.

"Food! Drink!" Valentin yelled into the tremulous hope. "Today, we celebrate a united clan!"

Cheers thundered through the Cavern, coming first from those who'd never left, but joined only seconds later by those who had—many of whom were red-eyed and shaking. Valentin's arms were open to all, his big body a sturdy oak against which they could find strength.

When people kept glancing at Silver with wide eyes, she went with instinct and extended her hands to show them that contact was welcome.

The offer was taken up by many. "I always knew he'd pick a mate as strong as he is," one woman whispered with a deep smile.

Another said, "Trust Valentin to nab not just a Psy but Silver Mercant herself. He's always made his own rules." There was pride in those words, respect in the eye contact.

Sergey remained aloof, but he was a bear; he couldn't hide his torment.

Walking over to him once she was free, Silver spoke before he could say a word. "You have only two choices."

He held her gaze in an aggressive challenge.

Silver was intimidated by no one, least of all a tortured bear. She did not look away. "You can hold on to your fear and let it drive you to hate, or you can trust in the bonds of clan. There is no middle ground."

"You know *nothing* of what this clan has suffered." Fisted hands, a clenched jaw.

"I'm your alpha's mate," she reminded him with icy precision. "I know this clan is full of warmth and a wild kind of love that doesn't hold grudges. To StoneWater, family means everything." Was it any wonder she'd fallen for the entire clan? "You chose to fracture that. Your choice now is to either fix that error—or walk away."

"You have no right to say that to me."

"I will do anything to protect Valentin. If that means eliminating a threat, I'll do it without compunction and without a single ounce of guilt." She made sure he saw the deadly truth on her face. "His heart is huge, but that doesn't mean you get to kick it. *Choose*."

Sergey swallowed . . . then subtly broke the aggressive eye contact. A second later, he walked toward Valentin and when Valentin drew him into his arms, he didn't resist. Instead, he held on hard, his body shaking as tears streaked his face.

The others gave them space.

Silver, too, shifted away, going to help two of the clan who were setting up tables for the food and drink Valentin had ordered. Moira, her baby strapped to her chest, sat with them. "I don't know what you said to Sergey," she murmured, her tone a little awed, "but that ornery bear has never showed submission to anyone but his alpha."

Yakov looked up from where he was on his knees putting up a table. "Valentin found a mate worthy of him."

Silver took that as the compliment it was meant to be—but she was also bear enough now to say, "I'd say I found a mate worthy of me."

Eyes amber, Yakov grinned. "Will Valentin punch me if I kiss you?"

"He is more likely to rip off your head."

"Might be worth it."

Silver considered the mood in the Cavern, considered the life she'd never have, considered what it was to be a bear—and leaned down to grip Yakov's jaw. She'd pressed a kiss to his mouth before he recovered from his surprise. Clanmates laughed as the dominant bear fell back on his ass. "Definitely worth it," he said, a happiness in his eyes that had nothing to do with the skin privileges.

The same happiness infused others around them.

Even Valentin when he ordered Yakov to keep his sneaky paws to himself.

It was about clan, about family, about bonds of the heart.

She understood so much now, saw how it could be, how she and her alpha bear could walk side by side, taking both the Mercant family and StoneWater into a dazzling future. But the noise inside her head, which had dimmed for an hour that had given her a false hope, it started to grow again. And grow and grow.

When Valentin found her sitting on the edge of their bed a half hour later, he was smiling. "There you are. Nova said you popped in here to—"

Cutting himself off midword, he hunkered down in front of her. "Starlight, you're crying."

Silver lifted a hand to her left cheek, touched the moisture there. "Oh." She hadn't known, hadn't realized. "The noise, it hurts."

THE quiet words from his strong Silver broke Valentin.

Gathering her into his arms, he sat down against a wall with her in his lap. "What can I do?" he asked, because he had to do something. "I'll take you out of Denhome, deep into the—"

"*No.*" She raised her head, her eyes still damp and her pupils hugely dilated but her will as steely as ever. "This night is important for our clan." Her fingers over his lips when he would've spoken. "And my range is phenomenal now. I can hear for miles, sound layer on sound layer."

Valentin's bear pounded its paws in primal frustration. "Can Nova knock you out?"

"I've considered it, but drugs have unpredictable effects on Psy senses—they could smash open my remaining shields." She took a deep breath and wiped away her tears. "I can hold on."

So fucking strong.

He rose with her, kissed tiny kisses all over her face until her lips tugged up. "You handled Sergey like an alpha bear."

No doubt the irritable older bear and Valentin would still butt heads, but the other man had come to him, and Sergey wasn't two-faced about anything. He'd been blatant in his distrust, and now he'd be as open in his choice to trust Valentin.

"You need to scream, you scream," he told his Starlight. "This is a bear party. Everyone will think you're having a great time."

Silver's smile deepened, lit her up. "Perhaps I will be rowdy tonight. I am now mated to a bear, after all. It's required."

"Exactly." She was so beautiful in her strength, he wanted to go to his knees, wanted to worship her. "Now let me show you how bears party."

Pain lingered in the fine lines that had formed at the corners of her eyes, but as he watched, she took a deep breath, lowered her lashes, and when they lifted back, her pain was gone. Shielded. Hidden. Except from Valentin. Inside him, he felt all of her, all her glory and all her hurt.

They walked out to join the party hand in hand. It began in a muted form as reunited friends and family cried and hugged, but then the beer began to flow—along with champagne for the fancy ones in the clan—and the laughter started.

Clanmates caught up, they danced. The small bears were allowed back into party a little past their bedtime, before being laid down on makeshift sleeping nests around the party area. The cubs fell contentedly asleep despite the chaos, happy being in the heart of clan.

Valentin joined in the celebration.

He laughed, he talked, he even entered a beer-drinking contest, but all the while his mind was on the woman with hair of moonlight who had fit so naturally into StoneWater.

When it came time to dance, he danced with her first, tucking her close to his body so she could go limp and abandon her teeth-gritting control for a fragment of time. He held her as she shuddered in pain, the movement hidden by his body and the energetic dancing all around them. "I've got you, *moyo serdechko*," he whispered, because she *was* his heart, the idea of a life without his Starlight by his side a nightmare beyond bearing. "I've got you."

He said the same things that night, as she slipped into unconsciousness after putting herself out using a psychic technique. And he held her all night long, his bear's heart tearing itself into a million pieces.

Chapter 38

I have often been asked what gave me the courage and the hope to continue the peace negotiations in the face of so much terror and bloodshed. The answer is love.

Even in the depths of the wars, even in the deepest horror, I saw lovers kiss and parents hug their babies, I saw brothers and sisters laugh together and I saw enemy soldiers raise an orphaned child as their own.

Love, this maddening, joyous creature of light—it refused to die. So how could I give up?

—From the private diaries of Adrian Kenner: peace negotiator,
Territorial Wars (eighteenth century)

THE CALL CAME at six forty-five a.m. the next morning, while they were still in bed. Silver was awake and curled into him, her hair a cool moon-lit river over the arms he'd wrapped around her.

This call, however, had to be answered.

Ashaya Aleine's face was drawn with fatigue, but her eyes were crystal clear. "We think we've come up with a solution that has a chance of long-term success."

Valentin closed his hands over Silver's shoulders from behind, the two of them speaking to Ashaya via Silver's organizer, which she'd propped up on a shelf at the right height. "How dangerous is your solution?" Valentin asked.

"Dangerous," Ashaya said flatly. "Silver could die on the operating table."

His entire being rebelled, his claws threatening to erupt from his fingertips.

"I'd like the details." Silver raised one hand to close it over his.

"Frankly, it's experimental." Ashaya folded her arms, her upper body clad in a light blue shirt with long sleeves. "You're the first and maybe only ever patient."

"Not if it works," Silver responded, sounding far calmer than Valentin felt. "If this works and if audio telepaths are identified soon enough, they can be saved."

Ashaya pursed her lips, then shook her head as if shaking off an unwanted thought. The dark curls of her unbound hair bounced around her head. "Samuel Rain was the one who put us on this path."

"What did he suggest?"

"It wasn't so much what he suggested as that he brings a wild card into the situation that makes me and Amara both think in new ways. In this case, that's led us to consider rerouting your neural pathways."

The scientist brought up a diagram. "Since we're working on the assumption that emotion and audio telepathy are linked—and it *is* still an assumption notwithstanding the data we've been able to gather—it follows that if we disconnect the two, the Tp-A part of your brain may simply stop working."

Silver's next question made Valentin want to wrap her up and hold her close where nothing and no one could ever hurt her. "I'd still be able to feel?"

Ashaya's expression was grim. "I don't know. Despite hundreds of years of research, the exact mechanisms of psychic power aren't well understood. It could be that one can't exist without the other. You've done enough research on your own to know the other risks."

"Yes, there are myriad possible complications." Silver still sounded far too calm.

Not calm at all, Valentin gave in to need and wrapped her in his arms from behind. "Explain them to me."

"It's possible that in rerouting my pathways," Silver said, "they could damage my primary telepathic ability."

"The brain is a complex mechanism." Ashaya unfolded her arms, her expression pensive. "Things are linked in ways we don't fully understand. The operation *could* succeed in permanently shutting down Silver's audio telepathy, erasing her ability to feel emotion at the same time—or it could give her audio telepathy a far larger pathway." She paused. "The latter risk is low given all we know, but it is present."

Valentin's bear rose inside him, agitated and angry. "Cutting the link between Silver's secondary ability and emotion seems like a simple solution. Why hasn't anyone else ever thought of it?"

"My family considered it long ago," Silver told him. "But the risk at that time was catastrophic and, with my shields working to block my audio channels, I had no need to take that risk."

"The technology just wasn't there," Ashaya added, before bringing up more detailed diagrams of the proposed operation. "As you may be aware, Silver, I'm Designation M."

"With the ability to manipulate DNA itself."

Ashaya's lips tugged into an unexpected smile. "Of course a Mercant would know that. This would be much safer if I could manipulate your DNA, but I have no idea which part of your genetic code to target, given the mysteries that still surround psychic abilities."

"I understand." Silver inclined her head. "When can you operate?"

Ashaya shook her head. "I'm no neurosurgeon. We've lined up a brilliant one whose discretion is unimpeachable, but I'd like to take several further scans, keep you under close observation for—"

"I don't have much time, Ashaya." Silver's voice was crystalline in its precision.

Valentin crushed her closer, aware the pain was ripping her to pieces. He willed the mating bond to take more, give it to him. He could take it, take anything for his Starlight.

"The sound level is close to unendurable," she continued. "I'm having trouble distinguishing your voice from the others screaming in my head. Valentin's is the only clear one."

"That's the mating bond kicking in to assist." The other woman picked up an organizer, appeared to be flipping through pages of data. "How long before you can no longer maintain?"

"Twenty-four hours."

Valentin's bear staggered. "Can you organize the operation that quickly?" he asked Aleine.

The scientist pinched the bridge of her nose between her forefinger and thumb, thinking so hard he could almost hear it. "Yes," she said at last. "But we need Silver for those twenty-four hours for scans, observation, brain mapping."

"Tell me where," Valentin said. "I'll make sure she gets there."

Surprisingly, the operating suite proved to be only a short drive away, the surgeon having already been in the region when Ashaya contacted him. It was in the same private hospital where Silver had had her scans. Owned by Krychek as it was, Valentin had no concerns about the staff's discretion—the cardinal might be ruthless, but as Valentin had noted long ago, he inspired loyalty among his people.

"How will you and the others get there?" Silver asked Ashaya.

"Don't worry about us. Just make your way there ASAP."

"Let's go," Valentin said, already moving to grab his socks and boots.

"You can't come with me," Silver argued, even as she changed. "The clan needs you today more than it ever has."

He wanted to roar at her like one of the damn lions who went around telling people they were the kings of the jungle. He'd like to see the peacocks strut if they pissed off an alpha bear. All Valentin's bear would have to do was sit on one and he'd win. "My mate comes first!" It came out a yell. So did his next words. "That's how a clan works! It all flows from the top!"

Of course she didn't give in, his Starlight with her spine of steel and her capacity to embrace an entire clan as family. "Your clan—*our* clan— is hurt, Valyusha. The normal rules don't apply."

"Fuck yes they do." Ignoring the mess of his own hair, he pushed his hands through the silk of hers. "I am not letting you go through this alone." It was a growl of sound.

"They'll be testing for the entire day." Silver stood toe-to-toe with him, the infuriating, beautiful woman. "Arwen can stay with me for that, and you need to allow him that. He's an empath. He's had me within telepathic contact his entire life."

Valentin kissed her lush mouth. "You don't have to convince me about family, you maddening woman. I understand." It was obvious Arwen adored Silver, idolized her. Valentin understood family. Understood that, sometimes, a man had to share his greatest treasure. "Scans and tests only?"

A nod. "I'll contact you the minute they confirm the time of the operation itself." This time, she was the one who kissed him. "You can be there in under an hour."

The latter was true, Krychek having located his private facility on the outskirts of Moscow, on land that was otherwise unoccupied except for trees and wildlife.

"Before I go," Silver added, "I need to see the clan, quietly tell my friends that I have to be away from Denhome for a while."

He sensed no sadness or bleakness in her, only a fierce determination. "Don't betray your secret," he said. "It protects you." It wasn't that he didn't trust his clan, but they were a big group, and people could let things slip without any bad intentions behind the slip.

"Agreed." Silver smiled. "We'll do this. We'll beat it."

"Hell yes, we will."

EXHAUSTED by the tests and the level of noise in her head, Silver nonetheless continued to hold on to hope. It was hard, but she refused to surrender, to give in—if she did, it was Valentin who'd hurt. And that was simply unacceptable.

After the long day, she was almost surprised when the surgeon stated that he had enough data to perform the operation. "Three hours," Dr. Bashir told her. "You should inform the large male who dropped you off. I certainly don't want him coming after me for lack of notice."

Silver nodded and, sitting up on the examination table, waited for
the surgeon to leave before saying, "Arwen." Her brother had waited outside
while Dr. Bashir completed his final examination—a full-body workup.

Her overall health would factor into her recovery.

Are you clothed? her brother asked.

No, I'm stark naked and looking to involve you in an incestuous orgy.

Pushing aside the privacy curtains, her brother walked in with a faint
scowl, his designer gray suit paired with a tie in a darker gray, his shirt
white. "Those bears are a bad influence on you." But there was no humor
in his face, in his eyes. "So?"

She just nodded. And opened her arms.

He jerked into them, holding on so tight she could barely breathe. She
held him back as closely, her sensitive, gifted brother who had kept her
"human," even in the depths of Silence. The empath who would make
sure she didn't turn into a psychopath, even if she lost the capacity to feel.
"I'm Silver Fucking Mercant, Arwen. This won't beat me."

Arwen's jerking tears came to a sobbing stop before turning into muffled laughter against her shoulder. "Those bears again?"

"Valentin." The thought of him made joy fill every cell of her body,
made her know what it was to be fully alive. "Are you saying he's wrong?"

Arwen shook his head, his arms still locked around her. "You *are*
Silver Fucking Mercant."

She stroked his hair until he lifted his head. Wiping off the remnants
of his tears, she said, "I love you, Arwen." She'd never said that to him,
to her twin who wasn't a twin.

His throat moved as he swallowed convulsively. "Me, too," he said,
his voice a rasp. "You know Grandmother will never forgive you if you
do this without telling her."

"I'll talk to her after I tell Valentin the time of the operation. Grandmother will handle it much better now that I can present her with a
solution."

Arwen's eyes held hers. "Come back, Silver. I can't do life without you."

"You should call Pasha. He knows how to do life, and I'm sure he
wants to do certain things to you, too."

Color flooded Arwen's cheeks. "You've definitely been corrupted by the bears." Lifting her phone off the side table with that accusation, he handed it to her. "You'll want to call Grandmother and your alpha bear yourself."

"Yes." She waited until he'd stepped out before making the call to Valentin. Then, she called the woman who'd been the defining force in her life.

TWO and a half hours later, Silver sat prepped and ready on a hospital bed, Valentin in front of her.

"Promise me something," he said.

When she tilted her head questioningly to the side, he said, "If the operation takes your emotions, I want you to promise me ten dates afterward. A chance to win you back."

"I promise," Silver said without hesitation. "But Valentin, you understand nothing will win me back if my emotions are permanently suppressed?"

She touched her lips to his before he could answer, the kiss a gentle thing. It was so strange, how powerful touch could be. She could keep this big man in place with a butterfly caress. Once, she'd have taken it as a sign of weakness on his part, power on hers. That was before she understood the touch would have as deep an impact on her, that she'd do anything to make him smile, make him feel pleasure.

Today he shuddered, this strong bear who had hands twice as big as her own, and whose physical strength dwarfed hers many times over. "You'll lose me," she said because she had to prepare him for the hurt she might inflict. "The surgeon believes there's a seventy-five-percent chance of success—"

Valentin's face cracked into a huge smile. "Damn that's good."

"There's also a *very* high chance that the operation will permanently deaden the part of me that feels." Ashaya and Dr. Bashir had come to that conclusion earlier today. "I'll be gone. You'll lose me."

"You'll lose yourself, too." Valentin's voice came out raw. "The woman you are without Silence, the full brightness of you, *solnyshko moyo*, it'll be shoved into a small box."

Silver went motionless; she'd been so worried about him that she hadn't thought about the consequences to herself. It slammed into her with brutal force. If the surgeon did turn off the part of her that felt, it would permanently turn off a part of *her*. The part that could hug and tease her brother. The part that could kiss a child's cheek, the part that felt not only loyalty toward her grandmother, but also a deep, *deep* love and an unending pride.

The part that loved Valentin until loving him was an essential element of her being.

"Oh." A shaky sound of acknowledgment.

Powerful arms wrapping around her, a bass heartbeat against her cheek. "I'll die," she whispered. "Part of me, a part I've barely had the chance to explore, it'll die."

"But you'll live." Her mate's voice was barely human. "You'll live and you'll be Silver Fucking Mercant who owns her enemies and who I'll get to see shining bright for the rest of my own life."

Silver blinked back the staggering sense of loss. "I'll be able to protect my family in the coming decades of uncertainty." So many lives, so many futures. "And I'll be there for StoneWater. I vow this. Even if I forget my emotions, I'll remember the vow. So long as I draw breath, the clan will always have a friend in the Mercants."

Amber eyes stared into her own, her Valyusha's forehead pressed to hers. His generous heart deserved to never again feel pain, but she knew he'd endure it because that was who he was. An alpha to the core. A man who would never let her down.

"Silver Fucking Mercant, Ice Queen and my mate. *Lyubov moya*." His voice shook on the words of love. "You will be that to me to my dying day. If the worst happens and if you ever need me, call. I'll be there. I'll always be there."

Chapter 39

Death comes in endless forms. Of the body. Of the soul. Of the heart.

—Catriona Mercant, philosopher and warrior (circa 1419)

THEY'D COME FULL circle, Valentin thought as he sat beside Ena Mercant in the waiting room of the private hospital early the next morning. Once again, he waited to see if Silver would wake up, while beside him sat a regal woman who reminded him too much of the brilliant, driven telepath who was his other half.

"You've made a sacrifice." Ena's voice was as cool as always, as cool as Silver's could get when she wanted to make a point.

"Grandmother, I have no idea what you're talking about."

"My granddaughter holds you in high esteem," Ena said. "You could've convinced her to make a different choice."

His head snapped toward her. "Hell no! I would've never done that!" Gritting his teeth, he rose to his feet, stalked across the small space and back. "We're talking about her *life*. If I could give up my own to save hers, I'd do it in a heartbeat."

Ena's eyes lifted to his, alpha to alpha. She gave a regal nod right as his bear was starting to rumble in his chest. "Regardless of today's outcome, I won't forget what you were to my granddaughter."

Valentin thrust his hands through his already wildly tumbled hair, fought the urge to pull. Sitting down beside Ena, he did something he probably shouldn't. He reached out and put his arm around her. She stiffened but didn't pull away. "She's magnificent. And she's ours. We'll do whatever we have to, to protect her."

"Yes."

That was all that needed to be said. They sat in silence until the doors to the operating theatre opened hours later. Ashaya and Amara Aleine walked out together with the surgeon, a fortysomething man of medium height. As expected, Amara broke off to head down the corridor in the opposite direction, while Ashaya and Dr. Edgard Bashir came toward them.

All were dressed in surgical white, though they'd removed the transparent gear that would've covered their heads and faces during the operation, as well as all other accoutrements of the surgical suite.

A man with disheveled dark blond hair exited in their wake, jogged to catch up with Amara. *Samuel Rain*. No one came after him, the nurses still inside.

Valentin and Ena had both risen to their feet at the first sign of the doors being opened. "How is she?" Valentin's bear wanted to rampage through those doors, grab hold of his Starlight.

"Stable." Ashaya's answer made him stagger inside.

"Then why aren't you smiling?"

Blue-gray eyes held his, sadness swirling in their depths. "I'm sorry, Valentin, but there is a close to hundred percent chance that her Silence will be flawless when she wakes."

"She's alive." That was what mattered. "And she still has her telepathy?" Silver would rather die than lose that.

"Unless there are unforeseen complications," Dr. Bashir said, "her telepathy should remain unaffected."

A single curl escaped the bun at Ashaya's nape to dance against her cheek. "The operation didn't go exactly as planned."

Ena stirred. "Explain."

"We couldn't cut the link between her audio telepathy and her emotions, couldn't even see the pathway that appeared to exist in the scans," Dr. Bashir began, the silver threads in his dark hair glinting in the overhead light. "As a result, we had to isolate the part of her that feels emotion."

"Dr. Bashir based his surgical intervention on the neural information Amara and I collected during the creation of the chip," Ashaya added, a fine tension to her jawline. "I just hope we weren't wrong."

"There's no reason to believe that," the surgeon said firmly. "The logic of the surgery is sound. We effectively sealed off every conduit going from the emotional center of her brain—it's now an island unconnected to any other part."

Ashaya's eyes never left Valentin's, the understanding in them stark. "Since the—albeit limited—data we have supports the assumption that audio telepathy does not exist in the absence of emotion, I feel confident in saying it's been neutralized."

"She's safe?" It was the only question to which he needed an answer.

Ashaya and Dr. Bashir both nodded.

My mate, my heart's sun, is safe.

It was Ena who spoke, and she spoke to him. "We knew it was a possibility that Silver might lose her emotions."

Valentin told her with his eyes that it was all right; he'd do everything in his power to help Starlight through this new part of her life. Even if it was one that meant leaving him behind.

Valentin didn't know how to stop loving someone.

Ena inclined her head very slightly in acknowledgment.

Ashaya's voice broke the silence filled with an unspoken understanding between an alpha bear and an alpha Psy. "The possible total loss of her emotions is why we discussed a remedial option with her."

The surgeon was more blunt in his response. "I seeded her brain with fine biofusion tendrils . . . though I think filament is the better term in this case, because these aren't offshoots of a larger biofusion implant."

Valentin didn't like the sound of any of that. "Why?" It came out so deep, he saw Dr. Bashir wince.

"The filaments integrate into the brain," Ashaya said, "become fused to it. Samuel and Dr. Bashir both saw the effect in the brain of another patient."

"You two need to be clearer," Ena said, her tone flat.

"In the course of his continuing work on creating a prosthetic—"

"—for Vasic Zen," Ena interrupted. "I assume the experimental bio-fusion gauntlet left the Arrow with artefacts in his brain that make ordinary options difficult. Why does any of that matter in Silver's case?"

"Because," Ashaya said, not taking Ena to task for having that privileged information, "Samuel inadvertently made a breakthrough that means his new second-generation filaments respond to conscious commands."

Valentin would be the first to admit he was no scientific mastermind, but he could put two and two together. "These things will let Silver, what, create new conduits?"

Dr. Bashir gave a hard nod, his dark eyes shining with a scientific fervor that told Valentin he'd enthusiastically embraced the fall of Silence. "With how untried the filaments are, the risk wouldn't be worth it to most people, but Silver's situation is unique—and she was adamant."

Valentin had no doubts at all about the latter. His Starlight knew her own mind. Always had. Always would.

"For example," Dr. Bashir continued, "if we did inadvertently damage her telepathic channels, she should be able to reintegrate them." The older man drew in the air with his hands. "We seeded her entire brain with the filaments—she has the materials to create bridges wherever necessary."

"Since Silver is more than smart enough not to want her audio telepathy back, that connection shouldn't be made." Ena stared at Ashaya rather than the surgeon. "Exactly *how* experimental are these filaments in my granddaughter's brain?"

"No ordinary medic would ever think of using them," the scientist said frankly. "The only reason we even offered Silver the option was the minor but possible risk of damage to her telepathy."

Ena continued to watch Ashaya without blinking. But Ashaya Aleine was mated to a very dominant leopard for a reason. She had the same kind of steel as Valentin's Starlight.

Not flinching under Ena's icy regard, she said, "Samuel has been obsessively testing the new filaments since he discovered what they can do. To ensure their safety, Dr. Bashir didn't insert anything like a battery into Silver's brain, nothing that would create energy or reroute her own energy to the filaments."

She paused, her eyes going from Ena to Valentin. When neither one of them interrupted, she continued, "That means it'll take intense focus on Silver's part to use the filaments, but it also means that if they fail, they'll simply lie dormant."

"How sure are you of that?" Valentin demanded, fighting the urge to grab the surgeon and scientist both and shake them for offering Starlight such a reckless choice. Didn't the idiots know that his Silver was a risk-taker? She hid it well under that cool, composed exterior, but his mate had a wild streak in her.

Look how she'd ended up in bed with a bear.

Dr. Bashir took a step back, his excitement fading under the force of Valentin's silent fury. "The only risk," he managed to say, "is that long-term, their presence might cause a reaction in the brain. Silver knew that, accepted it."

Squaring his shoulders, the doctor cautiously returned to his previous position. "I've seen dormant first-generation filaments in another brain— Vasic Zen's, since Mercants apparently know everything, exactly as rumored," he added sourly. "I have no qualms in saying the danger is negligible. The brain doesn't seem to notice them unless they're active."

Valentin glared at the surgeon, even as hope bounced up inside his heart like a hyperactive puppy. "Let me get this straight—if Silver chooses to feel emotion, she could do it without risk?"

It was Ashaya who answered. "As she'll be able to sense and test her own psychic pathways in a way no surgeon can, she could conceivably reconnect the emotional network to the rest of her brain *without* reconnecting the audio telepathy."

"Like a road built around a swamp," Dr. Bashir dared put in. "It'd still be there, but safely isolated."

"Or that's how it's supposed to work." Ashaya, her face drawn, slid her hands into the pockets of her surgical smock. "It's an experiment, but it's the best chance we could give her."

"I can see her in the Honeycomb." Ena's frigid voice. "How is that possible?"

"Her brother ensured the connection didn't fail during the operation, though I don't know the technical details of how," Ashaya replied. "Once she's conscious, she'll know it's in her best interest not to resist it. It should ameliorate the danger of sociopathy arising from a total lack of emotion."

Valentin thought of Arwen's smile when Silver had hugged him right before the operation, of the puppyish way the slick Psy male hung on his sister's every word. He'd be devastated by the change in her, now that he'd seen who she could be with emotion. But, as it did to Valentin, Silver's life meant far more to Arwen than his own happiness or sense of loss.

The only reason he wasn't waiting with Ena and Valentin was because he was covering for Ena's unexplained absence.

"*Spasibo*," Valentin said to both Ashaya and Dr. Bashir. "You saved an extraordinary life today." Of a woman who was already changing the world, and who would grow ever more brilliant as she grew into herself and into her strength. Valentin's heart would burst with pride for her, even as it broke. "Can we see her?"

"The nurses are moving her into an isolation room using a connected lift"—a nod back toward the surgical suite—"but Arwen will alert her to come to consciousness as soon as Dr. Bashir judges that she's stable enough to be awake," Ashaya told him. "You can see her then."

That time came too quickly and far too slowly. Ena gave Valentin an extraordinary gift by permitting him to be the first inside Silver's room. His mate's face was pale but beautiful under the network of monitoring wires woven into her hair. They'd shaved that glorious hair in a small square patch that would be easy to hide until it grew back—that'd be important to his Starlight.

Not because of vanity, but because it was part of her armor.

Her lashes lifted at that moment, the fuzziness of a psychic deep sleep rapidly replaced by acute intelligence.

"Hello, Starlight." He went to take her hand.

She curled it away from him.

A punch with a stone fist wouldn't have hurt more. His bear dropped its head, backed off. Swallowing the hurt, because she was alive, was breathing, he curled his own hand to his side. "You're okay?"

When Silver spoke, her voice was raspy but otherwise strong. "My mental acuity and telepathic reach are undamaged."

"The audio telepathy?"

"Dead." A long pause, her eyes on him. "I remember our relationship together," she said at last, "but I feel no compulsion to re-create it. I can no longer even understand why I acted in such an irrational manner." She stopped speaking only long enough to swallow, wet her throat. "I recall asking for biofusion filaments to be put in my brain."

The puppy inside him, the hopeful innocence, it trembled. "Dr. Bashir got them in."

"I won't be using them." Silver's voice was toneless in a way it had never been, not even when she was shutting her apartment door in his face. "I don't know why the woman I was wanted to feel emotion again—her memories are like those of another species altogether. Do you under-stand?"

"Yes, *solnyshko moyo*, I get it." It crushed man and bear both to hear her speak to him as if he were some random person on the street, but seeing her chest rise and fall, seeing her free of the agony that had brought her to tears, it was worth every second of heartache.

"I just came to see for myself that the operation was a success." Unable to resist, he sneaked a touch of a strand of her hair that was spread out on the pillow. "Remember what I said—if you ever need me, all you have to do is say the word."

Silver Mercant, the woman who was his and yet, paradoxically, who might never be his again, said, "I appreciate all you did for me, Alpha Nikolaev. Without you I may never have contacted Ashaya Aleine. I am in your debt."

He went to say there were no debts between them, decided to hell with that. Fighting fair wasn't on the agenda. Not today, not any fucking day until his heart physically gave up. His bear, wounded but determined, rose up on its feet, stared out of eyes he knew had shifted to amber. "Ten dates." He rumbled deep in his throat. "You owe me those."

"I'll keep my word," she said in the toneless voice that made him want to bellow in uncivilized rage, "but the outcome is guaranteed."

"Then you have nothing to lose by holding to our terms."

Chapter 40

Love will find its way
Through paths where wolves would fear to prey

—From "The Giaour" by Lord Byron, Psy, poet, lover, & soldier (d. 1824)

IT WASN'T UNTIL Valentin was on his knees in the forest a day after the surgery, a bearish roar erupting from his mouth, that he realized one critical thing: His heart was battered black and blue with bruises, but it wasn't broken . . . because the mating bond was gone and *not* gone at the same time.

What?

He froze in place.

Silver's frost and fire was missing inside him, but he didn't feel empty. He *should*. He poked at the wound. *Blya*, it hurt! But he wasn't numb, wasn't lost. He poked again, just to be sure. "Fuck!"

Sulking at the pain because it meant his mate wasn't with him, he sat there in the fallen leaves and tried to make sense of something that didn't make sense. Changelings who lost their mates through death or other causes, yet managed to hold on to life, were faded shadows of themselves. Valentin's mother wasn't whole even after all these years. She functioned, but that was it.

In contrast, Valentin was so angry and in pain and missing Silver as if he'd lost a limb, but he wasn't fundamentally broken. His bear wasn't anywhere close to insane. In fact, that bear was decidedly grumpy . . . but it remained firmly convinced that Silver was its mate.

That puppyish hope sat up again, wagging its stubby tail. If the mate bond wasn't broken, then Silver couldn't be totally Silent, no matter what everyone believed. They'd said it themselves—the brain was a complicated organ.

Valentin scowled at the puppy. He was a damn alpha bear; he wasn't a puppy. *"Zatknis'!"* But the stupid thing wouldn't shut up. "Yip, yip, yip!" It danced inside his heart. Getting up off his knees because it was annoying him, he threw back his head and made a loud sound that caused the smaller creatures in the forest to go motionless.

That shut the puppy up—for about a minute.

Then . . . "yip."

"Grr!" Giving up, he found his phone, which he'd managed not to mangle—Silver might call him on it—and contacted Arwen.

Silver's brother had given Valentin his code before the operation, saying, "You love my sister. You'll hurt when she's Silent. Call me if you wish to talk."

Valentin had the feeling the other man was the one who needed to talk. Right now, Valentin wasn't in the mood to talk to anyone except his mate, but he needed this question answered. "Arwen," he said without explanation when Silver's brother accepted the call. "Can you still sense my bond with Silver?" Silver had told him she'd hidden it to protect it from curious eyes, but that Arwen, connected to her in the Honeycomb, could "see" it through his empathy.

"No." The empath's voice was carefully gentle. "It's gone."

No. It wasn't.

"It's there." Valentin set his feet apart, prepared to become an immovable wall. "I don't know how, but it's there."

"I wish I could say it was, because that would mean my sister was whole and herself, but it's not, Alpha Nikolaev."

Valentin's scowl grew deeper. "The audio telepathy? It's definitely dead?" That mattered more than his hope or Arwen's need.

"Oh, yes." Arwen's voice dropped. "My sister is . . . different, more Silent than the Silent. More Silent than I've ever known her to be." A long pause, the next words shaky. "I miss her."

So did Valentin. Every second, every minute, every hour. "You doing okay?"

"Yes."

"Stop lying. You're hurting." Bruised though it was, Valentin's alpha heart responded to the pain of a man who was now part of his family. "You know I won't betray you. Silver loves you. I'll protect you for that alone."

A shuddering breath. "Yes, I'm hurting." The answer was fractured. "I'm trying to contain it for my grandmother's sake, but it feels as if I've lost part of myself. Grandmother is as strong as always, but— I shouldn't be speaking of family matters with you."

"You know I'm family, Arwen." No matter what, his soul was linked forever to Silver's. "Ena having a tough time?"

"Tougher than I expected. I thought she'd appreciate Silver's perfect Silence, but . . . she's sad that Silver's lost part of herself. Grandmother would never describe it as sadness, but I know it's there, like I've always known she would fight to the death to protect me and Silver."

"I'll talk to her."

"Grandmother isn't likely to appreciate it," Arwen said, his tone distinctly dubious.

"Don't worry, Arwen. I have a way with tough Mercant women." Hanging up to a strangled sound from the other man, Valentin headed to Denhome.

Sergey was the first person he saw. The other man gave him a stiff nod, followed by a scowl. "It's not my business, Valya, but where's your mate? Did you make her angry enough to leave you already?"

Had the question been asked in aggression, Valentin would've given him a response no one would've ever forgotten. But Sergey had spoken with unusual hesitation, with worry from a senior member of the clan to his alpha.

Valentin clamped him on the shoulder. "She's as dangerous as a bear when she's riled." The clan would understand a pissed-off mate. "I'm working on it."

A laughing grin. "In that case, I wish you well. I once had to chase my mate halfway across Siberia so I could beg her forgiveness. Worth the frozen balls."

TWO hours later, when Valentin got into the car to drive to the hotel where Ena was staying in Moscow, he wished this was as easy as Silver being angry with him.

Courting her the first time around wasn't exactly easy, he reminded himself.

He was an alpha bear.

He had balls big enough to handle rejection.

Even as he grinned, even as his bear postured inside him, his heart ached. Because he, more than anyone, knew that sometimes, love wasn't enough.

Sometimes, people changed so deeply that the change broke love itself.

PART 2

PART 2

The Human Alpha

BO WAS RUNNING late for the early morning meeting with Krychek. The Psy telekinetic had messaged him only minutes earlier to ask if they could talk at a nearby building where he had another meeting; he'd asked Bo to bring Lily along, as he wanted to discuss a forthcoming Ruling Coalition media announcement.

Bo had tried to call him to see if they could reschedule for a little later in the day, but it had gone straight to voice mail. Given the importance of what Krychek probably wanted to discuss, he'd sent through a message that he was on his way. Halfway there, he got a confirmation message from the telekinetic: In meeting. Will be done by the time you arrive. I appreciate your time.

Odd that Krychek hadn't just teleported to him, but perhaps the other man was trying to be extra polite. Bo snorted. Yeah, right. Likely Krychek was trying to tread softly in an effort to keep Bowen and the humans of the Alliance talking.

Sliding away his paper-thin but highly resilient phone that had survived water, fire, small children, and dogs, he smiled at spotting his sister. Lily had been meant to come in late to the office today, had been in the opposite part of the city from him, so they'd agreed to meet midway.

She was standing on the bridge where they'd arranged to connect, but instead of her usual serene sweetness, she was leaning over the side of the bridge and having an enthusiastic conversation with the gondolier below. The two had to shout to be heard over the music of a busker on this side of the canal, so he could hear her voice, though not what she was saying.

Whatever it was, it had her laughing before she waved good-bye to the gondolier; the man poled away to pick up a couple of excited tourists. "Flirting with Piero?" he teased on reaching her. "What will your tattooed doctor say?"

"Ha ha. You know Piero's wife would brain me with her hockey stick if I dared make eyes at him." Stepping forward, she hugged Bo.

He squeezed her back. They weren't talking about the degrading chip in his brain, the one that was likely to lead to his death in a matter of weeks, but that bleak reality was there every time he looked into his sister's face. As was his own knowledge that Lily's death would follow his if they didn't find a solution. She'd been implanted after him but was now well outside the safe removal period.

Their parents didn't know—that was something the two of them had to decide soon. Whether to warn them . . . or to let them enjoy this time with Bo and Lily without that dark shadow hanging over every moment.

"Have you eaten?" He flicked her hair back from her face after they broke the embrace. "Your favorite bakers have just put out a fresh batch of pastries." The place was a few minutes' walk from the other side of the bridge, on their way to the meeting with Krychek.

"Are you Psy now?" She poked at his abdomen. "How can you have seen that on the walk from the office?"

"Social media," he said with a straight face. "They post a picture every time a fresh batch comes out of the oven."

Her lips twitched. "Who told you?"

"Niall." He grinned. "He passed me as I was walking here. He was stuffing his face with a hot-from-the-oven croissant at the time."

"Done. Let's go." Turning on her heel, she began to stride away, her black coat sleek and her feet clad in little red boots. "Hurry up, slowpoke!" She threw him a laughing look over her shoulder . . . and that was when he saw it.

The red dot centered on her forehead.

Ice crashed through his system, but Bo didn't freeze. He ran. "Get down!" The words were barely out of his mouth when he slammed into his sister, intending to take her to the ground.

They didn't make it.

The bullet hit his back, smashing through his body in a blast of searing pain that seemed everywhere at once; the momentum crashed them through the old bridge wall and into the canal below. He took Lily with him, her body held tight in his arms. She'd be safer in the water, where she could use the light and shadows to disorient the shooter.

The water closed over their heads, bubbles everywhere.

He kicked up, released her. He didn't think the bullet had gone through his flesh to hers, but he searched for damage nonetheless. "You hit?" he asked, finding it a little hard to breathe.

Shaking her head, Lily gasped for air. "How did you know?"

"I saw—" Bo began when his heart gave a jerking thud and the world blurred.

Lily screamed at the same moment. *"Bo!"* He felt his body sliding down into the water, felt Lily clutch at him to keep him afloat. Other hands joined hers soon after, hauling him up, but he couldn't speak, his vision nearly all black.

"Bo! Hold on! Help is coming!" Desperate hands searching for the cause of the pain shredding his flesh.

In the back of his mind, a mind that had a deep knowledge of weapons, Bo knew the bullet had been designed to fragment inside the body, causing maximum damage. "Lily." It was nearly soundless but she heard.

"I'm here, Bo." Her voice shook. "Just hold on."

"My brain," he managed to say. "Use it."

His vision collapsed. He felt his heart give one more beat.

Then . . . nothing.

Chapter 41

Hope, you audacious beast, you dancing moonbeam, you loyal canine, I miss you.

—Adina Mercant, poet (b.1832, d.1901)

A WEEK AFTER her release from the hospital—a full month following the operation—Silver knew intellectually that she'd lost a part of herself both she and others had valued, but she didn't experience any sense of loss. She felt nothing even when she went through memories tagged as powerful by her previous self, the concept of emotions just that: a concept. Foreign, difficult to grasp.

Her mind was cool clarity, devoid of anything extraneous. At least when she was awake. It was only when she was asleep that things went awry.

She dreamed.

She'd always dreamed, even in Silence. Arwen's impact. The truly Silent didn't dream. Or that was what the populace had always been told. If that were true, Silver shouldn't be dreaming. It wasn't as if she had any intention of willing the biofusion filaments to create a new, safe pathway to her emotional core. Silver saw no reason to feel when she was so much more efficient in her current state.

Her decisions during her emotional period were difficult for her to comprehend.

Why, for example, had she found the bear alpha so intriguing? Genetically, he wasn't a male she should consider for reproductive purposes—the children were unlikely to be high-Gradient Psy . . . though they *would* also have the ability to shift. Having a Psy-changeling child would be to her advantage as someone who worked with the other races, but it wasn't a big enough advantage for her to attach herself to a bear clan for life.

Look at how laissez-faire the bears were in how they lived life. It simply did not mesh with her measured, calculated approach. She found it impossible to understand why she'd been happy living in an enormous cave system. Happiness itself, of course, was a concept she no longer understood. She had the words for it, but not the internal comprehension she'd once had. It was a lack she was willing to live with given the myriad advantages.

Her logic was sound.

Yet, night after night, she dreamed of Alpha Nikolaev—and in those dreams, she sensed his hair-roughened skin sliding against hers, drew his earthy scent into her lungs, woke feeling as if she'd been entwined with a big, warm male body. Her sleep was deep and calm. It was only when she woke that confusion caught her in its grip.

"It's apt to be an echo of emotion," her grandmother had told her when Silver mentioned her dreams two days earlier. "The brain often fights losing pieces of itself."

It made perfect sense. Ena's next statement, however, hadn't been as rational. "Are you certain you don't wish to attempt to reactivate your emotional center?"

"Of course I'm certain. I'm far more efficient this way."

"Efficiency isn't everything, Silver. I learned that when Arwen was born."

Silver was still attempting to process her grandmother's statement as she dressed to return to work. She'd overseen her team remotely to this point, but had decided it was time to go into the office. It was too early according to Dr. Bashir, who continued to oversee her healing, but Silver felt capable—though she would maintain a close eye on her stress levels to ensure she didn't sabotage her return to health.

It was also why she was still home at nine forty-five.

A slightly less intensive schedule wouldn't be problematic, since it had become clear to her that she could achieve even more now than she had prior to the operation. She hadn't realized how much energy caging her Tp-A abilities sucked up until the act was no longer necessary.

Ready, she walked into the kitchen area of her apartment to mix up a nutrient drink. The kitchen was large, full of sunlight, the build optimized for the changelings who were the main tenants of this complex. The latter was how Valentin must've got in to slip a card under her apartment door two days earlier.

That card sat on her small dining table.

The picture on the front was from a children's story: a laughing blonde girl riding on the back of a huge bear. She knew the memory it represented, and that memory haunted her in her dreams. But it was the words inside that she found the most incomprehensible.

> *Silver Fucking Mercant. I told you nothing would keep you down.*
> *Happy twenty-ninth birthday.—V*

It wasn't that she didn't understand the words; it was the impact those words had on her. She should've thrown the card in the trash as soon as she'd finished reading it, but instead, she kept it in a place where she'd look at it every single morning.

"Throw it away," she ordered herself.

But when she left for the office fifteen minutes later, the card was still exactly where it had been since she received it.

Her reaction had to be part of the emotional "echo" effect. It'd wear off.

Once outside her third-floor apartment, she walked carefully along a path that rose up above the lush grass of the huge central green area. The path had no railings or other handholds and was challenging in heels.

Which was why Silver had made it a point to master the task, until her changeling neighbors gave her a thumbs-up when they passed her.

"Yo, Miss Silver!" The call came from a teenager whose family was living temporarily in the city while his mother undertook a lucrative short-term contract. The children would've usually been left with their pack, but as both teenagers had wanted to experience city life, they'd been permitted to enroll in a local school for the duration.

Silver knew all that because the changelings insisted on treating her as one of their own. Not because of who she was, but because of the relationship she'd had with Valentin Nikolaev. Uncertain what effect a denial of that relationship would have on Valentin's status, she'd said nothing.

He was no longer her mate, but she owed him and StoneWater a certain loyalty. More, she'd given her word that she would protect the clan to her dying day.

Silver did not break her promises.

As a result, people continued to treat her as his mate. The reaction held true regardless of whether it was a bear or wolf or nonpredatory changeling with whom she was interacting.

"Christof. Why aren't you readying yourself for school?" She had a vague memory of hearing that they were starting at ten thirty today because of a teachers' meeting.

The wolf male jumped up onto the path from the grass below, his grace that of a predator's, though his landing was shaky. "I got plenty of time," he said with a covert glance at his timepiece after shoving his long black bangs out of his eyes. "I figured I'd get in some jumps."

Silver had no need to ask what he was talking about—she'd seen him jumping down from a number of the high pathways. She'd also seen him fall badly, and had rendered first aid. "You do realize you're a wolf not a cat?"

The teenage boy made a face, his eyes deep blue against skin of wintery white. "Yeah, yeah, that's what Dad said when I fractured my ankle that time, but I hate those smarmy cats at school, always jumping off shit and trying to scare us."

"I didn't realize there were any big cats in this region." The question came from the part of her that had once been mate to an alpha bear.

"They're not big," he said derisively. "Just wildcats—transferred because the dad's some fancy-deal professor. They got permission to be here. But they're so smug." Thrusting his hands into his pockets, he slumped his shoulders forward and curled his lip. "They called me a 'feral wolf.' Can you believe that?"

"I see. Did you respond?"

"Of course I did." A growl that was nothing like Valentin Nikolaev's deep rumble, the sudden amber of Christof's eyes a much darker shade. "I couldn't let that insult stand. I put kitty litter in their lockers." His laughter was bright, but it didn't fill the air, didn't steal her breath. "You should've seen their faces."

Disturbed by the direction of her thoughts, Silver took a firm mental step off that unproductive path. "Your action may escalate the conflict."

"No. I got detention, but so did they because they threw the kitty litter at me." A distinctly self-satisfied look. "Second strike means an automatic expulsion, and I'm not done with the city. Neither are the kitties, so we've agreed on a truce." Having reached the end of the path, the teen lifted a hand. "Mom's calling. I better boost."

She turned to ensure he landed safely after his jump, but at the same time, she *listened*. She picked up no hint of his mother's call—clearly, whatever the teething problems with her operation, her Tp-A abilities were well under control.

. . . assassination attempt.

The fragment of breaking news came through her preset telepathic filters just as she reached the curb outside the complex. Before she could follow up on the news a familiar rugged all-wheel drive stopped in front of her.

The driver, a heavily muscled man with impressively broad shoulders, reached across to push open the passenger side door. "Hop in. I'll give you a ride."

Silver entered the vehicle without hesitation—one thing she'd learned from the memories of her time with Alpha Nikolaev was that he'd never harm her. Since getting to the office earlier would allow her to complete more work, it was a good decision to accept the ride rather than taking the skytrain. "Thank you."

He swung smoothly into the traffic. The fresh scent of his aftershave drifted across to her, layered over the natural scent of his skin.

That scent triggered a highly tactile memory of his hands skimming over her body, his muscled thigh pushing between hers, his hair falling forward and his smile an invitation. He'd been so warm, his weight heavy on her but not crushing, his chest hair rasping against her nipples.

She considered the memory with detached focus, every detail clear in her mind from the way his smile caused grooves to form in his cheeks, to how his breath whispered over her before his lips took her own, to the firmness of his mouth and the aggressiveness of his tongue.

Despite the richness of the sensory detail, she was still in control, her pulse normal, her breathing even. She remained stable.

"You still doing okay?" A gruff question.

Silver thought of the card she hadn't thrown away, the one that sat in the center of her dining table in a silent taunt. "I've had no unwanted auditory input since the surgery."

"The apartment? Everyone leaving you be?"

"For changelings, yes." Had they been Psy, she'd have considered their behavior incredibly intrusive, but she'd successfully adapted to changeling norms. "As there are only a few bears, it's relatively calm. Only one window broken in the past three days."

Valentin chuckled and the sound wasn't quite right, wasn't what she remembered. As if he were muting himself. Valentin never muted himself. "And you?" she asked. "You lost a mate."

His hands, big and powerful, clenched on the steering wheel. "Right now, my mate is sitting next to me, alive and breathing and with that brilliant brain going a hundred miles an hour. So yeah, I'm doing okay."

Silver looked at the traffic he was dodging with such ease. "Turn right here. It's a shorter distance to EmNet HQ." The words didn't seem right, either, didn't seem to be what she should be saying.

"So, now that you're pure Silence," Valentin said after making the turn, "you ever think about rerunning the sex experiment?"

"Whatever compelled me to do that, it's been shut off by the operation."

"What about the scientific benefits? Regular sexual contact with a willing partner is meant to improve health and general well-being."

Ignoring that deliberately provocative statement, Silver gave him another direction choice. This time, he ignored it. "If we go this way," he said, "I can show you something."

"I have a schedule to keep," she said. "There's just been an assassination attempt on Bowen Knight. He was shot."

Valentin's muscles bunched, all playfulness erased. "How bad?"

Silver knew he considered the other man part of his extended family, but she had no good news to give him. "Early reports say it may be fatal."

"You need to mobilize EmNet?"

It was a good excuse, but Silver couldn't lie to this bear. "No. It's a political situation, not a humanitarian emergency." If Bowen Knight did die, it could plunge the world into chaos, but for now, the peace was holding. "I'm sorry for the impact this may have on your sister."

Valentin's hands flexed on the steering wheel. "Nika is tough—she'll be there for her mate. But I'm going to give Stasya a heads-up." A glance at her, their eyes colliding. "I might be alpha, but Stasya's the big sister who can bully Nika into telling her if she needs clan help."

Silver didn't interrupt while he used the vehicle's system to make contact with Anastasia Nikolaev. "Make sure Nika's mate and his family know StoneWater will offer any assistance we can," he told his second.

"I'll call her now," Anastasia said before hanging up.

Silver spoke into the quiet. "How is the situation with Sergey and the clanmates who returned with him?"

Valentin shrugged. "We're growing stronger together as a clan. They're loyal, just scared."

Silver found herself turning to look at his profile, taking in the harsh angles of his face. He'd never be called beautiful, but Valentin Nikolaev had a presence that demanded attention. "You have a deep ability to forgive."

"Prerequisite of the job. You've seen the shit bears pull—imagine how crazy I'd be if I held grudges." He brought the vehicle to a stop in front of a shop with a pink awning.

She stared through the car window. "I've had my nutrition for the morning."

"Yeah, but have you had waffles with maple syrup and strawberries?" He was out of the vehicle before she could respond.

Opening her door, he said, "It's looking like the world might soon go to hell again, but today there's time for waffles." Deep, dark eyes locked with hers once more, his big body blocking out the light.

"Remember your promise," he said, and though she'd lost her emotional core, she had memories to draw from, knew it was a profound hurt he was trying but failing to hide.

The bear inside him was badly wounded. And she was the cause.

"I remember," she said. "Ten dates. That was the promise."

A ring of amber around his irises, his body a muscled wall.

She took a breath and his scent washed over her. Wildness and soap and warmth. So much warmth. Like that which kept her safe in her dreams. "I can't get out of the car if you block my way." He was so close, she could count each individual eyelash. "Why is your bear rising to the surface?"

"It wants to lick you up like honey," he said, his voice a rumble and his attention that of a predator's. "It's missed you."

Silver knew that, despite the memories between them, there was only one answer she could give. "It needs to get over that." Because she wasn't his mate any longer, couldn't ease his hurt.

A smile that didn't reach his eyes. "Come on then, Starlight. Let's go eat waffles."

Starlight.

The address clicked into place inside her. Unable to process the sensation or to explain it, she waited for Valentin to step back. He took his time, until she wanted to lift her hand and shove at his chest. Her palm tingled, remembering all the times she'd done exactly that—not just to Valentin but also to other bears who'd tumbled into her. It hadn't been done in anger. That was simply how bears interacted, tactile and a little rough.

Never too rough with her, however. As they were never too rough with the cubs.

Stepping back at last, Valentin said, "After you."

Silver was expecting Valentin's steadying hand on her waist, knew it was a stabilizing gesture done out of habit. "I can exit on my own."

He severed contact at once. "Whatever you say."

Suspicious of his quick agreement, Silver had her guard up when they entered the waffle restaurant. The maître d' looked Valentin up and down with a jaundiced eye. "Break it and you pay for it."

Valentin's response was startling. Grinning, he grabbed the stern and well-built brunette up into his arms and off her feet, pressing a kiss to her lush red lips. "Nice to see you, too," he said after setting her down.

Smile wide, she slapped at his chest. "I mean it. I'll send you an invoice if you so much as bend a spoon."

"I only did that once." Valentin released her with that scowling statement. "You got a table for us?"

The brunette tilted her head, the smile she bestowed on Silver blindingly warm. "It's good to finally meet you. I'm Victoria."

"Thank you for fitting us in," Silver said, waiting until she and Valentin were seated and alone to ask her question. "Do you kiss all maître d's?"

"Sure, why not?" His eyes were bear again, amber and challenging, his voice bad-tempered. "It's not like my mate's kissing me."

Chapter 42

"YOU DON'T HAVE a mate."

"Semantics."

Silver stared pointedly at her organizer. "How long will this take?"

Reaching over, he grabbed her organizer, switched it off. "Confiscated for the duration." He placed it beside his cutlery. "You promised to go on ten dates with me. No fair if you spend it with your nose in your organizer."

Silver knew he was playing a dominance game. And she knew never to let an alpha bear win. "I can have my nose in my telepathic senses. How will you confiscate that?"

He leaned back in his seat, sprawling to take over all available space, his booted feet on either side of her chair. Shoving his hand through the windblown strands of his hair, he said, "*Starlichka*. You know I'd never take away part of what makes you, you."

"Alpha Nikolaev—"

"Valentin." A firm word. "You know you've been calling me Valentin since the day we met." In his eyes, she saw the more intimate name he didn't say: *Valyusha*.

"Things have changed."

"My name hasn't." Primal amber eyes held hers.

Silver refused to blink. "You're being difficult."

"That's my other middle name. Valentin Mikhailovich Difficult Nikolaev." Stubborn words, but the hurt he was trying so hard to hide, it remained.

"Valentin then," she said, deciding this small capitulation didn't send the wrong signal when he was wearing his heart on his sleeve. "You *must* understand that I'm not the Silver you once knew." While she didn't feel emotion, it was important to her that Valentin didn't have his pride crushed.

He was alpha; he needed that pride.

"I know," he said with a slow smile. "You're Silver Mercant point two. Even sleeker and sexier."

"Alpha Nikolaev."

"Valentin," he said in a mock-stern voice accompanied with a wink. "Here are the waffles."

The male server put a large plate in the center of the table. It was piled high with waffles doused in what appeared to be a sweet syrup, as well as sliced strawberries and cream. He then placed a single smaller plate in front of Valentin.

Silver went to state she had no plate and only then realized they'd forgotten to give her cutlery, too. Before she could point that out, however, the server was gone—moving so fast that it had to have been planned. "I thought you brought me here to eat waffles."

Valentin cut off a corner that was relatively clean of syrup and cream. "I did." He held out the piece on his fork. "I know what you can handle. Trust me."

"We're in a public location."

"Changelings know you're my mate—"

"I'm not."

"—and the rest of the world already thinks we're having a hot and heavy affair." His lashes shadowed the amber glow of his gaze. "Run with it, *solnyshko moyo*. It's good for your image."

That he was right didn't alter the fact he was once again playing dominance games with her. After taking a second to consider the situation, Silver moved without warning to grab the fork right out of his hand. She then fed the piece into her mouth. "Interesting." She no longer had trouble with most foods, a holdover of her experiences in StoneWater.

Valentin held out his hand. "My fork?"

"I think not." Using the edge of the utensil, she cut off a piece that was thick with syrup, before picking it up along with two slices of strawberry. "Here."

Valentin's eyes sparkled. Leaning in, he ate the offering. "Good," he said. "But that was a girly bite. I'm a bear."

Silver thrust the tines into the top waffle and held up the entire thing to him, syrup and strawberry slices dripping off it onto the plate. "Better?"

Throwing back his head, Valentin laughed. And the sound, it filled the air, filled the room, filled her up. Disturbed by the powerful intensity of her reaction, she went to lower her hand, but Valentin moved with that unexpected speed to grab her wrist. Tugging her forward, he took a huge bite out of the waffle she'd speared.

His throat moved as he swallowed. Then he was back to take another bite. And another.

He'd demolished it in under a minute. "That's more like it."

Applause erupted into the air. When Silver glanced around, she saw they were the center of attention. Each and every face wore a smile. As if taking Silver's glance for permission, the red-lipped maître d' came over. "I have to admit, I wondered how it would work when I heard Valya had mated a Psy, but you can clearly handle a big hardheaded bear."

Silver didn't respond except to incline her head; her and Valentin's relationship—or lack of one—was their business. Waiting until the woman had left, she lifted an eyebrow in a deliberate action. "I think we've eaten enough waffles."

"Hell no. Try this." Picking up a whole strawberry, he held it out.

Silver could have ignored it, but doing so would once again call their relationship into question. She bit into the fruit, allowed the burst of flavor to explode onto her tongue before lowering her voice to a level only he'd pick up. "I'm not her." Not the woman he'd fallen in love with, not the woman he'd mated, not the woman who'd ridden on his bear form through the forest. "I'll never be her again."

Shifting forward, Valentin grazed her cheek with his knuckles. "I know," he said, his voice gritty and that huge heart of his in his eyes. "You're alive, Starlight. Everything else is secondary."

She felt the truth of that in every syllable; for her life, Valentin Niko-laev would do anything.

"But," he added, "I can't just let go. Give me the nine more dates you promised me. After that, I'll only bother you once in a long while when the urge to see you, scent you, becomes overwhelming." A faint smile, too faint for a man as brash and as wild as Valentin. "You can get security to kick me out."

Silver knew she'd never do that. Not to this man who had given her sanctuary and who'd helped save her life. "You ordered enough waffles for a herd of bears."

Appearing mortally insulted, he picked up the fork she'd dropped onto the plate. "Bears are never in a herd, Starlight," he said censoriously. "That's for the four-legged leaf eaters." He shuddered. "Have another bite."

Silver acquiesced. By the time they left the café, she was receiving a steady stream of telepathic alerts on pieces in the human/changeling media about her and Valentin's "adorable breakfast date." The *PsyNet Beacon* had printed a curter description but had given it more space than she'd expected, especially in light of the news on Bowen Knight.

When she mentioned that to Valentin, he shrugged. "We're the bright, sunny life-interest story to balance out the dark." Amber retreating from his eyes, his next words were harder. "Stasya messaged me while you were in the restroom. It's touch-and-go with Bo."

"That's not good news for world stability." Keeping an eye on the PsyNet for further news on the topic, she said, "How have you explained why I'm no longer living in Denhome?"

Valentin touched his hand to her lower back as she got into his mon-ster of a vehicle. She should've reminded him of her earlier comment, but it seemed a petty response to what she was certain had been an uncon-scious act on his part. Valentin touched the people he loved; it was part of his nature.

Asking him to stop was like asking a tree to stop giving shade under its branches. Impossible.

"Our clanmates think you're staying in the city because you need to work on a big EmNet project that makes it hard for you to be at Denhome," he said. "They just assumed and I didn't correct them." He closed the door and came around to get into the driver's side. "We'll keep that going for a while, then I guess . . . I'll have to tell everyone we've separated because you're *really* mad at me."

Silver blinked. Changeling mates didn't separate. "No."

"No?"

"To effectively say you were unable to court your mate back to you, it'll damage your standing in the eyes of not only your clan but other changelings. StoneWater doesn't need that." It was the stability of the region, she told herself, that was driving her decision. "We'll think of something else."

"Silver Fucking Mercant." Valentin began to drive on those admiring words. "I'll leave the solution up to that beautiful brain of yours." Even as Valentin said that, even as he played with her as the puppy inside him wanted to do, he was *scared*.

It wasn't an emotion with which he was familiar. He was an alpha bear, had been born that way, confidence flowing through his veins. Even when Silver had been in the operating theatre, he'd been grimly hopeful, not afraid. He'd flat-out refused to feel fear.

But this Silver, she was different in ways he'd never expected. She blazed as bright, her intelligence cutting, but she wasn't the woman who'd kissed him, who'd been so patient with Dima's tendency to cling to her, who'd admitted she loved her brother and that she'd lay down her life for her grandmother.

Neither was she the woman he'd courted and teased at the start. That woman had been ice, but he'd felt the warmth of the fire beneath, his bear drawn to the heat. This Silver was endless ice, no hint of the fire. Even when she'd reacted to his challenge with the waffles, he hadn't been able to feel *her*.

It was a staggering blow.

Part of him—a huge part of him—had been convinced the strange dormant mating bond between them would speak through the massive changes in her brain. Not once had he allowed himself to so much as consider that he'd have to let her go after their ten promised dates.

He swallowed the tearing hurt that wanted to grab him by the throat, permitting himself to feel only a fierce pride and relief. Everything he'd said to her was true: for her life, he'd accept any pain. In the years and decades to come, she would change the world, and she'd do it without being crippled by an unwanted ability that had caused her so much pain it had driven his tough Starlight to cry.

For that outcome, man and bear both would accept a lifetime of the most intense loneliness if that was what awaited at the end of this road.

"Am I allowed to suggest one of the nine remaining dates?"

"As long as it's not staring at matching organizers while drinking tasteless concoctions." In truth, he'd do exactly that if she asked; both parts of him just wanted to be close to her. Some of the dates he planned would be for the bear, so it could sit next to her, drink her in. Later. Not yet. The bear was still too hurt to act rationally in her presence.

Silver didn't reply for two long minutes. "My apologies," she said afterward.

"Telepathic call?"

"A developing situation in Bahrain. A landslide that may have done major damage." She checked something on her organizer. "Ripples are also beginning to develop from the attack on Bowen Knight."

Anger boiled in his blood once again at the fact a good man had been taken down by a *mudak* who couldn't even look him in the eye. Bears did not have any time for those who murdered from a distance. "I'll get you to your office." Moscow traffic wasn't bad, with the majority of commuters choosing to use the sleek skytrains that crisscrossed the air high above the streets—it was the drivers who were insane.

Like the man who'd just stopped his vehicle in the middle of the street to exchange insults with a pedestrian. Creative insults, too. Someone's mother was apparently a goat. No, a goat who ate shit.

Normally, Valentin would've found it funny. Not today.

Getting out of his vehicle, he went to lean one arm on the roof of the insult-spewing driver's car. "My mate needs to get to work, and you're in the way," he said in a very reasonable tone of voice.

The bearded driver gulped. "Alpha Nikolaev." It came out a squeak. "I'll move."

"*Spasibo.*"

Silver shot him a thankful glance once he got back in the vehicle and they continued on their way. "I'll be liaising with my team about the situation in Bahrain for most of the journey."

Saving hundreds, possibly thousands of lives in the process. Being Silver Fucking Mercant. His mate, and the most incredible woman he'd ever known.

Bringing the vehicle to a stop by her office, the area in front a strip of green planted with evergreens that spoke of the city's changeling influence, he went to open her door. She swiveled around and stepped out. "*Spasibo.*" A pause. "The date I intended to suggest? It was to go out for ice cream." Eyes of clear silver held his. "It seems only right."

His bear rubbed against his skin, wanting out, wanting to wrap itself around her. "We'll save that for last."

Silver nodded. "I have to go—it looks like there's been a second slip in a more remote region." With that, she was striding into her office in those ridiculous heels she wore as if they were boots—so stable on them that he wanted to pounce on her just to see if she'd wobble.

He didn't think she would, not his mate.

The Unknown Architect

THE ARCHITECT OF the Consortium looked at the reports feeding out through the media. Bowen Knight had been shot. Some of the articles said he'd died at the scene. Others, that he was critically wounded. No official confirmation either way from the Human Alliance. A grainy video taken by a tourist was the only available visual.

It showed a knot of people around what must be Knight's body. His sister, Lily, was the most recognizable, her hands on her brother's chest and her wet hair hanging around her face as she either did CPR or tried to stem bleeding. Reports said Knight had been shot in the back, however, so that'd be the exit wound. Unless, of course, the latest report out of Venice was true and the bullet had been designed to fragment inside him, causing catastrophic damage.

Chances of survival in the latter scenario: close to zero.

Knight's violent death hadn't been in the Architect's plans. Yes, Knight had to die, but it was meant to be a stealthy elimination that could be put down to an accident or natural causes. The Consortium wasn't a radical organization out for notoriety. It was a shadow organization designed to secure maximum gains for those in the group. Had the Architect's plans gone as intended, no one would even be aware of their existence.

However, that was done. What was important now was keeping as low a profile as possible while they brought the rest of their plans to fruition.

Did one of us order the recent high-profile hit?

The Architect sent out the message via the anonymized chat room they currently used to communicate. It was clunky and old-fashioned, but it was also close to impossible to hack.

Each of the members would've received a phone alert of the Architect's posting.

No confirmations.

That didn't mean it hadn't been masterminded by one of the group. The Architect had made an excellent decision in bringing together the world's most ruthless and power-hungry people, people who cared nothing for morality or peace when those things didn't serve their bottom line, but there was an inherent weakness in any such group: these individuals could not be trusted. They were also fully capable of taking an action that went against the better interests of the group if such an action would help them on a personal level.

The Architect was particularly interested in the possible motives of one member of the Consortium. He'd been approached to join the group not simply because of his position of power, but also because of his vocal dislike of racial integration on any level. He wanted Psy, humans, and changelings in their separate worlds.

It was only during Silence, he'd said, that humans had come to any kind of power.

However, the outspoken male was by no means the only possible suspect. Others believed Bowen Knight was dangerous and should be removed from the playing board. He'd proven too effective at uniting the human race into an ever-bigger financial juggernaut.

More and more family groups and businesses were adding the Human Alliance logo to their own. Bowen Knight had also managed to build strong relationships with a growing number of powerful changeling packs—*and*, crucially, he'd begun to meet with Psy family groups to see if business cooperation was possible between the two disparate races.

The Alliance called him its security chief, but he was its effective CEO. The ostensible leader was seventy years old, a man who was respected for his advice, but who turned up only on those occasions when the Alliance needed a media-friendly talking head to represent them. Apparently the older male was very happy with this arrangement—the Architect knew because Consortium spies had subtly sounded him out with the intention of flipping him with promises of power.

Every single spy had reached the same conclusion: *Giovanni Somme is unshakably loyal to Bowen Knight. He understands he's a figurehead, but Bowen speaks to him often and has taken his advice on more than one occasion. Before being raised to his current position, he was consigned to an obscure desk job despite his experience and decades of service to the Alliance. There is nothing we can give him that will make him turn against his leader.*

Somme, however, could not step into Knight's shoes. Knight's loss would cripple the Alliance, but it would most probably also turn the spotlight firmly back on the Consortium, wrecking the Architect's plans. Because, unlike the others in the Consortium, the Architect didn't just want money or a certain level of political influence. The Architect wanted *power*.

If that meant cleaning house and eliminating some of the looser cannons in the Consortium, so be it.

Chapter 43

Don't shortchange your legacy by settling for a mediocre match. Accept only the gold standard.

—Advertisement for Qui & Charleston, genetic fertility specialists

SILVER RETURNED TO the apartment complex at eleven thirty that night. She was psychically and mentally exhausted, the dual natural disasters having had a far worse impact than anyone had predicted. Evacuations were still in progress, notwithstanding that every single group and individual she'd contacted had pitched in to assist.

At this point, there was nothing EmNet or Silver could do. As always, their job was to coordinate resources in the immediate aftermath and get the correct people in position, then back off unless further assistance was requested. EmNet would remain on call, of course, but now that all necessary parties had been connected, the local coordinators held the reins.

Despite Silver's immediate action in initiating a disaster plan, casualties were forecast to be in the hundreds.

Silver knew the result EmNet had achieved was far better than any possible outcome prior to the creation of the worldwide emergency network. Rescue had been underway in a matter of minutes, with more help coming in from across the region. None of that made the outcome a good one in her personal ledger. Losing even a single individual went against her perfectionist tendencies.

She had to learn to manage that. Today, her fierce concentration in attempting to do the impossible, save every life, had led to a pulsing headache behind her eyes. It had no doubt been exacerbated by the fact she hadn't stopped to intake any nutrition. That wasn't about to change—she'd forgotten to order a delivery of nutrition bars and drinks after finishing the final items in her pantry this morning.

That food had come in a hamper courtesy of StoneWater.

Silver wasn't used to forgetting such essentials, but she wasn't concerned, aware she was still regaining her equilibrium after life-altering surgery. The thought had just passed through her mind when she entered her home to the soft glow of a light she'd turned on via her organizer.

Placing her workbag on a nearby chair, she removed her heels and walked toward the kitchen to get a glass of water. She went motionless at first sight of her dining table. Sitting on it was a large jar of nutrient mix, beside it an even larger box of protein bars. A bowl of glowing gold glass veined with bronze sat next to that—it held a number of shiny red apples.

The variant Valentin had fed her slices from as they discussed her conditioning.

All I'm saying is, how can you possibly have all the data if you've never let go of your Silence to see what happens?

Deep and a little rough, his voice echoed in Silver's head.

She took a breath when her lungs began to protest, walked on quiet feet to the table. The note was propped up beside the card she hadn't thrown away. Picking it up, she read words written in a strong and messy black scrawl that was deeply familiar: *I heard you haven't had a food delivery. I stocked you up. All seals initialed so you know they haven't been tampered with. Eat.—V.*

Silver didn't even bother wondering how he'd gotten in. This was a changeling complex, and he was an alpha bear. After mixing up a tall glass of the nutrient drink, she picked up a protein bar and an apple, then went to sit in the padded window seat that looked out onto the green space that was the heart of the complex.

Despite the late hour, a group of adults lingered below. They had beers in hand but weren't really drinking, the interaction more about socializing than alcohol. At this time of night, even the usual bear-wolf animosity was dropped in favor of a quiet drink to round off the day.

Silver knew she'd be welcomed with open arms should she wander down, but she wasn't in the correct frame of mind for casual social interaction. She'd learned to do it as a teenager to put those of the emotional races at ease . . . and she'd come to like it during her stay with Stone-Water, but her memories of that time were blurred outlines, distant echoes viewed through a thick pane of glass.

She stared at her meal.

And found herself choosing to pick up her phone. The number was preprogrammed. Valentin answered within seconds, his voice a deep rumble that sank into her veins.

"*Spasibo* for the food," she said. "I needed it tonight."

"You never need to thank me for feeding you," was the gruff response. "Have you eaten?"

A pause, a harsh inhale. "I had a burger an hour ago, before I came out for my patrol shift—Chaos made the kids' favorites today. Burgers and fries and pizza."

"A healthy spread."

Laughter, loud and unrestrained. As Valentin *should* always laugh. His next words, however, were in no way light. "You must've had a brutal day. I saw the extent of the disaster on the news bulletins."

"Too many people died."

"A lot more people lived."

Silver realized she'd drunk more than half the nutrient drink. Setting it aside, she unwrapped the protein bar without hanging up on a conversation that should've been over in thirty seconds at most. She'd thanked the alpha for his courtesy, achieved the purpose of her call. "Are you running the patrol alone?"

"Yes. Didn't want to inflict my mood on anyone else."

Silver knew there were many layers to that statement. Part of it had to do with her, but not all. "Is there a problem in Denhome?"

"Nothing major. Normal idiocy."

"Tell me." It was a command.

A grumbling sound came over the line. "I'm the alpha here."

Silver knew how to hold her own against him by now. "I'm an alpha-in-waiting."

"Yes, you are." Was that pride she heard? "Sergey's having a difficult time accepting he's no longer part of the command structure. He's dominant enough that his position as a senior isn't in doubt, but—"

"You can't trust him like you do the men and women who supported you from day one," Silver completed. "He must understand that."

"He's a bear, Starlichka." An exasperated tone. "Why are you expecting him to be reasonable?"

"I'll explain it to him if you wish."

"What? By killing him?"

"I've gained control over my murderous impulses."

"Hmm," he said suspiciously. "I won't take you up on the offer just yet. This is about union not division—I'll give him chances to prove himself, regain his place at his alpha's side."

"You're an excellent alpha." Silver didn't know why she said that. Valentin knew his own worth.

"I'm an excellent mate, too." Words that held more than a little of the bear's possessive wildness. "Never forget who you are to me. You say the word and I'll be at your side, no matter the battle."

Silver put down the empty protein-bar wrapper. "Even though I can give you nothing that changelings value? Not companionship, not touch, not children?"

"No. Matter. What." A heavy pause, followed by, "Though I wouldn't say no to a couple of pint-size Silver-Valentin hybrids. Psy do genetic matches, right? We'd make seriously tough, seriously smart kids together. Think about it."

Silver didn't tell him she'd already thought about it. "You're right."

"I am?" She could almost see his mouth drop open. "I think I'm hearing things. Give me a minute to thump sense into my skull."

Ignoring his playful words, she told him the rational reason for her response. "The child of an alpha bear and beta Mercant is apt to be a threat on multiple levels. Also, I've concluded that despite those who would stop the tide, the future will be shaped by individuals who are the embodiment of Trinity."

"You're beta nothing."

"As long as my grandmother lives, she is our alpha." It was a matter of respect and of a position earned.

"Okay, I'll give you that—I'm too scared of Ena to argue."

Silver knew full well that Valentin Nikolaev was scared of no one.

"So," he said, "you're up for mingling supersmart Mercant genes with supertough, slightly aggravating bear genes?"

She rubbed her fingers over the shiny red flesh of the apple. "As long as you understand it will always be a full co-parenting agreement."

"Huh." A rasping sound that told her he was scratching his jaw, her mind filling with countless other times she'd seen him do the same. "I figured a Mercant—*my* Mercant—would be possessive and ask for full custody."

"Attempting to take an alpha bear's child from him would be a recipe for certain disaster." Valentin would *never* give up rights to his child. "And a child with you and me as committed parents, and my family plus the clan as interested parties, would be safer than if we put that child in a vault."

Valentin took too long to reply, so long that she thought he was about to reject her offer. She began to think up counterarguments because now that she'd decided on the clear advantages of this course of action, she refused to be thwarted.

"Sorry." Valentin's deep voice in her ear. "Had to pick up and relocate a wild bear cub that decided to go exploring and nearly fell into a small crevasse."

The image reminded her of Dima and of how Valentin would throw the child high up in the air, then catch his screaming, laughing body in arms so safe, no child was ever scared when he was in the vicinity. "How is Dima? Has he recovered from his twisted ankle?" It was Nova who'd told her that bit of information during one of Silver's calls to check on the clan.

StoneWater still considered her their alpha's mate; it was her responsibility to live up to that status. If she didn't, it would reflect badly on Valentin.

"He's running around attacking unsuspecting clanmates like a champ," Valentin confirmed. "And anytime you're ready to create that hybrid of ours, just say the word."

"I'll consider the optimum timing." Silver's eyes fell on her timepiece. It was well past midnight. She needed to sleep so she could function at her best the next day, but she was having difficulty ending the conversation. The words "stay safe tonight" exited her mouth without her conscious volition.

"You get to bed. Dream beary dreams."

She hung up before she could make any more inexplicable statements. When she slipped into bed not long afterward, the apple on her bedside table, it was to the realization that her headache was gone.

HUMANS Against Psy Manipulation mounted another series of attacks the following day, beginning at five a.m. Moscow time. None in the city itself, but Silver and her team were kept busy coordinating the massive emergency response that strained resources in several corners of the world.

Rapidly considering their options, she contacted BlackSea using the code she had for them under the Trinity Accord. While the water-based changelings were nominally part of the Accord, they were openly wary of it. To date, she'd only requested their help on rare occasions, because most of their people were out at sea.

At least two of today's attacks, however, had taken place near large bodies of water, so BlackSea might have people who could assist.

The voice that answered was curt and male. "Malachai Rhys."

"Silver Mercant on EmNet business," she said before laying out her request.

"We'll assist anywhere we have people," Rhys responded at once. "What do you need?"

Silver read out her list.

Rhys told her which ones were doable before saying, "The first location is impossible. Too inland for any of our people to call it home—but there's a small owl wing within a half hour's flight. Not officially part of Trinity, but they'll respond to a call for humanitarian aid."

"Do you have their contact details?" After noting them down, she said, "If your people need resources on the ground, contact EmNet."

"We can take care of ourselves."

"EmNet has supply lines across all three races. Don't be foolish because of pride or isolationist tendencies."

A short pause, the next words Rhys spoke holding what might've been bemusement. "When I heard Valentin Nikolaev mated you, I thought it must be a mistake. Now I see you're more than capable of handling an alpha bear. As you said, Ms. Mercant, we won't be foolish, and we will access resources as needed."

He hung up.

Silver continued to work.

"Silver?" Devi stuck her head around the corner of Silver's office, the StoneWater clanmate having asked if she could intern at EmNet. Silver had cleared it on the understanding that the internship wouldn't lead to a permanent position. Devi had to put in her time, gain the same level of experience as others on the team before she could apply for any such position.

"You've completed the phone contacts I asked you to make?" she asked the younger woman.

"Yes, but I have a call for you from Lily Knight. She says she can't get through to you on your direct line."

Silver glanced at the small mobile comm on her desk. Every single line was running hot, the calls going to her team while she dealt with the most critical matters. "Put her through on my private phone."

The call came in on visual.

"Lily," she said, taking in the gray-eyed woman of Asian descent who was the Human Alliance's highly photogenic communications liaison.

Over their acquaintance, Silver had come to appreciate that Lily Knight wasn't only a pretty face; the other woman had a titanium spine and an unflinching work ethic that Silver had relied on more than once already—but even the expert makeup on Lily's face couldn't hide the deep purple shadows under her eyes. "Is it Bowen?"

Chapter 44

If a male bear attempts to feed you, narrow your eyes and take a hard look. Unless that bear is related to you, chances are high that he's being devious and branding you as his without ever saying a word.

—From the March 2080 issue of *Wild Woman* magazine: "Skin Privileges, Style & Primal Sophistication"

LILY SHOOK HER head. "No change." Her cheeks were hollow, her skin devoid of its usual health. "I wanted to let you know we're hearing rumors that the anti-Trinity human group might have been funded by the Patel Conglomerate."

Silver did a quick PsyNet search, found the data. "The Patel Conglomerate's major assets are in energy resources—they'll suffer no negative effects should Trinity succeed." United or divided, the world needed energy.

Lily ran a hand through her hair, the silky black strands falling back perfectly in place around her face afterward. "I don't think this had anything to do with economic factors—not like with the Consortium."

Silver ignored the messages flashing up on her organizer and lighting up her telepathic senses. "Why?" she asked Lily, just as her search brought up another Patel asset: a small pharmaceutical company that specialized in the development of cutting-edge drugs.

An easy source of a unique poison.

"Akshay Patel," Lily told her, "the CEO, has consistently opposed integration when we've raised it within the Alliance. He believes humans can only thrive if we shut out the other groups and grow strong behind impenetrable walls."

"Do you want me to pass on this information to Kaleb?" From where it would go to the Ruling Coalition of the Psy.

"No. The situation is being handled." Lily's eyes flicked left and down. "I wanted you to know in case you run into roadblocks where the Patel Conglomerate controls the workforce. They employ a lot of people in certain areas."

"Thank you."

"But," Lily added, "you can tell your mate—it'll save me looping him in. According to my brother, the bears have claimed us as family and can be trusted to look out for our interests." Lily's voice hitched. "Until Bo wakes to say any different, I'm going with his judgment calls."

After rubbing at her face, the drawn woman glanced at her watch. "I have to go. Press conference in two minutes. Anything you want me to put out there?"

"If you could drop in a mention of EmNet's work dealing with the current emergencies, it would help increase our standing in the eyes of the world." The less red tape and intransigence Silver had to deal with, the better.

"Consider it done." Lily signed off.

Making a note to tell Valentin about Akshay Patel, Silver began to check the backlog of messages and data. She wasn't the least surprised when she looked up some time later to find an alpha bear seated in the large chair on the other side of her desk. It was as if some part of her had known he was coming.

"Here." He pushed across a disposable cup. "Got it at the Psy place down the road."

The experimental Psy café, Silver knew, had been created by Sahara Kyriakus as a place for Psy to learn to socialize with those of all races, hopefully leading to more interracial pairings, *particularly* between Psy and humans. The PsyNet needed humans, but their compliance couldn't be forced. Sahara was of the opinion that love would win the day. The menu had everything from tasteless protein bars to triple-chocolate mochas with whipped cream and sugared almonds on top.

From what Silver had seen, it was a thriving success among college-age adults. Curiosity was a powerful force. At least for Psy and changelings. In humans, it was tempered by more than a century of distrust when it came to the Psy. Sahara hadn't yet worked out how to ease human minds so they'd patronize the café.

Valentin, however, clearly had no compunctions about walking into it.

Picking up the disposable cup, she took a cautious sip: hot nutrient drink lightly flavored with what might've been peach. "*Spasibo.*"

"What did I say about thanking me for feeding you?" His smile took the sting out of the rumbling chastisement. "Can you break for a minute?"

"Yes." A pause to intake the drink and loosen her tense muscles was only sensible. "I'll have to stay connected to the Net and take any urgent calls that come in."

"No problem. I just have someone with me who was missing you." Turning back, he whistled.

A little body ran pell-mell into the office. Dima's face lit up at first sight of her. "Siva!" Running around her desk, he lifted up his arms.

It would've been honest and rational to tell the cub that she was no longer interested in such tactile contact, but she'd never been cruel. Not under Silence and not outside of it. This child didn't understand the change in her, saw her only as the woman who'd treated him with care during their acquaintance.

"Dima." Easily lifting him up despite his dense changeling build, she placed him on her lap. "Have you been behaving?"

An enthusiastic shake of his head. "I climbed up the side of Denhome until Mama said if I didn't come down, I'd be in time-out for a *week.*"

"I see." She redirected a telepathic contact to one of her team who was also telepathic. "Did you obey her instructions?"

A gleeful grin. "I *fell* down and Mama caught me." Curling up into her lap, he said, "Wanna see my bear?"

Used to the bear desire to show off, Silver nodded. And the neatly dressed little boy in her lap turned into a shower of light that formed itself into the shape of a small white bear who stood up and growled at her—as if saying "boo!"

"He's a polar bear." Silver had not been expecting that.

"Chaos's genes," Valentin said with a smile.

Her comm rang at that instant with a call she had to answer. Instead of being impatient, Dima lay quietly in Silver's lap, her hand on the pristine white of his fur. Valentin, meanwhile, sat across from her doing something on his own phone, a scowl on his face. Halfway through, Dima shifted into a naked little boy who started to draw on the blotter on her desk while she made sure his small body didn't slip off her lap.

"Thank you, I appreciate the promptness of your response," Silver said, finishing off the call.

Dima turned to face her the instant she was done.

"Did you come to the city to visit me," she asked, "or do you have other plans?"

"Just to see you!" An exuberance of smiles before he whispered, "I hid in Uncle Mishka's truck, but he smelled me." Wriggling up after that breathless recitation, he wrapped his arms around her neck. "I miss you, Siva. Are you gonna come back to Denhome soon?"

Silver's gaze met Valentin's over the top of the little boy's head. And that huge heart, it was right there. "Come on, Dima," he said. "We'd better let Silver finish her work."

The child known for being a barnacle immediately let go, the tone in Valentin's voice clearly that of an alpha speaking to one of his clan. "Bye, Siva." A big kiss pressed to her cheek. "Did you drink your food? Uncle Mishka says it'll make you strong."

Releasing the boy's weight as he scrambled off her lap, Silver picked up the cup and took a long drink. "I'll finish it," she promised. "Try not to fall off any more walls. You're only a small bear."

"I'm going to be big like my papa!" Running around to Valentin on that determined declaration, he said, "I got no clothes now."

"What're you going to do?" Valentin asked. "We are in Moscow—you might be busted for public nakedness."

Dima shifted again.

Laughing, Valentin picked him up, holding the cub against his chest. "You think you'll be free tonight?" he asked Silver.

She shook her head. "I'm likely to be here all through the night." She'd have to send her assistant home for a change of clothes at some point.

Valentin just nodded and left holding Dima, who was waving madly with one paw over his shoulder. Her office felt strangely empty after they were gone, as if all the air had been sucked out of it. Silver tried to shake off the odd sensation, but she found herself getting up and standing by the large window behind her desk, the drink in hand.

Valentin and Dima exited the building a few minutes later. Valentin paused, looked up. So did the small white bear. They both smiled and waved. Silver lifted her cup in a silent salute, her free hand rising to press against the glass. Seconds later, they were gone, swallowed up in the flow of traffic around the building—or they should've been. She saw them every step of the way, irrespective of how many others walked around them.

When they finally disappeared into the bullet-train station in the distance, Valentin likely having left his vehicle in the parking garage below the station, she felt the loss like a cut inside her. The wrench was startling and it had her *listening*. But there was nothing she wouldn't normally hear. Her audio telepathy was dead.

Her comm began to beep. A telepathic alert sounded in her brain.

Turning away from the window, she got back to work. But she made sure to finish the drink. Right when she would've begun to run out of energy again, a delivery was made to the office from the same café. Sandwiches and drinks for the entire office.

"Signed for by Alpha Nikolaev," the Psy deliveryman said. "All prepared under the watch of a StoneWater employee."

Devi took care to scent all the food regardless. "Valentin told me to make sure," she said to Silver. "It's sooooo cute how he looks after you. I hope my mate feeds me, too."

Silver ate the sandwich marked with her name—the spread was the same one she'd enjoyed in Denhome—and she drank the accompanying nutrients.

When Valentin messaged her two hours later to check how events were developing, she removed her earpiece and took the call on her personal phone. "The humanitarian situation is under control," she told him. "The death toll currently stands at five hundred and seven." That was five hundred and seven too many for Silver. "The majority died in the initial blasts, but we've lost at least a hundred people as a result of the injuries they sustained during the attacks."

"You doing okay, Starlight?"

"Given my tiredness, my efficiency is no longer at its peak, but I haven't made any errors." Silver's eye fell on the empty drink container on her desk. "The food was appreciated."

"You're being sneaky, thanking me by using fancy words."

Silver toed off her heels, flexed her feet. "I was brought up to be polite."

"Hang around with me long enough, and we'll change that."

Hearing a horn in the background, she said, "Are you in the city?"

"Ran in some of the young clan soldiers for a party. One of us will be coming back in to pick them up in a few hours."

"If you'd rather just stay in the city, you can use my apartment." Her offer had nothing to do with emotion; she was just repaying the favor StoneWater had done her.

"You know what, Starlight? I'm going to take you up on that. I need to crash anyway—did a double shift yesterday."

"I'll call complex security, clear you in. Not that you need it."

A deep chuckle. "Hopefully my bigfoot-sized body won't break your couch."

"Take the bed. You'll be uncomfortable on the couch." Not thinking too hard about what that would mean for her when she went to bed, she said, "I have some information I need to give you. It's from Lily Knight."

Another urgent call lit up her comm screen just as she finished briefing him about the Patel Conglomerate. "I have to go." It was ten minutes later that she contacted complex security to let them know Valentin was cleared.

They laughed, delight in their tone.

"Of course he is," the woman on the other end said. "He's your mate. Your scent imprint is all over him."

Silver was still thinking about the latter when she finally left her office. It was now five in the morning, and she'd sent her local staff home three hours earlier. They'd return to the office at eight, while she'd come in at nine—and she'd be on call to her human deputy her entire rest period.

Her phone rang just as she reached the complex. "Sergeant," she said. "A problem?"

"No. I saw you'd logged off and wanted to let you know I appreciate the vote of confidence. I know this incident is way beyond anything else I've handled."

Silver wasn't used to delegating, but her team wouldn't function at peak efficiency if she insisted on doing everything herself. "I trust your readiness for the task," she told the human male. "But don't hesitate to call me if it's something that needs my input."

"Will do."

"I'll speak to you after I wake, so please make sure you're ready to deliver a concise briefing to bring me up to speed."

"Consider it done, Chief." He signed off before she could remind him her actual title was Director of EmNet—not that she expected her team to use that. She'd learned from watching Valentin lead, understood that informality did not mean a lack of respect and that it could form deeper bonds over time.

Clearing herself into the complex using the retinal scanner, she didn't jump when a wolf prowled up off the grass inside and, loping up to the pathway, padded beside her all the way to her apartment. She recognized that black coat with its fine threads of bronze as Margo Lucenko, head of complex security and senior member of BlackEdge. "*Spasibo*," she said once she reached her apartment.

The wolf didn't leave until Silver had opened her door and it had padded inside to check out the scents. Only after Margo was satisfied the area was safe did she step back and give Silver a nod before heading out. Silver shut the door, kicked off her shoes, and, going into the bedroom, placed her organizer and purse on the bedside table.

Her bed was made, with no visible signs of Valentin's presence. But when she slipped into bed after completing her nightly routine, the warm, earthy scent of him seeped into every cell of her body. Silver slipped into sleep in a heartbeat, Valentin wrapped around her like a blanket.

The Human Alliance

There are those who call me the bridge between disparate interests. I hope
that is my legacy. That my children and my children's children into the future
become the bridge whenever violence and horror threaten the world.

—From the private diaries of Adrian Bowen Kenner: peace negotiator,
Territorial Wars (eighteenth century)

LILY HAD BEEN asked to take over the communications officer role in
the Alliance because she had a natural ability to put people at ease in any
given situation. She was also very good at judging the media currents and
had the technical skills to ensure the Alliance's message got through
without disruption.

The work suited her, but she'd always understood that she was the
conduit, and that was fine with her. She didn't want to be the person who
made the decisions. That was Bo's role and he'd been born for it.

"We need you," she said to her brother, her hand locked tight with his
where it lay against the white sheet of the hospital bed. "The others want
to bring Akshay Patel in, torture the truth out of him, even though all
we have are rumors." She swallowed. "They're angry and hurting, and it's
pushing them into unconscionable decisions. I've managed to pull them
back for now by reminding them you wouldn't green-light something like
that."

Once, he might have. Her brother wasn't perfect—he'd made mistakes, many of them. But he'd learned, become a true leader, one who understood that a society couldn't be built on shadows and lies. "We're watching the Patels and their associates very closely. I've done some hacking, gotten a line into their communications systems." Beyond her being the face of the Alliance, that was her greatest skill.

"I don't think Akshay Patel is connected with the Consortium. From everything we know, the Consortium is made up of the power-hungry from all three races, and HAPMA wants humans to stay separate." She paused. "Of course, he *could* be a part of the Consortium for his own ends. They do both want Trinity to fail, after all."

And Akshay Patel was ruthless enough to work with his enemies and to use HAPMA so long as their goals aligned with his. "This isn't what I'm good at, Bo." She could see those facts, but she didn't know how to use them to get the answers they needed. "The others on your team are so angry that they're blinded by their rage. You're our center and our compass."

Her brother had single-handedly brought humans out of obscurity. He *was* the Human Alliance. Lose him and they'd lose everything. "*I* need you." A raspy whisper. "Wake up, Bo. Please."

But her strong, powerful brother remained silent, his body quiet, when Bo was all tightly controlled energy, vividly alive even when he wasn't in motion. The doctors had told her there was a high chance he might never wake—and if that ended up being their final conclusion, she'd follow Bo's wishes and pull the plug. Her brother had made it clear that if he was ever in this position, they were to harvest his brain and find out what was happening with the telepath-blocking chip.

"Not yet," Lily whispered. "I know you're too tough to die. We'll wait."

Chapter 45

It takes a lot to anger a bear, but when enraged, they are merciless foes.

—Found in the notes of Adrian Kenner: peace negotiator, Territorial Wars
(eighteenth century)

VALENTIN THREW PAVEL against one wall, his twin against the other.
They both took the impact with audible "oofs" of sound, shook themselves
off. Pavel was the one to speak. "What the hell, Valya?"

"The baby is sleeping." He pinned them to the spot with his gaze.
"Keep it down."

The other man settled his abused shoulders, a scowl on his face. "Yasha and I were just wrestling. Not being loud."

"Your audience was being loud." He glared at the sheepish-appearing
group of bears now looking anywhere but at him; most were still in their
pajamas as they geared up for an early start. "Did I hear bets being placed?"

Yakov rubbed the back of his neck, a blush of color across his cheekbones. "Sorry." He and Pavel came to join Valentin. "How's Silver?"

Of all Valentin's clan, only his seconds and Nova knew exactly what
had happened. "She's driving herself hard." It infuriated him that she
wasn't taking care of herself as she should, but he was more than capable
of picking up the slack—hell, he'd pet and cosset her if she wouldn't strike
him dead where he stood for daring.

Damn but he loved her. "She's agreed to have kids with me."

Yakov blinked. "Huh. Really? Even after they rewired her brain?"

"Yes."

Pavel's dimpled smile was pure joy. "That's great news, Valya."

Valentin nodded, the puppy inside him a little bruised but not broken. Because she'd invited him into her home, told him to sleep in her bed, eaten the food he sent her—*and* banned him from telling anyone they weren't mated anymore. Not that Valentin believed the latter. Her cold, beautiful starlight might be missing inside him, but it wasn't *gone*.

"What's the situation with the BlackEdge border?" he asked after forcing his mind off his mate with conscious effort of will.

"Juveniles playing 'I dare you.'"

"Bet they weren't as good as we were when we played that game," Pavel said.

"Of course not." Grinning, Yakov bumped fists with his twin. "Anyway, I cracked the heads of ours; Stasya told BlackEdge of theirs. It's sorted."

"Good." Valentin's phone buzzed with an incoming message.

Reading it, he felt his heart kick.

Monique Ling has just arrived.—Ivan

Ivan Mercant was Silver's cousin and part of the security team at the apartment building where she'd lived prior to the attempt on her life. Valentin had reached out to the man after he'd spoken to Grandmother Mercant and confirmed that Ivan had finally been cleared of any involvement in Silver's attempted poisoning; it had taken so long because he was the one Mercant perfectly placed to get the poison into Silver's apartment.

Ena had fully briefed Ivan as soon as he was eliminated from the suspect list.

As for Monique Ling, she'd thrown Ena by turning out to have a powerful natural shield.

"You would've scanned her if she hadn't?" Valentin had asked, his arms folded and his opinion of the breach of privacy clear.

"Integrity is a useless relic when my granddaughter's life is at stake."

"Silver wouldn't thank you for it." He knew his Starlight; she'd made her own choices, and they weren't always the same as Ena's.

"The point is moot since I couldn't get into Monique Ling's head."

Ena was certain she'd gained all possible information from the woman regardless, but Valentin wasn't so sure. Conversational interaction was not Ena's forte.

I'm on my way, he messaged back.

After telling his seconds what was up, he left for the city. It was pure chance that he spotted his mother moving through the trees in her bear form; Galina Evanova didn't normally come this close to Denhome. Heart thundering, he halted the car, stepped out . . . and she pounded away.

Valentin could've caught her, but that would've achieved nothing.

His soul full of a sadness that was more than a decade old, he got back into the rugged all-wheel drive and drove on.

It took Monique Ling three minutes to open the door after he knocked. Her mahogany brown hair was damp but combed straight, her bangs a thick wedge across her forehead, and her body clad in loose white pants and a white top. "Oh!" Her bow of a mouth curved. "You're Silver's man! I saw it on the comm channels!"

"I am." Valentin leaned against the doorjamb, arms folded and a smile on his face. Bears could be charming. Today, he'd be charming. He had a feeling Monique would react better to charming than to Ena's brand of frosty politeness. "I was wondering if I could talk to you?"

"Sure!" She opened her door wide, all girlish happiness, despite the fact she was thirty-three years of age. "How's Silver?" Big and round brown eyes looked at him with an earnest expression. "She's icy, you know, in that Psy way. But she was always nice to me, even when I bothered her about random things like which color of cream was her favorite."

Valentin quickly reevaluated his first impression of Monique Ling; she was far more emotionally perceptive than she might appear on first glance. "She's my mate," he said with a wicked smile. "So by definition she's doing great."

"Ha! That's bear logic for you." Clapping her hands, Monique walked him in. "I dated a bear once. Most fun I had in *years*."

Monique's living area was set up in a way similar to Silver's neighboring apartment, with the windows overlooking the city. But that was where the similarities stopped—where Silver's was elegant gray and pristine, Monique's was a startling chaos of colorful clothes and objects against white: white sofas, white walls, white table, white chairs. One shoe he could see was bright red, a purse on a sofa vivid blue.

"Excuse the mess," Monique said with the bubbly insouciance of a woman used to men doing as she wished.

Valentin found her sweet the same way he found other pretty, harmless things sweet. His bear would eat her alive in a second. That same bear wouldn't dare even take a bite out of Silver unless they were playing. His mate was titanium fire to Monique's gentle flame.

"This is nothing compared to Denhome after a big party," he said with a grin. "Imagine a whole clan of drunk bears and party decorations. I once saw my second-in-command fast asleep in bear form—some wit had decorated her with string lights and crepe paper after painting her claws pink." Stasya had *not* been amused at the twins' stroke of drunken genius—after she stopped laughing. "Just when the bears responsible thought she'd forgotten the incident, they happened to get drunk at a party and woke to find themselves encased in melted chocolate that had gone hard."

"Oh, that sounds like so much fun." Monique glowed. "You want coffee? I was just making some."

"I wouldn't say no." He followed her to the kitchen area, keeping things casual. "You know Silver's moved out?"

"I heard." Monique's lips turned down. "I really liked her as a neighbor—she was the kind of person I knew would respond if I ever screamed, you know? She wouldn't just ignore it."

Yes, that was his Starlight. "Part of the reason she moved was because of a possible security breach."

"Her grandmother asked me about that on a comm call." Monique pushed the Start button on her coffee machine. "I was so surprised—this place is locked up tight." She turned, leaning her hip against the counter. "Did they steal anything important?"

Valentin knew from Ena that she'd framed the breach as aimed at stealing restricted data rather than an attack against Silver. "Doesn't look like it. Silver had taken all her electronics to work with her, so they were out of luck."

"I do that, too," Monique confided as the rich scent of coffee filtered into the air. "I deal with so much classified corporate information that it's just not worth the risk."

"Silver said you had a high-powered position." He couldn't quite marry this bouncy woman with a suit-and-tie corporate. "In fashion, right?"

"She remembered!" A beaming smile as she turned to pour their cups of coffee, her machine one of the fastest brewers on the market. "I wish I could help you figure out who might've breached her security, but I swear I didn't see anyone suspicious. I would've remembered—my mom always says my mouth might be a runaway train, but my memory is a steel trap." She handed him a mug of coffee. "And the people I've brought home with me have all been people I trust."

There it was. "You're searching for a mate?" He quickly followed with, "My eldest sister's doing that at the moment." Rolling his eyes, he added, "I have to mop up all the broken hearts she leaves in her wake." Thankfully, Pieter's wasn't one—a single kiss and the two had realized they were meant to be friends. "The woman's giving bears a bad name."

Laughing, Monique said, "I just can't find the right man or woman." She took a sip of her coffee, sighed. "I'm totally open to anyone, but most people can't handle the fact I easily earn five times a normal income. Or if they *can* handle it, they want me to spend all my money on them. I love buying gifts, don't get me wrong, but I don't want it to be expected."

Valentin nodded, suddenly realizing he and Silver had never once discussed finances. She probably made *ten* times a normal salary. As alpha of StoneWater, he was the CEO of their business ventures, but he didn't think of that money as his—it was the clan's. He drew the same income as his senior staff, nothing extravagant. The rest of the money went toward raising and educating their cubs, keeping their territory strong, and further developing their business interests to the betterment of the clan as a whole.

He wondered what Silver would say to that . . . and realized she'd understand exactly how the clan worked. From all he'd seen, the Mercants functioned the same way. "I had the same trouble until I found Silver," he said to Monique. "Then, boom." He thumped his fist against his chest.

Monique made a melting face. "Oh, that is *so* romantic."

"Of course, she made me work for it," Valentin admitted before casually asking, "You didn't have any luck the last time you were in Moscow? There might've been an earlier attempt to get into Silver's apartment, so we're looking at anyone who was in the building during the time frame."

"Not really." Monique bit her lower lip. "I mean, there was Jai Shivani from work, but it never went anywhere and he's hardly the type to do industrial espionage. Straight as a ruler, you know?"

Valentin's instincts stirred. "Was he the only one?"

"Yup. I was really busy with work, hardly any time to play. Even Jai was only here maybe four times." A conspiratorial grin. "One time, the power went out when some big-deal processor melted down or something. That was fun. Too much fun. I ended up with the worst hangover."

Power didn't usually go out in buildings like this one; there were fail-safes upon fail-safes. Which was why Ena had come to suspect that someone had made *very* sure the power would hiccup that night. To date, however, she'd found nothing to confirm that Silver had been the target of that hiccup—the building housed countless high-profile individuals.

"Vodka?"

"What else? I'm in Russia!" Monique giggled. "Actually, there might've been a bottle of tequila involved, too."

Valentin grinned. "You weren't worried about mixing business with pleasure?"

Monique waved a hand. "Jai is in accounts. We hardly ever see each other except at the company Christmas party."

Valentin stayed another fifteen minutes but didn't learn anything else that might be useful. His next stop was the security-control station, where Ivan Mercant brought up the security feeds from the night of the power cut.

Ena and Arwen had already been through these, but that was before Ivan was cleared. The other man's demeanor changed from all business to ruthlessness camouflaged by a flawless black suit the instant he saw the gap in the recording. "This shouldn't happen," Silver's cousin said, his blue eyes hard. "The security system has multiple redundancies. It should always stay on, power outage or not."

"Why didn't you notice this at the time?"

Ivan found his organizer, checked the dates. "I was on leave a week on either side of the incident. My return briefing wouldn't have covered this." He put down the organizer. "I would say I can't believe this was missed, except that the individual noted as being on duty that night was a man I had to fire only a month later when he came to work high."

"Could he be the inside man?" Valentin asked. "Someone had to turn off the security system."

"If he was," Ivan replied, "we can't question him. While high one night, he fell into the Moskva and drowned. He was also a talker—I wouldn't have trusted him with any kind of a conspiracy that required keeping his mouth shut. I'll have Arwen trace his finances regardless."

Valentin stared at the blackness of the missing footage. And thought of what Silver had told him of a family with strong ties to the energy market—and access to complex chemicals—whose leader was against racial integration, against *Trinity*, to the point that he might be funding a terrorist organization. "Anyone on your team connected to the Patel family?"

"Human conglomerate headed by Akshay Patel?"

Of course a Mercant would have that information in his perfectly coiffured head. "That's the one."

"Not according to my current data, but I'll do some digging."

"If the cameras went off, does that mean Silver's internal security devices would've also gone off?"

"Yes. I helped her with the setup, and we locked them into the power grid to guard against failure." His face displayed no expression, but had the very dangerous and highly trained man been a bear, Valentin would've said he was pissed. "I never considered that an enemy would take down the entire power grid to get to her—that shouldn't even be possible with the safeguards in place."

Yet someone had pulled it off, and the end result was that for twenty minutes that night, Silver's apartment had been open to intrusion. "Someone really wanted her off the chessboard." Valentin's claws shoved against the skin of his fingertips.

"I'll work on unearthing the traitor in our midst," Ivan said flatly.

Valentin had a feeling that if there was a traitor, his cover wouldn't last long with Ivan Mercant on the trail. The man reminded him of a spy from the silver screen, suave and handsome on the surface, deadly underneath.

Leaving the other man to his task, Valentin went to his car, used the car's system to call Pavel. "I need you to find out about a man named Jai Shivani who works in the Moscow branch of the same company as Monique Ling. Look for any connections to the Patel family—of the Patel Conglomerate, headed by Akshay Patel."

"Gimme a few minutes." The other man hung up.

As it was, Pavel didn't return the call until Valentin was about to get out at Silver's complex, the dash clock showing it was eight forty. She wouldn't normally be home at this time, but given how late she'd worked, Valentin was hoping she'd gotten some extra rest. He wasn't sure he could control his protective instincts if she was running herself ragged. The possibility of a telepathic whack on the head or no, he might throw her over his shoulder and kidnap her to his lair.

"Jai Shivani is related to the Patels. Third cousin twice removed," Pavel said. "But, distant relatives or not, he went to the same boarding school as Akshay Patel, and they seem close in the school photos I was able to unearth."

"Boarding school probably made them closer than many siblings."

"Fewer connections between them in their adult lives," Pavel added, "but they both go to certain parts of the world at the same time every year. Family reunions maybe."

Or planning sessions.

"Send me everything you have." Once that information came through,

Valentin had a decision to make: He knew the Human Alliance had asked everyone to wait, but it was focused on Akshay Patel. Jai Shivani was a small fish not even on their radar, according to the information they'd shared with Silver. The man was also in Moscow. Literally a ten-minute drive away.

Valentin's instincts raged at him to head that way, eliminate a possible threat on his mate's life. But Silver was also the head of EmNet and couldn't afford to lose the Alliance's trust.

Claws releasing, he gritted his teeth, made a call.

"I want to talk to him," he said bluntly to Lily Knight after explaining that Jai Shivani's name had come up in the course of another investigation. "I'm right here, and I can be a scary bastard." He was very careful not to promise to hand the man over to the Alliance—if Shivani had orchestrated the attempt on Silver's life, his own life was forfeit.

Bears didn't take prisoners.

"I can't make that decision," Lily replied. "I need to talk to the leadership." She returned his call five minutes later. "They want a human observer with you. Your mate has one working for her in the main EmNet office, a man named Erik Jahnssen."

"Done." Valentin knew he could drive away right now and Silver would never know about the upcoming confrontation. Of course, that kind of secret was how stupid bears lost their women.

Valentin was not a stupid bear.

He walked to her apartment, knocked.

Chapter 46

SILVER OPENED HER door seconds after Valentin's knock, already dressed in a gray pantsuit with a white shirt and sky-high heels. Her hair was also up in that fancy twist that made his hands itch to mess it up. "Valentin." Her eyes scanned his face. "Is something wrong?"

He wanted to yell at her. She had lines of exhaustion on her face, shadows under her eyes. "You have a half hour?" It came out a rumbling growl, his bear was so mad at her. "It's important."

She glanced at the complicated timepiece on her wrist, the face a large square that displayed all kinds of data. "My deputy is meant to log off at nine. I'll ask him to take an extra thirty minutes."

That she'd cleared her schedule without asking him why he needed her time, it crashed right through him, slayed him. Angry though it was, his bear rubbed against the inside of his skin, wanting her fingers running through its fur, her weight on its body as the bear took her for another ride. "Eat first," he ordered.

"I'll grab a bar." She did exactly that and was in the car with him two minutes later.

"We also need Erik Jahnssen from your office."

Again, she made the call without questioning why.

"You should be resting." The words burst out, a loud thunder of sound. "This is not how you recover from neurosurgery!"

She chewed a bite of her bar, swallowed. "I'll take that under advisement." A calm statement that made it clear she'd do nothing of the sort.

"Grr." Valentin made his claws slide back in. "You are an infuriating woman, Starlichka."

When he stopped at the Psy café and grabbed her a hot nutrient drink, she took it but gave him a stern look. "Valentin, the bar was enough nutrition. You'll increase my weight if you keep feeding me."

He fought the urge to tumble her into his lap, kiss her, and kiss her until she laughed and became his Silver again, the one who said things like that to him but who also loved him. "Because I'm a gentleman bear," he grumbled, "I won't point out that a woman who barely sleeps is never going to get there. But if it ever happens, it'll just give me more of you to cuddle."

Silver focused pointedly on her organizer, drink in hand. "Are we crossing off another date on your list, this time with an observer?"

"Very funny." His worst scowl had zero effect on his mate. It was like she was immune. "Do you think I'd waste a date by putting a time limit on it?" Snorting, he shook his head . . . just as she took a sip of her drink.

Bear satisfied, he said, "No, I just had a very interesting conversation with Monique Ling."

"Monique?" She took another sip. "Everything I know of her—and I dug deep when I first met her—says she has no political or fanatical leanings."

"No, but at least one of the men she brought home might."

When he told her what he'd learned, she turned off the organizer and angled herself to better face him, her fingers still around the drink. "Have you told Grandmother?"

"No. I want to know if we're right first."

Silver nodded at once. "Agreed." The possibility of Silver's poisoner being a Mercant had caused a deep schism in Ena, calling all her beliefs about family, about loyalty, into question.

To heal that schism and return her grandmother's absolute trust in the bonds of family, they had to give her categorical proof that no Mercant had been involved. "Erik is waiting outside his apartment down this street."

Silver briefed the rawboned human male after they picked him up— even after a short acquaintance, she knew he could be trusted to keep the secret. According to the psychological profile run by a previous employer, if Erik had a flaw, it was that he tended to be loyal to people long after they'd failed to live up to that loyalty.

At this point, after watching her work from her hospital bed to handle crises with no bias motivated by race, creed, or any other divisive factor, he'd given that loyalty to Silver.

"I have to make sure you two don't torture this dude?" Erik made a face, his eyes—a pale brownish-hazel—dubious, and stubble rough on the red-flushed skin of his jaw. "If he tried to poison Silver," he said in his Dutch-accented Russian, "I'm happy to help you pound the *mudak* into dust."

"I like you," Valentin said with a baring of teeth, just as his phone rang.

Tapping an earpiece Silver knew he couldn't stand but that was useful for private conversations, he said, "Pasha, what have you got?" He listened, asked several more questions before hanging up.

She wasn't the least surprised when he pulled out the earpiece and threw it onto the dash. Shoving a hand through the thickness of his hair, he said, "The possible asshole is still at his apartment—surfing the news sites on his comm. His focus seems to be the recent spate of HAPMA attacks."

"Pavel does realize hacking is illegal?" Silver curled her fingers into her hand when those fingers wanted to reach out and straighten the strands of Valentin's hair about to fall into his eyes.

"Who said anything about hacking?" Valentin's innocent look wouldn't have fooled a four-year-old. "Here's how we do the interrogation—you be scary and I'll be scarier."

"To a human with ordinary shields," Silver said coolly, "I am far scarier than you."

Valentin's claws sprung out, curved and razor sharp. "What do you want to bet?"

Silver took in those deadly claws. "If you sharpen them to a point, perhaps."

Both men laughed, but it was Valentin's laughter that sank into her bones. "Silver Fucking Mercant." An affectionate look as he pulled into an open parking space on the street.

Getting out, he went around to open her door. "Ready?"

"Let's do this." She held eyes that had gone amber when he laughed, still held the bear's delight. "The loser in the scariness stakes has to eat the other's choice of food for a day. Erik is the challenge witness and judge."

A grinning Erik clapped his hands once. "I accept."

Valentin shuddered. "Now I *have* to be super scary." He lifted her out of the vehicle, the move so absentminded she didn't think he was being purposefully aggressive.

As she and Erik walked with him into the secure apartment building, their way cleared by Pavel in some no-doubt illegal fashion, she was glad she'd worn her highest heels. With Valentin wearing work boots, it put them on a somewhat even footing—he was still taller and much bigger, but they . . . matched.

Match or not, however, it felt as if Valentin took up all the room in the elevator, his big body brushing against hers. Heat and earth and warmth, that was Valentin. Silver told herself to step away, but they were already at the correct floor, and the doors were opening to reveal a neatly carpeted hallway.

Jai Shivani's apartment was at the very end.

Valentin had Erik push the doorbell, while nudging Silver out of the way of the security camera that allowed the inhabitant of the apartment to see who was standing at his door. The touch was gentle, very unbearlike if you didn't understand that bears could be tender with those they loved.

The bear, who stayed out of sight of the camera with Silver, loved her deeply.

"Yes?" The clipped query came through the intercom.

"Oh, hi. I'm, er, your neighbor from downstairs." Erik sounded appropriately hesitant. "Could we speak?"

A telling pause. Followed by, "About what?"

"My wife and I were hoping to talk you into selling your place."

"It's not for sale."

"Just listen to my offer."

The camera swiveled without warning, focusing on Valentin and Silver.

"Why has your scent become pungent with fear sweat?" Valentin rumbled. "We simply wish to talk."

"Get out or I'm calling security." This time the tremor in Shivani's voice was unmistakable.

Valentin turned to her and Erik when Jai Shivani hung up. "I asked nicely."

"You did," their human observer said. "Verified. I even got it on tape." He held up his phone.

Smile dangerous, Valentin slammed his body into the door. It crumpled like tin. Two seconds after that, he was inside the apartment.

Silver made her way more sedately through the wrecked door—quite confident of Valentin's ability to lock down their target and Pavel's to blind security. Erik entered behind her. "You're both scarier than me," he said. "I'll just observe like I'm meant to."

Silver arrived in time to see a man with light brown skin and dark eyes, his rounded belly pushing at the buttons of his blue shirt and his hair caught back in a tail, put up his hands. His phone lay smashed in a corner. Valentin's clawed hand was around his throat. "Don't hurt me,"

Jai Shivani whimpered, perspiration dotting his brow. "I haven't done anything."

"This should be easy to clear up, then," Silver said with her iciest smile. "I'll do a telepathic scan."

Erik didn't interrupt, the human member of her team well aware of Silver's ethical lines.

Jai Shivani didn't have that advantage. All the blood drained from his face, his skin going a sickly pasty shade. "Silver Mercant." It came out strangled.

Ignoring him, Silver spoke to Valentin. "Should I rip his mind apart, find out if he knows anythi—"

"No, please." Shaking, Shivani swallowed and shifted his attention desperately to Valentin. "Please, you're not like her. Don't let her rape my mind."

Valentin flexed the hand he had around the man's throat. "Talk." Eyes aglow, voice a bearish growl. "You know about what."

Jai Shivani was no hardened criminal. He crumpled.

When he next opened his mouth, it was to unleash a river of words. "I was following instructions, that's all. I was told to get into your apartment"—his eyes cutting to Silver—"on a particular day. I had to put something from a sealed packet into the weird food jars all Psy use."

"Why were you confident you could get in?" Silver asked.

"I"—a rapid swallow—"I wasn't. Just got lucky with a power cut." Chest heaving, he held up his hands palms out. "That's it, that's all I know."

Silver glanced at the organizer she'd brought in with her. "He's lying. I'll take the truth from his mind—the depth of the scan will, unfortunately, leave him a vegetable."

Valentin shot her a scowling look. "But I wanted to play with him a little."

"Wait! Wait!" The would-be poisoner turned to the only human in the room. "You're like me. Help me."

Folding his arms, Erik leaned against the nearest wall. "I've never poisoned anyone in my life, so nope, I'm no sniveling coward."

Denied his final hope of mercy, Jai Shivani began to babble out every

piece of information he had. He confirmed the power cut had been manipulated and, of his own volition, told them it was Akshay Patel who'd
given him the order to doctor Silver's food.

He also had proof of the latter.

"I recorded our conversation," Shivani blubbered. "I trust Akshay like
a brother normally, and we vacation together at least once every year, but
he's gotten secretive over the past few months—I wanted to cover myself
in case he was into something shifty."

"Really?" Valentin's voice was rapidly becoming all bear. "You didn't
get a clue when you were asked to break into an apartment and put an
unknown substance in the food? I should kill you for terminal stupidity."
A deadly pause. "Maybe you did something even worse that night. To
the woman who got you into the building."

"I didn't take advantage of Monique, I swear!" Tears filled Shivani's
eyes, his lower lip quivering. "I just put drugs in her drink to knock her
out. Akshay gave me two pills to use, but I wanted to be sure they wouldn't
hurt her if mixed with alcohol, so I got some over-the-counter stuff
myself."

Fat tears rolled down his face. "I really like her, but they said I couldn't
go back after that night. I had to pretend we were just work colleagues
who'd had a fling"—his eyes shifted to Silver—"so I wouldn't be connected
to the powder I put in your food."

Silver checked her organizer again without seeing anything. It was a
prop to further cement her pitiless reputation. "That additive was a fast-
acting poison. Which means you are an accessory to attempted murder."

Shivani fainted.

Valentin managed to catch the heavyset man, throwing him on the
bed as if he weighed nothing. "I win. He fainted when I pressed in my
claws."

"I think not. He fainted after I stated the depth of his culpability."

They both looked at Erik.

Throwing up his hands, the tall human backed off. "Hey, I am not
getting in the middle of a lovers' quarrel." His grin was huge. "Though I

am going to tell everyone I know that you have a scariness contest going on."

"You're an insult to judges everywhere." Valentin's grumble just made Erik's grin deepen. "Go make your report to Lily. Starlight, you already give him the code?"

"No, here it is." After doing that, Silver stepped over to stand next to Valentin, both of them looking down at Jai Shivani's passed-out form. "We are, however, now in a quandary—it's not to my advantage to have the news of my near-poisoning get out." Robots were meant to be invulnerable. "Also, we didn't exactly question him in a legal way. Calling Enforcement will be problematic."

Valentin rubbed his jaw, his skin unexpectedly smooth today. "I really want to tear off his head."

Silver stared at him, realizing the rough statement was dead serious. *"Valentin."*

"He nearly succeeded." His voice was as deep as a bass drum, his eyes pure bear. "I saw you collapse after that poison hit your bloodstream. I felt your body convulse."

Silver gripped his smooth jaw between her fingers, forced him to look at her and not Shivani. "But he *didn't* succeed. We don't punish attempted murder the same as murder. And we don't punish the pawns worse than the kingpins."

Valentin rumbled dangerously at her before finally giving a hard nod. "I'm not letting him get off scot-free," he said, his voice difficult to understand. "He hurt you."

"Agreed. But you know what I realized in this room today?"

"What?"

"That, because he has no psychic shields, I have the power to cause him terror with a simple bluff." Silver had never before understood humanity so clearly. "Imagine what that does to a person, how the fear must eat away at you, *especially* when some Psy do violate human minds. The human race has a very good reason for hating the Psy."

"No argument," Valentin said in that painfully deep voice. "But he didn't attack a Psy who'd raped his mind. He attacked you, a woman he'd never met, and who would never touch a single thought in his head." Breath harsh, Valentin shook his head. "Human assholes don't get a free pass just because there are worse Psy assholes."

Blunt and angry he might be, but Silver knew he was also right. As humans weren't a homogenous entity, neither were the Psy. "Each individual makes their own choices."

"Damn right."

Releasing her hold on him when he pulled in his claws, she considered their options. "My family has the financial power to take much of what he values—and we'll also make it clear to him that any further such acts will mean being subject to changeling justice. I don't think he has the willpower or aptitude to defy us."

"I'm going to keep an eye on the piece of shit, too." Valentin's eyes were still deeply bear, but his voice was becoming less deep, more human. "In fact, I think he'll be moving into a building controlled by changelings so he can be closer to the bear business where he's about to start work." He took out his phone. "I'll arrange for someone to take charge of him for now."

Silver stayed silent, her hands at her sides, one holding the organizer, the other free. When Jai Shivani woke midcall, she calmly, coldly laid out his punishment. "You may, of course, attempt to fight our judgment," she said. "In which case, Alpha Nikolaev will take you into bear country and challenge you to fight for your life." That seemed a reasonable guess. "Do you think you'd win?"

The human male shook his head so hard it almost spun off. "I swear, I won't ever do anything else bad. I'll work hard, be law-abiding. I'll think good thoughts."

"Your thoughts are your own—no one will be scanning you," Silver said, because constant fear of violation was too cruel a sentence: human, Psy, or changeling, the mind should be inviolate.

Two StoneWater bears arrived minutes afterward. Both greeted Silver with smiles and said they hoped her work would let up enough that she could soon move back to Denhome.

Erik caught a ride with them when they left with Shivani.

Silver got into Valentin's vehicle instead. His primal anger vibrated against her skin.

"Akshay Patel," he said. "Where the fuck is that man based?"

"Mumbai, but he has a house in Milan and another one in New Caledonia. The Conglomerate also has offices worldwide." Silver had traced that data while they'd been in Shivani's apartment. "According to media reports, however, he is currently utilizing his main residence."

"Chert voz'mi!" His claws erupted again. "A tiger pack controls changeling access to Mumbai. They're pissy with everyone—damn Bengal tigers, always mad about something. I need Akshay in my territory."

"Having you tear off his head will hardly be conducive to getting him to divulge his motives and/or the names of any others involved."

Amber eyes flashed to hers as the deep bass of his anger filled the vehicle. "He can still talk if I tear off his arms."

Realizing she was attempting to have a rational conversation with a currently very irrational bear, Silver metaphorically threw up her hands. "Grandmother must be the one to have this meeting with Patel. You know it and so do I." It was the only way to achieve balance, to heal that schism inside Ena.

Valentin gritted his teeth so hard she could hear it, his biceps bulging as he squeezed the steering wheel. She expected an argument. What she got was, "Your grandmother can be as scary as fuck."

"So you agree?"

A nod.

"I need to talk to Lily first."

When she did, the other woman said, "Screw it. I'm not asking the board. You break Patel, and you find out if he's the reason why my brother is fighting for his life."

"I'll make sure we pass on any data," Silver promised. "Bowen?"

"His heart's failed." Lily's voice caught. "They've got him on a machine."

"There are mechanical hearts that function as well as organic hearts," Silver said. "If you need access to any cutting-edge medical intervention, call me. I'll make it happen. The world needs your brother."

"Thank you, Silver. I just . . . I need to wait a little longer. Bo wouldn't want intervention if all hope is lost."

After the difficult conversation with Lily, Silver contacted her grandmother telepathically, her range blinding. She'd gone up at least two Gradient points—to 9.5—since the operation. Either her audio telepathy had been utilizing part of her psychic "bandwidth," or the strength it had taken to contain the Tp-A had used far more energy than she'd realized.

Ena's telepathic voice was crystalline, her response to Silver's revelation simple. *I'll take care of it.*

Silver had the strong feeling she'd exchanged one dangerous predator for another. The one in the driver's seat was still rumbling in his chest, a furious mountain about to erupt. Ena sounded like ice in her head, but that ice cut like a blade.

Grandmother, she said, *we must know not only if he has other associates, but also if he is the head of HAPMA or if it's connected to the Consortium.*

I haven't suddenly turned senile, Silver.

And I've just talked Alpha Nikolaev out of ripping off Akshay Patel's head. You are sounding very much like him.

Valentin thinks like a predator. He fits well into our family.

Silver wondered how she'd ended up with an enraged bear on one side and an equally enraged—even if Silent—Psy on the other. *Grandmother.*

I will be circumspect, Ena said at last, *but you must understand this man will not survive the interview. He tried to kill my granddaughter.*

Silver wanted to reach out across the psychic void and hold her grandmother, tell her she was all right, that Akshay hadn't succeeded. A very un-Psy thought, but Silver's mind remained safely quiet. No audio from beyond the normal spectrum.

The final decision is yours, she said. *But remember, Akshay Patel may have set in motion events far more dangerous than my attempted murder. Bowen Knight is currently on the verge of death, and there are major emergency incidents all over the globe where countless people are dying. I am not the only grandchild involved.*

You are mine.

I am also the director of EmNet. Any lives lost because we didn't fully debrief Akshay Patel are on my head.

You take too much on your shoulders, Silver, was her grandmother's cool response. *But rest assured, I will not make a final call until I have wrung him dry of all possible information.*

You understand the critical need to get anything we can on the attempt to assassinate Bowen Knight?

Of course. We wouldn't have Akshay Patel without the Alliance's assistance.

Don't go alone, Silver ordered. *He may be human, but he's ruthless and powerful.*

I won't be going anywhere. I think the family's newest member will wish to offer his services to expedite this.

The connection severed.

"My grandmother is about to ask Kaleb to abduct Akshay Patel and put him in a cage she controls." Silver tapped a finger on her knee. "I believe I talked her out of torturing him to death, but I'm not certain."

The large predator in the driver's seat smiled. "I've always liked your grandmother."

Chapter 47

To kill to protect family is an act of honor and fidelity.

—Lord Deryn Mercant (circa 1514)

ENA HAD SURVIVED this long because she made it a point to know her enemies. So before she contacted Kaleb to organize a teleport for Akshay Patel, she did her research. What she uncovered was illuminating: Akshay Patel was forty-three and the head of his family group. That family group was a serious economic power. And, according to the records she discovered in what had once been Council-restricted files—not that it had ever stopped Ena—a large percentage of the Patel family had natural telepathic shields Psy couldn't breach.

Not an unexpected development. Powerful human family groups were rare because ordinary humans, the ones without shields, were vulnerable to Psy manipulation, their ideas stolen before they'd ever had a chance to truly bloom. While Ena would strip a mind bare to protect her family, she didn't believe in such underhanded methods to increase one's power or wealth—being a shadow power didn't mean being without ethics.

Mercants had always understood that honor defined a family.

The Patels' strong genetic tendency toward mental shields went some way to explaining their rise in power, even during the time of the Psy

Council, but that wasn't the only thing that marked them as different. They'd consistently displayed strategic thinking that left their competitors in the dust, a skill that had very clearly been passed on from the time of Akshay's great-grandfather.

The current head of the family was as smart as his predecessors. Akshay Patel also had a habit of supporting causes that were all about human advancement: scholarships, funding for scientists, grants. None of that was unusual. Many human companies did the same, believing the Psy and changelings had advantages enough.

What *was* unusual was that in the time since Akshay took over as CEO, the Patel Conglomerate had steadily cut ties with Psy businesses, in stark contrast to the vast majority of human businesses. Everyone wanted to get *into* the lucrative Psy market. The decision was especially surprising since the Patels were in an advantageous position in that they controlled energy to which certain Psy companies needed long-term access.

While Akshay Patel had maintained his family's wealth and business success by creating alternative sources of income, he'd also given up sure bets when they involved Psy. Each time a Psy contract came up for renewal, Akshay said no. That didn't speak of business tactics but a strong ideological viewpoint: Akshay Patel was anti-Psy.

Since the business news media had reported on a recent situation in which Patel had refused to do a deal with a changeling group, he was also turning anti-changeling. Most likely, he saw himself as neither.

No, to Akshay, he was pro-human.

Ena stood in the elegant gray of her living area, looking down into the crashing waves beneath the cliffs on which the architecturally designed house was perched. Her abode was all angular lines and glass, clean and functional, and yet it made a statement. That described Ena as well.

The only things that broke up the internal lines were the dark red roses that grew wild behind the house and that she cut and put in vases. At one point in the past, she'd considered why she did that and realized the answer was both simple and complex. Part of it was Arwen. She hadn't been this Ena until his birth. She'd been harder. These days, she wasn't soft . . . but she understood certain subtleties in life.

So she understood that Akshay Patel hadn't come out of the womb this way. Neither could it be a simple case of nurturing designed to skew his viewpoint—his predecessors had all been happy to work with anyone who brought a good offer to the table. Even Akshay had followed the same path in his youth. Something had drastically changed his viewpoint. Knowing what that was would give Ena the upper hand.

It took her another three hours to find the answer.

That was when she got in touch with Kaleb. As expected, he didn't blindly obey her request. His implacable will was part of why she'd once thought Kaleb and Silver would make an extraordinary power couple. She should've known neither would follow the well-trodden path, both masters of their own destiny.

After explaining the situation to Kaleb, she said, "I'd like to speak to him in a place he can't control but that is civil." Violence wasn't always the best tactic with someone of Akshay's power and likely arrogance. "I have a location." She sent him a telepathic image.

Kaleb asked several further questions before saying, "When?"

"Twenty-five minutes." That would give Ena enough time to prepare a pot of tea and make her way to the windowless cellar bathed by a lighting system that made the room glow as if in sunlight. Set up like a conversational nook, it was welcoming but private. If necessary, it could also become a cage.

"Do you need backup?" Kaleb's cardinal eyes spoke of power most Psy could never comprehend.

Ena was nearly certain he was a dual cardinal, a creature of Psy myth, but she'd never been able to confirm. "No, I'll handle this. But I need you to find another piece of information for me."

Giving a curt nod when she stated her request, Kaleb signed off. Ena made her way to the cellar, was seated in one of the six antique chairs in the room when Kaleb teleported in her guest. He left without a single word. "Please," Ena said to the man behind the attempt to poison her granddaughter. "Take a seat."

Tawny brown eyes scanned the room before settling on her. "Ena Mercant, I presume."

Ena inclined her head. "Would you like a drink?" She held up a bone-china teapot that sat on the graceful white table between them. "Tea?"

Taking a seat across from her with no sign of concern, one of his feet propped on the knee of the other leg, Akshay Patel shook his head. "Nothing personal. I don't trust Psy."

Ena wasn't startled by the elegantly spoken rudeness. She'd expected that after having researched his bargaining tactics. "How can you know the motives or personal beliefs of all Psy?" Lifting a cup of the herbal tea she'd already poured for herself, she took a sip out of the delicate china.

Akshay Patel tugged down the sleeves of his pinstriped navy jacket, aligning them with the pristine white cuffs of his shirt. "Maybe I'm psychic."

Ena lowered the fragile cup to a saucer as delicate. "You have no fear."

"Of an old woman with delusions of power?" A mask of faux civility, the smile on his handsome face silent mockery to accompany his insult. "Why should I?"

"How do you expect to get out of this room?"

A gun was suddenly in his hand, the weapon sleek and metallic. "Psy, human, or changeling, a bullet punches through flesh, spills blood hot and red."

"As occurred with Bowen Knight?" Ena lifted her teacup again.

Akshay Patel's mask slipped, revealing turbulent emotions. "He wasn't the target—Bo has done a lot for the human race, but he was being sucked into this takeover of our race described as cooperation. I just wanted to give him a wake-up call."

"I fail to see how a human-on-human attack would've woken him up."

"They'll find data on his phone linking the hit to a meeting with Krychek." A tight smile. "Bo would've already been acting on it if he wasn't so badly wounded. That's my fault and I take full responsibility for the fallout and the damage to the Alliance—I should've sent the shooter after Lily when Bo wasn't around to protect her."

"You didn't do it yourself? I wouldn't have thought you'd trust anyone with such a critical task."

A shrug. "I'm no marksman, and there are people I trust with all I love. Not something you'd understand."

Ena's research gave her the answer. "Your brother-in-law, a former special operative and close friend. He is, I assume, driven by the same motive as you—the psychic rape of your wife."

Akshay Patel's eyes grew hard. "Connecting into that Hivenet of yours, I see. How are the plans for the subjugation of the human race going?"

The fact he didn't deny her supposition, added to his body language, gave her the answer she needed. That answer cleared the Mercants' debt to the Alliance and to Lily Knight in particular. Ena telepathed the data to Silver, shutting down the link before her granddaughter could ask any questions. "Is that why you're so against Trinity? You believe it'll leave humans in a worse position?"

"It'll leave humans in a position of *no* power." Akshay's hand remained on the gun he'd placed against his thigh. "That's what the Psy have always wanted, always done."

"From your recent business moves, it appears you believe the change-lings will come to feel the same way."

The mask back on, he lifted a shoulder. "They're sure getting chummy with Psy these days. Lucas Hunter pretends to be evenhanded, but he's the father of a half-breed child. Psy and changeling. *Not* changeling and human." His expression was granite. "Now I hear the precious Mercant scion has mated one of the two most powerful changeling alphas in Russia. What a stroke of luck for you. I guess the poor schmuck will never know you fucked with his mind."

Ignoring the latter part of his rant because she wasn't ready to talk about Silver, Ena sipped more of her tea. "Lucas Hunter has multiple packmates who identify as both changeling and human. One of his senior people is mated to a human."

"It doesn't matter." A blood vessel stood out prominently on his temple. "Now that the changelings have access to Psy corporations, I can see them cutting off human contracts."

"Has that happened?"

"Not yet, but it will." Lifting his weapon, he deactivated the safety using his thumbprint. "Now, I think our conversation is over."

"Talking of conversations, my granddaughter had an interesting one with your cousin Jai recently." Ena's cup made a quiet clinking sound against the bone china of the saucer when she put it down.

Akshay's left eyelid flickered. "He's always been a disappointment to the family. I used to think he'd be at my side as I took us to greatness, but he never quite achieved what he should have."

While Ena respected Akshay Patel's desire to avenge his wife, that he'd insult a member of the family to an outsider lessened his standing in her eyes. "Yet you used him to get to Silver."

"Why not? He was available and in the right area."

"And disposable," Ena guessed.

"That, too. It was worth the gamble—and it'll be worth other gambles in the future. If I take down Silver, I crash EmNet for long enough that certain other measures can be taken and will be far more successful than if Silver's pulling in help more efficiently than any computer program." He aimed the gun at her head. "Sorry. Can't risk you telepathing the information."

He pressed the trigger.

Or he tried to.

Grimacing, he tried until the veins in his temples began to pound, the finer blood vessels in his eyes bursting to give them a crimson tint. Ena poured herself another cup of tea with tranquil precision. "It doesn't matter how hard you try," she said in the same tone she'd used the entire conversation. "You won't break my hold."

Akshay Patel spoke through gritted teeth. "I have a natural shield."

Not answering, Ena drank her tea.

Sometimes, the win came from perception rather than reality. Akshay Patel thought she was a telepath, which she was; however, she also had just enough of a strange little power for it to be useful. A power so erratic in its appearance in the population that it had no official subdesignation. Not quite telekinesis, but on the spectrum. She could affect a specific number of elements, including those used in the manufacture of weapons.

The human CEO thought she was controlling his mind. What she was actually controlling was the weapon itself—*it* was repelling Akshay through a little subtle manipulation on Ena's part. "You'll give yourself an aneurysm if you keep attempting to break free."

Akshay finally threw aside the weapon. But rather than giving in, he jumped up from his seat, his hands reaching out as if to strangle her. In his eyes, she saw the moment he realized he could move freely. Ena shot him with the stunner she'd kept in her lap. His body spasmed as he fell to the floor, his limbs twitching with residual energy.

Looking down at him from the table, she held the bloody tawny brown of his gaze. "You're about to die. You know that and so do I. Will you protect your co-conspirators?" That he couldn't have gotten to Silver on his own wasn't in doubt.

To cut off electricity to an apartment building that secure with that many redundant systems would've required help from various highly placed sources. The Patels might control a large number of energy systems, but they had no footprint in Moscow. Kaleb held the controlling interest in the largest energy company, and the smaller ones serviced areas that didn't overlap with Silver's apartment.

Akshay Patel simply *could not* have arranged for the power to be disrupted in a company under Kaleb's banner unless he had someone on the inside. Even then, he'd need a second person inside the building itself who could override the redundancies.

Ivan would take care of unearthing that individual, but as for the employee at the energy company, Ena had requested Kaleb check the records to see if any of his hires had connections to the Patels. He'd telepathed her the results ten minutes ago, having found three employees who'd previously worked in businesses held by the Patel Conglomerate— not an unusual circumstance in the same industry.

Crucially, however, none of the three had been on duty the night the power went out in Silver's apartment. Kaleb had seen that, dug further, and discovered that the workers on duty at the time of the blackout were all long-term, experienced, and skilled. One of those employees had a wife who'd received a six-figure payment into her account immediately prior to the incident.

That employee was Psy.

Yet Akshay Patel made it a point not to have Psy contacts. "Do you think your co-conspirators would be as loyal to you?" she asked conversationally when Akshay didn't speak, his eyes boring into her. Hate foamed in their depths.

A spasm crossed his face.

"The pain will continue to increase," Ena told him. "The muscle spasms will eventually cause you to lose control of your bladder, then your bowels. You'll begin to drool. A second blast on the same setting will ensure you lie in your own waste for hours before your brain finally shuts down."

She took a sip of tea. "Or you can answer my questions, and this ends with me putting a shot directly into your brain. You'll die before you know it. And it ends with me and you. I won't go after your son or daughter."

Fear crawled across his face. "You wouldn't," he managed to grit out between spasms. "They're children."

"Silver is the child of my child." Ena let him see her implacable will. "Like for like. Except I'll be successful in my extermination efforts."

"Y-you're a monster."

"Perhaps, but I'm a monster who's giving you a choice. Will you sacrifice your children to protect your co-conspirators?" Ena knew the choice she would've made, though no one outside the family could ever know that. The Mercants were safe and successful partially because others believed that while they worked together as it was more effective, they were snakes who'd swallow one another should it come down to it. "You have ten seconds before the offer is off the table."

Water shone in the human man's eyes, his will broken. "Don't let my family find out I died this way," he said, his vocal muscles having relaxed enough for him to form the sentence.

"Give me what I want and your body will be discovered in a vehicle, broken beyond repair as a result of a single vehicle crash."

A shudder that didn't seem controlled, rather the product of the voltage still arcing through his body. "No faces, no names. Consortium."

Ena was unsurprised at the words, but she wasn't certain she believed them. "I thought you were against interracial cooperation."

"Don't have to like them to use them," Patel said, his breathing starting to turn jerky. "Consortium is short-term. Psy in charge pretends to be evenhanded, but she'll betray us all to hold on to power."

Ena's senses went on high alert. "She? The head of the Consortium is a woman?"

"No faces, voices distorted, that's how it works." His chest spasmed, his hands drumming against the floor before he brought himself under control. "But her software glitched for a couple of seconds once. I record everything. Went back and listened. Woman."

It was far more information than anyone else had about the individual behind the Consortium. "How did she contact you?"

"Hard-copy letter. Inviting me to join because I'd been public in my distrust of Trinity."

"Did you keep the letter?"

"I keep everything." His eyes held hers, his will impressive given the hit he'd taken. "Bottom left drawer of my satellite Amsterdam office."

Ena put down her cup again. "Do you expect me to take this on faith? Your son's name is Vahan, isn't it?"

A shuddering panic. "*Please.* Don't hurt my children. I've told you all I know."

"How do you communicate?"

"Internet. Throwaway e-mail addresses. A defunct chat room about entertainment stars." He gasped a breath. "If we need a comm conference, we leave a message there, with the current channel settings. Different every time." He gave her the web address without prompting. She didn't look it up, in case there were safeguards in place tracking where a member was logging in from.

"I requested a power failure in a certain wide area. Someone with the right connections organized it." His breathing was a touch better now. "I handled Silver's building myself."

"How did you find a traitor in the security team?"

A sudden smile with a touch of arrogance. "Not security. Maintenance. Lower pay, but had the right access and skills after I got him a coach. Psy junkie who's good at pretending to be normal. People never do penetrating security checks on maintenance staff."

Ena telepathed the information to Ivan. "You're a clever man, Mr. Patel." She meant that sincerely. "Tell me about HAPMA."

"They asked for money, I gave them some." He flexed his hands as control returned to that part of his body. "I thought they might be useful, but they've exceeded my expectations."

"You expect me to believe you're not the founder?"

Fear turned his face bloodless. "*Please*. They're only children." He stopped trying to regain control of his body. "HAPMA's grassroots. Only contact I had was with a man named David Fournier. Survival trained." He swallowed. "I was open in being anti-Trinity, caught his attention like I caught the Consortium's. Only difference is that the Consortium bitch is stone-cold sane while I'm not so sure about David."

"Yet you gave him money."

"Fanatics aren't always the sanest people in the room."

"Unfortunately, that's all too true." She picked up the stunner and shot him again.

Chapter 48

I had a five-year plan once. It was a good one, too. Then life happened.

—Unknown street philosopher

SILVER.

Silver sat up straight at her grandmother's telepathic voice. *Grand-mother.*

Across from her, Valentin tapped the side of his head. He'd asked her if she had time for a date that afternoon and, since EmNet was currently in standby mode while Ena was dealing with Akshay Patel, she'd said yes. He'd told her to change into StoneWater clothes—she'd chosen jeans and a fine vee-necked sweater in palest green with narrow horizontal stripes of silver that Nova had given her and told her to keep.

When Valentin arrived, it had been with a truckful of cubs excited to go to an amusement center where they got to play in a pit of foam balls.

Now she nodded to confirm she was having a telepathic conversation. He grabbed hold of the two cubs who'd been seated beside him and said, "Who wants to be thrown into the pit?"

"Me! Me!" The cubs next to Silver scrambled out, too, running after Valentin as he carried his gleeful cargo toward the large pool made up of colorful balls that were soft enough to do no damage to children, but deep enough that the kids could get "lost" in them if they ducked down. Which was why Valentin had booked this pool privately—so he knew exactly how many kids were in there at any one time.

Anyone caught ducking down to hide would be summarily banished to the benches to watch mournfully while everyone else played. Valentin's threatened punishment was apparently an effective one. As she watched, the kids thrown in popped immediately back up, laughing and asking to be thrown in again.

Grandmother? she said again when Ena stayed silent after that initial contact.

My apologies, Silver. I'm having to deal with a secondary telepathic matter. I'll get back in touch once that's completed.

The contact cut off.

Not surprised by the interruption—Ena was the matriarch of their family and, as such, was the first port of call for all of them—Silver was nonetheless . . . impatient. It had been hours since Kaleb confirmed he'd delivered Akshay Patel to Ena. Since rushing her grandmother was an impossibility, Silver slid out of the bench seat and headed toward the pool.

Watching Valentin's arms move in his old white tee, his biceps bulging and his face full of laughter as he picked up the cub who'd just scrambled out of the foam pit, she felt a strangeness in her stomach she remembered from when she hadn't been Silent.

Silver stopped, listened.

Nothing beyond the children's voices and the sound of their play.

"Throw me, Mishka! Throw me!" The words were delighted, the childhood nickname used in innocence.

Many a man would've chastised the cub that he was speaking to an adult—that he was speaking to his *alpha*, and should be more respectful— but Valentin pretended to growlingly bite Arkasha before doing as demanded. He had no need to worry about respect. She'd seen how he was treated by the teenagers and older children. They loved him as deeply as these cubs, but they never called him Mishka. It was understood that was a privilege reserved for the very young, the very old, and his sisters.

"Siva!" The smallest cub, Dima, saw her on his way out of the pit, ran toward her after he exited. "Will you throw me?"

Reaching down, Silver gathered his warm, solid body into her arms. "I don't want to do harm," she said to Valentin.

"He'll be fine." He grabbed Fitz, who was jumping up and down next to him. "Throw just hard enough to get him into the balls—and watch for the other five in there. They know not to move when someone's about to be thrown in."

Having already noted the positions of those five, Silver watched Valentin throw his cub, noted Fitz's landing position, then looked down at the little boy she held in her arms. "Ready?"

A quick nod, eyes bright.

She threw.

Screaming in joy, Dima sank into the foam, bounced up an instant later, chortling so hard he fell back down and his friend—a cub who'd returned with the dissenters—had to pull him up. "Is there a trampoline below?" Silver asked, realizing the children were bouncing around like rabbits rather than heavy-boned bears.

"Not quite, but close enough." Valentin came to stand beside her as the children began to throw the foam balls at one another. "Part of the safety system—not a single accident here in the twenty-five years it's been running."

The furnace of his large body tempted her to edge nearer, sink into his warmth. "You did your research."

"I'm alpha," was the simple answer.

And these cubs were his responsibility.

She went to answer when a ball hit her on the nose. Startled, she looked toward the pool, saw several innocent faces. Arkasha began to giggle a second later, the sound quickly spreading to all seven cubs. "Come play!" sensitive little Sveta said. "Siva, Mishka, come play!"

Silver never saw it coming. One minute, she was standing on her own two feet disturbed by her compulsion toward the large bear alpha with whom she'd once shared skin privileges; the next minute, she'd been scooped up in his arms and was being launched into the air. He'd thrown her so gently that she barely felt the impact before she was bounced up. Much taller than the children, she ended up with her head above the balls even sitting down. Her hair tumbled out of its twist.

Around her, the children began to swim over. Valentin, meanwhile, was standing outside the pool laughing. She blew the hair out of her eyes, closed her hand around a ball. When the children reached her, she whispered, "Let's get Mishka." That was all the encouragement they needed.

They pelted Valentin with the foam balls.

Throwing out his arms and making the face of an enraged bear, he jumped into the pool and began to chase the cubs. They screamed and ran from him. Silver, meanwhile, continued to pelt him with balls. Valentin suddenly changed direction and dived toward her. She twisted out of the way, but he was too fast and she found herself pinned under him, his body keeping the foam off her face and his arms caging her on either side.

"Gotcha," he said, the bear in his eyes, a playful presence.

Silver couldn't speak, her stomach suddenly so tight it was difficult to breathe. The laughter faded from Valentin's face, a slow slide into something deeper, more tender. *"Lyubov moya, solnyshko moyo."* A harsh whisper colored in unconcealed, primal emotion . . . before he was assailed by balls from every side, the cubs coming to her rescue.

Backing off with a lionish roar that delighted the children, he began to chase them again. Silver, her heart a drum, simply sat in place. Her ears caught the sound of the children's laughter, Valentin's growls of mock pursuit, the odd noise from other areas of the play center, but nothing unusual. Her audio telepathy was under control.

The rest of her, however . . .

"Siva?" A small body scrambled into her lap. "I'm tired." Giving a big sigh, Arkasha collapsed against her.

She wrapped her arms around his body and said, "I think you need a drink of water." Getting up with the tiny gangster trustingly holding on to her hand, she walked to the edge of the pool and they got out. Arkasha drank deep of the glass of water she poured at their table, his eyes on the play in progress.

He was back in the pool seconds later.

Silver should have gone, too. She'd promised to participate. But it was too dangerous to her sense of stability, her mind in confusion, caught between who she believed herself to be, and who she was becoming. Though it was impossible not to watch Valentin, not to hear his deep voice as he played with the cubs, she stayed by the table using the excuse of being ready to give the children any sustenance they needed.

That afternoon passed by in a heartbeat—and it stretched forever.

Lyubov moya, solnyshko moyo.

My love, sun of my heart.

Valentin didn't touch her again, but when he dropped her off at the complex, the children having been picked up by Yakov and Anastasia, he said, "Remember who we were, Starlight. Choose us." His voice was unusually solemn, his gaze amber.

Silver couldn't reply, her blood a roar in her ears. She certainly wasn't in the right frame of mind to receive a telepathic contact from Ena. *I'm just leaving Alpha Nikolaev's vehicle,* she said when her grandmother asked if she was free to talk.

Valentin needs to hear this, too. Ask him if he is available to meet at your current home. Kaleb will bring me in.

Silver's fingers curled into her palm, her body half-out of Valentin's vehicle. "Grandmother is asking if you're free for a meeting."

His expression changed, became deadly. "Akshay Patel?" Not waiting for an answer, he said, "I'm free. Where?"

"My apartment."

This time, she didn't wait for him to reach her, jumping out of the vehicle and beginning the walk to her apartment before he'd opened his own door. It didn't take him long to catch up to her, of course. He was a big and warm presence at her side, his energy so vibrant she could almost touch it.

"Valya!" The call came from across the grass and two floors up, the woman hanging out the window a beautiful blonde Silver had seen around the complex but never met.

The blonde blew Valentin a kiss.

"Careful, Irina," Valentin called back. "My mate is the jealous type."

Clearly unabashed, the woman blew Silver a kiss, too. "Any woman worth my alpha would be!"

"She's clan?" Silver asked after the woman drew back inside the apartment.

"Half human, all bear." He winked. "Fariad has the biggest crush on her I've ever seen a man have on a woman."

"Oh? Does he knock on her door at the crack of dawn?"

A scowl. "I didn't have a crush. I was courting you. There's a difference."

"Right," Silver said, her shoulder brushing his arm as they walked.

Valentin pretended to bite her. "Grr."

"I quiver in terror."

"I'll have you know I do make people quiver in terror," Valentin pointed out with a sulky look on his face that made her want to—

Silver shook her head, attempted to calm her skittering pulse.

Searching for a distraction, she pointed out the sun-lounging area below. "Look." Several bears—in that form—lay lazing about on the lush green grass. The wolves lay on the other side of an invisible line of demarcation.

Every so often, they'd give one another a dirty look, then get back to sun worshipping. The first snowfall was forecast to hit any day. It wouldn't stop either bears or wolves from being outside, but they were making the most of the grass while it still existed.

Several bear heads went up at that instant, their noses turning unerringly toward Valentin. They began to rise; she knew they wanted to come to him, touch him, have that tactile alpha-to-clan-member contact all bears needed. But Valentin waved them down. "I'll be back after I take care of my mate."

His deliberately provocative response made several bears "laugh" before they settled back down. The wolves, too, were looking *very* interested. Apparently being mortal enemies didn't mean you weren't intrigued by gossip about the other party.

When she didn't say anything in response to his words, Valentin gave her a distinctly wary glance. "What are you planning?"

"You'll find out when you fall victim to it."

Valentin's smile was more real than she'd seen it since her operation, his bear right there in his eyes, so close to the surface that she could almost touch its fur. "You're a scary woman, Starlichka." Lifting a hand, he brushed tendrils of hair off her face.

Silver broke contact with a jerk that had those bearish eyes narrowing, a predator on the hunt. He closed the inches between them, until her sneakers brushed up against his boots. "Scared?" A challenge.

His body was a furnace, but Silver didn't back off. This wasn't the first time she'd tangled with this particular bear. "I don't get scared. I'm Silent."

"You sure you haven't been willing those filaments in your brain to build bridges?"

Silver thought of the card she still hadn't thrown out, of how she hadn't washed the sheets on which he'd slept, of how she kept permitting him physical contact . . . and how she hadn't ordered any food since she moved into this apartment. "Why would I exchange perfect efficiency for the messy chaos of emotions?"

"Wild-monkey skin privileges."

Silver stumbled into him at the rough words spoken against her ear.

Valentin caught her. "Was it something I said?" This time, his eyes were laughing, his body a muscled wall that invited her to snuggle in.

And her stomach, it did that strange thing again. "Must be the uneven floor," she responded, because to let him win this verbal battle would set a bad precedent.

Bear that he was, he'd think he could win all their arguments by bringing up physical intimacy. She broke contact, started to walk toward her apartment again. "Speaking of wild-monkey skin privileges—"

"Naked wild-monkey skin privileges."

"As I was saying, speaking of naked wild-monkey skin privileges," she repeated without a hitch, "are there changeling primates?"

"Nope. Nothing from that part of the animal tree." He glared at her. "You're trying to distract me from seducing you."

"According to *Wild Woman* magazine"—to which she now had a subscription, strictly to further her understanding of changelings—

"bear males have delicate egos. I don't want yours crushed when I kick you out."

The deep rumble of his displeasure at her back, a big, dangerous presence that made her feel deeply safe, she cleared them into her apartment. The door slid back to reveal a room full of natural light. Greenery cascaded beyond the windows, while she knew from her orientation that the roof was a living carpet.

"I see you went wild with the décor, Starlight." The affectionate words had her looking at the apartment through his eyes; light and spacious, it was fitted out with modern furniture covered in oat-colored fabric.

That, however, was how it had come. Silver had added nothing to it, simply putting her clothes in the bedroom closet. Which was why she looked askance at the giant pink teddy bear sitting on her couch. "How did you manage that?" she demanded. "It wasn't there when we left."

"Don't look at me." His expression was affronted. "I would've gotten you a *brown* teddy bear." Folding his arms, he curled his lip. "There are no such things as pink bears."

Walking over, Silver looked at the furry thing. "Who does it smell like?"

Valentin looked pained but drew in a breath. "Yasha and Stasya."

Spotting the little bag that hung from the bear's neck, Silver tugged it off. Inside was a handwritten note folded into a small square.

> *We all thought you might be missing your bear, so we got you a substitute. (Honestly, he's probably just as good to cuddle up with in bed. Plus, his feet aren't boats and he doesn't snore.)*

Valentin, who'd come to read over her shoulder, made a loud noise and, picking up the bear, went as if to tear it limb from limb. She touched her hand to his arm. And he stopped.

"It's a gift. Don't ruin it."

"It's *pink*." His chest rumbled. "And it is *not* as good as me."

She tried to pull the bear from his grasp. He held on. *"Valentin."* She tugged again.

The stubborn bear refused to let go. "Release this now, or you'll be facing Kaleb and Grandmother while holding a pink teddy bear."

"So?" he said, but released his hostage at last. "I'm going to dye that bear brown when you're not looking."

Leaving him scowling in the living area, Silver managed to get the plush toy into her bedroom and return right before her grandmother and Kaleb teleported in. Valentin still had a glare on his face, but he inclined his head respectfully at Ena. "Grandmother."

His greeting to Kaleb was a curt nod. "Krychek."

"Nikolaev," Kaleb responded in the same vein, sliding his hands into the pockets of his black suit pants, his shirt a simple white.

"Grandmother, please sit," Silver said, only taking her own seat once Ena was seated.

Valentin came down on the couch beside her, while Kaleb took a seat across from them. Ena sat to their right. They looked at her as one, waiting to hear what she had to say.

"I have," she began, "completed my meeting with Akshay Patel."

"I think you meant to use the word 'interrogation.'"

Ena gave Valentin a speaking look. "A meeting is far more civilized."

"My apologies," Valentin said with such perfect politeness, Silver had to check he was the one who'd spoken.

Then, as they listened, Ena told them what the CEO had confessed—and what he'd betrayed. "The Consortium did have a role to play in this," Ena said toward the end of her briefing, "but only in the sense it gave Akshay Patel tools to pull off actions he already wanted to take. The Bowen Knight incident was wholly Akshay and his brother-in-law—he didn't want to involve outsiders in human matters."

Valentin's claws had slid out long ago. When he spoke, his voice was gravel. "Tell me he's dead."

"No. He's more useful to us alive."

Chapter 49

SILVER STARED AT Ena. "Grandmother, you're not known for mercy."

"A slight understatement," Kaleb said in his usual emotionless way, which terrified people with its very calmness. "For many, the name Ena Mercant is synonymous with the words 'cold-blooded' and 'ruthless shark.'"

"I believe your picture would also suffice for that dictionary entry," Ena said without missing a beat.

Kaleb's smile was faint but real.

"Grandmother," Valentin said, his body a storm of turbulent energy barely contained, "I respect you, but that bastard tried to murder my mate. He needs to die."

"He might be able to give us the Consortium."

Her words filled the room with a potent silence . . . broken only by the noise of play from outside. The apartment was fully soundproofed, but that soundproofing wasn't a default, had to be switched on, since most changelings preferred to live in proximity to others.

Silver had never turned it on.

"I've had the briefing." Valentin flexed, then fisted his hands after retracting his claws. "Those bastards don't show each other their faces."

"Akshay Patel is extremely paranoid and distrustful. He's done everything in his power to discover the identity of the individual behind the creation of the Consortium. Already he's told me that the one who sits at the center—the spider in control of the web—is a woman."

"Interesting." Kaleb leaned back. "You believe him?"

"A man will do many things to protect his children." Her words were arctic. "Whatever his faults, Akshay loves his son and daughter."

Kaleb didn't move. "How will you control him once he's with his children and able to spirit them into hiding?"

"Our family's greatest strength is our intelligence network." Ena's words were directed at all of them. "Akshay is well aware that wherever he goes, it will never be far enough—and I have given my word that his children will be safe so long as he cooperates with us."

Silver could feel Valentin's body vibrating next to her, his shoulders knotted and thighs rigid against the denim of his jeans. "Patel's a murdering bastard," he said in a voice so deep it echoed inside her. "But it's not right to make a man's children pay the price for his crimes."

"If he does what we want, that will never be an issue." Ena's eyes were ice when they met Valentin's. "He has willingly bargained his freedom for their lives. He's the one who will pay." A pause. "You would've taken his life, and the children would've lost their father. Our moral compasses are not so different, Valentin Nikolaev."

Hands fisted, Valentin nodded at last. "You're right. But I wouldn't have won his compliance by threatening his children." He held Ena's gaze with the wild amber of his own. "That line should never be crossed."

Silver had never seen her grandmother back down against anyone. She didn't today, either, but Ena also did not stare Valentin down in the way she did those who didn't have her respect. "We have different lines, Valentin, but we both protect those who are our own."

Valentin nodded slowly. "I don't like leaving him alive—a man who uses poison, he's not the straight-up kind."

"He's broken," Ena said flatly. "I made sure of it. He is my puppet."

Kaleb tapped a finger on his knee, his voice flawless midnight when he spoke. If Silver hadn't seen him with Sahara, and if she didn't know the other woman well enough to understand the passionate way Sahara embraced life, she, too, would've believed him wholly without heart. "Can he actually be useful to us?" Kaleb's cardinal eyes were unreadable. "If he starts betraying Consortium plans, they'll know they have a mole."

"How we use him will require careful thought, but this is the closest we've come to the Consortium since they shied away after making initial contact with me," Ena said. "Silver, you'll undertake tracking their communication methods."

"I've already sent word to our people." Three of her family had trained in covert online operations. "They're working on it now, but the setup is clever, and the Consortium could switch to a different chat room without warning—should the individual behind the group once again utilize physical letters to achieve that aim, we'll be right back where we started."

"Understood."

"We should ask for Arrow assistance," Kaleb said. "Unearthing the Consortium is a shared goal."

"I'll contact them," Silver said without asking her grandmother; Ena had long ago given Silver carte blanche over network operations. But that wasn't the topic at the forefront of her mind. "Grandmother, you must make a promise." Even as she spoke, she ran her hand down Valentin's back, over the rigid knots of his muscles.

Her grandmother's gaze took in the placement of Silver's hand. "Ask."

"Whatever happens, Akshay Patel's children are not to be harmed." She made her tone as implacable as Ena's had been. "He can keep on believing the same, but you are not to follow through on your threat."

"Ena Mercant is not known for making toothless threats."

"It was my life he tried to end," Silver said. "I make the call."

Valentin's head turned toward her, his muscles unbunching under her touch.

Ena looked at her for a long time. Silver didn't flinch. Finally, her grandmother inclined her head. "So be it. I won't harm the man's children. But should he step out of line, his life is forfeit. Does anyone disagree with *that* decision?"

Silver held her silence. Valentin didn't. "Silver Fucking Mercant," he said. "Granddaughter of Ena Fucking Mercant." A grin at Silver. "Do I want to meet your mama, Starlight?"

"Those particular genes skipped a generation," Ena said coolly. "I have no argument with the Arrows knowing of the chat room, but the information about *how* we came by that data needs to be kept within a very small circle. The fewer the number of people who know Akshay Patel is ours, the lower the chances someone will let it slip."

"I haven't shared it with our own tech team," Silver said. "They don't need to know to chase the communication channels."

"Lucas Hunter and Aden Kai need to know," Valentin said. "None of us would be aware of the Consortium without them."

The resulting discussion was over quickly, the highly selective short list arrived at after mutual agreement. It was at the end of the meeting that Ena said, "Walk with me, Silver. Show me this complex."

Silver had no trouble standing up to her grandmother when required, but she also understood that certain orders were to be followed. "Of course, Grandmother. You're welcome to stay the night here, if you wish," she added.

"I may do that." Ena looked at Kaleb as they all rose. "Thank you for the assistance."

Kaleb nodded, then glanced at Valentin and Silver. "Sahara," he said, "has invited you both to dinner next Friday."

"You look like you'd rather chew nails," Valentin remarked with a very bearish gleam in his eye.

"My mate, as changelings term her, is insistent I learn to socialize."

"How's that going for you?"

Kaleb slid his hands into the pockets of his suit pants. "It makes Sahara happy."

The simple answer had Valentin holding out a hand. "No further explanation needed."

Kaleb, who rarely made physical contact with anyone aside from Sahara, shook it. He was gone the next second, a cardinal telekinetic of such power that teleportation took less than a heartbeat. But despite Kaleb's power, it was Valentin's wild charisma that made Silver's body hum with a primal awareness.

He tugged on a strand of her hair. "I'm going to see the clanmates who live here." His irises were onyx again, but rimmed by amber.

And he looked at her as if he wanted to eat her alive. The hurt she'd seen in his eyes, it was gone, erased by an emotion so huge, it demanded that she feel in return. His bear's fur rubbed inside *her* skin.

Her heart slammed into her rib cage, memories that had once been flat suddenly taking on color and texture and depth. She wet her throat. "We'll talk later."

"Kiss me later," he dared in a whisper for her ears alone. "Prove you can keep your distance. Prove you're Silent."

It wasn't a playful challenge. It was deadly serious.

ENA didn't say anything until they were outside, strolling along one of the gently curved walkways. "You made a request of me for Valentin's sake."

"He's my mate." The possessive claim was instinctive . . . and it ran bone-deep. "I've decided to have children with him."

Her grandmother took her time answering. "An intelligent choice. It will strengthen your position as the head of EmNet. Pity Valentin doesn't have human blood, or you'd have the trifecta."

"Grandmother, *you* have human blood. As do I."

Ena came to a full stop, looked at Silver with an unblinking expression. "Of course, I do," she said after almost thirty seconds. "And the reason for glossing over that fact no longer exists." She began to walk again, her calf-length coat a camel shade that suited the copper of her tunic and wide-legged pants.

"I will allow it to leak that your great-grandfather was a human engineer who chose to remain with his wife even after Silence came into effect, and she did everything in her power to subjugate her emotions. The idea of true love running in the Mercant line will further boost your credibility with the emotional races, while your track record will reassure the Silent."

"I did some research as a teenager." Silver stopped herself from looking over to where Valentin was no doubt roughhousing with their clanmates. "I believe your parents did indeed experience true love. They were together since they were fifteen, and she was twenty-five when Silence went into effect, too old for Silence to ever truly *take*." Ena had been, for that time period, a late-in-life baby.

"My parents were never disciplined for breaching the Protocol," her grandmother said. "I certainly never witnessed anything of the kind."

"Yes, but when I dug through the physical archives below your residence"—a place Silver had spent a lot of time in as a teen, Ena the only one in the family who could teach her the telepathic skills she needed to know—"I found an old diary kept by a human relative who maintained bonds with them throughout her life."

"That would be my aunt Rose, my father's youngest sister. She bequeathed me her estate."

"I always wondered how the diary ended up in the archives," Silver said before continuing on with her original topic. "Rose wrote that though the two followed the rules of Silence in the hope it would help their violently psychic children, they shared the same bedroom all their lives."

Ena nodded thoughtfully. "For me, that was simply the way it was in the family. I never thought to question it through the lens of Silence. I know for certain they slept in twin single beds, a foot of distance between them."

"Yes," Silver said, "but, according to Rose, when they died"—Ena's parents had died at the same time, though only her father had suffered a long illness—"they were discovered holding hands, as if they'd reached out to one another in their final moments."

As a teen, Silver had been intrigued by the report, but she hadn't actually understood the gift of love and the sacrifice of her ancestors' lives. That she did today told her a lot about her own emotional state . . . and the choices she had to make.

Her grandmother's voice broke into her thoughts. "I was never told that. It would've been erased from any official record." A heartbeat before Ena spoke again. "You should digitize the relevant parts of the diary if you haven't already. Your great-grandparents' love story will make excellent media fodder."

"I'll get you the whole diary." Silver saw nothing wrong with Ena's request or with how mercenary it sounded—her grandmother had been protecting the family for decades. All her thoughts were about how to achieve that aim. "Grandmother?"

"Yes?"

"Now that Silence has fallen, are you ever tempted to experience emotion?"

"Temptation is an emotion," Ena said, her voice as difficult to read as always. "I would, however, choose to experience it for the simple reason that information is power. Ignorance is the opposite. The problem, of course, is that emotion and Silence are not things that can be switched on and off. To become Silent is a long and arduous process. Emotion is naturally chaotic."

The words made Silver think of the foam balls that had been thrown around the play area that day, of how the cubs had gleefully attacked Valentin. She wondered if the exhausted cubs had curled up into furry snoring balls on the ride back with Anastasia and Yakov, or if they'd found a second wind and the ride had been full of noise and belly laughter.

"I have a request of Valentin," Ena said without warning. "Let us speak to him."

Dangerously ready to see Valentin again, despite how problematic he was to her equilibrium, Silver accompanied her grandmother to the central green space. The wolves had all left—perhaps because there were too many bears, or perhaps so the bears who lived in the city could be free with their alpha. Silver had noticed that though the two sides were never friendly, they were respectful. It was the only way a complex like this could work.

"It appears we have a problem." Her grandmother came to a stop on the edge of the path, just before the grass.

Silver went to ask what, then realized it. "Oh, Valentin is that very large one with the scar on his left ear." She pointed him out where he sat in the center, his clanmates around him—the physical description had been for Ena's benefit; Silver *knew* Valentin whatever his form. "The bears here don't see him as often as those in Denhome."

"I will take but a moment of his time." Her grandmother stepped onto the grass and walked straight toward Valentin, ignoring the other large bears in her path. They, in turn, lumbered out of her way when she would've otherwise had to go around them.

As Valentin had said more than once, Silver's grandmother was an alpha; she demanded respect by her simple presence. Silver, too, was an alpha personality, but when she stepped onto the grass to make her way to Valentin so she could hear what her grandmother intended to ask him, the bears didn't get out of her path.

They came to her instead.

One midsized bear leaned up against her, would've pushed her over without meaning to if she hadn't set her feet apart to steady her balance . . . and if she didn't already have another bear on her other side, his warmth heavy against her. Her hands rose, rested on their fur. They leaned a little deeper into her.

She stroked.

It was her responsibility as Valentin's mate to see to the welfare of clanmates who needed contact from their alpha pair.

When she lifted her gaze, she found the largest bear in the clan looking at her. The sense of pride that burned in those eyes was a rough kiss.

The connection broke only because Ena had reached him. He turned to her grandmother, listened to whatever she had to say, then gave a single nod. Ena inclined her head in return and began to walk back. When she reached Silver, she said, "I will be accompanying Valentin to Denhome. I wish to see where my grandchildren will spend much of their time."

"Much? I don't think Valentin would trust his cubs out of his sight."

"He will when they are with me."

Silver had no argument to that—her grandmother's ethics might not be Valentin's or Silver's but she knew how to protect children of the family. "I'll come with you," she said, without having thought about what she was about to propose. "My deputy has things well under control, and I need to reconnect with my clanmates."

Her grandmother made no comment on Silver's choice. "I will walk until your mate is ready to leave."

The bears who'd been pressing into Silver stepped away, as if aware she needed to walk with her grandmother. She and Ena didn't speak much as they walked, but they reached an understanding nonetheless. When Valentin drove them to Denhome, the ride was quiet, the words Silver had to say to Valentin a heaviness that pulsed.

It was time to end this.

Chapter 50

The choice we make at the fork in the road can define our very existence.

—Lord Deryn Mercant (circa 1506)

"TELL ME OF your family, Valentin," Ena said from the backseat of Valentin's large vehicle. "It is surprisingly difficult to research changeling clans. You keep your records off any major network."

Silver saw Valentin's shoulders bunch, went to head off her grand-mother, but he caught her eye, shook his head. And then, he told Ena the dark secret of his clan. He contained his pain behind a gritty control until he spoke of his mother. "She wanders the wild, a bear who will never be at peace."

A hard swallow, his hurt so apparent to Silver it was as if he were inside her. "When Nova had Dima, I spotted her lingering close by, brought him out for her to see, but she disappeared into the trees before I could reach her. I've seen her near the den recently, but for all intents and purposes, she is lost to us."

Ena asked penetrating questions. Valentin answered all of them. "What will you do with our secrets, Grandmother?" he said softly at the end.

"What do you think, Valentin?"

He smiled through the echo of a terrible series of events that had scarred his huge heart but not changed its warmth or its ability to love. "I think you'll bury them in the same deep, dark hole where you bury Mercant secrets. We're family now and family protects. It never harms."

"I have always appreciated your intelligence," Ena said regally. "Now, tell me about this Pavel individual who is distracting Arwen from his duties."

Chuckling, Valentin shook his head. "I'm not touching that with a ten-foot pole."

"Neither am I," Silver said before Ena could ask. "If you wish to poke into Arwen's private life, Grandmother, you are on your own."

Valentin's hand lifted as if to play with her hair, his fingers curling into his palm halfway as he pulled back. It didn't matter. The raw power of his presence, his dare an invisible visitor between them, it wrapped her up in possessive arms. She felt as if she were vibrating within by the time they arrived at Denhome.

She walked into the Cavern to find it relatively quiet. It was soon apparent why. An exhausted ball of cubs—some in bear form, some in human—lay in the center, snoring in short bursts. Clanmates walked around them, throwing them the odd smile, but otherwise not worried about their choice of sleeping position. Someone had managed to get a thick rug under them, so they were well cushioned at least. She saw Nova bend down to pet one, causing the cub to smile in her sleep.

That was when the healer saw Silver. Welcome lit up her whole face. "Silver!" She ran over, her feet clad in deep blue heels, her dress a vibrant cerise, and her hair precisely curled. "It's so good to see you." A hug before Nova jerked back. "Oh, I forgot—"

Silver touched her hands to Nova's. "It's all right, Nova." The warmth of the other woman's skin against hers, it didn't feel wrong. And her heart, it felt so strange inside her chest. "I'd like you to meet my grandmother. Grandmother, this is Nova, the clan's chief healer."

"Grandmother," Nova said respectfully. "You are most welcome."

Ena received the same response no matter which part of Denhome she visited, until they reached Sergey; the older bear was helping build a bed in the area of Denhome set aside for carpentry and other such projects. He held Ena's stare without welcome. "Come to see how the lesser races live?"

"Your low opinion of your own race is not my concern," Ena said, cold as ice.

Sergey narrowed his eyes . . . then threw back his head and laughed a big bear laugh of which Silver wouldn't have believed him capable. "That'll teach me to poke a bear straight out of hibernation." He swept out his arm in a wave. "Would you like a tour of our workshop?"

Ena took her time answering. "I suppose," she said at last, "a bear of your years is apt to have at least some useful knowledge. You may proceed."

Silver felt a living warmth at her back as Ena and Sergey walked off deeper into the cavernous space. "He seems in a far better mood." Even though he had baited Ena, the man had given Silver a welcoming glance.

Curving his hand over her hip, his chest brushing her shoulders, Valentin said, "I'm his alpha—he needed to understand that and accept it. We had a discussion. It's done."

"By discussion, do you mean a fight?"

His chuckle vibrated against her, the heat of him sinking into her to warm parts she hadn't known were cold. "Since your grandmother has a guide, do you want to catch up with your clanmates? Nova and the others are making drinks so you can sit and chat."

Shifting on her heel, Silver looked at the hard edges of his face, touched her hand to that thick black hair he never bothered to comb, felt her heart squeeze. "Valentin."

He lowered his head, his hair rough and tumbled. "Starlight." A ragged word.

She touched her fingers to his lips, saw her hand was trembling. "Who are you to me?"

"Yours," he said. "I'm yours."

AN hour later, Nova showed Silver into her old room. Ena had made the unexpected decision to stay at Denhome overnight, so Silver didn't have to return to Moscow—especially since she could hook into EmNet systems using her devices or the StoneWater network. The latter she knew she could trust; to these bears, she was half of their alpha pair.

No one would treat her as an enemy.

No one would spy on her.

No one would do anything but defend her to their last breath.

And Valentin . . . he'd die to keep her safe. She felt that knowledge in the very core of her being, as if she were inside his mind, inside his *soul*.

"I made sure all the clothes you left in Denhome stayed in good condition," Nova told her. "I figured you could change here, and then if you and Mishka . . ." A sudden pause, her smile fading. "I don't know what to do or say. Mates are usually for life unless one dies."

"He's still mine," Silver said at once. "He told me so himself."

A dangerous edge to her that Silver had never before seen, Nova said, "Don't break my brother's heart, Silver. He's a big lug, but where you're concerned, that heart of his, it's like glass. You could shatter it with a few careless words."

The visual was an unforgiving one, shards of glass crimson with Valentin's blood lying at her feet. "I would *never* hurt Valentin." The words came out hard, a rebuke as brutal as Nova's words.

Nova's eyes went amber, searched Silver's face. "You still love him," she whispered. "My God, Seelichka. Even though they cut into your brain, even though they rewired you, you held on to him. No wonder Mishka calls you Silver Fucking Mercant."

Silver didn't answer the healer, but after Nova left, she exited her bedroom and looked until she spotted Pieter. Making her way to the quiet male after ensuring Nova and Stasya were nowhere nearby, she said, "Petya."

A suspicious scowl. "Why are you calling me Petya? You always call me Pieter."

"You asked me to call you Petya."

"But you never do."

"I'm doing it now."

"Why?"

Bears.

Deciding not to go any further down that rabbit hole, she said, "Will Valentin return soon?" He'd made it a point to find her after dinner, tell her that he had to go speak with Selenka.

In his gaze had been an unhidden need that clawed at her, his love worn openly, though she might yet kick at it. He wasn't budging in that love, wasn't building walls behind which he'd be safe, wasn't doing anything but inviting her back into his warmth, despite the pain she'd caused him.

Alpha bear he might be, but he had no self-protective instinct when it came to the people he loved. If he wouldn't protect himself, she'd do it for him. That was why she'd hunted out Pieter.

"Valya? I'm guessing he'll be back in two hours." Hazel eyes watched her, Pieter the most difficult to read of all of the seconds. "Why?"

"I need you to take me to Galina Evanova."

No change in Pieter's expression. "Why do you think I can track her?"

"You're one of Valentin's best friends," she said, gaze resolute. "You keep an eye on her because it matters to him and his sisters."

Folding his arms, he looked bear-stubborn for a second before admitting, "We all do—Inara spotted her a hundred meters from Denhome earlier today." Flinty eyes. "If you get hurt, Valya will tear off my head and stomp on it."

"I'm a high-level telepath, Petya. I can smash back a rampaging bear." It'd stun the bear, but it wouldn't do harm unless she literally sought to kill. Psy couldn't breach changeling shields, but they *could* kill changelings with a massive psychic surge.

"A-hem."

"And, of course," Silver added at that pointed cough from the bear in front of her, "I'll have your big, strong self with me."

Scowling at her, Pieter nonetheless snuck her out of Denhome and into the trees. "You won't be able to approach her," he said in the soft dark green of the trees, the sky above dotted with stars. "She doesn't even let Dima close, and he's her only grandson."

"Leave that to me." Silver had things she wanted to say to Galina Evanova.

A glance from Pieter, his eyes glowing a faint amber in the darkness. "You could wipe the floor with me, couldn't you?"

"What do you think?" she asked, steel and ice in her tone.

"I think," he said with unexpected solemnity, "my alpha chose well." He raised his hand a second later, then put his finger to his lips.

Nodding, Silver tried to walk in his footsteps, so she'd avoid crunching a branch or making any other noise. He stopped five minutes later and, hunkering down, pointed into the darkness. Silver didn't have changeling night vision—it took her a full minute to see the outline of a bear seated under the branches of a tree with a large canopy.

She put her hand on Pieter's shoulder, whispered so low she could barely hear herself. "I need privacy."

He looked outraged. Putting his hand to his hair, he pulled up the strands and drew a line across his throat, demonstrating what Valentin would do to him if she got hurt. Having half expected that response, Silver dug out the earplugs she'd requisitioned from the medical supplies while Nova was away from the infirmary.

Pieter scowled when she held them out, but put them in his ears. Now he'd be able to see her, but not hear her conversation with Galina. She rose to her feet, stepped forward, deliberately making a noise. The sleeping bear woke, her head jerking up.

She began to lumber to her feet seconds later.

"Do not run," Silver said flatly. "I'm an extremely strong telepath. I will slam you into unconsciousness as many times as it takes." It wasn't that easy, of course, but Ena had taught her that sometimes, belief was all about projection.

She set her feet apart and stared into the wild amber eyes facing her, daring the other woman to defy her.

When the bear rumbled at her, she folded her arms. "Try it," Silver said softly. "I will put you flat, then I'll tie you up and drag you to Denhome."

The bear just stared at her. As well it might. Silver was currently a tiny percentage of its overall weight. But it was listening, and it hadn't run. Nostrils flaring, it suddenly jerked forward before stilling. Behind her, she felt Pieter ready himself, but he held back when the bear froze.

"Yes," Silver said softly. "I'm your Mishka's mate." She used the pet name deliberately as a reminder of the boy whose heart this woman was breaking every day that she wandered out here. "I've also had enough of this bullshit." She spit on the ground for emphasis, the act not natural to her, but in a negotiation, every move counted.

"You're in pain, I understand that," she said in the same hard tone. "But that does not give you permission to brutalize your children's hearts." Never again did Silver want to see that pain in Valentin, his big body held so fiercely rigid as he contained his emotions. "Get out of sight, or come in," she said flatly. "Those are your only choices."

Bear faces might be hard to read, but Silver had been around them enough to know this one was as outraged as Pieter had just been. "If I see you lingering around Denhome but not coming in, if I so much as *hear* a report from a sentry that you've been spotted, I will track you, and I will put you down. Is that understood?" Of course, Silver wasn't about to murder Valentin's mother, but this was a hardheaded bear she was trying to reach. It required tough talk.

"Your children's wounds need to heal," Silver continued. "Each time they see you, and you turn away from them, it rips the scabs wide open. *Enough.*" She sliced out her hand.

The bear actually scrambled back.

"If you want to wallow in your pain, you do that. But you *do not* get to hurt Valentin or his sisters." She took a step forward.

The bear backed away.

"The next time I see you," Silver said in her most icy tone, "you'd better be walking into Denhome."

Shifting on its paws, the bear turned and lumbered off into the trees.

"These earplugs don't work that well, you know," Pieter said softly from behind her.

She shot him a flinty look. "Say a word, and I'll bury you beside her."

A rare grin from this reserved bear. "You're the scariest woman I've ever met. I think I'm in love with you."

Bears. "Let's get back."

As they made their way through the forest, Pieter said, "You've taken a risk." It was quiet. "They hurt seeing her, but they also need to know she's all right."

Silver knew that. She also knew that StoneWater bears would've never called Galina Evanova on her behavior. Valentin, with his big heart, would've never been so pitiless. He looked after the people he loved. He'd looked after Silver even after she hit his heart with blow after blow. "She's a bear, Petya. You really think she'll listen to me if she wants to see her children?"

"Huh." He ran a hand through the sunset of his hair. "Never knew a mama bear to let anyone stop her seeing her cubs, but you did say some pretty harsh things."

"They needed to be said." She didn't think Galina was manipulating her children and clanmates on purpose, but she *was* doing it. If Silver had to face her down again and again until the other woman understood the damage she was doing, so be it.

No one was allowed to hurt Valentin.

Not even Silver.

Chapter 51

Love is no rose. It's a goddamn weed that digs its roots in so deep, there's no hope of getting it out.

—Nina Valance, human novelist married to a telekinetic (circa 1977)

SILVER AND PIETER made it back fifteen minutes before Valentin returned.

Having gone to her room to dress for bed, Silver waited another ten minutes before leaving that room and going next door to Valentin's. She pushed open the door without knocking because he was hers and she had every right to go in.

He was standing shirtless in front of the bed, his hands on his hips and his hair damp from a recent shower that scented the air with soap. Wearing blue jeans on his lower half, he was staring at three different shirts laid out on the mattress: one white, one black, the third a steely blue.

"Why are you getting dressed?" Silver asked, closing the distance between them.

He'd gone motionless the instant she entered, watched without moving as she picked up the blue shirt. "Put on this one." Shaking it out, she walked around behind him and helped him shrug it on, smoothing her hands over the muscled breadth of his shoulders before she came around to the front. "You didn't answer my question."

"I'm planning our next date." He raised a hand, caught a lock of her unbound hair, tugged her gently closer. "I need to have a swanky outfit for that."

She didn't offer to button his shirt for him, though the strip of skin and crisp hair on his chest was highly distracting. "What are we doing that requires formal clothing?"

"A dinner date at a fancy restaurant."

"I would suggest we swap that date for a different one."

Valentin folded his arms, jaw set. "No trickery."

"Let's exchange naked skin privileges."

Valentin ripped off his shirt so fast she heard fabric tear. She was on her back on the bed the next second, a bear in human form looking down at her. "Done," he said, but froze with his hand halfway down her side. "Hold on—is this Silver-and-Valentin-wild-monkey skin privileges, or is this biological-exchange-of-fluids-so-we-can-create-a-cub skin privileges?"

She felt the tremor in his body, heard the hope twined with fear in his voice. And knew, no matter what, there was no turning back. Hurting Valentin was simply not acceptable to any part of her.

"This is Silver-tasting-Valentin all over again." Breasts aching and her core hot, she touched her hand to his cheek, things unfurling inside her for which she had no name. "This act, it's so raw, so primal, so intimate. I need to know if I have the capacity to process it along the new pathways in my brain."

VALENTIN'S heart pounded like a bass drum. Sliding his hand under Silver's head, he pressed his face against the side of hers as his body shook. She'd *come to him*. They'd rewired her brain, and still she'd come to him. He could work with that.

She wove her hand into his hair, wrapped her legs around him in an open possessiveness that gripped his heart tight. "Valyusha, you're shaking."

He kissed her, hot and deep and full of all the love he'd had to contain while she woke from her long sleep. He'd missed her *so much*. Crushing her to him, he told himself to slow the fuck down, to not rut on her like a damn feral bear. But then Silver licked her tongue against his, and he had no hope in hell of doing that.

He tore off her clothes.

She didn't give him a cool stare and remind him that clothes cost money. Her body arched under his, her skin flushing a creamy rose. He kissed his way down her throat, over her right breast, to her nipple. When he bit, she pulled hard at his hair. He shuddered, did other bad things to her.

His tongue in her pussy made her scream; his fingers digging into her butt had her fighting him for control; his stubble rubbing against her breasts had her locking her legs so tight around him that he felt owned. "Fuck, I missed you."

Silver didn't speak.

She scratched him, she bit him, and then she pushed at his shoulders until he let her be on top. He took the chance to squeeze her ass as she undid his pants. Drunk on her scent, he gave up on the momentary good behavior and hauled her up with a single powerful motion to press his lips to her pussy once again.

She gave another little scream.

Valentin was more than strong enough to hold her in place while he lapped her up like honey. She came so hard her body shuddered. He would've kept going forever if his cock hadn't been a stone rod in danger of snapping in half if he didn't get inside her.

Throwing her limp body onto the bed beside him, he tore off his pants and underwear and rose over her. One hand on her breast, he squeezed, fondled, branded. *Mine*, said the bear. He didn't realize he'd spoken the guttural word aloud until Silver's eyes, eyes gone that mysterious dark, locked on to his mouth.

Still fondling her breast, he kissed her. Not gentle and loverlike. Uncivilized and bearlike. Releasing her breast only so he could stroke down her body to grip her hip, he bit at her lower lip before rising above her. "Are you wet enough for me?"

She spread her thighs for him, her hands on her knees and her core slick.

His brain lost all thought. He sank into her in a single thick thrust, gathering her close and crushing her to him as he filled her body with his—but as her arms and legs came around him while her pussy clamped down on his cock, he was the one who was claimed. By Silver Fucking Mercant.

"IT wasn't the skin privileges," Silver said to him some time later, his well-satisfied mate lying with her head on his shoulder, her hair sweeping across him. He, of course, had his hand on her butt. Why the hell not when she was naked in bed with him, and he was sweaty from being totally and utterly wrung dry?

"Hmm?" he play-growled. "Sure felt like naked skin privileges to me."

Silver stayed lax against him, pure satisfied female. He smiled, smug. Okay, yes, he'd lost it and rutted on her exactly like a feral bear, but he'd also made her come three times. Not his best effort, but he planned to make up for it.

He slid his hand from her ass to between her legs, cupped her. "Are you sore?"

"You are rather well-endowed, but the ache is one I like."

He kept his hand right where it was. Possessive? Him? "What were you talking about before I got distracted by how soft you are"—he ran his fingers through her folds—"and how good you smell." Rolling over onto her, he nuzzled and bit at her neck.

Silver pulled at his hair again to make him pay attention. His displeased rumbling had zero effect on her. His mate would never fear him. His bear swaggered around like an asshole, pleased with his choice of this strong, sexy woman.

"I've been feeling more and more," she said, her eyes locked to his. "And I've been trying to justify my responses in various ways."

Valentin couldn't hide his hurt. "Why would you do that, Starlight?"

Her hand on his jaw, a petting caress. "Don't you understand, Valyusha? I was justifying it to *be* with you, to do things with you. I couldn't explain why when my emotions were meant to be gone."

"Bears are stubborn fools," he said with a baring of his teeth. "The mating bond wasn't about to let go." It was anchored in a part of the psyche so primal even the operation couldn't sever it.

"Neither was I. You're mine." Flat, no room for argument.

Hurt retreated under a wave of smug pleasure.

"I want no confusion about that." Silver's fingers gripped his jaw hard. "I want *no one* believing we might not be a unit. Not our clan, not your family, not mine. And never, ever you." Her gaze was pure steel. "If that means embracing emotion, so be it."

Happy as he was, Valentin worried. "Your audio telepathy?"

"Nonexistent, though I've clearly reaccessed my emotions far faster than anyone could've predicted." Playing with his hair again, Valentin's dangerous, beautiful mate said, "I've always had a sense of it at the back of my mind. That sense is gone."

"And physical contact?" he asked, remembering how she'd overloaded in his arms. "Not just skin privileges with me, but tactile contact with the clan. Since you and I, we're forever"—it was hard to breathe through the joy crashing through him—"we need to protect you from overloading."

"There's no need," Silver replied. "My time in Denhome taught me that I can manage the impact—our bears are baffled by but respectful of a clanmate who needs time alone now and then." Fingers still in his hair, her touch proprietary. "And I have a strong feeling the mating bond helps, too. We balance each other."

Valentin's happiness threatened to explode out of his skin. "I can't wait to grow old with you—and to see you turn into a hard-ass like Ena."

She didn't smile. "I hurt you. I'm sorry."

Not liking the pained guilt on her face, he shifted onto his back again and hauled her up on his chest so he could cuddle her close. "It was tough having you distance yourself from me, but it wasn't as bad as I thought it would be."

He tangled one hand in her hair. "Partly because I was too fucking stubborn to believe you when you said you didn't want me, didn't want us, but mostly because you were always right here." He tapped a fisted hand against his heart.

Silver propped her chin up on her hands, looked inside her mind. There it was, the primal bond that connected her to Valentin. It dared anyone in the PsyNet to touch it, just *dared*. She hadn't thrown a shield around it this time, and following her lead, neither had Arwen.

Silver had a feeling anyone who got too close would get a riled-up bear's welcome. "I don't know where our bond was hiding all this time," she murmured, "but I have my suspicions."

The lazy-eyed bear who was now stroking her back, all the way down to her buttocks and back up, demanded a kiss. She gave it, demanded another one herself. "The PsyNet is alive in a way most people don't understand," she told him afterward.

"Of course it is." Her bear rolled his eyes. "All those brains in one big psychic network. If it wasn't going to become a sentience of its own in some way, what else was it going to do?"

Silver narrowed her own eyes and moved until they were nose to nose. "You're much, much smarter than you like to make out, Mr. I. M. A. Medvezhonok." Not that she hadn't known that from day one.

Smiling at her in that smug bear way, he fondled the side of her breast. "Tell me more about this sentience in your PsyNet. What do you think it did?"

"I think the NetMind and its more erratic twin, the DarkMind, make decisions for the good of the entire network." The majority of Psy didn't know about the NetMind's dark twin, but Silver was a Mercant. "And— *Oh.*" She scrambled up to sit astride him.

Hands firmly possessive around her hips, Valentin scowled at her. "Now my chest is cold. Aren't your pretty tits cold?"

"Focus." She glared at him, but her body missed his, too, so she snuggled back down. "I've just realized something."

"What?"

"We know the PsyNet must need changeling energy, too, even if at a lesser level than it needs humans." Their world had always been a trium-virate. "But we've been thinking that means pulling others permanently into the PsyNet."

She shook her head. "There would've been Psy like me in the past, Psy who needed to remain in the PsyNet. I see it, Valyusha. I see how it was meant to be." Excitement was a heated river inside her. "Bonds *across* networks were once the norm. The energy can flow from one to the other."

Valentin frowned. "I know I have a bond with my seconds and my healers that you'd probably see as a psychic network, but what about humans?"

"Humans fight and die for those they love," Silver whispered. "Bowen Knight put his body in the path of a bullet to protect his sister, put a dangerous implant in his brain for the sake of his people."

"We've been so arrogant all this time," she said, furious with herself for falling into the same trap. "We've assumed that because we can't see a human psychic network, that means it doesn't exist. Stupid when there's so much evidence that it does."

"Fascinating."

She dug her nails lightly into the chest of the bear whose hands were lazily mapping her body. "It is fascinating."

"Not when you're naked and my cock is hard and I want to eat you up like candy." A slow smile. "I missed you, Starlight. Come be with me."

Silver had no chance against this bear. Never had.

"SOMETHING'S happening," Valentin said an hour later, while the two of them were lying sweaty and boneless in each other's arms. "There's a commotion in the Cavern."

Silver got up with him, quickly pulling on clothes as he tugged on his jeans. Bare-chested, he took her hand and the two of them walked out. Valentin froze partway to the Cavern. "I can scent her," he whispered, eyes wild. "My mom."

"Good, I'm glad I didn't have to carry through my threat of stunning her with my telepathy and dragging her back to Denhome."

Valentin's mouth fell open. She waited to see if he'd be angry at her interference, but he threw back his head and laughed that huge, generous laugh. "Silver *Fucking* Mercant." A hard kiss, her body crushed to his. "She's going to be pissed at you for the next decade."

"I don't care." It had never been about her. Only him.

His expression when they walked into the Cavern and he took in the dirty woman with long, tangled black hair who sat wrapped in a blanket . . . it was everything.

Later, when he kissed Silver and kissed her and kissed her until she was drunk on him, she knew she'd do anything for him. Face down feral bears. Face the chaos of emotions. Battle the world itself.

"I love you, Valyusha."

"I'll be your teddy bear anytime, Starlight." Taking her hand, he pressed it to the bass beat of his heart. "It's yours. Forever and always."

Shadows

AKSHAY PATEL'S BODY was found in his study, the CEO dead of an apparently self-inflicted gunshot wound. Silver scanned the photos and report her grandmother had been able to gain from her Enforcement contact, Valentin reading over her shoulder as she sat in the computer center of Denhome.

"He didn't do that to himself." Valentin's tone was definitive.

"It's a picture-perfect scene," Silver said. "That alone makes me doubt it, but why are you so sure?"

"Patel was a man used to power, but he bargained away his freedom for his children—yet according to this, he shot himself while his children were home and the door to the study unlocked."

Silver nodded. "You're right." No loving father would want his children to discover his mutilated body, the high-power projectile weapon having destroyed most of the back of his head. "Further to that, Akshay Patel might've been broken, but he was an intelligent man. I would've expected him to begin thinking about how he could somehow make the situation work to his family's advantage."

"Consortium?"

"It makes the most sense." She tapped her finger against the desk. "But it's far too soon for them to have known he was broken by my grandmother. We kept the information within a trusted and extremely small circle. And I'm certain Patel wouldn't have told anyone."

"Too proud," Valentin agreed. "Maybe the Consortium never knew Patel had been turned." He began to play with her hair, Silver having kept it down for him since they were in Denhome, where she didn't have to wear her armor. "Cracks might be appearing among the co-conspirators."

"The psychological profiles of the kind of people who'd join a group like the Consortium are also not those of people who'd do well in a group that requires long-term cooperation." Arrogance, narcissism, control, they were the hallmarks of the Consortium's higher echelons. "The ones we've run to ground have all been the heads of their family groups or business empires, people used to making their own decisions."

Bear claws touched her neck but she didn't flinch. Valentin would cut off his own hand before harming her. Sometimes the bear just rose to the surface and wanted to play. Reaching back from where she sat in the work chair, she ran her fingers along his thigh. "The person who created the Consortium would've done better to reach out to people in my position."

"You can't be bought, Silver."

"No." She gave her loyalty not for power or influence but because it was deserved. "I meant people who are close to those in power—the seconds-in-command or the senior aides. The vice presidents. People with ambition but who aren't yet used to being in charge.

"Collect the right personalities into a group, and the leader of the Consortium could've had a stable and powerful network." Instead, that person had gone for those at the top, believing they could control the vicious dogs she—if Akshay Patel had been right in his deduction that the architect of it all was a woman—had brought into the mix.

"I'm glad you're not on the side of evil," Valentin said, rubbing his jaw against her cheek. "You'd make a deadly evil genius."

"I will put that on my résumé."

Laughing, her bear mate scooped her right out of the chair and threw her up before catching her snugly against his chest. She glared at him, though her lips wanted to curve at the joy on his face. "I am not a cub."

"Grr." He pretended to bite her.

"Valyusha!" She pulled at his hair to get him to stop.

He tickled her.

And Silver laughed so hard that she snorted. Throwing her hands over her mouth at the inelegant sound, she found her eyes locked with those of a bear who was delighted with her. She dropped her hands, wrapped her arms around his neck, and kissed the life out of him. "Let's go or we'll be late."

"Definitely can't be late for ice cream."

It was after their ice cream date, as they were walking through the fading light of Moscow, the air bitingly cold, that Silver updated Valentin on her search for information about his father, specifically whether Mikhail Nikolaev had been the subject of a terrible Psy experiment. "I haven't yet discovered anything concrete," she said, "but I'm following several data threads."

"You're being careful?"

She didn't chide him for his rumbling concern. Her mate was an alpha bear—he couldn't help being protective of those he loved. Neither could she. "Yes," she said. "This data is old, that's why it's so difficult to unravel. I don't think there's any real risk of attracting dangerous attention, but I'm taking maximum precautions."

"Good." He ran his hand over her hair, a wild peacefulness to him even as they discussed this emotionally wrought topic. "No information is worth your life."

Silver interlaced her fingers through his. "I know, but as *you* know," she added in a cool tone, "I can be just slightly relentless in pursuit of a goal."

His chuckle was warmth wrapping around her, an acceptance so deep she knew nothing could ever shake it—Valentin Nikolaev saw every part of her and he loved every part of her.

Before he could speak, however, her phone lit up with a call from Lily Knight.

"Bo is degrading," Lily told them, her face stark on the small screen, but her voice clear. "The doctors are giving him days at most."

"I'm very sorry, Lily." Silver had a brother she loved; she knew Lily would be devastated by Bo's death—but the impact of his loss would spread far beyond the other woman. First and foremost, it would leave the Alliance with a huge power vacuum. The previous leadership had been swept away by Bo and his group when they came in fighting for the Alliance's future, and Bo hadn't had long enough to train a successor.

The Alliance stood in real danger of collapsing right when it was needed most. Their world was a triad; it could *not* stand strong if one part of that triad was missing. "Is there any way EmNet can assist?" Their mandate was to offer help in all emergencies; to Silver's mind, this qualified.

"Smoke and mirrors if you can," Lily said. "Anything that'll keep the focus off the Alliance and off Bo." Huge gray eyes met Valentin's. "If it all comes tumbling down, we may need a place to hide certain vulnerable people."

"No need to ask, Lily," Valentin said. "StoneWater will protect them."

"We're standing on a precipice," Silver said after Lily signed off.

His face grim, his fingers warm and rough around her own, Valentin spoke her concerns aloud. "Trinity, EmNet, your PsyNet, it could all collapse if humans withdraw from the playing board."

"Yes." Humans needed Bo, needed the Alliance, needed to know they had someone in their corner who'd protect them should the Psy or changelings become aggressive. "Right now, all we can do is give Lily what she's requested. Any ideas for the smoke and mirrors?"

Her mate's eyes gleamed just as soft flakes of winter's first snowfall drifted out of the sky. A second later, she found herself bent over a bear alpha's powerful arm while his laughing mouth covered her own right there in the center of Moscow.

MOSCOW DAILY: MORNING EDITION
SILVER MERCANT WITH ALPHA NIKOLAEV! EXCLUSIVE PHOTOS WITHIN!!

ACKNOWLEDGMENTS

I'd like to thank all the people who helped me with research questions for this book, most of them to do with translating Latin and Russian.

Before I do that, I'd like to say that I did take some liberties with the information provided: for example, as Russian is written using Cyrillic script, where the spellings of the translations varied, I've chosen a spelling and run with it.

Those of you familiar with Russian naming conventions—where many surnames have a different form, depending on the gender of the bearer—will have noticed that Valentin and his sisters all bear the name Nikolaev (rather than Nikolaev/Nikolaeva). This is because not all the naming traditions in the Psy-Changeling world are identical to our own.

One Russian custom seen throughout *Silver Silence* is the way diminutives are used to show affection. A single person can have multiple nicknames, some used by friends (Valya), others by family (Mishka)—and, of course, there are the special names a lover might think up and use (Valyusha).

My thanks to everyone who helped me find the right diminutives for the characters.

As for the Latin maxim, as one of my translators pointed out, because it's a dead language, there's no one around to ask if a translation is perfect. The final translation used in this book is the result of several people's input.

Without further ado, I'd like to thank (in alphabetical order): Tatiana Agapov, Teresa Anderson, Lana Calinin, Rachel K., Galina Krasskova, Cathleen Kuznesoff, Lori Jo Levy, Melissa Martinez, Tetiana Matsypura, Father Nick, Irim Sarwar, Jenny Sliger, and Julia Sullivan.

An extra-special thanks to Karen Lamming and Vladimir Samozvanov for their detailed explanations of the structure of the Russian language and how Russian culture so often impacts particular words and the way they're used.

As always, any errors are mine—I hope you'll forgive them!

ABOUT GOLLANCZ

Gollancz is the oldest SF publishing imprint in the world. Since being founded in 1927 Gollancz has continued to publish a focused selection of bestselling and award-winning authors. The front-list includes **Ben Aaronovitch**, **Joe Abercrombie**, **Charlaine Harris**, **Joanne Harris**, **Joe Hill**, **Alastair Reynolds**, **Patrick Rothfuss**, **Nalini Singh** and **Brandon Sanderson**.

As one of the largest Science Fiction and Fantasy imprints in the UK it is no surprise we have one of the most extensive backlists in the world. Find high-quality SF on Gateway written by such authors as **Philip K. Dick**, **Ursula Le Guin**, **Connie Willis**, **Sir Arthur C. Clarke**, **Pat Cadigan**, **Michael Moorcock** and **George R.R. Martin**.

We also have a strand of publishing in translation, which includes French, Polish and Russian authors. Gollancz is home to more award-winning authors than any other imprint, with names including **Aliette de Bodard**, **M. John Harrison**, **Paul McAuley**, **Sarah Pinborough**, **Pierre Pevel**, **Justina Robson** and many more.

The SF Gateway
More than 3,000 classic, rare and previously out-of-print SF novels at your fingertips.
www.sfgateway.com

The Gollancz Blog
Bringing you news from our worlds to yours. Stories, interviews, articles and exclusive extracts just for you!
www.gollancz.co.uk

GOLLANCZ
LONDON